WITHOUT A TRACE

by

Lesley Pearse

Magna Large Print Books
Long Preston, North Yorkshire,
BD23 4ND, England.

British Library Cataloguing in Publication Data.

Pearse, Lesley
    Without a trace.

    A catalogue record of this book is
    available from the British Library

    ISBN   978-0-7505-4280-7

First published in Great Britain in 2015 by Michael Joseph
an imprint of Penguin Books

Copyright © Lesley Pearse, 2015

Cover illustration © Ildiko Neer by arrangement with
Arcangel Images

The moral right of the author has been asserted.

Published in Large Print 2016 by arrangement with
Penguin Books Ltd.

Magna Large Print is an imprint of Library Magna Books Ltd.

Printed and bound in Great Britain by
T.J. (International) Ltd., Cornwall, PL28 8RW

For Barry Greenwood,
you have enriched my life, dear friend

Chapter One

2 June 1953

'Where on earth could Cassie and Petal have got to?' Molly Heywood was shouting out to Brenda Percy, landlady of the Pied Horse, because the village hall was so noisy.

It was Coronation Day and, due to heavy rain, the long-planned and highly anticipated street party had had to be moved into the hall at the last minute. Molly and Brenda were working their way down the long row of excited seated children, offering sandwiches.

Brenda paused to admonish a little boy who was about to douse the girl sitting next to him in orange squash. 'Oh, I expect the rain put Cassie off,' she said, once she'd told the boy he was heading towards getting sent home in disgrace. 'I don't think I'd have come to help if I didn't live right across the road.'

'But Cassie isn't like that, and she'd made Petal a super fancy-dress costume,' Molly shouted back.

Brenda heard the anxiety in the younger woman's voice, and felt like barking back at her that she should just enjoy herself and stop fretting about other people. But Molly Heywood took everyone's troubles on board and always tried to help people, which, considering how bleak her own life was, made her almost a saint.

9

Molly had wanted to go on the village coach trip to London to see the Coronation procession, but her father hadn't let her go. Brenda knew most people would say that a young woman of twenty-five should just ignore what her father said and go anyway, but Jack Heywood wasn't the kind to be disobeyed: he had a vicious temper, and he would make Molly pay dearly for it if she went against his wishes.

Brenda had been the landlady of the Pied Horse for twenty years and, as Jack, the village grocer, came in every single day, she knew just how cantankerous, stubborn and mean-spirited he could be. It was a common knowledge that his older daughter, Emily, had left home after a beating and had never been home since. His wife, Mary, was a sweet-natured woman who was well liked by everyone, but she was a bag of nerves and too weak to stand up to such a bully.

Aside from the men who had been called up in the war, most of the residents of the Somerset village of Sawbridge had never been more than ten miles from their homes in their whole lives. Even going into Bristol or Bath was a challenge for them. So, in the main, they tended to be narrow-minded and insular, making assumptions based on nothing but their own limited experiences.

Their assumption about Molly was that she was as weak as her mother and something of a doormat, but this wasn't the case. Her fault – if it could be claimed to be one – was that she had a kind heart. She didn't oppose her father in order to protect her mother from further stress. She liked to help people, to be at the centre of things, so when she couldn't go on the trip to London she took on the role of street-party organizer. She wanted to make the occasion very special, to ensure that every child in the village remembered Coronation Day for the rest of their lives.

Molly deserved praise for her efforts. The high street was decked out with bunting, much of which she'd run up herself on the sewing machine. Apart from bullying just about every adult in the village to make cakes, sandwiches or jellies, she'd also planned races on the cricket ground, a treasure hunt and the fancy-dress competition. But when the day began with rain and showed no sign of letting up, there was no alternative but to drag all the trestle tables and chairs in from the street and quickly decorate the village hall. There was a suggestion that the bunting put up the previous day should be used for this, but it was dripping wet, and too difficult to get down.

Considering that all the new decorations for the hall were borrowed Christmas ones, and many were past their best, it looked quite jolly. Brenda thought that, after all Molly's efforts, it was churlish of so many of the adults to stay at home, merely sending their children to the hall for Molly and anyone else who was mug enough to be willing to entertain them.

But those adults were missing out on seeing forty-five children between the ages of two and fourteen staring wide-eyed at the spread before them. After years of deprivation both during and since the war, the government had given everyone a very welcome, bigger sugar ration because of the Coronation. The village women had pulled out all the stops to flaunt their cake-making skills. Most of the younger children here today, born during the war or since, wouldn't even have known their mothers were capable of baking such wonders.

The fancy-dress competition had created almost as much excitement and competitiveness. Looking around, Brenda could see several queens, King Arthur, the Pope, a Pearly King, and a Queen of Hearts playing card. The latter was finding it hard to reach around her stiff card costume to eat her sandwiches, and Brenda predicted that the costume would be torn off before long.

There had also been a competition for the best village shop-window display. Molly should have won it for her effort at Heywoods, the grocery shop. But, of course, she wasn't allowed to win, not when the competition had been her idea.

It was marvellous. The centrepiece was a big plaster-of-Paris cow she'd found in a shed. She'd painted it white, made a crown out of card and tinsel with fruit gums for jewels and draped it with a purple coronation cloak. Then, in straw all around it, she'd invitingly placed various British food items: a large Cheddar cheese, baskets of eggs, punnets of local strawberries, stone flagons of cider and pots of jam, marmalade, chutney and honey.

But, right now, Molly didn't look a bit happy. She may have been responsible for the glee on the children's faces but she was worrying about the one child who was missing.

'Cheer up, Molly,' Brenda said, slinging her arm around the girl. 'You know Cassie is a law unto herself – she'll have taken Petal somewhere else, somewhere more exciting maybe. She's too good a mother to just sit indoors and look at the rain.'

Brenda had always had a soft spot for Molly. There was something about her sweet, country-girl face, rosy cheeks, soft blue eyes and lovely smile that brightened any day. She was the reason Heywoods grocery shop was always busy; she was warm, funny and a great listener, too. Jack Heywood believed the shop's success was because of him but, in truth, if Molly ever left, he'd lose most of his customers overnight.

'She wouldn't do that, Brenda,' Molly said with a shake of her head. 'She spent days making Petal's costume, and even if she hadn't done she would've come just to support me, as I organized the party.'

Brenda remembered how everyone had talked when Cassandra March arrived in Sawbridge village two years earlier. They had looked at the voluptuous redhead with deep suspicion. She wore no wedding ring and had a half-caste four-year-old girl in tow. That the child was called Petal only raised more eyebrows. After all, what sort of person would give their child such a name?

'She'll be a whore,' Jack Heywood announced that night in the Pied Horse and, even though Brenda firmly believed that you should never label anyone before getting to know them, she had to admit that the woman's flaming red hair, pencil skirt, tight sweater, high heels and excessive make-up conformed to the image of a fallen woman.

No one had imagined Cassandra March would want to stay in the village; it was assumed she'd come to see someone here and that, once that was done, she'd leave. But, to everyone's amazement, she began looking for a place to rent.

It was no real surprise that Molly befriended her – even as a young girl, she'd collected up the kids that everyone else shunned. But, to be fair to Molly, Brenda also found there was a lot to like about this mysterious young woman who didn't appear to give a fig for what people thought of her. And Petal was a bewitching little girl, with her big eyes, toffee-coloured skin and shiny, curly hair. She was a poppet. Even some of her mother's most voluble critics passed on outgrown clothes and toys from their own children to Petal.

Somehow, against all the odds, Cassie had managed to persuade cantankerous Enoch Flowers to let her live in an old farm cottage he owned in the woods. A rumour went around that she'd offered him her body for it, and perhaps she had. But Brenda thought it was more likely the old man let her have it as he found the idea of a city girl living in isolation, cooking on an open fire and using an outdoor privy very amusing, just as most people in the village did.

Yet they were all wrong about how she would cope with country life. She made the little cottage a home and she stayed. The high heels and tight skirts were brought out only for trips into Bristol, but Cassie still managed to look like a pin-up girl in a cotton frock, with a scarf tied around her head and wellington boots.

'I'm getting really worried now,' Molly admitted to Brenda. 'I saw Cassie yesterday when she gave me some bottles of orange squash as her contribution to the party. She promised me she was coming today – she said Petal had had her cos-

14

tume on and off about a hundred times. Cassie had even got a new dress to wear. So why aren't they here? What if one of them is ill or has had an accident?'

'Oh, no. It won't be that.' Brenda patted Molly's cheeks affectionately. 'Most likely she was put off coming because they'd have to tramp through mud to the village. Or maybe they went to some-one's house this morning to watch the ceremony on television and decided to stay on there. Stop worrying. There's enough to do here to keep us all on our toes!'

She was right about that: two six-year-old boys were pushing cakes into each other's faces, and Brenda rushed off to separate them.

Molly handed round some sausage rolls, as-tounded at how quickly the huge tray was emptied, but her mind was on her friend. Cassie wasn't normally too keen on joining in village acti-vities because, even after two years, she was still treated with suspicion by many people. But she would've braved it today for Petal, as the little girl was excited about dressing up as Britannia. Cassie had scoured the shops in Bristol until she found a suitable helmet and had sewn the dress by hand.

Mud would never have put them off; Cassie would just have packed the costume into a bag and changed Petal when they got to the village. As for watching television at someone's house – who was there? The few people who had tele-visions – and Molly's own parents were part of that select group – wouldn't invite someone like Cassie to watch it with them.

As it was, Molly had only watched the actual

crowning in Westminster Abbey, because there was too much to do for the party for her to see anything more.

She caught hold of Brenda's arm. 'Look, I must go up to Cassie's, to satisfy myself that Petal and her are okay,' she said. 'I'll go on my bike, so it won't take long.'

Brenda pursed her lips. 'If you feel that strongly, I suppose you must. But you'll get drenched,' she said, looking anxiously at Molly's new blue gingham dress with its full skirt and her white, strappy sandals.

'I've got my raincoat and my wellingtons in the cloakroom,' Molly assured her. 'I'll be back long before we start the party games, and I'll enjoy them then without worrying.'

Taking one last look around the crowded village hall and satisfying herself that there were enough mothers helping, Molly put a few sandwiches, sausage rolls and cakes in a cardboard cake box, found a spare party hat, flag and hooter, then rushed off to fetch her raincoat and boots.

It was hard to cycle up Platt's Hill in the driving rain, and her raincoat kept blowing open, so her dress was getting soaked, but Molly reminded herself it would be easy coming back down. She was always cycling up this hill to deliver groceries for people, but the narrow, rutted lane which led down to Stone Cottage, where Cassie lived, was almost at the top of the hill, well past the last of the village houses. From there on, it was only fields and woodland.

On reaching the little lane and seeing it was too muddy to ride down, she left her bike and, carrying the box of party food, made her way gingerly down to Cassie's house.

In sunshine, Stone Cottage and the surrounding woodland looked idyllic; a place of utter peace and beauty. More than once Cassie had told Molly that it made her heart glad every single morning she woke here. This suggested to Molly that Cassie had lived in a very bad place before, but Cassie wasn't one for confidences. Molly wondered if this was because her father was a tyrant, much like her own, and had thrown her out when he discovered she was pregnant. Admitting such a thing would be hard for someone as proud as Cassie.

But whether this was the case or not, Stone Cottage was still lovely even in the rain, albeit with a slightly sinister tinge, because the birdsong halted and the tree trunks took on a fairy-tale menace.

Molly came out into the clearing, Stone Cottage was to her left, built with its rear against a solid rockface. Presumably, when the cottage had been built a hundred or more years ago, it made good sense to utilize this wall of rock, and the roof began where the rock ended. Ivy and other plants had crept up and over the cottage roof, hiding it, so a stranger coming down through the wood above the cottage wouldn't know it was there until they found themselves stepping on to the roof.

Cassie had often mentioned that she'd heard badgers and other night creatures walking around on it.

It was a simple little place, one room down and one up, the staircase between the two floors little more than a ladder. Four windows to the front, two on each floor, either side of the front door, which was framed by a dilapidated rose-covered porch. On the side of the cottage was a second door, with the pump beside it and a well-worn brick path to the privy, which also leaned against the rockface. This door had clearly always been the preferred way in and out of the cottage. Cassie had been unable to open the front door because the lock had seized up with lack of use.

'Cassie!' Molly yelled out as she got close. 'Where are you?'

There was no reply, but Molly noticed the side door wasn't shut properly, only pulled to, the way someone might leave a door if they were indoors or had just popped out for a minute.

Molly had been brought up to respect other people's homes. When she was delivering groceries, she would never walk into someone's kitchen uninvited. Cassie had often teased her about the way she always hovered on the doorstep, even if the door was wide open, never stepping over the threshold until she was asked in. In this case, though, it was unlikely Cassie was outside in the rain and, furthermore, Molly had a slight feeling of unease, which made her push the door open a little further and call out again, louder this time.

No reply. All Molly could hear was dripping rainwater and the wind in the trees. She couldn't see much through the partly open door, as there was an old sofa covered in a multicoloured crocheted blanket with its back to the kitchen area. It struck her that she'd never known Cassie go out before without locking the door, even though nearly everyone in the village left theirs unlocked. But then Cassie had come from London, and it was said people were very different there.

Putting aside her usual reservations in the interests of leaving the party food in a dry place for Petal, Molly pushed the door open further and went in, placing the box on the uncleared table.

The first thing she noticed was Petal's Britannia costume on a coat hanger on a hook on the stairs, the silver-coloured helmet gleaming brightly. Judging by the bread, plates with crumbs, teapot and two dirty cups on the table, something or someone had interrupted Cassie before she could clear the table. As Molly walked past the sofa into the main part of the room, she saw Cassie on the floor and screamed involuntarily.

She was sprawled, on her back, one leg slightly twisted. Her head was on the hearth and her blood had spilled out across it on to the floorboards in a shiny, dark-red pool.

Molly clamped her hands over her mouth to stop her scream and stared in absolute horror, not really believing what she was seeing. This was something which happened in films, not in real life. And, although she had never seen a corpse before, she felt absolutely certain Cassie was dead.

She was wearing the old floral print dress she wore most days and she still had a few curlers in her red hair, as if she'd been in the process of taking them out. Her arms were splayed out and her blue eyes were wide open.

'Cassie, Cassie, what happened?' said Molly, dropping down to her knees and taking her friend's wrist to feel for a pulse. Tears ran down her cheeks unchecked when she found none.

Cassie's skin felt very cold, too, so whatever it was must have happened some time ago. She knew she had to run to get the police, but horror rooted her to the spot.

She'd had so many laughs and in-depth conversations here in this cottage. Through Cassie, she'd learned so much about the world outside this village – about people, books, art and music. So many evenings with Petal sitting on her lap reading to her, or playing board games. Cassie was, without doubt, the best friend Molly had ever had, but more than that, too: she was her teacher, confidante and soulmate.

Then, all at once, it occurred to her that Petal wasn't here.

Where was she?

Petal was a shy child, nervous of people until she got to know them, and Molly had never known her to stray far from her mother's side. But, surely, if she'd seen her mother fall and all that blood spurting out, she would have run for help?

'Petal!' she called out. 'It's me, Auntie Molly. It's okay, I'm here now, and you'll be safe.'

But when there was no reply, not even a little whimper of distress, a dreadful thought crossed Molly's mind.

Was Cassie attacked and Petal so terrified that she ran to hide?

Molly forced herself to act, running up the narrow stairs to look in the bedroom. She was distraught, tears almost blinding her. Her whole being wanted to run away from this scene; she couldn't deal with it.

There was a double bed at one end of the room

and a small single at the other. Both were neatly made, and Cassie's new red-and-white dress was lying on the double bed ready for her to put on. But Petal wasn't there. Molly looked under the bed, but there was nowhere else Petal could hide herself.

She went back down the stairs and checked the child wasn't hiding in the privy or the woodshed, calling loudly, even though her voice was croaking with emotion. But there was nothing, not a rustle of leaves or a crack of a twig, to break the quiet in the woods.

Molly's stomach heaved and she vomited again and again into some undergrowth. Nothing in her life so far had prepared her for something as bad as this and, somehow, the fact it had taken place on a day the whole country was celebrating their new queen being crowned made it far, far worse.

'The police,' she said aloud, and forced herself to straighten up, wiping her tears away with the back of her hand. 'No time to lose.' Staggering, and with the heavy rain mingling with the tears streaming down her cheeks, she began to make her way back up the muddy track to her bike.

Chapter Two

Molly fled up the rutted lane to the road. It was hard going through the mud, so she climbed up on to the bank and forced her way through the bushes. On reaching the top, she jumped on her bicycle and freewheeled through the rain all the way down to the village, barely able to see for tears.

The high street was deserted but she could hear children in the village hall singing 'The Farmer's in His Den'. When she reached the police station she flung her bike down outside and ran in.

PC George Walsh was on duty behind the counter.

'What on earth?' he exclaimed when he saw her. She was soaked through, wild-haired and crying. He lifted the counter top and came through to her, holding out his arms. 'Has someone attacked you, Molly?'

They had been at school together from the age of five, and George now belonged to the same drama group she did. She liked him a great deal, not just because he was nice-looking, with grey eyes and curly brown hair, but because he could always made her laugh, and he was sensitive.

'I've just found Cassie March dead,' she blurted out. 'And Petal is missing! I can't find her.'

George caught hold of her elbows and moved her away from him so he could see her face. His eyes were wide with shock. 'Cassandra? Dead? Where did you find her?'

Molly sobbed out what she'd seen, and George put his arms back around her, holding her to his shoulder. 'I'll have to report this to the sergeant, and he'll have to get on to the DI. We're a few men down, with the Coronation and all. I'll be a few minutes. Will you be all right on your own for a bit?'

'Yes, of course. Thank goodness it was you on

22

duty and not someone I don't know,' she said, trying to brush away her tears. 'You will find Petal? She's only six.'

'As soon as I've reported it, a search will be started. I'll get you a cup of tea,' he said, went back behind the counter and disappeared through a door.

It occurred to Molly as she sat on the bench waiting that most girls of her age and in these circumstances would run across the road to their parents for comfort and support.

Heywoods grocery shop was right opposite the police station, and from the sitting room above the shop her parents might have seen her running in here, or spotted her bicycle outside. But, even if they had seen, they wouldn't come over. Her mother would want to, but her father would sniff and say, 'If she's in trouble, she can get herself out of it.'

There would be precious little sympathy from him when he heard that she'd found Cassie dead. He disapproved of Cassie on every level. Being an unmarried mother with a mixed race child was, in his bigoted view, beyond the pale, and because Cassie didn't creep around hanging her head, that was evidence she was no good. He often called her 'that red-headed whore', angering Molly, because that was such an ugly and untrue label. In fact, he was very likely to relish Cassie's death and he wouldn't be concerned about Petal being missing either. Molly often thought that whatever part of the brain it was which gave people compassion and empathy was missing in him. Her mother didn't share her husband's views, but she was afraid of him and wouldn't dare do or say anything he disapproved of.

Molly put her elbows on her knees, held her head in her hands and began to cry again, this time because of the situation with her father. He was a tyrant, and he sucked all the joy out of everything, growing nastier with each passing year. Yet she couldn't leave because of her mother.

With hindsight, she should've left home at sixteen, as her sister, Emily, did, even if that meant moving into a girls' hostel for a year or two, or getting a live-in job like a mother's help. But what she had planned after that was to go to drama or art school when she was eighteen, and she stupidly thought she could save some money by living at home and working in the shop.

As it turned out, her father had never paid her a proper wage. All she got was the odd half-crown as pocket money, and she had to beg for money for a new dress or shoes. He poured scorn on her plan of drama school and insisted it was her duty to help in the shop and look after her mother.

Nothing could've been less appealing to Molly than a life of slicing bacon and stacking shelves, but she loved her mother dearly. She was a timid, gentle person and she suffered from her nerves, often having such bad attacks that she could barely breathe and had to go to bed until it passed. She needed calm, love and encouragement to bring her out of it, and she certainly wouldn't get that from her husband.

Emily was far braver than Molly was; she'd gone after their father had given her a good hiding for seeing a boy he considered a lout. He broke two of her ribs and one of her front teeth, and when she left she vowed she'd never return. She had been true to her word. There was the occasional letter, which their father tore up if he saw it. In one, which got through unseen by her father, Emily had written that she'd got a job as a secretary for a solicitor. Both Molly and her mother had written back immediately, explaining this was the first letter they'd received in months, and begging Emily to let them have a telephone number so they could ring her, or for her to ring them after eight in the evening, when her father would be at the pub. But she never did give them a number or ring them, and the chilly tone of her subsequent rare, brief letters implied she had decided that her mother and sister were as bad as her father, so it was difficult for Molly and her mother to know what to do. In the last couple of years there had been no further letters; they didn't even know if she still lived at the same address.

Now, at twenty-five, Molly virtually ran the shop. Jack Heywood sat in his office out the back all day and did crosswords and smoked his pipe, and Molly never got a word of praise from him for all she did, only sarcasm and abuse.

˙ It was a terrible thing to hate and fear her own father, but she did. He was a bully, a bigot and a complete hypocrite. She couldn't help but wish he would have a heart attack and die. Perhaps then her mother could learn to laugh again instead of trembling with anxiety every time he had that scornful expression on his face.

George came back through the door behind the desk. 'Sergeant Bailey has gone up there now. I expect you heard him drive off. I've spoken to the guvnor on the phone, and he'll be joining Sarge up at Stone Cottage. He asked that I take a statement from you, and said he'll talk to you when he gets back.'

George held up the flap in the counter for her, then led the way through into the back of the police station.

'I'm going to get you that cup of tea first,' he said. 'You look as white as a sheet, so just sit there while I get it.'

Molly sank down gratefully on to the chair he pointed out. She felt very shaky and faint.

George didn't take long, and came back with tea on a tray. 'Luckily, Sarge had put the kettle on, and his wife brought us in some rock cakes. Come on. We'll go to the interview room.'

The room he took her into had grubby green walls and stank of stale cigarette smoke. George noticed her wince as he put the tea tray down, and he turned to open the window.

'Sorry about that,' he said. 'You and I must be the only people in the village who don't smoke, and it comes hard when you have to live with the pong.'

'I don't normally find it so bad, but I feel a bit sick after finding Cassie.'

'I'm sure you do,' he said, indicating she was to sit down opposite him at the table. 'You've had a terrible shock, so have your tea and, when you feel up to it, we'll start on your statement.'

The tea and George's gentle manner did help to calm her a little. If she'd had to talk to any of the other officers she wouldn't be able to cope.

'What a wash-out for the Coronation,' he said to distract her. 'As it turned out, perhaps it was as well we didn't get the coach to London to see it.'

Even through her distress, Molly remembered that one of the reasons she hadn't minded too much about not being allowed to go to London was because George had told her he'd be on duty that day. He'd even made a little joke about his disappointment at not being able to sit next to her on the coach. For several days afterwards she kept thinking about it and wondering how she could engineer being somewhere alone with him. But she hadn't intended it to be here in the police station like this.

'Well, Molly,' he said, once he thought she was ready. 'We'll start first with your full name, age and occupation, which of course I already know, but I need you to tell me officially, then tell me why you went to Stone Cottage.'

Molly told him, and he wrote it down.

'And what time would you say it was when you found Cassie?' he asked.

'Well, the children's tea party began at three ... I suppose it was quarter past when I began to worry that Petal wasn't there. I spoke about it to Brenda Percy and left soon after. It must have taken me at least twenty-five minutes to get to Stone Cottage, so it was probably ten to four when I found Cassie.'

'Did you touch anything?'

'No. Well, apart from the door and maybe the rail on the stairs. I went up there to look for Petal, and in the privy and woodshed.'

'What made you think Cassie was dead?'

Tears started up again in Molly's eyes. 'There was so much blood and her eyes were open. But I felt for her pulse, too, and couldn't find it.'

'So, after you'd looked for Petal, you left and came back to report it at the police station?'

Molly nodded and wiped her eyes.

'Did you see anyone, either on the way up there or on the way back?'

'No. No one at all,' she said.

'When did you last see Cassie alive?' he asked. 'Was it today?'

'No.' Molly shook her head. 'It was yesterday afternoon after school. She came into the shop for some tea and bacon. Petal was really excited about the party.'

'Excited' didn't really cover the mood Petal was in. She had rushed into the shop, dark eyes blazing with excitement, flung her arms around Molly's waist and gabbled something so fast Molly couldn't follow what she was saying.

'Say it slower, sweetie,' she said, holding Petal's arms and pushing her a little away from her.

She was wearing her blue-and-white checked school uniform dress. Her curly hair was like a halo round her sweet face and her teeth were brilliant white against her brown skin.

'Mummy's made me a Britannia costume,' she said, still gabbling, but a little clearer now. 'She made the dress from an old sheet, it's kind of like a Roman toga. But the helmet is the best, all silver and gleaming. I think I'm going to win the prize for best costume.'

Molly hugged Petal. She adored the little girl. 'Now, don't go banking on it, will you?' she warned her. 'Some of the other mummies can make good costumes, too, and the vicar is the judge and he can be a bit old-fashioned.'

'She's been like this for days,' Cassie said, grinning with pride at her pretty daughter. 'Look, Molly, I'm no cake maker, so let me pay for four bottles of orange squash as my contribution to the party.'

'Are you sure you can afford it?' Molly asked, because she knew Cassie had very little money to live on.

'Of course! I don't want those Holier than Thous pointing out I'm mean, as well as being "no better than I should be".'

The way she laughed as she said this proved that, whatever people said, it was water off a duck's back to her. 'I'm going to doll myself up and flirt with any man who so much as glances at me,' she went on. 'That should give everyone something to talk about after I've taken Petal home.'

Molly admired Cassie so much for her attitude. She wished she could be so daring.

Now, remembering that last brief conversation she'd had with her friend, she wished she'd told her what she thought.

'I took the money for the orange squash and said I'd take it to the hall instead of her carrying it home and bringing it back today,' Molly told George. 'The last thing I said to her was to remind her that the party started at three, and I said that maybe we could have a bit of a chat after it.'

George nodded. 'Do you know of anyone Cassie might have visited today? A friend, relative? Maybe she left Petal with them.'

'Cassie doesn't have any relatives here, and she wouldn't have left Petal with a friend, not when there was a party in the village.' Molly paused, looking hard at George. 'Cassie was killed, wasn't she? I mean, it wasn't just an accident.'

'I can't possibly say from just what you've told me,' he said, looking at her with rather mournful eyes. 'That's for the investigating officers to decide, and the coroner, too. Now, to save time later, what can you tell me about Cassie's friends? Male and female.'

'You must know that she didn't have any real friends in the village aside from me,' Molly said reprovingly. 'People were mean to her. They said nasty things because she was on her own with Petal, and because Petal wasn't white.'

'I am aware of that.' He sighed. 'Village people tend to be very narrow-minded. But do you know if anyone was particularly nasty to her? Threatened her? Called at Stone Cottage uninvited? Someone that bothered her?'

'She often said she'd grown so used to getting the cold shoulder on the bus or outside the school that she barely noticed it any more. But I think she would've told me if anyone was doing something more than that.'

'You were very close friends?' he asked.

Molly frowned, not sure how to explain how it was. 'Cassie wasn't really one for closeness. I know she liked me, and was glad I wasn't mean like everyone else, but I still couldn't have dropped in to see her any old time I fancied. She kind of held back, if you know what I mean.'

George half smiled. 'Yes, I do,' he said. 'I ran

into her recently and I found her even more guarded than most people are when talking to a policeman. It was only when I said you and I were at school together that she warmed up. It was plain enough to me she was fond of you. What do you know about her family?'

'That wasn't a subject she encouraged,' Molly said. 'I kind of got the impression she'd brought herself up because her mother wasn't up to much. I used to think that her father might be a bit like mine, but I was wrong about that because just recently she mentioned he'd been killed in the war.'

'Where was her childhood home?'

Molly shrugged and pulled a face. 'I don't know. It must seem very odd that we were good friends yet I don't know all that background stuff about her, but she talked about here-and-now stuff, like the past wasn't important. But the reason I got the impression her mother wasn't up to much was because she once said she wanted Petal to have the stability in her life that she'd never had. And Cassie did give her that. She was a great mother and home-maker. That cottage was awful when she moved in, but she made it nice.'

'So when was the last time before today that you went to Stone Cottage? And tell me about her men friends,' George asked.

Molly didn't want to repeat anything Cassie had told her about the men in her life, but she knew she had to, in case one of them was responsible for her death.

'The last time I went there was last Saturday,' she said. 'I'd been delivering an order to the

Middletons up Platt's Hill. I dropped in to see her afterwards.'

She paused, thinking about how everything had looked and seemed that day.

It was around eleven in the morning, very warm and sunny, and as she bumped down the track to Stone Cottage she thought how picturesque it looked. The ivy dappled the mellow golden stone walls, and the pink roses around the porch looked beautiful.

Petal was playing outside with a doll, wearing the pair of faded red shorts she always wore when it wasn't a school day. She was small for a six-year-old, but well rounded, which made liars of those who claimed her mother half starved her. Her light-brown skin had a sheen to it, and her features were small and neat, except for her dark eyes, which were huge and soulful. Molly had only seen about three or four black people in her life, and then only in passing in Bristol, but she knew their hair was usually wiry, with tight curls. Petal's wasn't like that. It was curly but it felt silky, easy to put a comb through, but Cassie normally plaited it in neat little braids. That morning it was loose and hadn't been brushed, as it stood up like a dark fuzz around Petal's face. She had one front tooth missing, which gave her bright, welcoming smile a lop-sided look.

She shouted with delight to see Molly and ran towards her. Molly got off her bike, hugged the child and then lifted her on to the saddle and wheeled her over to the cottage.

'I like Saturday best of all 'cos I don't have to go to school,' Petal said. 'And it's the best Saturday because you've come.'

Cassie must have heard Petal speaking, because she came out of the cottage. She was wearing a loose, flowery smock and had bare legs and feet. She often wore this dress while doing her chores. It looked like a maternity dress, but Cassie said it was comfortable and cool.

'Great to see you!' She beamed. 'Petal said just a little while ago she hoped you would come to see us today. Would you like some ginger beer? It's home-made, and good.'

'Go on, then,' Molly replied, and lifted Petal down, laid her bike on the ground and sat on an old bench.

Cassie disappeared into the cottage, and Petal came and perched herself on Molly's lap, leaning into her shoulder. 'You don't come here enough,' the child said.

'I can't. I have to work in the shop and look after my mum,' Molly explained.

'Yes, I know. Mummy said everyone puts on you. I don't know what that means really, but I think it means you are a nice person, and I wish you could come here more.'

Molly chuckled, because Petal was such an old-fashioned little thing. They had a brief conversation about school and reading. Petal could read very well; it seemed Cassie had begun teaching her before she went to school. Then Cassie came back with the ginger beer and she began to tell Molly how she made it, a long, quite involved process using yeast and sugar.

Molly had become aware during their friendship that this was one of Cassie's tricks, to talk

33

about something random and complicated rather than anything personal. It usually meant she had a problem.

It had been a surprise to Molly that Cassie was a real homemaker. The cottage might not have any modern conveniences, but she'd made it homely with jumble-sale finds and things that had been given to her. An old wardrobe had been transformed by Cassie painting it white and stencilling flowers all over it. The chairs around the scrubbed wood table were all painted primary colours, there was a colourful old blanket over the shabby sofa, bright cushions, and the walls were covered in pictures she and Petal had painted.

Outside, she'd fixed a checked table cloth up like a sun shelter over the old table and chairs. There was even a vase of wild flowers on the table, and cushions on the chairs. She made her own bread, wonderful soups with vegetables she grew, and during the winter there was always a pot of rich, tasty stew simmering on the fire.

'Right, out with it,' Molly said. 'What's the matter? You only tell me long, boring things like how to make ginger beer when you've got something on your mind.'

Cassie sighed. 'Oh, it's nothing really, just that bastard Gerry I've told you about. He got a bit nasty with me yesterday. He thinks I'm seeing someone else.'

'Are you?' Molly asked.

'Yes, of course, I've told you before I like different men for different things. Gerry is good in bed, but he's a mean bastard and no fun. Brian is boring, but he's kind and lovely with Petal. Mike is

34

really good fun, generous, too, but he's as unpredictable as the weather and I never know when he'll turn up.'

'Did you admit to Gerry that you were seeing other men?'

'Yes, no names, of course, and I said they are just mates, not lovers. But Gerry went mad, saying I was a tart, and a whole lot more, which I won't go into.'

'Did Petal hear all this?'

'No, at least I don't think so. We were outside. She had gone to bed and was asleep before he arrived. She was still asleep when he left.'

'How did you leave it with him?' Molly asked.

Cassie shrugged. 'Told him he had no right to tell me who I could or couldn't see, and if he didn't like the way I was he could sling his hook. Or words to that effect. He took a step towards me like he was going to hit me, but I picked up a bottle to let him know he'd have a fight on his hands. He left then.'

Cassie dropped the subject and began to talk about the vegetables she was growing, and Molly left soon afterwards to get back to the shop.

She realized she had to tell George about this, but she didn't know how to. Cassie was the only person she'd ever met who talked about sex openly; other girls either didn't mention it at all or used prim little euphemisms. Molly knew that if she repeated what Cassie had told her word for word, George and the other policemen would think her friend was a common tart, and she couldn't bear the thought of them sniggering about her and making crude remarks.

'I only stayed for about half an hour with them,' she said carefully, trying to give herself time to think of a way to tell George what she knew. But just as she was preparing herself, the door opened and Sergeant Bailey came in. He was a burly man in his fifties and he'd been at Sawbridge police station for as long as Molly could remember.

'How are you bearing up, Molly?' he said, crouching down by her chair, his big face soft with sympathy. 'It must have been an awful shock to walk in on something so nasty. You were right, Miss March is dead, and I'm very sorry to have to tell you, but we think it was murder.'

'No!' Molly shrieked in horror. It was one thing thinking it, but quite another to have it confirmed. 'Why would anyone want to kill her? And where is Petal? Has she been killed, too?'

'There is nothing at the cottage to suggest Petal has been hurt. We made a quick search of the surroundings, but found no sign of her. I've called in some of my men and some reinforcements from Bristol to do a thorough search, but I doubt they will arrive today. As to your question about why would anyone want to kill Miss March, that's what we need to find out. And you can help us with that by telling us all you know about her.'

'But all your men should be searching for Petal now,' she burst out. 'She's only six, she must be terrified; cold and wet, too. You can't leave her out there till tomorrow.'

Sergeant Bailey and George exchanged glances. 'Molly was telling me about the last time she spent some time with Miss March,' George said. 'But I could go up to Stone Cottage now and

36

start searching if you like.'

The sergeant looked from George to Molly, then patted her on the shoulder. 'Carry on talking to PC Walsh. I have to get in touch with CID at Bridewell in Bristol, and talk to people to see if anyone saw or heard anything unusual today. Couldn't have picked a worse day for a serious crime – half the force are on leave and the rain is likely to wash away evidence. But we'll try to get a search going today, I promise you.'

Molly still thought that finding a missing young child should be the priority, not questioning villagers. But she could hardly argue with him.

George touched her elbow as the sergeant left the room. 'Before Sarge came in, I got the feeling there was something you wanted to tell me about Cassie,' he said. 'Am I right? Was it about a boyfriend?'

Molly was still a virgin and had every intention of staying that way until she got married, so she was crippled with embarrassment at having to tell George what Cassie had told her. But one of those men might be the murderer, so she had to spill it out.

Keeping her eyes downcast, she began to tell him what Cassie had said about the men in her life.

'She said Gerry was "good in bed", but mean,' she managed to get out, not fully understanding what the first phrase meant

From sixteen until she was eighteen she'd been courted by Raymond Weizer. They occasionally went to the pictures but mostly just went for walks. When he was called up for National Service, it fizzled out. And, as she had once confided in Cassie, there hadn't even been any fizz to start with; they'd never done anything more than kiss. Her parents had approved of Raymond because his family were farmers and he would inherit the farm in due course. Raymond married Susan Sadler six months after he was demobbed and they now had three children. Since then Molly had been to the pictures and to the village dance lots of times with various young men, but kissing was still as far as she went and, with just one exception, none of the men had been exciting enough to make her wish she dared go further.

However, realizing that the men in Cassie's life were vital to the investigation into her death, she had to tell George exactly what Cassie had told her, albeit blushing and stumbling over her words sometimes.

George looked a little embarrassed, too.

'It was hard to tell you something like that, which was a confidence,' she admitted when she'd finished. 'Especially as, sometimes, I didn't fully understand what she was telling me, and I didn't like to ask her to explain.'

'You did very well,' he said, and she noticed he had a little dimple in his chin when he smiled. 'I don't suppose you know these men's surnames, or where they live,' he asked.

'No, but they can't live far away, not if they just turn up when they feel like it,' Molly said. 'Have you looked to see if Cassie had an address book? I've seen her in the phone box lots of times. She could've been phoning one of them.'

George gave her one of those 'you don't need to

38

make suggestions to the police' looks.

'Sorry,' she said. 'I'm being bossy.'

'It's okay. Better to be bossy than say nothing. Would you be able to tell us what Petal was wearing today?'

'No. Yesterday she was wearing her blue checked school dress, but Cassie didn't let her wear her school clothes at any other time. My guess is that she was wearing red shorts, but I could probably tell you better if you let me look in the bedroom. I could see what was missing.'

'Has Cassandra ever said she was troubled by anyone?' George asked. 'Someone that turned up there, made a nuisance of themselves – maybe someone from her past?'

'She never said – well, except about Gerry,' Molly replied. 'But she was tough, George! If someone was being a nuisance, she'd see them off. She wouldn't just put up with it.' She almost added, 'like I would'; after all, she'd put up with her father saying the most horrible things to her for years, and hitting her, too. Cassie had been very blunt about it, saying her father was a brute and her mother almost as bad for letting it happen, so Molly should walk out on the pair of them.

'Did she tell you where she lived before she came to Sawbridge?' George asked, breaking across her thoughts.

Molly pondered the question; it was something she'd always been curious about. 'I can't give you a straight answer because Cassie never told me, but I think she'd spent most of her life in or near London, because she would mention art galleries and theatres there in a kind of personal, knowledgeable way. I think she was in Bristol, too, for a short while before she came to Sawbridge. She mentioned Devon, Glastonbury, Wells and other places sometimes, but I got the impression she was wandering around the area looking for a permanent place to bring up Petal and, when she got to Sawbridge, she felt this was it. She once told me she'd dreamed of a home like Stone Cottage for years.'

All at once Molly felt exhausted, as if all the energy in her body had drained away. She didn't want to talk any more and, anyway, she had nothing more to say.

'Go on home after you've signed this,' George said, as if he'd picked up on how she was feeling 'You look all in – not surprising after what you've been through – and I know you were up and about at seven o'clock this morning. I saw you carrying an armful of stuff to the village hall as I came on duty.'

'I've got a feeling nothing is ever going to be the same after today,' said Molly sadly as she got unsteadily to her feet. 'Is that silly?'

PC Walsh caught hold of her two hands in his and looked down at her. 'We've known each other a long time, Molly,' he said. 'Perhaps nothing will be the same again, but that doesn't necessarily mean it will be worse than before. Sometimes it takes something bad for us to see where we want to go, and who with.'

Molly smiled weakly. She wanted to think he was expressing an interest in her but, after all that had happened, it wasn't appropriate to think like that.

'I'll see you tomorrow, Molly,' he said. 'If you think of anything else that might be useful to the investigation, jot it down so you don't forget.'

Chapter Three

It was just after seven and still raining when Molly came out of the police station. Hearing music coming from the Pied Horse, she stopped in the middle of the road. She knew that the Percys had booked a small band to play tonight. If the weather had been good, they'd have played in the street and Molly would be helping to serve drinks.

She was astounded that the Percys hadn't cancelled the band the minute Sergeant Bailey had informed them at the village hall that Cassie was dead. It wasn't right to carry on with all the jollity when a young woman had been murdered and her child was missing.

Rage bubbled up inside her at the thought of people laughing, chatting and drinking at such a time, and the tears that welled up in her eyes were scalding. She already had a picture in her head of Petal stumbling around in the woods, hungry, soaked to the skin and too scared to go to anyone because she'd seen her mother being killed.

Yet now there was an even worse picture nudging out the previous one. That of Petal's small body shoved hastily under a bush to conceal it. Killed purely so she could never identify her mother's murderer.

41

Molly's usual timidity left her, and she marched across to the pub, flung the door open wide and, holding it like that, she launched into a loud and bitter tirade.

'You should not be in here drinking tonight!' she shouted out at the top of her lungs.

The band stopped playing and everyone turned to look at her. The blank expressions on their faces incensed her even further.

'Surely you all know that Cassandra March was found dead today and her six-year-old daughter is missing? Little Petal may have been murdered, too, but just in case she ran away from the man who killed her mother, is there anyone in this pub who feels able to carry on drinking and chatting while a frightened six-year-old is hiding in the woods in this rain?'

She let her question sink in for a few seconds. 'Right, who is going to come and help me search? It won't be dark until nearly ten tonight. We've got three hours to find her.'

There was a buzz of discussion. Normally, there would've been very few women in the pub but, because it was a special day, there were around twenty or so this evening. Yet they, the very ones Molly had expected to urge their husbands to join the search, looked indignant at the request.

'Come on!' Molly called out, wondering where on earth this new courage had come from. 'Imagine if it was your little girl alone in the woods.'

The first two men to make a move were in their fifties: John Sutherland and Alec Carpenter, both farm labourers.

'Thank you,' Molly said. 'You are true gentlemen. Now, who else is coming?'

It took a while, and a great deal of whispered discussion with their pals but, gradually, the men began to come over and join John and Alec. In the end, there were eighteen of them.

Three dropped out as soon as they realized they would have to walk up the hill. Halfway up, another four turned and went back down.

'So a pint is more important than a child's life, is it?' Molly called scornfully after them.

When the remaining eleven reached the track that led down to Stone Cottage, they stopped and looked at the mud in alarm.

'I'd like to look for her, but I'm not dressed for it,' Ted Swift admitted, looking down at his highly polished brogues. 'You need wellingtons to walk in that.'

'There's a big police search arranged for the morning, I heard,' Jim Cready, the local window cleaner, said. 'We should wait for that, Molly. None of us is dressed for tramping through rain and mud.'

Like sheep, they all turned and followed Jim back down the hill.

'What's a bit of rain and mud compared with saving a small child?' Molly yelled out as they retreated, then burst into tears of frustration.

She stomped down to Stone Cottage and followed the well-worn small track into the woods made by Cassie and Petal. But the track petered out after about two hundred yards; this was clearly as far as mother and daughter were in the habit of going.

Molly had been calling out for Petal as she

walked, but it occurred to her that no child would stay so close to home if something had frightened them there; they would run to somewhere they perceived as safe – school, the church or a favourite shop – so there was no sense in staying in a wood where the undergrowth was too thick to walk through.

Reluctantly, she turned round and made her way back to the road. She felt foolish now that she'd tried and failed to organize a search party. She would search the church, look in the schoolyard and along the backs of the shops, but maybe she should wait for the police search tomorrow morning at first light to go further afield. After all, they were pulling in men from both Bath and Bristol.

It was gloomy in the church, and the usual smell of polish and damp had a layer of rose scent added to it from the two very large vases of roses either side of the altar.

She looked around, including in the vestries, calling out Petal's name, but to no avail.

On an impulse she sank down on to her knees at the altar rail and prayed that Petal would be found unharmed.

As she got up she remembered that the last time she'd made a plea to God was when Emily said she was leaving home after their father had given her that beating. They were in the bedroom. Emily was sobbing; her face was swollen and red where he'd slapped it, but that was the least of her injuries: he'd hit her again and again on her back with a cane. As she was only wearing a thin blouse, her back was a mass of weals, and some were bleeding.

'I hate him!' Emily sobbed out. 'I'm going and I'm never coming back and, what's more, I'm going to steal the week's takings to teach him a lesson.'

Molly had always looked up to her big sister, because she consistently stood up to their father and had stuck up for Molly hundreds of times. But this beating wasn't just because Emily had carried on seeing Bevan Coombes, 'the lout', as her father called him, after she'd been warned she wasn't to but because she'd dared to tell Jack Heywood he was a deranged bully who ought to be locked up in a loony bin.

Molly did everything she could that night to sooth Emily's wounds, gently applying antiseptic cream, cuddling her sister and stealing some of their father's brandy to help her sleep. Later, she got on her knees to pray for a miracle; that Jack would wake up a changed man and beg Emily not to go. It didn't work, of course: her father was still as nasty the next morning. Emily waited until Saturday night when he'd gone to the pub, opened the shop safe and pocketed the week's takings, then picked up her suitcase and went to catch the last bus into Bristol.

She didn't tell Molly or their mother when she was going, and neither of them knew she'd found out what the combination number for the lock on the safe was. Jack found a note from her inside it. It said, 'Treat people badly and they'll behave badly. You deserve this and more.'

That last defiant act of Emily's still impressed Molly. Time and again when her father hit her, she wished she could find her older sister's guts.

Now, as she walked from the church to her home, she thought about the prayers she'd just offered up. They were simply that she wanted God to keep Petal safe, and that if someone was holding her to let her go without harm. She hadn't prayed that her father would be pleasant when she got home, because she knew he wouldn't be.

News travelled fast in the village so, by now, even people who hadn't been at the hall or in the pub would know exactly what had happened. Her parents may have even watched from the window as Molly passed the shop with the men as a search party.

Molly let herself in the side door, passed along the corridor by the stock rooms and went up the stairs to the flat. She was tempted to go straight to her bedroom instead of going into the sitting room where her parents would be, but if she did that her father would only come in and ask her what she was playing at. So there was nothing for it but to join them and get it over with.

Opening the door to the sitting room, she found her parents sitting just as they always did. Her father was in the wing-back armchair to the right of the fireplace and closest to the new, small, cube-like television placed on a table in the alcove. Her mother was on the left side, her back to the window overlooking the high street. Her chair was smaller, and rather hard, but she claimed it supported her back well. Neither of them ever sat on the couch, and the cushions on it were arranged with precision.

Jack turned his head as Molly came in, his mouth already twisted into a sneer rather than a

46

welcoming smile.

'I always knew that little tart would come to a sticky end,' he said, his accent broad Somerset. 'Good riddance to bad rubbish, that's what I say.'

Molly's eyes prickled with tears at his nastiness. She hadn't expected him to show any concern for Cassie but, even so, delighting in her death was appalling.

'That's very cruel, Dad,' she replied, wishing she had the courage to say something stronger. But she could see the glint of malice in his eyes, and knew by the way his mouth was twisted that he had plenty more to say on the subject and that one wrong word from her could make him flare up. She always promised herself that the very next time he was horrible she would tell him what she thought of him, but the truth was she was far too scared of him, so much so that she usually fled when she thought he might be about to hit her.

Mary, her mother, put her finger to her lips to warn Molly. With her back to the light from the window, she looked younger than her fifty-five years, but that was only because she'd had her brown hair permed recently and was wearing a flattering duck-egg-blue twinset and a little powder and lipstick for what was a special day. Close up, her face was very lined, and there was a deep sadness in her eyes that was very aging.

Jack Heywood was sixty and, although her mother always said he'd been a fine-looking man and old photographs bore this out, bitterness, thinning hair, bad teeth, a paunch and a greyish tinge to his complexion had taken those good looks.

Molly felt bad that she didn't like him, much less love him, but then he'd never been a real father. He'd never played with her and Emily, never taken an interest in their schoolwork or hobbies. All they'd ever got from him was criticism and scorn. Maybe if he'd had a son he might have been different, but he saw all females as his inferiors, and there to be used and abused.

Even the decor of their flat above the shop was evidence of his laziness and lack of interest in the home.

Paint and wallpaper had been in very short supply after the war, and most ordinary working people didn't have the money to spend on non-essential things. The more affluent people soon began making an effort to spruce up their homes and businesses, but not Jack Heywood, even though he could easily afford it.

The parade of shops in which his business stood had been built back in about 1850, and in 1910 the previous owner had extended his shop, Greville's, into the one next door and the flat above. The older residents in the village often said what a high-class establishment it was. The installation of a bathroom and a large kitchen and other renovations to the living quarters had made it an attractive and spacious home. But it hadn't been redecorated since then, and the Edwardian wallpaper, although probably once lovely, was now stained and shabby. All the furniture – a mixture of handed-down and wartime utility pieces – looked as if it had seen better days.

'Cruel! I'll give you cruel,' Jack snarled at Molly, rising in his chair a little as if about to strike her. 'Everyone but you knew that girl was a wrong'un. You're just too stupid to see it.'

'Yes, I suppose I am stupid,' she said meekly, thinking she must be stupid to work so hard for him for nothing. She moved out of his reach as a precaution. 'But even if you didn't approve of Cassie, I'm sure you feel some concern for Petal. She's missing, you know, and for all we know she could be dead, too.'

'Petal!' he exclaimed. 'What sort of a name is that to give a child?'

Molly knew it was an odd sort of name but she'd never known one that had fitted a child better, and anger rose up inside her that just this once he couldn't show a little concern for a child in danger.

'The name suits her beautifully,' she said in a quiet voice. 'I can't believe that you can't say you hope she'll be found soon, and how terrible it is that a young woman should be murdered in our village.'

She turned on her heel and left the room swiftly, ignoring his protest that he knew the truth about people and that Cassie had probably brought her death on herself.

Going into the kitchen, Molly paused for a moment to take a deep breath.

The kitchen was a large, pleasant room, the walls lined with glass-fronted cupboards which her mother kept immaculately, with her best glass and china on display. On the central, scrubbed-top table was the special cake Mary had made for today. She'd put a model of the Coronation coach on to the white icing but it had sunk to halfway up its wheels because the icing was too soft. Molly had noticed some plates of vol-au-vents, cheese straws and other food on the sideboard in the living room; the cake must have been intended to be the centrepiece. But as no one had cut into it she guessed that her father had been so scathing about it that her mother had brought it into the kitchen to hide it from any visitors.

Aware that she'd eaten virtually nothing all day, Molly cut a slice of it. Like all her mother's cakes, it was perfection, a soft and moist fruit cake, and very delicious. Molly stood for a moment or two eating it, thinking about how many people in the village really liked Mary Heywood. Before her nerves got the better of her, she had been involved in everything from singing in the choir to being a leading light in the Mothers' Union. Jack had no real friends, only people who toadied around him because he owned a shop and was on the parish council and therefore a useful person to keep in with. Some of them must have been around this afternoon, and it was likely that's how he'd heard about Cassie.

Molly was just putting the kettle on for some tea when her mother came out of the living room, shutting the door carefully behind her.

'I'm so sorry about your friend,' she said once she was in the kitchen. She held out her arms to her daughter. 'I'm sorry, too, that your father had to be so nasty about it.'

Molly allowed herself to be drawn into a tight embrace, remembering that, just before Emily left for London, she'd remarked that it was shocking that their mother couldn't even hug or cuddle them in their father's presence. As she pointed out, a man who resented his own daughters being shown affection was worryingly strange.

'Oh, Dad's just a grumpus,' Molly said lightly, because she knew her mother's nerves got worse when she thought her youngest had been hurt by him. 'I'm sure he doesn't really mean to be that way. I'm really tired now, so I'm going to bed. I hope you don't mind?'

'You're such a good girl,' Mary said, holding her daughter tighter still. Her voice sounded as if she was about to cry. 'I wouldn't blame you if you went off like Emily did. I know it's no life for you here.'

'How could I leave you?' Molly replied, forcing herself to laugh, as if she'd never even considered leaving home.

'Go and get into bed,' her mother said. 'I see you've had some cake, but I'll bring you some tea in and you can tell me all about what happened earlier. John and Sonia Burridge called round and told us you'd found Cassie dead and were in the police station giving a statement. They heard it from Brenda Percy. Then Mrs Pratt rang and said you'd gone into the pub to try to get a search party together. Your father scoffed, of course, but I thought it was very commendable of you. Poor little Petal, I do hope she will be found.'

Molly went into her bedroom then, got undressed and into her nightdress, and she was just getting into bed when her mother came in.

She sat on the end of the bed, and Molly related the whole story, excluding only what she'd told the police about the men in Cassie's life. She knew that would offend her mother.

'Cassie was murdered,' she said once she'd finished. 'My first thought was that it was an accident, but I soon realized she wouldn't have fallen backwards onto the hearth, she'd have gone face down. Besides, if Petal had seen her fall, she would have run and got help, wouldn't she?'

'Yes, I suppose she would,' Mary said thoughtfully.

'So it stands to reason that whoever killed Cassie took Petal so she couldn't identify him.'

Mary moved closer to her and took one of Molly's hands in hers. 'Your dad believes Cassie was selling herself and she upset one of her customers.'

'Trust him to think of something like that,' Molly said indignantly, pushing her mother's hands away, irritated that she might be inclined to believe her husband's theory rather than thinking for herself. 'People are so narrow-minded and stupid, especially Dad. Just because she was an unmarried mother and was a bit unconventional doesn't mean she had to be a criminal or a prostitute. She was a good mother to Petal; she taught her to read even before she started school. I've never known such a happy child.'

'From what I saw of her, I'd agree totally,' Mary said, twisting her hands together, as she always did when she was agitated.

Molly relented and took hold of her mother's hands to stop her. 'There's nothing for you to worry about, Mum,' she said. 'But I'm going out on the search first thing tomorrow, so Dad can bloody well take care of the shop.'

'Don't swear, dear! And he wasn't always this way,' Mary said in a small voice, a tear rolling down her cheek. 'He was never the same after he was attacked.'

Molly had heard the story a hundred times of how her father was hit over the head with an iron bar and robbed. She was only four in 1930, when it happened. Her father had been on his way to the bank with the week's takings from the furniture shop he managed in Bristol. He was badly hurt, needing a great many stitches in his head, but it was still rumoured that he was in league with the thief. This was later proved to be untrue, when the police caught the culprit, but by then Jack had been fired from his job and his reputation was in the gutter.

'We had such a hard time for over a year,' Mary said. 'He was in pain from his injury, he couldn't get another job, our landlord threw us out because we couldn't pay the rent. We'd have ended up in the workhouse if Jack hadn't managed to get a job on a farm out here, with a little cottage for us all to live in. I know you and Emily enjoyed it at the farm, but for me and your father it was like slavery. He worked from four in the morning till late at night, back-breaking work it was, too. I had to help him milk and muck out the cows, along with caring for you and Emily.'

'Yes, I know all that, and it must have been awful for you,' Molly said impatiently. 'But Dad got a public apology from Dawson's, the furniture-shop people, didn't he? And they compensated him, too; they gave him enough to get this shop.'

'But you don't understand how much he suffered, and I did, too. That takes a lot of getting over,' her mother said, her eyes welling up with emotion.

'It was twenty years ago, Mum! High time he stopped wittering on about it and realized he was lucky, just as he was lucky being turned down when he went to enlist in the First War. That's another thing he goes on about as if he'd been deprived. What man in their right mind would resent missing out on that?'

'He said he hated the way people looked at him because he wasn't in uniform.'

Molly shook her head in disbelief. 'He'd have preferred to lose an arm or leg, or be blinded, then? Though I suppose that would have given him something worthwhile to moan about. But, getting back to the attack: if it hadn't been for that, he would never have got a business of his own. So why should he still be angry and take it out on us?'

Mary hung her head. 'I think it changed him mentally, and I haven't been much of a wife to him in the last few years. That doesn't help.'

Anger welled up inside Molly. 'I'd say he was the one who caused your problems,' she said sharply. 'If only you'd stood up to him years ago, he might not be ruining all our lives now.'

Molly lay awake for a long time after her mother had gone back into the living room. She felt bad that she'd blamed her mother; after all, Jack Heywood was a very frightening man. But her father was the least of her worries right now. The possibility that Petal was cold, wet and frightened in the woods was her main concern.

It seemed almost unbelievable that she'd lost Cassie in such a dreadful manner, and when she tried to close her eyes, all she could see was her friend lying on the hearth, her blood pooling on to the floor.

No one could appreciate what light Cassie had brought to Molly's life. Until she arrived in Sawbridge, Molly had felt like a horse wearing blinkers must feel, seeing only what was directly in front of it. Her life was so narrow. All she had was her work in the shop, small roles in the drama club, and singing in the choir. She never went anywhere; even Bristol, Bath and Wells were like distant lands. She spent hours dreaming of finding a wonderful husband who would whisk her away to a home of her own where she would never again have to clean the bacon slicer or deliver people's groceries.

But even if, by chance, a really nice, single man happened to come into the shop and be attracted to her, Molly knew her father would pull out all the stops to ruin it for her. Over the years he'd put off several potential boyfriends by being aggressive towards them. She felt that his reputation was so well known now that no local young man would even attempt to ask her out.

Cassie was the first person she'd ever met who looked beyond the normal and the humdrum. She had told Molly she wasn't to dream of a man coming to change her life, she was to do it herself. As her sister, Emily, had done. But even if Molly wasn't yet brave enough to change her life, Cassie had opened it up for her because she knew about so much more than other people. Not just world news, films, books or music, but about customs in other countries, different religions, about science, history and all manner of other subjects. Yet, despite being clever and knowledgeable, she was also great fun, and so interesting. An hour in her company always felt like only a few minutes.

And she also gave good advice. She'd told Molly over and over again that she should leave home. She said if she stayed in Sawbridge she'd either marry the first man who asked her just so she could have a home of her own or end up the noble spinster who looked after her parents and missed out on everything.

Molly had often wondered if Cassie's understanding of her situation came from similar experiences. Her father had been killed in the war, but she might have had memories of him being a bully, or there could have been a nasty grandfather. It could even have been her mother who hurt her, and perhaps that was why she didn't want to say anything at all about her past.

Along with offering good advice, Cassie had also pointed out how many talents Molly had, that she was brilliant at window dressing, a good actress with a lovely voice, and that she could run a business single-handed if necessary. 'You don't see the big picture because you are far too close,' she had said on more than one occasion. 'Your father is grinding you down, making you think you're worthless. In fact, you're multi-talented. I believe you could do anything you put your mind to. But if you stay working for that ogre for much longer you'll become as pathetic as your mum.'

Molly didn't like Cassie saying her mother was

pathetic, but she knew her friend had a point. Yet what could she do about it? What sort of a daughter would walk out and leave her mother alone with Jack?'

She hoped so much that the police had already found Petal, and that the search tomorrow would be unnecessary, but that only solved one problem. Petal would still need to come to terms with the death of her mother and, unless close relatives could be found who were willing to take her in, she'd have to go to a children's home. She remembered Cassie's strong views on such places, the way her face would darken and her eyes flash. Molly wished she was in a position to take care of Petal. She couldn't bear to think of how awful it was going to be for her.

At five thirty the next morning around forty people were gathered outside the police station, ready for the search. It was still raining and quite cold, making everyone all too aware of how important it was to find Petal quickly. Molly was wearing her raincoat, sou'wester and wellington boots; it didn't bear thinking about how badly the child would be faring if she was out there somewhere dressed only in shorts and a blouse.

Molly knew everyone there. They were mostly men, including three or four who had joined her on the previous evening, but there were around ten women, too. Over half were the same people who always turned out when asked, whether to help at the village fete, tidy up the churchyard or raise funds. The rest were younger, in their late twenties and early thirties, and Molly knew almost all of them had young children themselves. Normally, a band of such volunteers would be laughing and chatting, but not this time. The seriousness of the situation was etched into the faces of each one; they were barely even speaking to one another.

A police officer Molly didn't know came out of the police station. He was tall and slender with a pock-marked face and a slightly hooked nose.

'I'm Detective Inspector Girling,' he said in a loud, clear voice. 'Thank you all for turning out this morning. I'm sure I don't need to tell you how important it is to find this little girl. Half of you will be starting the search from the village, working up towards Stone Cottage. The other half will be driven up there by bus, and you will search the woodland area above and around the cottage.

'You will not only be looking for Petal,' he said, looking at each face in the crowd in front of him, 'but for clothing, shoes, hair ribbons – anything, in fact, that either doesn't belong in the woods or which looks out of place and suspicious to you. Should you find something, I ask that you don't touch it but stay at the spot and call out to alert the officers searching with you. Does anybody have any questions?'

The only question was about how long they would be searching, from someone who had to go to work later that morning. There was a hum of conversation at that, some saying they would search until Petal was found, however long that took.

Molly had put some sandwiches, some water and an apple into her small haversack. She noted that most people had something similar. She had barely slept at all for imagining Petal alone and frightened out in the dark, but that image was preferable to the one of finding her dead in some undergrowth.

A green-and-white coach drew up, and Molly was told to get on it, along with about twenty other people and some policemen, all of whom were strangers to her, because they had been drafted in from Bristol. There were dog handlers, too, but they were using their own transport to get themselves and the dogs to the cottage.

The coach dropped them by the track down to Stone Cottage, because after that it was so narrow. It was even harder to walk on than it had been the previous day, because all the vehicles going to and from the cottage had churned up the mud.

Molly was put into a group that was to go directly north, up behind the cottage. In her group was a man who had only moved into the village a couple of months ago. Customers had been talking about him in the shop; it was said he was a writer and a bachelor. His looks alone were enough to make women chatter, because he was tall and very nice-looking, with a mane of curly brown hair and lovely dark-grey eyes. At any other time Molly would have welcomed an opportunity to speak to him, but it seemed all wrong even to smile at him under such sad circumstances.

The dog handler who was leading their group explained that they needed to remain within six feet of the people to the right and left of them as, that way, they could thoroughly search the area.

'Don't rush. Scan the ground for anything unusual. Rake through the undergrowth with your sticks,' he said. 'Disturbed ground, a shoe, a handkerchief or some other small thing could help us work out what happened here. Yell out if you do find something, but don't pick it up or touch it.'

Molly had brought a walking stick from home, as had many others. A walker had left it in the shop; it was a slender, lightweight, metal one with a spike on the end to get a grip in muddy conditions.

They set off immediately. The new man was to her right; on her left was Maureen French, a middle-aged, rather horsey woman who sang with Molly in the church choir.

The dog was very busy at first, going here and there, and sniffing wildly. Molly thought this must be because Petal had played close to the cottage and he was getting her scent strongly. But by the time they'd gone about a hundred yards into the woods the dog appeared to lose the scent. This wasn't surprising, as Cassie had always told Petal not to go out of sight of Stone Cottage and, as the undergrowth was very thick – in places, really hard to get through – Molly couldn't imagine a little girl with bare legs attempting to force her way in.

'Tough going, isn't it?' the writer man said to her after about an hour. 'I believe you know Petal well. Do you think it's likely she would have come this way?'

'Not if she was on her own, but then, if she was taken, the person might have carried her,' Molly replied. 'The police must know what they're doing. By the way, I'm Molly Heywood. I don't think we've met before.'

'I've seen you in the grocer's,' he said, pausing for just a second and leaning on the stout stick he was carrying. 'I'm Simon Fairweather.'

At nine they stopped for refreshments in a field. Mr Henderson, a retired schoolteacher who lived close to the field, announced that they'd covered two miles. He had a pedometer and had measured the distance. 'It seemed a lot further than that,' Molly said, with some surprise. She knew the area pretty well, but she hadn't ever walked right through the wood before to get to where they were now. 'But then it was such hard going, climbing up one minute, then climbing down, and through all those brambles and shrubs.'

'It didn't look to me as if anyone had been through there in months,' Mr Henderson said. 'No broken branches or trampling underfoot. I saw a few tracks made by small animals, but nothing by a human.'

'You trained in tracking under Chief Sitting Bull, then?' Simon asked teasingly.

Mr Henderson laughed good-naturedly. 'Well, all those cowboy-and-Indian films I watched as a kid must have taught me something,' he said.

'Cassie used to take Petal out in the woods to find wood for the fire,' Molly said. 'They used to follow animal tracks. I went with them several times, but Petal hated being scratched. I don't think she'd flee into thick undergrowth, not even if she was scared. She'd have run for the road.'

'I think you're right there,' Simon agreed. 'From what I've seen of Petal, I'd agree entirely.'

'You knew her and Cassie then?' Molly asked.

Simon nodded. 'I like walking, and I often do a

61

circular walk, coming back past Stone Cottage. Cassie always spoke to me, offered me a drink or whatever. I stayed for supper with them once.'

Molly thought it a little odd that Cassie had never mentioned him. Simon Fairweather was most definitely the kind of man you would mention meeting.

'Did you go to the police and tell them that?'

He looked startled, his grey eyes widening. 'No. Well, why would I? I didn't have a relationship with Cassie, it was only the odd chat.'

'But you must have formed an opinion about her, picked up little snippets that might be useful to the police?'

He looked doubtful about that, and it crossed Molly's mind that he may have had a bit of a fling with Cassie. She was very easy about sex. Just a couple of months ago she'd cheerfully admitted to having sex in a field with a man she'd met an hour before in the library.

'Don't worry. It was a one-off.' Cassie had laughed at her friend's shocked expression. 'He didn't have a clue, and I didn't like him enough to coach him.'

Remembering that admission made Molly wonder if she should tell the police about it; she didn't want to portray Cassie in a bad way but that man could be her killer.

'I think you ought to talk to the police, Simon,' she said. 'I keep remembering little things that may or may not be important. One thing I was just reminded of is a bit embarrassing, but I think I ought to pass it on.'

'Someone she slept with?' he asked.

'Umm...' Molly hung her head.

'I didn't sleep with her,' Simon said. 'I liked her, but that was all.'

Molly felt she believed him. 'What did you talk to her about?'

Simon smiled. His eyes were very twinkly and she noticed he had lovely full lips. 'About books, mostly. I write, you see, got my first book published last year. Cassie wanted to know all about it.'

Molly remembered then that Cassie *had* said she met a man she talked about books to. For some reason, Molly had assumed he was elderly; she certainly hadn't considered that it could be the writer so many women in the village gossiped about. 'Tell me about it. What kind of book is it?'

'It's a thriller called *"Shadows"*. It didn't exactly set the world alight, but I'm just doing the final editing on a second one, which I hope might.'

Molly liked the light way he spoke; he didn't seem to take himself too seriously.

They set off on the search again then, circling round an hour later so that they came back to Stone Cottage soon after one. The other search parties arrived back a short while later, everyone looking very wet and weary. DI Girling got them to gather round so he could speak to them.

'We've covered a vast area this morning, far further than it would be possible for a six-year-old to walk, and we have found nothing to prove that Petal has been in that area. Thank you all for your help, and, although I know many of you were intending to continue searching until Petal is found, we need to stop for now while I reconsider what needs to be done. We will call on you should we need to conduct another search.'

Simon looked at Molly, and shrugged. 'He's right. She couldn't have walked beyond the area we searched.'

'Then that means she was taken,' Molly said, tears springing involuntarily to her eyes. 'I just wish there was something more I could do.'

Simon reached out and put his hand on her arm in sympathy. 'Me, too,' he agreed. 'Will you introduce me to one of the cops you know so I can tell them I knew Cassie a bit?'

'I'll take you to George Walsh,' she agreed. 'He interviewed me last night, and he's a good sort.'

George Walsh had been in a different group to them. When she went over to speak to him he took off his helmet and wiped the sweat from his forehead with a handkerchief. Molly introduced Simon, explaining that he'd known Cassie.

'I think you might be the right people to help out the DI,' George said. 'Just wait here while I have a word with him. I know the others are going to get the coach back to the village, but someone will run you back down later.'

'What do we know that might help the DI?' Simon asked Molly as PC Walsh walked away.

'Just stuff Cassie told us, I suppose, but I could murder a cup of tea, so I hope he doesn't keep us long,' she replied.

After speaking to DI Girling, PC Walsh left with the others, walking up the track to the lane and the waiting coach. DI Girling came over to Molly and Simon.

'I hear you both knew Cassie quite well and have

been in her home. PC Walsh thought you could help by looking around it and seeing if you notice anything missing, something that wouldn't normally be there, or anything that doesn't seem right. Miss Heywood, I believe you were very close to Miss March and her daughter, so maybe you could tell if any clothes or toys have been taken?'

Molly was very apprehensive as she stepped into Stone Cottage. Cassie's body had been taken away, but the bloodstain on the floor by the fireplace was still there and immediately brought back all the shock, fear and revulsion she'd felt when she found Cassie the previous day.

Simon and DI Girling stayed downstairs looking around, and Molly went upstairs. She pulled out the drawers in the chest next to Petal's bed first.

As neither Cassie nor Petal had a great many clothes, it didn't take long to go through them. She checked the laundry basket, too, to make sure that anything she thought was missing wasn't in there.

'I'd say some underwear, socks and a red cardigan has been taken,' Molly said to DI Girling when she'd finished and was walking back down the stairs. 'Also, a red-and-white spotted dress with short sleeves, and I can't see Petal's red shorts anywhere, so my guess is that she was wearing those, ready to change into her Britannia costume. Are her yellow raincoat and wellingtons still here?'

'I haven't seen them,' the policeman responded. 'There's a scruffy, off-white adult raincoat on the hook by the back door. Is that Miss March's?'

'Yes, and Petal's yellow coat is usually next to it. So she must be wearing that. It doesn't look like

Petal ran out of here in fright, does it? No six-year-old picks up a change of clothing, including clean socks, do they? I doubt Petal would even think to put on her coat.'

'Umm! Yes, you're right there,' DI Girling said thoughtfully. He took a notebook from his pocket and wrote down the items she'd identified as missing. 'Can you think of anything else that might be missing?'

'I can't see her toy dog, a floppy, brown-and-white thing, she used to cuddle it when she was tired, or if you read to her. Cassie never let her take it to the shops or anywhere like that, it had to stay on her bed.'

Simon came over to Molly. 'Did you see Cassie's diary up there?'

'No, it wasn't there,' she said.

Simon looked at DI Girling. 'Have the police already found it and taken it away?'

DI Girling looked suddenly more animated. 'There was no diary on the list of items which were taken away. What was it like?'

'Big, seven by ten inches, I'd say, a dark-blue leather cover with a metal clasp. It was a five-year one, and Cassie said she wrote it up every day.'

'Where did she keep it?' DI Girling asked.

'I saw it on the table when I came for a meal one evening,' Simon said.

'It was mostly on the dresser,' Molly said, going over to it and looking in the drawer. 'Cassie told me that maybe she'd use it one day as a basis to write a book.'

'She said that to me, too.' Simon nodded. 'We used to talk a lot about writing when I came by.

She asked me how you know where to begin a book, and whether it's better to write in the first person or the third.'

'Did she let you read any of the diary?' DI Girling asked Simon.

'Oh no, she hated the idea of anyone looking at it,' Simon said firmly. 'She struck me as a very private person. She said once that, if she did ever write a book, the most daunting thing for her would be getting someone to read it when she'd finished to give a critique.'

DI Girling turned to Molly. 'Did she say anything about her diary to you?'

'Only that writing down what happened to her helped her rationalize things. She said she wrote down stuff like people being nasty to her because she was an unmarried mother with a mixed race child. She said that seeing it on the page made it clear to her that they were ignorant and bigoted, and they were to be pitied. She claimed that stopped her hurting.'

DI Girling looked a bit bemused at that. 'She kind of put her head on the chopping block coming to live here in an all-white area, didn't she?' he said. 'Now, if she'd gone to live in Bristol, no one would've turned a hair. Did she ever say why she came here?'

'I got the idea she wanted to hide away,' Simon said. 'Did you get that idea, too, Molly?'

Molly nodded. 'Yes, she was a bit of a hermit. She'd go into Bristol once a week on the bus, and in the school holidays she'd take Petal to Wells, or Bath, but the rest of the time she was just here in the cottage. She grew vegetables, she'd cook, knit

67

and read. She didn't even have a wireless.'

'What did she live on? Did she ever say?'

'Very little,' Molly said. 'She had to count every penny. She had a cleaning job in Bristol, and that's why she went there every Thursday. She usually came into the shop for food after she got back, too.'

'Did she tell you who she worked for?'

'No, and I never asked,' Molly said. 'I did think it was funny that she dressed up to go there, though.'

'What do you mean, "dressed up"?'

'Well, she looked really smart, glamorous even: a tight skirt, her hair up and high heels. If I was doing a cleaning job, I'd go in my oldest clothes.'

'Did you ask her about it?'

'I teased her,' Molly said. 'I said she was the smartest cleaner I'd ever seen. She just laughed and said she had an overall and some plimsolls in her bag but she liked to make out she was going somewhere lovely.'

'So she might have been lying and, in reality, she was meeting a lover who gave her money?'

Molly frowned. 'Yes, I suppose she could've been, but she always looked awfully weary when she got back. Besides, if there had been a man, I think she'd have told me about him. She told me about the other men in her life.'

DI Girling looked long and hard at Molly, as if weighing up whether she was telling the truth. 'Getting back to the diary, it's very strange that it's gone,' he said, pulling cushions and the gaily coloured crocheted blanket from the sofa to look underneath them. 'It suggests to me that the

68

person who took Petal thought there might be something in it to incriminate them. A family member, perhaps. Petal's father?'

'But I don't think Cassie had any family,' Molly said. 'As for Petal's father, she said it had been a brief fling, over long before she knew she was going to have a baby, and she never saw him again. She added that she didn't regret it, though, as Petal was the best thing that ever happened to her. And, really, if a black man had come to the village, someone would've seen him, wouldn't they?'

DI Girling was silent for a moment, just standing there staring into space. Simon winked at Molly encouragingly.

'You said it was a five-year diary?' DI Girling said after a little while. 'People who keep diaries on a regular basis tend to have a stack of old ones, too. Did she?'

Molly shrugged her shoulders. 'I don't know. She never said she did.'

'No, nor to me,' Simon said. 'But tell us, Detective Inspector, was Cassie's death definitely murder?'

DI Girling sighed deeply. 'We're not absolutely sure – it could be manslaughter, a fight that got out of hand. But I heard this morning from the pathologist that there are indications of a fierce struggle, bruising on her arms, face and to her neck, and he didn't think falling back on to the hearth would result in death, only if her head had been banged hard against it, perhaps more than once. Then, of course, the daughter's disappearance and the fact that some of her clothing has been taken adds another perspective. Someone intending to kill a child wouldn't bother to take clothes or a toy. So it looks to me as if the target was Petal.'

'You mean that this person wanted to take Petal away? But Cassie tried to stop them and got killed trying?' Molly asked.

'That may be the case, but I shouldn't be talking to you about any of this so I'd be obliged if you'd keep my opinions to yourselves.'

Molly told DI Girling about the man Cassie said she had met in the library, and then Simon told him a little more about how he had got to know her. 'What about fingerprints?' Simon asked. 'Did you find any here?'

'I'm not at liberty to divulge that,' DI Girling said. 'But on that note I'd like you both to come to the police station now to give me yours, so they can be compared with any others we might have found. After that, I trust neither of you will leave the village, in case we need you to answer further questions.'

Simon and Molly turned down the offer of a lift back to the village, both saying they'd walk. Molly wanted to delay going back to work and seeing her father. Simon gave no reason.

'I don't get the impression the police are going to try very hard to solve this,' Simon said thoughtfully as they made their way up the muddy track. 'For a start, he never asked me where I was at the time of Cassie's death.'

'No, he didn't, did he?' Molly said. 'How odd! In fact, he ought to have taken you in for questioning, not just chatted with us both in the woods.'

'Exactly! Hardly first-class detective work. But,

as it happens, I have a cast-iron alibi. I was staying with some friends – a doctor and his wife – for two days before Coronation Day. I watched the ceremony on their television, along with some of their family. I only left there at five in the evening, and heard about Cassie in the Pied Horse last night.'

'Well, that puts you in the clear then,' she said.

'Yes, but isn't it awful to think that the prejudice there was about Cassie when she was alive is still there now she's dead, and that any investigation will only be half-hearted?'

Molly hadn't thought of that. She had always believed that the police would take the same care with every case they were trying to solve.

'Maybe we can whip up a bit more concern, if not for Cassie, for Petal,' Molly suggested. 'I mean, most people thought she was a very cute little girl. I'm sure they'd want to know where she's gone.'

Simon grimaced. 'I've got a feeling, Molly, that you and I are the only people who give a jot about either of them. I'd love to be proved wrong, of course, but I don't think I will be.'

Chapter Four

Two weeks on from Coronation Day Molly and her mother were stacking a delivery of canned goods in the stock room behind the shop and talking about the investigation into Cassie's death

71

and Petal's disappearance, which appeared to have ground to a halt.

'Maybe something new will be revealed at the inquest,' Molly said.

'Perhaps, and I hope they can release Cassie's body for burial after that,' Mary replied. 'Thank goodness the vicar stepped in and agreed the cost of the funeral would be met by the church, as she had no known family.'

The first week after the tragedy, it had been the main subject of conversation in the village; even the Coronation, the wonder of television or Sir Edmund Hillary conquering Everest took second place. Most people had cast Petal's father into the role of murderer. Without knowing anything about him, where he came from, or what he did for a living, suddenly he was the murdering child-snatcher and possibly responsible for every unsolved crime in the country.

That first week there were police everywhere. Door-to-door inquiries were made across a ten-mile radius of the village, and dozens of people with only the most tenuous link to Cassie were questioned. It seemed to Molly that Simon had been wrong in saying he didn't think the police would make much of an effort to solve the crime.

The national newspapers had all taken up the story, and published pictures, urging people to come forward if they had seen Petal or knew anything at all about Cassie.

Then, suddenly, like a light being turned off, everyone lost interest.

The journalists who had been knocking on doors to try to get extra titbits of information, disappeared, and so did all the extra police brought in from Bristol.

To Molly, who was still grieving at the loss of her friend, this was an outrage. She couldn't sleep at night for worrying about Petal, and she couldn't understand how anyone could just forget a small child in danger.

She was particularly incensed by the indifferent attitude of the parents of children who were at school with Petal. She felt they should all be scared for the safety of their children, if nothing else.

'Even the local police don't seem to care much any more,' she said bitterly. 'George does, of course, but he's far too junior to influence anyone higher up. He told me they didn't get one lead about Cassie's background from the pictures of her in the papers. As for Petal, all the sightings reported turned out to be false. But someone, somewhere must have seen her, she's a distinctive-looking child. They should be putting up posters of her face everywhere and running the story again in the newspapers to keep it fresh in people's minds.'

All at once her father appeared in the doorway through to the shop, his face flushed with anger. 'If I hear another word about that dead tart and her darkie kid, I'll throttle you!' he yelled out.

Molly quaked. Normally, she would've said nothing; anything to keep the peace. But this time she had to speak out.

'She was my friend, and I was very fond of Petal,' she said, trying not to show her father how scared she was of him. 'Besides, I was talking to

73

Mum, not you.'

'How dare you!' he roared, stepping forward and striking her hard across her face. 'You've been hanging around with that uppity tart so long you're becoming just like her.'

Molly reeled, but did what she always did when he hit her: curled her arms over her head to protect herself and looked for the best way to run to escape him, because she was terrified. But when she looked towards the door at the end of the stock room which led to the outer side door, she saw her mother cowering against the shelves, shaking with fright.

Molly's cheek stung from the blow. She knew there would be more unless she got out, but she couldn't leave her mother to take the brunt of her father's violence.

'No father should hit their daughter for voicing her opinion,' she said, biting back tears and aware her voice was shaking. 'If you don't apologize right now, I'll leave. And it will be for good, too.'

'You'll never leave home,' he sneered at her. 'You wouldn't last a day without your mother fussing over you. You're pathetic and weak, like her.'

Something snapped inside Molly. All her life she'd lived with his sarcasm, violence and sheer nastiness. She'd had more slaps from him than she could count, but enough was enough. He had no right to treat her and her mother this way.

'The only pathetic thing about Mum is that she's stayed with you all these years,' she said, standing up straight to face up to her father. 'Not through weakness, but because she truly believes that marriage is for better or worse. And she did

74

get worse, didn't she? You are a lazy, whining bully with no joy in you at all, and I'm ashamed to be your daughter.'

He stood still, staring at her open-mouthed while she made her impassioned speech, and she thought when he turned from her that he was going to skulk away with his tail between his legs.

But he didn't. He picked up the long, metal pincher-like gadget they used for reaching packets on high shelves and, before she could move away, he brought it crashing down on her head.

'You dare to oppose and insult me!' he snarled, while raining blows down on her. 'I am the head of this household and you will do as I say.'

The first blow had felt like she was being branded with a red-hot poker, and was quickly followed by more, and Molly screamed at the top of her lungs. Mary yelled at him to stop and tried to catch hold of his arm, but he pushed her away, sending her crashing into a shelf unit and sliding down to the floor.

'Stop this, Mr Heywood!'

The deep male voice took them all by surprise, and they turned to see PC George Walsh standing in the small passageway which led to the shop. He was in civilian clothes, had clearly come into the shop to buy something and, hearing a commotion coming from beyond the door which led to the stock room, had decided to investigate. To Molly and Mary's good fortune, he was in the nick of time, and before Jack could move or speak George lunged forward, caught hold of the older man's arm and shook it till he dropped his weapon. 'By rights I ought to give you a taste of your own

75

medicine,' he growled, pushing Jack away from Molly and towards the wall at the back of the store room. 'Men who hit women disgust me.'

'You don't know what she said to me,' Jack said plaintively, but he was already shrinking under the look of revulsion on the face of the young policeman. And Walsh had manhandled him as if he was capable of doing him serious damage.

'I wouldn't care if you told me she'd stolen a week's takings or burned your shop down; there is no justification for any man hitting a woman.' George went over to Mary, who was still on the floor, and helped her to her feet, then he turned to Molly and put his arm around her protectively. 'You come home with me,' he said. 'We'll talk about pressing charges while I see to your injuries.'

Molly wanted to go with him. She couldn't think of anywhere safer than being with George, and she hurt all over, but she couldn't leave her mother alone with her father.

'Thank you for the offer, George, but I can't leave my mum,' she said, as tears of shock began to run down her cheeks. 'But I promise you, if Dad takes one further step towards either of us, I'll ring the police station immediately.'

They all looked towards Jack. He had slumped down on to a chair in the corner and was holding his head in his hands as if he was very aware he'd gone far too far.

'He might be sorry now, but I'm still going to report what I've just witnessed,' George said forcefully. He went over to Jack and prodded his shoulder. 'You lay just one finger on either of them ever again and I'll see you get locked up.

Like I said, I'm off to report you now.'

'I didn't mean to hit her, but she got my goat,' Jack whined. 'You don't know what I have to put up with.'

'You should be down on your knees thanking God for such a devoted wife, and a daughter who has made your business so successful.' George's lips curled back in scorn. 'If Molly had any sense at all, she'd leave home right now. She deserves so much better than this.'

George left, then, slamming the shop door so hard the bell jangled furiously. Jack scuttled into the shop, not even glancing at his wife or daughter.

Mary and Molly looked at one another fearfully. 'He'll put the "CLOSED" sign on the door now and probably go off to the pub,' Mary whispered. 'I can't imagine what he'll be like when he comes back. Maybe you should've gone with George.'

Molly was shaky and nauseous with shock and hurting from the beating her father had given her, but George's intervention had dispelled her fear. 'I meant what I said, Mum: I'll ring the police if he does anything more to either of us, and I'll press charges. He's got away with stuff for far too long. We have to stand up to him. Now, let's go upstairs. He can go and hang himself for all I care.'

Upstairs, Mary got Molly to sit down while she put a cold compress on to the red weals on her head and neck. One had caught her on the side of her face and drawn blood, and the skin around her eye was already swelling up.

'You're going to have a real bruiser in the morning,' Mary murmured, and when Molly looked up she saw that her mother was crying silently.

'Don't, Mum. I can't bear to see you cry,' she said.

Mary hugged her daughter close to her breast. 'Oh, my darling. I think George was right – you should leave. This is no life for you, and I can't even promise things will get better after today.'

'I'd leave if you came with me,' Molly said, moving her head slightly so her voice wasn't muffled. 'We could get a little flat in Bristol and I could work in one of the big shops. I'm sure you could get some part-time work, too.'

Mary shook her head. 'I couldn't do that. It would mean I'd be dependent on you, and that isn't fair to you either. You couldn't look after us both, and I wouldn't let you try. I'd just ruin your life.'

Molly thought that was the saddest thing she'd ever heard. How could her mother believe that she'd ruin her own daughter's life?'

'I can't leave you here alone with Dad. You're already a bag of nerves. Even if he doesn't hit you, he'll make you do all the work I do now, and he'll be on at you constantly.'

'I just won't do all the work,' she replied. 'I'll ignore him. He'll have to get someone else to help, or the shop will go under. Maybe I can persuade him to sell it and retire.'

Molly thought that retirement would be even worse for her mother: her father would have nothing at all to do, and he'd grumble, demand and find fault even more. But she couldn't say that. Her poor mother had to be left with some hope for the future.

Mary Heywood knew what her daughter was thinking as she hugged her to her breast. Molly was right in believing Jack wouldn't change; he couldn't, he was too set in his ways. But she had to find a way to make her daughter see that she wasn't responsible for either of her parents and that she was entitled to choose her own path in life.

Of course, Mary knew she was partly to blame for this state of affairs. She should've put her foot down with Jack long ago, at the first sign of violence and nastiness, instead of caving in and allowing him to do it. Maybe if she'd walked out years ago he would've come to heel when he realized what he stood to lose. But, instead, she'd just kept quiet, and that had added more fuel to his fire.

It might be too late now to change Jack, but it wasn't too late for Molly to start out afresh. Emily had made the break and got away; Molly could, too. Mary knew she had to be a real mother now and protect her child, whatever the cost to herself.

She moved back slightly from Molly and, putting one hand on each side of her daughter's face, she lifted it to look at her. Such a sweet face, wistful blue eyes, a neat, up-tilted nose and a generous mouth. She would never be a beauty queen, but the warmth of her personality and the way she cared about people meant she would always be liked and admired. Mary hoped she'd find love soon with a man who really deserved her.

'Listen to me,' she said. 'You *are* leaving home, Molly. Not today or tomorrow, but as soon as we can make the arrangements without your father finding out. I won't sit back any longer and watch you working without being appreciated or being given a fair wage. I want you to have fun, to make new friends and be happy. So please don't refuse.'

'But I'll need money—'

Mary cut her short by putting a finger on her daughter's lips. 'I'll get you the money, and in the next few days we'll work out together where you're going to go. Now, I suggest you go and have a lie down for a bit. You've had a nasty shock.'

After two days of lying around nursing her wounds and trying hard to think of where she could go if she did leave home, on the afternoon of the third day Molly decided to go and see Simon. She might hardy know him, but he seemed to be a man of the world, he'd liked Cassie, too, and she thought he would give her good advice.

She put make-up over her bruised eye, hoping he wouldn't notice it, and, taking a pot of local honey and a few buns her mother had made as a little present, she walked down the high street to his flat, which she knew to be over Weston's, the funeral directors.

There was a concrete staircase up to his flat, reached from the back of the building. Molly remembered that when she and her friend Christine had been about seven they came round here to find out where Mr Weston kept the dead bodies. He'd caught them trying to peer in a window of an outhouse, and he'd taken them back to Heywood's grocery shop, holding each of them by the ear.

'You should teach your child to have some respect for the dead,' he had raged at her mother.

'Death is not a sideshow at the fair, something to snigger about.'

She was very lucky that her father was out of the shop that day and he never got to hear about the escapade. She and Christine never dared go to the undertakers again, though.

Molly rushed up the stairs, hoping Mr Weston hadn't seen her from a window. She didn't want him informing her father about this either.

'Molly!' Simon exclaimed as he opened the door. What a delightful surprise. Come on in. I was getting very bored writing and was just going to make some tea. Nice to have you to share it with.'

Molly handed him the buns and the honey. 'A little present in return for some advice,' she said.

She loved Simon's posh voice, and he looked lovely, in a creased, open-necked shirt and grey flannel trousers, with his feet bare and his hair all tousled.

His flat was just a bedroom, a living room, a kitchen and a bathroom, all rather shabby and untidy. She glanced through the open door to his bedroom and, seeing the unmade bed, guessed he never made it.

'Yes, I know I live in squalor!' He laughed, guessing this was what she was thinking. 'I really ought to get a house-keeper; I'm quite useless at the domestic stuff.'

'I'd offer to come and do it for you,' Molly said, 'but I doubt my father would approve of that.'

'Did he do that?' Simon indicated her black eye.

Molly hesitated; she might have known the make-up wouldn't fool anyone. She wanted to

81

deny her father had done it, but she guessed that Simon had already heard that her father was a bully. 'Yes, and that's why I need some advice. I want to leave home.'

'Well, I don't know if I'm the best person to give advice, but I'll do my best,' he said.

'Obviously, I can't go right away, I've got to wait, as I'll be called as a witness at Cassie's inquest. Mind you, if they are as slow at organizing that as they are at finding out what happened to Petal, I might still be here at Christmas.'

They sat at the kitchen table, which Simon hastily cleared of books and dirty tea cups, then, over tea and the buns, discussed the lack of effort the police had put into finding Petal. Like Molly, he didn't think the police had been very thorough.

She told him her idea about posters with a picture of Petal on them being printed, stuck up in post offices, railway stations and other public places.

'I agree,' Simon said. 'A six-year-old isn't that easy to hide. Someone must have seen her – unless, of course, she was killed and buried very soon after Cassie was killed.'

'If the murderer was going to kill her, surely they would've done it at the same time as killing Cassie? It makes no sense to risk taking a child somewhere else,' Molly said. 'That's why I think she's alive.'

'Then, logically, Cassie's killer has to be someone who would care about Petal, like her father. If only we knew about him, and what happened between him and Cassie. It must have been something seriously bad for her to come and live in Sawbridge like a hermit,' Simon said.

Molly nodded in agreement. 'Have the police tried to find her diary? Or who Cassie worked for on Thursdays? As I see it, there are many things they could follow up, but they haven't bothered. I bet if Petal was the child of a policeman or a schoolteacher they wouldn't have given up so quickly.'

'What does your policeman friend say on the subject?'

'I haven't really had any opportunity to talk to him and, anyway, I think he'd tell me that was police business. But he did intervene the other day when my dad did this.' She pointed to her face. 'He warned Dad he was going to report him, and I think he scared him a bit, as Dad hasn't been so nasty since. But then that's what I came for advice on. I know it's time for me to leave.'

'You must,' Simon said, nodding his head. 'There's a big, wonderful world out there waiting for you. Sawbridge is fine for a writer like me who wants quiet, but not for a pretty girl in her prime.'

'I'm not pretty,' she said.

'I think, then, you must have a distorted mirror,' he retorted, leaning forward and touching her cheeks lightly. 'You are also bright, kind and adaptable. I know girls are conditioned into thinking that getting married and having babies is the be all and end all. But that isn't so. Since the war ended there are so many opportunities arising for women. Everyone knows how well women coped when all the men were off in the army, and I don't think any right-minded person would want to push you all back into the kitchen.'

'You sound like Cassie,' Molly said.

'She made me aware of things I'd never considered before,' he admitted. 'I hadn't ever noticed that women got a different deal to men, not until I met her. I suppose I was like every other male, brought up to think women were there purely to serve us.'

'Yes, Cassie was quite militant. She raged on about women getting a lower wage than men when they did the same job. That was something I hadn't even thought was unfair – I just accepted it.'

'I got the impression she'd been pushed around, and that was why she was the way she was. Maybe she'd had a tough childhood, or it could've been her experiences since she had Petal. Mind you, she always evaded questions about her past. I'd have given anything to have got her full story. Did she tell you much about it?'

Molly shook her head. 'No, she could never be drawn on it. I asked her once where she'd met Petal's father and she told me very bluntly that it wasn't something she wanted to talk about.'

Simon chuckled. 'She could crush you with a couple of words, couldn't she? But then she must've taken an awful lot of stick for having a mixed race baby. I don't know why that should horrify people so much. I think I'd prefer a black one – they're very cute, with a better finish than white babies.'

Molly laughed at that. She'd always thought Petal was far more attractive than any other child of the same age she knew. 'People seem to be scared of anything or anyone that's a bit different.

84

I heard a couple of women talking in the shop a while ago about someone they knew who was going to Italy for a holiday. "I wouldn't want to eat any of that foreign muck," one said. The other one said she'd be afraid she'd catch something nasty. You could go to Weston-super-Mare and catch something nasty, couldn't you?'

Simon smiled. 'During my stint in the army, lots of the other chaps had a real phobia about trying any food different to what they'd had at home.'

'I can't imagine you in the army,' said Molly with a smile. 'You just don't seem the type.'

'You mean I look like a milk-sop?'

'No, of course not,' she insisted. 'It's the guns thing, and needing to be very fit.'

He laughed. 'I'm stronger than I look and, for your information, I learned to use a shotgun at eleven and used to shoot rabbits and ducks. But if you'd seen the lads who were called up at the same time as me, you'd have thought none of us would make soldiers. But then it was the same in the First War – farm lads, bank clerks, carpenters and plumbers, not fighters. Few of us welcomed call-up, but we had no choice so we buckled down and made the best of it.'

'It must have been scary thinking you might be killed.'

'I never allowed myself to dwell on that. The army was the making of me. It made me more self-sufficient, I learned to value what it is to be English, and to be grateful to my parents for giving me such a good start in life. If you'd seen the plight of all the refugees in Germany at the end of the war! They'd lost everything – their homes, families, their health – they were hanging on by a thread. I tell you, Molly, it made me realize how lucky I was that England was safe and I had a home and family to go back to.'

She was touched by his sincerity. 'I can imagine. Cassie often talked about articles she'd read about how it was in Europe – all those displaced people, cities smashed to pieces. Did you talk to her about it?'

'Yes, I told her about seeing survivors of the concentration camps and all the horrors that went with that. It was good to get it off my chest, as it had preyed on my mind. She was incredibly well informed. Goodness knows how she became so.'

'She used to go into the library and read the newspapers after she'd taken Petal to school. I asked her once why she hadn't gone to university, because it was obvious she was bright enough to go. But she just laughed.'

'I suspect she came from the kind of middle-class background where women don't have work,' he said. 'She never spoke about it, but she had that sort of genteel manner, didn't she?'

Molly thought about this for a moment. 'You might be right about that, but I'd say she went out of her way to hide it. She was such a mystery.'

Simon smiled at her. 'You're a mystery, too. I can't imagine why you haven't been snapped up by someone and got a brood of little ones.'

'My dad puts off any potential suitors.' Molly laughed. 'That's yet another reason to leave home and why I needed advice.'

'Is that about what to do, or where to go?' he questioned.

'Both, I think,' said Molly, blushing, because she knew she sounded a bit drippy. 'I've never done anything but work in the shop, and how do I find a place to stay and a job all at once?'

'First, you get the job,' he said. 'Seeing as you know shop work, you could apply to Selfridges, Harrods – or even Fortnum & Mason, the posh grocery shop. Once you've been offered a job you could get a place in a girls' hostel.'

'You make it sound so easy,' she said.

He smiled. 'The only tough part is making the decision to go and sticking to it. It will all fall into place once you know that's what you really want.'

She got to her feet, suddenly aware she'd been there for over an hour. 'I must go now, Simon, but thank you for the chat and the advice. Once the inquest is over, I'll do it.'

'You can come and talk to me any time, if it helps,' he said.

As Molly walked home, she realized that talking to Simon had had an effect similar to that talking to Cassie had always made on her. Both gave her the ability to see her life and the path ahead a little more clearly. He was such a nice man; a bit too posh and sophisticated for her – but a girl could dream.

The inquest was held in Bristol a week later. Molly had to be there to give evidence about finding Cassie's body. George took her in a police car because, although he didn't have to give any evidence, he had to drop off some papers at Bristol's Bridewell police station.

At the inquest, the pathologist who performed

87

the postmortem confirmed that Cassie had died of a fractured skull, the result of her head being hit against the stone hearth several times with considerable force. He said that there were bruises on her neck, arms and a blow to her cheek consistent with a violent tussle prior to her being knocked down on to the hearth and the final blows which killed her.

Molly had to confirm the date and time when she found Cassie's body, and she was asked a few questions about Cassie's private life. As Molly had never met any of Cassie's other friends, she could offer no information about them. All she could give were her views on her friend's character.

As a result of the findings, the coroner recorded the death as Murder by a Person Unknown.

Molly was glad of the verdict, as she thought it would force the police to renew the investigation, but when she met up with George afterwards for a cup of tea in a café near the Coroners Court, he sounded doubtful.

'There's a possibility that, if the killer is still holding Petal, it might make him panic and release her so he can get away,' he said. 'But it's just as likely he'll feel he must kill her, too.'

'Don't say that!' Molly exclaimed.

'I certainly hope it won't come to that,' George said. 'Everything about Cassie and this case is so mysterious. I know you think the police have done nothing at all, but that's not true. We can't find a record of her birth, trace her parents, find out where Petal was born – nothing. We don't think Cassandra March was her real name but, normally, when we make an appeal for information in the press with a photograph, someone comes forward. But no one has – well, except the four men who had got to know Cassie since she moved to Sawbridge.'

'Were they the ones I told you about? Her lovers?' Molly asked.

'Yes. They'd all had a relationship with her, but they knew precious little about her. They came forward voluntarily, and they all had firm alibis for the time of her death, so we could rule them all out. From what we've gathered from them, Cassie wasn't one for talking about herself and her past. She certainly didn't tell any of them who Petal's father was or why they weren't together. Each one of the men said she was fun to be with, didn't take life too seriously, that she was warm and amusing. I think we can assume that meant she was sexy, too.'

Molly blushed. She had a feeling these men in Cassie's life had cared more about the sex than anything else. 'We all – you, me, the whole village – assume it's Petal's father who took her. But what if we're all barking up the wrong tree?'

'We're assuming that because he's the most likely candidate. For one thing, he must have been a bad lot for Cassie to be hiding away from him in Stone Cottage.'

'But we don't know that is who she was hiding from. Petal's father could be just a man she slept with once and never saw again! Maybe the killer had some entirely different grievance with her? She'd run out on him, stolen his money, told his wife he'd been a naughty boy? Anything.'

'Yes, that's a good point. But can you tell me,

Molly, if the murderer wasn't Petal's father, why would they take her with them? She would only make the culprit's escape harder and, like you said earlier, it would be far less risky to kill her there in Stone Cottage.'

'Okay, so if it was Petal's dad, what do you think his plan was?'

'I don't think he had one. I suspect it was just instinct to flee with her.'

'He was organized enough to take some clothes and her toy with him.'

'Yes, well, maybe he stopped for long enough to think that through. And there are places that a black man could be invisible – an area like St Pauls, for instance,' George said. 'She'd be just another child of an immigrant. He could always say her mother had died or run off. So many people come and go there, no one would think anything of it. And they aren't likely to tell tales on anyone either.'

St Pauls was an area of Bristol quite close to the Coroners Court. With its elegant, large Georgian houses and close proximity to the city centre and the docks, it had once been a very desirable place to live. But back in the thirties the owners found their property too expensive to maintain and many sold it on to people who turned the houses into flats or lodgings. As there had always been a sizable proportion of black people in Bristol because of the docks, many of them gravitated towards St Pauls and its cheap rooms.

Bristol had suffered a great deal of bomb damage during the war and this had made housing very scarce. The local council had concentrated its efforts on building new homes in the suburbs of Bristol, ignoring inner-city areas like St Pauls. At the same time, immigrants from the West Indies were flooding into England, too, lured by the prospect of work as nurses, as bus and train drivers, and in factories. Unable to find homes in the better parts of Bristol, they, too, made for St Pauls, and unscrupulous landlords were quick to exploit the situation.

St Pauls was now a ghetto. The poorer tenants had no choice but to share their accommodation to pay their rent, and the ensuing overcrowding and unsanitary conditions were shameful.

'And I suppose there is no accurate record of everyone living there either?' Molly said.

George shrugged. 'It's impossible to keep tabs on everyone,' he said. 'We think there must be many babies born after the parents arrived in England that were never registered, purely out of ignorance. People come to join relatives, then move on to other cities. The children might be in school for a year, then they're gone. It's just not possible to check up on them all. I just hope that whoever it is that's got Petal – if someone has got her – he's taking good care of her. Of course, he could've taken her to London, Birmingham, or Cardiff – anywhere with a sizable immigrant community – and finding her will be like looking for a needle in a haystack.'

'But Petal was a very bright little girl. I couldn't imagine her not telling someone about her mother. And if she saw what happened to Cassie, she's likely to be distraught,' Molly said.

'That has occurred to me,' George said. He

looked hard at her face, as if taking in the fading but still visible black eye. 'It also occurs to me that you are avoiding discussing what you're going to do about your violent dad!'

Molly was embarrassed. 'I'm planning to leave home as soon as I can get a job. I'd put off applying for any until after the inquest, and now there will be the funeral. As soon as that's over, I'm going. But don't tell anyone, because if it gets back to Dad, he'll go mad.'

'I thought perhaps you were waiting for the posh writer chap to sweep you off your feet.'

Molly looked at him. Had someone seen her go into Simon's flat? She couldn't think of any other reason for him saying such a thing. 'Simon's just a friend,' she said indignantly. 'I'm surprised at you. I never had you down as a nosy parker.'

'I'm not, but I have to confess I've been keeping an extra sharp eye on you, what with the murder, and your dad.'

'That's very kind, but unnecessary now. Thanks to you, Dad has calmed down. I like Simon, and it's good to talk to him, because he's the only other person in the village who liked Cassie. But if you want to keep your eye on someone after I've gone, I'd appreciate it if it was my mum. Could you do that?'

George put his hand over hers. 'Of course I will, and if you send me your address when you're settled, I'll write and tell you all the gossip. I think it's the best thing for you, Molly, but I'm going to miss you, all the same. Have you decided where you'll go?'

Molly looked at his big hand over hers and

thought how nice it felt. 'London seems the best bet,' she said. 'Maybe I could get a job in one of the big shops? I believe Selfridges and Harrods are both very special.'

'You've always been a bit special to me,' George suddenly blurted out, his face flushing a bright pink.

Molly was surprised at him saying such a thing, but touched, too. 'What brought that confession on?' she asked.

He shrugged. 'I was just suddenly aware that I'll really miss you. But if you do go and you want to come back and see your mum sometimes, without having to face your dad, you can come and stay with my folks. They would love to have you.'

'That's such a kind thought,' said Molly, moved to find George so empathetic. She'd already wondered how she could see her mother away from her father. 'I might very well take you up on that.'

George smiled. 'I'll be hoping!'

'Not many people here are there?' George said in a whisper as he and Molly took a pew in the church for Cassie's funeral.

Molly glanced round and saw there were around twelve mourners in all, including Simon and Enoch Flowers, Cassie's landlord.

'I'm relieved to see this many,' she whispered back. 'I thought it might be just you, me and Simon, especially as it's raining so hard.'

It had been warm and dry for several days, but at seven this morning the heavens had opened and the rain hadn't let up since.

Molly's mind had been all over the place since

93

her long chat with Simon. One minute she could think of nothing but moving to London and working in a smart department store, the next she was plunged back into mourning for Cassie and feeling desperately afraid for Petal. She was finding it hard to dance attendance on the customers in the shop the way she used to, and she often forgot to order items they were low on. On top of this she kept slipping into little romantic fantasies about Simon.

He was so much more mature and articulate than the boys she'd grown up with. Most of them could barely string a sentence together, let alone talk coherently about the situation in Europe or equality for women. She knew, of course, that the attention he paid her was just his gentlemanly way, but she couldn't help but wish it was more.

Looking across the nave at him now, he looked so handsome in his dark, well-cut suit. She wondered what a kiss from him would be like, or even to be naked beneath the sheets with him, his slim body pressed against hers.

She pulled herself back from that titillating thought. It was entirely inappropriate in a church. She glanced sideways at George beside her, almost afraid he'd read her mind, but he was looking off into space. She wondered if he ever had such thoughts about her.

The organ wheezed and sighed before one of the Bach Preludes began. Reverend Masters had asked Molly what music Cassie would like, but that was just another thing Molly didn't know about her friend. Cassie hadn't even had a wireless, so the subject had never come up. But Molly had chosen 'All Things Bright and Beautiful' as the hymn, because she'd heard Petal singing it once, and, even though Cassie had claimed to be an agnostic, she would like that, just because of her daughter.

The responses to the prayers were muted, the hymn was sung only marginally louder, and Reverend Masters' eulogy could have fitted almost any average housewife. He mentioned Cassie's love of books and gardening, but not her indomitable spirit, her sense of humour or her intelligence – all things Molly thought she had impressed on him. He mentioned Petal being missing still almost as an afterthought, and didn't even speak out to tell the congregation that, if they knew anything at all about where she was, they should go straight to the police.

It was exactly the kind of funeral Molly had expected, yet she had hoped she would be pleasantly surprised and uplifted. As it was, she felt that, once again, she'd been slapped in the face with the knowledge that no one apart from her and Simon had liked Cassie. Even George hardly knew her. She guessed the other people here, with the exception of Enoch Flowers, had only come to the funeral to make themselves look good.

The second Cassie's coffin was in the grave and the last prayer intoned, they all scuttled off. Even Simon went, though, to be fair to him, as he'd seen her and George arrive together, perhaps he thought it inappropriate to hang around when no one else was.

Molly stood silently in the rain, looking down at the casket, which she knew had been paid for from church funds, and cried. It wasn't right that such a memorable, bright and fascinating woman should've such a weak and meaningless send-off.

George let her cry for a few minutes, holding his umbrella over her without saying a word. Finally, he touched her shoulder. 'Let's go and have a drink. Not here, where people will talk, but in Midsomer Norton.'

Molly smiled weakly at him, touched that he'd sensed that she really needed someone, or something, to delay her return home. It was bad enough having to say her last farewell to Cassie, but she was also anticipating a great deal of ridicule and sarcasm from her father when she got back.

There had been an atmosphere ever since he'd hit her. He hadn't apologized, not even when her eye was black and swollen and she had weals on her cheek and neck, but he had let her stay upstairs until the swelling went down without saying anything nasty again. It was tempting to think he felt bad about attacking her as, even when she went back to work, he restocked the shelves in the shop, a job he normally left to her, and unpacked several deliveries, too – he hadn't even admonished her when she'd forgotten some orders, but she thought it was more likely he was just brooding and waiting for an excuse to pounce again.

'I've borrowed Dad's car,' George said, pointing out the green Austin A40 Devon which was parked by the churchyard gates. 'He said if I scratch it he'll wring my neck.'

Molly smiled. Very few ordinary people in the village had cars yet, and she'd often seen people admiring Mr Walsh's when he parked it outside the pub or the post office. She felt quite honoured to be getting a ride in it.

'We'll have lunch at the pub I'm taking you to,' George said as he drove away from the high street. 'I always think that after something distressing you need food to lift your spirits.'

Molly half smiled. George was always making rather odd remarks and she rarely knew how to respond to them. 'Did you find the funeral distressing, then?' she asked.

'In as much as there were no family there to mourn Cassie,' he said. 'I hardly knew her, unlike you, but it is tragic for someone so young, with so much to live for, to lose their life in such an awful way. As for all the sadness and mystery about Petal, that's really getting to me. I know you don't believe we're doing anything about it down the nick, but I promise you I'll be keeping it in the forefront of everyone's mind.'

'So what would be your plan?'

'Well, it seems to me that one thing I could do is to try and find out what Cassie's real name was. I've already spoken to Miss Goddard, the headmistress, and asked her if she saw Petal's birth certificate when she enrolled her at the school. But she didn't. Miss Goddard said she asked Cassie to bring it in, but she said she had mislaid it. Unfortunately, Miss Goddard didn't chase it up. I'd say Cassie had made up both their names, and she'd only do that if she was running from something or someone.'

'What do you mean, "from something"? Something illegal?'

'Possibly, or maybe she got involved with villains and found out stuff they didn't want her to know. But I have other questions, too. What did she live on? Do you know?'

'No, I don't. She might have got some national assistance, I suppose, but she always struck me as too proud for that, and as the kind of person who manages on very little.'

George glanced round at her. 'However careful she was, she'd still need some money. I think she got it on her weekly trip to Bristol.'

'Out of a bank, you mean?'

'No, Molly, from some kind of work. But what kind of job only requires you to be there one day a week?'

'She did cleaning.'

'I don't think that would pay enough to keep herself and Petal.'

'So how do you think she got by?'

'Prostitution?'

Molly was shocked and surprised by him. 'No, she wouldn't do that,' she said indignantly.

'You're being a bit illogical, not to say naïve,' he said with a shrug. 'You told me about Cassie's lovers, and that she had very liberal ideas, compared with most women. You even said she had sex with a man she'd just met in the library.'

'Yes, but she wouldn't do it for money.'

'Why wouldn't she?'

Molly thought about that for a little while. She had never seen a prostitute, but she had always imagined them as raddled-looking women with tight clothes and too much make-up standing on street corners in slum areas of the cities.

'Cassie just wasn't the type to do that,' she said

at length.

George chuckled. 'Molly, all kinds of women over the years have turned to it when they have no money and children to feed,' he said. 'It's the oldest profession, as I'm sure you know. But maybe Cassie had just one man who paid her and that's where she went every Thursday. Is that any different, really, to having a lover who is a married man and buys you a dress or gives you jewellery?'

'Put like that, I suppose it isn't,' Molly said reluctantly. 'But Cassie was so independent.'

'It is very hard for any woman to be truly independent,' George said reprovingly. 'They don't get paid the same as men, most have problems getting childcare, and there's very little sympathy for an unmarried mother.'

'That's very modern of you,' said Molly with a touch of sarcasm. 'I never expected a boy I went to school with in Sawbridge to have sympathies with women's problems.'

He smirked. 'I'm not brave enough to voice them in the pub, though, so that makes me look like a knight in rusty armour.'

After the sadness of the funeral and the bad feeling at home, Molly was glad to put it all aside and just enjoy being with George. Despite knowing him all her life, she hadn't realized that he'd seen action in Germany after he was called up in 1944. She remembered, of course, him leaving the village, bound for an army camp to train, along with a couple of other local boys who were eighteen, too, and all called up together. For some reason she'd imagined he spent his time working in stores or something, because he never said a word about his experiences when he returned after the war was over. It pleased her that he was so modest, never seeking glory or feeling the need to boast. She realized she had underestimated her old schoolfriend.

'Then I joined the police force after I was de-mobbed,' he said. 'That snotty friend of yours, Simon, said it was because I needed to follow orders, like I was some half-wit, but at least I'm doing something worthwhile, not just sitting at a desk scribbling like him.'

'He's rubbed you up the wrong way,' Molly said with a smile. 'Don't tell me you've become, like so many around here, suspicious of strangers?'

'I've got nothing against strangers, or even writers. I just don't like the way he brags,' George said. 'He was holding forth in the pub about how he got wounded in Normandy, then when he recovered he went out to India to teach English. He spoke as if none of us had done anything and never been anywhere.'

'I haven't found him like that,' she said, but, in truth, Simon had been a bit dismissive of some of the locals. 'But you kept it very quiet about being in Germany. I didn't know that.'

'Everyone was doing something during the war,' he said. 'I don't think many of us knew what our old friends were up to.'

'I'd have written to you if I'd known,' she said. 'I suppose I thought you were stuck out at Aldershot or somewhere.'

George grinned. 'The night before I left there was a dance in the village. You were with John Partridge all evening – I couldn't even get one dance with you. I expected you to be married to him by the time I got home again.'

'John Partridge!' Molly exclaimed. 'He had goofy teeth and sticking-out ears! I only danced with him that night because I felt sorry for him. And I'm glad I did, because the poor man was killed by a V2 in early 1945. He was only in London for an interview.'

George's smile vanished. 'Gosh, yes, I'd forgotten about that. What bad luck! My mother wrote and told me. He was going to become a priest, wasn't he?'

'That's what he wanted to do, but he'd already been turned down by both Oxford and Cambridge, so that interview he was going for was for some far lesser college or training place.'

'Fate is a strange thing,' George said thoughtfully. 'We could be driving back to Sawbridge this afternoon and die in a car crash. Or I could get shot by some hoodlum tonight when I go on duty. You just never know what's in store for you.'

'A cheerful thought,' Molly said. 'But if I don't get home soon I know what will be in store for me. Dad will be on the war path.'

Chapter Five

Four days after the funeral Enoch Flowers came into the shop. Molly had been surprised to see him at Cassie's funeral. He hadn't spoken to her there, not even a nod, but that wasn't unusual, as he was famously silent.

Molly thought he looked like a gnome: short and tubby with a slightly too large head and deep creases in his face, like an apple that has been kept too long. No one knew exactly how old he was, but it was generally thought he was in his seventies. Yet he still ran his farm alone, milking over thirty cows a day, along with all the other chores.

As usual, he was wearing a very worn tweed jacket with leather patches on the elbows, mole-skin trousers held in at the ankles with gaiters and a grubby neckerchief of indeterminate colour. He brought into the shop with him a farmyard smell, and Mrs Parsons, who was getting Molly to slice some bacon rashers, wrinkled her nose in disgust.

'Good to see you, Mr Flowers,' Molly said. 'I'll be with you in a minute.'

Mrs Parson normally lingered to gossip after paying for her groceries, but the smell got too much for her and she hurried out, still with a wrinkled nose.

'I come to see if you want to go up to Stone Cottage and go through the young lass's things, take anything you've got a mind to?' Mr Flowers growled at Molly in his strong Somerset accent.

Molly almost asked him to repeat what he'd said. She couldn't really believe she'd heard right.

'That's very thoughtful of you,' she said cautiously, wondering if there was some kind of catch to his offer.

'Well, you were the only pal she did have, and I knows she appreciated your kindness. There ain't nothing there of value, but it struck me you was the kind to want a keepsake.'

Molly was astounded that he could be so sensitive, and that he'd obviously had a soft spot for Cassie. 'I'd like that. I really miss her,' she said. 'And maybe I could take a few of Petal's things, just in case the police find her?'

'I don't hold out much hope of that,' he said. 'Pretty little thing she were, too, a credit to her ma. I miss 'em both; they used to come up to the farm for milk and eggs. Always smiling, the littl'un. Her ma was a good'un an'all. She'd have made a fine farmer's wife.'

Such warmth from a man who normally communicated in grunts was astounding, and it made Molly glow to hear her friend praised.

'I wish everyone in this village was as kind about her. I find it very sad that they can't even say something nice now she's dead, or even show concern for Petal.'

'Most folks is like that,' he said. 'I've had plenty said about me. Anyways, Miss March came here to hide away from someone. I reckon he tracked her down. He'll have killed Petal now and buried her someplace,' he said.

'I'm really hoping that isn't the case.'

Flowers grimaced. 'I don't reckon he knew she had a kid till he got to the cottage. What else could he do with her? You can't let a kid tag along with you when you've just killed her ma.'

'Cassie never told me she was hiding from someone,' Molly said.

'Nor me, but I've been around long enough to recognize the signs. Any road, I gotta go now. I've left the key under a stone by the pump. You take what you want and I'll get rid of the rest.'

After Mr Flowers had left Molly went outside the shop to arrange the fruit and vegetables more neatly, and to let his smell disperse through the open door. She wondered what would be a good keepsake. As far as she remembered, Cassie didn't have anything remarkable.

She was just picking over the vegetables and taking out anything which looked past its best when her father came out of the shop. He stood in the doorway, puffing on his pipe and watching her. 'Your mother will make some soup with that lot,' he said curtly, looking down at the basket she was putting the rejected vegetables in.

'Okay,' she said, though no response was really needed, because her mother always made soup with anything they took up to her.

'Were you off with that writer fellow after the funeral?' he asked.

'No, I wasn't,' she said. 'Why do you ask?'

'In case you go making a fool of yourself over him,' he said. 'He's married.'

That was news to Molly, Simon had implied he was single. It was so typical of her father to try and humiliate her. He must have heard some gossip that she and Simon were friendly and decided to put a spanner in the works. The most annoying thing about it was that it stung. She had daydreamed about the man and, even though she knew she wasn't the kind of girl he'd go for, if he'd asked her out, she would've gone.

'I'm not likely to make a fool of myself over any man,' she said sharply. 'I've got more self-respect.'

'I was just warning you. I heard in the pub last night that his wife came looking for him. Seems he'd walked out on her.'

'Fancy that,' she said, picking up the basket of vegetables. 'Excuse me. I'll take these up to Mum.'

She didn't go upstairs, but went out into the backyard and sat on the bench in the sun to gather herself.

It didn't make any real difference to her that Simon was married, or that he'd walked out on his wife. Apart from a couple of friendly chats, there was nothing between them, whatever her father thought. He must've had his reasons for leaving his wife – she, of all people, understood that no one knew what went on behind closed doors.

But what this news had done was remind her that she could be an awful fool when it came to men, and that, if Simon had made a play for her, she'd probably be putty in his hands, just the way she'd been with Andy Soames.

Andy was a bricklayer. He'd come into the shop when he was building a new house just outside the village. She was nineteen then; he was twenty-five: tall, blond, blue-eyed and, to her eyes, utter perfection. He had flirted with her as he bought a pork pie and some apples for his lunch.

That afternoon she had taken off her shop overall, brushed her hair and put on some lipstick. A quarter of tea had been accidentally left out of a delivery to Mrs Rawlings that morning, so Molly told her mother she was going to drop it in to her. The house Andy was working on was, conveniently, in the same direction as the Rawlings place.

Andy was standing on the scaffolding around the half-built house. He'd taken his shirt off because it was a hot day, and the sight of his bronzed bare chest with its rippling muscles made her feel quite faint.

'Out for a walk?' he called out, leaning on the scaffolding rail and smiling down at her.

'Taking this round to a customer,' she called back, waving the tea. 'It's far too nice to be stuck in the shop this afternoon.'

He moved suddenly, catching hold of one of the vertical scaffold poles, and shinned down it at the speed of light.

'That was impressive,' she said. 'You didn't even look as if you were hanging on.'

'A trick of the trade,' he said, flashing a wide smile that showed his startlingly white teeth.

She ought to have known right then that he was out of her league. Men that looked like him wouldn't fall for a girl like her. But when he said he would walk with her to deliver the tea and perhaps take a stroll across the fields, she stupidly imagined he was smitten by her.

He kissed her as soon as they were in a field and tried to persuade her to lie down in the grass with him. His kiss sent her reeling, and she might have lain down with him if her father hadn't been expecting her back at the shop. As it turned out, after three or four such incidents, she began to see that all he wanted from her was sex. He never asked her out. Not a night out at the pictures or a dance when he was washed, shaved and in smart clothes. All he ever offered was a walk during the day, when he was all dirty and smelling of sweat. Yet each time she agreed to meet him up the road she came very close to losing her virginity.

It was purely the fear of having a baby that stopped her going the whole way. She knew her father would throw her out if she fell pregnant and, anyway, she'd seen other girls she'd gone to school with either being made to marry the boy responsible or sent away in disgrace and having the baby adopted.

But she had wanted him so much. Just the thought of his kisses made her tremble and her stomach flip over. Three weeks later his work in the village was finished, and he never even came to say goodbye to her.

It was a harsh lesson. She cried at night for weeks, feeling cheap and used. But maybe it was a worthwhile lesson, because she had never let any other man or boy treat her that way since. Of course, Cassie had said she saw nothing wrong in having sex before marriage, as long as you made sure the man used a Durex. As Molly couldn't imagine ever being bold enough to ask a man if he had one, she had told herself she wasn't ever going to go that far. Yet even at Cassie's funeral she'd been having erotic thoughts about Simon. If he had made a pass at her, might she have succumbed? She thought, to her shame, that it was likely.

A little later that morning her mother came into the shop and, between customers, Molly told her about Enoch Flowers.

'My word, that's a turn-up!' her mother exclaimed. 'He doesn't normally give anyone the time of day.'

'He's a bit of an outcast – I expect that's why he understood Cassie,' Molly said. 'I'll go up to the

107

cottage after we close and look around.'

Mary looked anxious. 'I don't like to think of you up there alone,' she said.

'Don't be daft, Mum. The person who killed Cassie and took Petal won't be hanging around there looking for another victim.'

'Perhaps not, but go now and get it over with.'

Molly was pleased to get out, and jumped on her bicycle. Ever since she had decided she was going to go to London she had found the days in the shop endless. Only last night her mother had told her she had withdrawn some money from her post-office account for Molly and that she ought to go soon. Molly's plan was to write to Bourne & Hollingsworth, a department store in London's Oxford Street, to ask for a job. The reason she'd picked that shop was because she remembered from Margaret, an old schoolfriend, who had gone to work there years ago, that they had a hostel where the staff lived. Margaret had worked there right up till last year, when she got married, and she had been very happy.

The bushes either side of the track to Stone Cottage had grown thicker since she last came up here and appeared to be doing their best to hide the footpath. It was also eerily quiet. Molly felt a little nervous, and looked all around her as she approached the cottage.

'Don't be silly,' she said aloud. 'There's nothing here to harm you.' Yet, all the same, she retrieved the key quickly from its place by the pump and hastily unlocked the door.

Looking around inside, she found a multi-coloured silk scarf in a drawer which she'd always

108

admired on Cassie, and put it to one side. There was also a pretty little gold-and-white hand-painted wooden horse she seemed to remember Cassie saying came from India. Amongst Petal's things she found a blue cardigan that Cassie had knitted for her daughter and embroidered down the front with daisies, and the book *Ameliaranne and the Green Umbrella* by Constance Heward, one Petal had wanted read to her time and time again.

In a small leather box she found some amber beads, a silver bangle and a gold ring with red stones set into it. She had no idea if the ring was valuable, but if Petal was ever found she would like something of her mother's, so she put the box with the other things.

There didn't appear to be anything else worth taking but, all the same, Molly pulled all the drawers right out to check behind them and looked at books on the shelves. Cassie had had surprisingly literary taste in books – Dickens, Thomas Hardy, Jane Austen and Ernest Heming-way – but she also liked A. J. Cronin and had got Molly to read *The Citadel*.

Seeing *Hatter's Castle* by the same author, Molly pulled it out to take home to read. As it came off the shelf, a letter fell out of it on to the floor.

There was no envelope, just a single sheet of paper with a London address at the top and no date. She had no way of knowing whether Cassie had received it here, or before she came to Saw-bridge.

'*Dearest Cassie,*' she read:

I was so very relieved to finally hear from you. I had been desperately worried about you and you have been in all my prayers.

I do understand why you felt you must go – the East End is not an ideal place to bring up a child. You said that you felt you were in danger, and I do so wish you had talked to me about this, as I'm sure the pair of us could've found a solution to whatever the trouble was. I can only hope that you are with good people now who are kind to you both. I miss you, and if it doesn't work out for you there I hope you know there will always be room for you both back here.

You are a remarkable person, Cassie. You've come through so much and yet somehow managed to keep your compassion for others and your sense of humour. Most would have crumbled or become very bitter. I wish I was in a position to help you more. All I can offer is my affection, a listening ear and the promise that God is with you. Kiss Petal for me and write back soon.

Your loving friend, Constance

Molly felt like shouting aloud in glee at having finally found something that was a lead into Cassie's past. She hastily pulled all the other books off the shelf and shook them to see if any other letters might be hidden there, but she found nothing more.

She stood for a few minutes looking around her, remembering Cassie. She could see her lying full length on the couch, her red hair shining in the light from the oil lamp, and hear her laughter as she related something funny she'd overheard or read in the paper. The brightly coloured crochet blanket she would tuck round Petal when she didn't feel well was there on the back of the sofa, and a pencil pot made from an old baked-bean can and covered by Petal in fabric and trimmed with braid sat on a side table. Everything in the cottage had Cassie's hand on it, and it hurt to think it would all be taken out and thrown away, wiping out the character of the strong woman who had been so dear to her.

What would the police do with the letter from Constance? Would they send someone to see her to try to find out more about Cassie? Maybe they would, but they'd almost certainly be heavy-handed, and Constance might just clam up on them, as she sounded, from the letter, like a very sensitive soul.

It might be better if she went herself, and if Constance did know anything useful about Cassie then she could pass her name and address over to the police and let them take it from there.

With nowhere else to search now, she picked up the few things she'd collected and left the house, putting them into the basket on her bike. Then, after locking the door and replacing the key by the pump, she rode home.

After supper she wrote to Bourne & Hollings-worth, and to Constance. The first letter outlined her experience in her father's shop and her interest in display, and asked that she be considered for a job interview.

In the letter to Constance she explained how

she had found her address and that Cassie was dead and Petal missing.

It is plain to me that you are very fond of Cassie and Petal, and I'm sure this letter coming from a total stranger is a huge shock to you [she wrote] *but I was very fond of Cassie and Petal, too, and I would so much like to talk to you and discover a bit more about her. I am hoping to come to work in London soon and, if you are agreeable, I could come to your home for a chat.*

Yours sincerely
Molly Heywood.

Finishing the letters at nine, Molly decided to slip out, post them and take the letter from Constance round to show Simon. He might have already left his flat, if his wife had made him go home with her, or she could even be there, but Molly really wanted his opinion about the letter and, besides, she needed to prove to herself that he was nothing more than a friend and, if he was leaving, to say goodbye to him properly.

She had thought that her father was watching the television in the sitting room but, after she'd gone downstairs and was about to open the back door, he appeared from the stock room.

'Who have you been writing to?' he asked, seeing the letters in her hand.

Molly's heart sunk. 'Just a couple of friends,' she lied.

'You haven't got any friends,' he said scornfully. 'Give them here and let me see.'

'Oh, Dad. One of them is to Margaret Goodie,

112

now Mrs Blake. I remember that you couldn't stand her,' she bluffed, forcing herself to sound light-hearted as she tucked the letters into her cardigan pocket. 'The other one is to Susan Eaggers. I'm sure you remember her family moving away last year.'

He looked hard at her, eyes narrowed with suspicion. 'But why the rush to post them now? They don't empty the postbox till after nine in the morning.'

'I wanted some fresh air,' she said.

'But it'll be dark soon.'

'There is street lighting, Dad,' she said. 'It's a lovely evening, and I've been stuck indoors all day.'

She waited, fairly certain he would point out she'd been gone for an hour that very afternoon. But, clearly, he wasn't aware of it. 'Don't go hanging around on street corners' was all he could come up with.

Molly held her breath until she was out of the door and the backyard. She wouldn't put it past him to come after her and take the letters to see if she was telling the truth. But, to her relief, he didn't, and she hurried down to the postbox and put them in.

She hesitated for a moment or two at the bottom of the stairs leading to Simon's flat, unsure whether he'd be pleased to see her or annoyed. But she took a deep breath, ran up the stairs and rapped on the door.

'Well, blow me down!' he exclaimed when he opened the door and saw her there. 'I was just feeling a bit sorry for myself, and you arrive to cheer me up. Come on in.'

'I did hear a bit of gossip today about you,' she said carefully as she walked in. 'But that isn't why I came, because that's your private business. I've got something to show you, and I want your advice.'

'I'm sure the whole village is buzzing with it, and making completely false suppositions,' Simon said, grimacing. 'The truth is that my wife and I were washed up years ago. She only came here today to talk about getting a divorce. Unfortunately, she couldn't find my flat, so went into your dad's shop, when it was busy, to ask where it was. I didn't realize omitting to tell the world that you are still legally married was such a heinous crime!'

'You know how people here love a bit of scandal,' Molly said lightly, a little surprised that such a man of the world should be upset by tittle-tattle. 'I bet they were disappointed you hadn't made a second, bigamous marriage or left some damsel in distress because you couldn't marry her.'

'Divorce isn't such a big thing,' he sighed. 'But never mind about that. Do sit down and tell me what advice were you looking for?'

Molly sat down at his table and explained how Enoch had told her to go and look for a keepsake from Cassie.

'I found this – it fell out of a book,' she explained, handing the letter to Simon.

He read it, but didn't comment for a moment, just rubbed his chin thoughtfully.

'I should tell you to take it straight to the police,' he said. 'This woman definitely knows something about Cassie's past, and she's obviously a good sort, and religious, too. But the police aren't noted for their delicacy, and I think you could get more out of her than they would.'

'But surely that would be tampering with evidence,' Molly said. She knew perfectly well that she'd already decided what to do, but she supposed she hoped he'd agree it was the right thing.

'All I can say to that is that if they'd done their job properly in the first place they would've found it themselves. I'm not saying you shouldn't hand it over to them when you know a bit more detail, Molly. But let's face it – I haven't seen any evidence of dynamic detective work, have you?'

'No, I suppose not,' Molly agreed. 'But how do we know this woman will tell me anything?'

'She sounds like a very nice woman who cared deeply about Cassie, so she's bound to want to talk about her to you. People do when they're grieving.'

Molly went on to tell him then about writing to Bourne & Hollingsworth to ask about a job. 'Their staff get accommodation in a hostel,' she said. 'I thought that would be better for me until I got to know my way around London.'

'That sounds like a great plan. London can be a lonely place but, living in a hostel, you'll get to know the other girls well.'

'Do you think they'll take me on?' she asked. 'Won't they take one look at me and see a country bumpkin?'

'I think they'll look at you with your shining hair, pink cheeks and that ready smile and be delighted to employ you.'

'You old flatterer.' Molly laughed. 'Now, what do

115

you think about the lady who wrote the letter?'

Simon looked at it again. 'There is something a little curious about her. She has beautiful handwriting, and the tone of the letter suggests that she's well brought up, but it's odd that such a person would live in Whitechapel.'

Molly looked at him blankly.

'Whitechapel is in the East End of London, and it's the rough part of the city. It was also very badly bombed during the Blitz.'

'Well, maybe she's a vicar's wife or doing something to help the people there.'

'That could be it,' Simon nodded. 'Let's hope she writes back quickly to you. In the meantime, how is it at home?'

Molly shrugged. 'Dad is as sullen as ever. He demanded to know who the letters I was posting were for. I lied to him, but I was scared he'd snatch them out of my hand. I can't wait to get away from here, but I'm so worried about my mother – she'll be at his mercy with no one to help her.'

'Your policeman friend will keep an eye on her. Molly, you aren't responsible for your parents. Your duty is primarily to yourself.'

'I'm not sure I agree with that. The world would be a terrible place if all everyone thought of was themselves.'

Simon smiled. 'There should be a balance, I agree, but you, my dear, have allowed your life to be completely taken over by your parents' wishes. At your age, you should be out having fun, falling in love and being reckless and silly. Stay at home much longer and you'll become a classic old maid.'

'Well, I've been reckless enough for one night, coming into your flat,' Molly said with a smile. 'If that got back to Dad he'd put me under lock and key. So I'd better go. I'll let you know as soon as I hear from Constance.'

Simon walked with her to the door. 'Be brave, little one,' he said as he opened it for her. 'Believe in yourself, too. You are a very special girl.'

Chapter Six

Molly waved from the train window until she could no longer see George standing on the platform at Bristol's Temple Meads Station. But when she sat down her heart plummeted.

On the drive to the station with him she hadn't been the least bit worried about her two-night stay in London. Yet now she was in a compartment with three total strangers, it came to her that, when she was in the city, there would be absolutely no one to turn to for help.

George had arranged for her to spend two nights in a small guest house he'd stayed at a couple of times when he had to be in court in London. It was close to Paddington Station, and he'd even drawn her a little map so she could find it easily.

Tomorrow morning at eleven she had her interview at Bourne & Hollingsworth. After that she would have to find her way from Oxford Street to Whitechapel to see Constance, then back again to Paddington for her last night there.

117

What had seemed so simple when George was talking about it now looked so scary. What if she got lost? People said London was dangerous. Supposing someone stole her handbag with all her money and train tickets?

Molly had never been to London before. In fact, the furthest she'd been from her home was a day trip to Weston-super-Mare. She recalled her disappointment when her father refused to let her go to London for the Coronation. He was going to be savage when he got up today to discover that, this time, she'd taken off without his permission.

She smiled at the thought of it. He hated anyone getting one over him and was smart enough to realize she would have been planning this for days. Of course, she'd be for it when she got home but, hopefully, she'd be able to inform him that he'd have no further say in her future, as Bourne & Hollingsworth had offered her a position.

It had seemed forever waiting for the replies to her letters; almost every day, she had had to make sure she was in the shop when the postman called, to ensure that any letter came straight to her. The one from Bourne & Hollingsworth came first, offering her an interview on 12 August. By that point, Molly had convinced herself that Constance wasn't ever going to reply. But she was wrong: the long-awaited letter arrived a few days later.

Molly took the letter out of her handbag to read again because each time she read it she gained comfort in finding that Constance cared as much about Cassie and Petal as she did.

Dear Miss Heywood [she read]

Please forgive my delay in responding to your letter, but the content was so upsetting that I found myself unable to think what I should say to you. I am deeply shocked and horrified that Cassandra is dead, and absolutely appalled that Petal was taken by her murderer.

To think of that sweet child crying for her mother is more than I can bear, and all I can do is offer up prayers that her kidnapper is treating her well, wherever she is.

Please do call on me when you are in London. We may be able to help one another through the grief and anxiety by talking about it together.

Sincerely yours
Constance

Molly had telephoned her yesterday and was surprised to hear a very frail-sounding voice on the other end of the line. She hadn't for one moment thought of Constance as old. However, Constance had seemed delighted that Molly would be coming to see her the following afternoon.

George had pressed a five-pound note into her hand just before she boarded the train. 'It's for unexpected expenses,' he said, waving away her protestations. 'If you get lost, or you feel threatened, it's money for a cab. It's a safety net.'

Molly had said she would give it him back if no emergency arose, but he'd laughed and kissed her cheek, saying all she had to do was come home safely.

Molly wished she knew how he really thought of her. He'd been part of her life since she was

119

five, and she'd always assumed he saw her like a sister, nothing more. But there did seem to be something more than that or why would he be so waspish about Simon? Like everyone else he had heard about his wife coming to the village to see him. George had spoken about the man as if he were a complete cad. Was it jealousy?

She might not know George's true feelings for her, but one thing was certain, she couldn't wish for a better friend. He'd rung the guest house in London and booked her room, driven her to the station and given her the encouragement she needed to make this huge first step towards leaving home. She hadn't admitted to him that she was scared of staying in a guest house because she'd never been in one before, or that the prospect of going on the underground filled her with dread. She certainly wouldn't have admitted that she didn't know how she was going to eat while she was away, because she was much too bashful to go into a café alone.

Was everyone like this on their first trip to London? Or was she just being a big baby?

The rhythmic chugging of the train was so soothing that Molly found herself wafting into a kind of torpor in which random thoughts and things people had said in the last couple of days kept popping back into her head.

George had warned her that the Braemar Guest House was a little shabby, but she was to keep in mind that the whole of London was that way, and it would be some time before it recovered from all the bomb damage during the war. He said she'd see bomb sites wherever she went.

There were a great many bomb sites in Bristol, too; almost the entire medieval shopping area of High Street and Wine Street was destroyed during the Blitz. Molly could remember the thudding noise from the bombs late in 1940 and the winter of '41, and seeing a red glow to the sky from the burning buildings. The horror of what was going on in the city was brought home even more closely by seeing 'trekkers', people fleeing for safety to the countryside, prams loaded up with their treasures as well as small children. Those people walked miles, many of them camping out under the stars however cold it was, fearing they would be killed if they stayed at home.

Molly had been twelve then, old enough to have a clear grasp of what war meant, to understand why food rationing was necessary and the terror bombing produced. She remembered how the children at school talked about their fathers and older brothers who had been called up. To her shame, at the time, Molly had always considered those children lucky, because their fathers were away, but she didn't know back then that some fathers were kind, gentle, affectionate men.

A couple of weeks ago she had run into George while delivering some groceries. It was a hot afternoon and they'd gone for a short walk across the fields together, because George was delaying getting back to the police station just as she was spinning out delivering the groceries.

He'd asked her what she'd been talking to Peter Hayes about in the street a few days earlier. Peter Hayes was a bit of a womanizer, and a bighead, too, and she'd responded a little brusquely, say-

121

ing something cutting about men who liked to throw their weight around.

'Maybe the reason you've never met Mr Right is because you suspect all men are bullies like your dad and you never give anyone a chance to prove himself,' George had said.

'I don't think that,' she said indignantly. She'd been a bit nasty about Peter; she had, in fact, stopped him in the street to remind him he hadn't been into the shop to pay for some groceries that had been dropped off with him several days earlier. She wasn't going to tell George that, though, because it was unfair to bandy such things around. 'If you must know, George, you've got it back to front. It's not that I'm "left on the shelf" because I'm frightened of men. It's just that my dad makes it impossible for me to keep a boy-friend.'

Except for Andy, whom Jack Heywood never met or even found out about, every other prospective boyfriend had been frightened off. Molly had tried to deter them from coming to the house to pick her up, but well-brought-up boys insisted on it. One encounter with her father was enough for most of them: his sarcasm and the way he belittled them was too hard to stomach. She'd had boyfriends who had tried to persist, but who could blame them for preferring to date a girl whose parents were pleasant?

All Molly's old schoolfriends had been allowed to invite boyfriends home for tea or Sunday lunch; sometimes their fathers even went to the football or to the pub with them. Courtship flourished where there was a climate of friendliness, trust and real interest. Molly knew this for certain, as all those same old friends were married now, and most had at least two children.

Molly yearned for love. She thought the nearest thing to heaven would be to have a husband and a home of her own. She liked to imagine the kind of wallpaper and curtains she'd have, the meals she'd cook, and sleeping in her husband's arms at night.

Yet, of all the men she'd met, George was the only one ever to stand up to Jack Heywood. He'd been marvellous that day in the shop when he'd turned on her father and taken his weapon from him. But then, he didn't seem to want her for his girlfriend, so maybe it could be said that her father put him off, too.

Molly knew deep down inside her that if she stayed in Sawbridge she'd probably settle for any man who wanted her, and the chances were he'd be as big a bully as her father. She had to go away and meet new people who wouldn't see her as a kind of Cinderella but as a competent, interesting girl with many talents.

These two days away were the first step to a new, completely different life. She would charm the manager at Bourne & Hollingsworth into offering her a job; she would work out for herself how to get around on the underground, conquer the fear of going into a café alone and make Constance like her enough to tell her all she knew about Cassie.

Molly had temporarily put aside thinking about Cassie and what might have happened to Petal because of her own problems, but she hadn't forgotten them. She was desperate to get some answers, and when she'd got them she would go back to the police and demand that they finish the job and bring whoever killed Cassie and took Petal to justice.

Molly had gone to see George at his home the day before to check he could still take her to the station in Bristol. Mrs Walsh had been so welcoming, inviting her in for tea and cake while she waited for George to get in, and it made Molly feel a bit guilty, because she hadn't told him about the letter and Constance.

George arrived back some twenty minutes later, apologizing for being late and telling her he'd been sent out to get some sheep off the road and, as fast as he got them back in the field, the rest of the flock in the field decided to make their escape, too.

'Luckily, old Enoch came along with his dog and rounded them all up for me,' George said. 'I told him you were going to London tomorrow for an interview for a job, and he wished you luck. "She's a bonny girl," he said. "London will be the making of her." I don't know why he thinks that – I doubt he's ever been.'

'Now, George, you don't need to go to London to know that it offers a lot more than Sawbridge,' Mrs Walsh said, reprovingly. 'And, besides, old Enoch did his bit in the trenches in the First War. So I expect he did go to London on the way to France. You shouldn't assume that no old person has ever done or seen anything.'

George just laughed good-naturedly. 'Molly's going to sail through her interview,' he said. 'She's the best sales girl I know. She always manages to make me buy more than I intended.'

'Let's hope they put you in the Fashion Department,' Mrs Walsh said, as if Molly had already got the job. 'I can just imagine you selling beautiful evening gowns to smart city ladies.'

'That would be lovely, but I'm fairly certain they give those jobs to experienced, more mature women,' Molly said. 'I'd like to be in Children's Wear, really.'

Mrs Walsh left the living room then; she said she had to get the tea on.

'You do know they call us "Swedes" up there,' George said once she'd gone. 'They snigger at our West Country accents. When I went on a course there, they never stopped pulling my leg. I thought most Londoners were far too full of themselves.'

'Oh, don't say that!' she begged him. 'I'll be afraid to speak. It's bound to be a bit strange at first. Maybe I'll hate it and I'll come back and settle in Bristol. But, whatever happens, I can't see me coming back here to the village, not while Dad's still around.'

She couldn't be certain, but she thought George looked a bit sad. 'Of course, I'll keep in touch with you, George.'

He smiled at that. 'Will you be keeping in touch with that writer chap?' he asked.

'No, I don't think so,' she said, secretly pleased that he was bothered at the prospect of a rival penpal. 'He's just a passing acquaintance, and he'll move on soon. I'll keep in touch with you, because you're special. I've known you all my life. Funnily enough, though, you've never so much as asked me to the pictures.'

She was surprised at herself for daring to be so outspoken.

'Would you have gone if I'd asked?' he said. He looked bashfully boyish and Molly's stomach gave a tiny flip.

'I think it's a possibility,' she said, leaning over to pat his cheek affectionately. 'The last time you held my hand was eleven years ago when we were leaving school. I thought you were going to ask me out that day, but you didn't. A girl has only so much patience.'

He blushed. 'I wanted to, but I was afraid you'd turn me down. Then there was the problem of how I'd find any time, because I had so many chores, with Dad being off at the War. Mum kept me busy with the vegetable garden, the chickens and sending me out shooting rabbits.'

'That's right, blame me,' Mrs Walsh called out from the kitchen. 'I'm the big bad mother keeping her boy close to home. As if! Mind you, I might have warned him off in case your dad skinned him alive.'

George looked at Molly, 'I'm not frightened of him. Even when I was fifteen I wasn't.'

Molly smiled. 'Then you were the only boy in the village that wasn't. I'm going to stand up to him, starting when I get back from London. But I am worried what he'll be like to Mum once I've gone for good.'

'We'll all keep an eye out for her,' George said, and the sincerity in his voice was touching. 'I'll whisper in a few ears, get my scouts out. He'll need to get help in the shop, and I think that woman who helps out in busy times will be anx-

126

ious to do more hours.'

Molly nodded. Her mother had said earlier that Hilda Swainswick had often offered to do more hours if she was needed. She would be good for the shop, too: she was hard working, loyal and very fond of Mary, and she had the kind of husband who wouldn't stand for his wife being bullied by Jack.

'It isn't for you to worry about my parents,' she said. 'But I appreciate it, and I must be going now. Eight o'clock tomorrow?'

George got up out of his seat, too, and in two steps reached her and took her hands in his. 'Be careful up there, won't you?'

On an impulse, Molly leaned in and kissed him, and all at once his arms went around her and he was kissing her back.

'I'm sorry to intrude,' his mother said from the doorway, making them jump apart, blushing furiously.

She didn't say what she'd come in for, perhaps too surprised at finding them kissing, and Molly and George just stood there feeling awkward.

'I must go,' Molly managed to get out, moving towards the door. 'I'll see you tomorrow, George.'

He didn't repeat the kiss at the station today, but remembering it now gave her a lovely prickles-down-the-spine sensation and, as she relived it, she got the stomach-flip thing again. How infuriating it was that George couldn't have kissed her like that two or three years ago! Why did it have to happen just as she was planning to leave?

Molly stood still and looked up at the Braemar

Guest House, 32 Sussex Gardens. It was identical to all the other houses in the once rather grand terrace: four storeys, steps up to an impressive door, but in desperate need of a coat of paint.

It had been a very long train journey; she was tired, stiff and her face felt as if it were covered in a layer of grit. Yet she wasn't scared now. Simon's map had been easy to follow and, although London was frantically busy, with its countless cars and buses and so many more people rushing around than she'd ever seen in Bristol, it wasn't as terrifying as she'd imagined. She thought it was exciting.

The door to the guest house was opened by an elderly woman with iron-grey hair, thick spectacles and a frilly white apron over a navy-blue dress. 'You must be Miss Heywood,' she said with a wide smile. 'Come on in, my dear. After that long train journey you must be dying for a cup of tea.'

Molly knew right away why George liked staying at the Braemar: it was cosy and clean and Miss Grady, the owner, was kind and welcoming. Molly's room was on the first floor at the back. It had a double bed with a cheerful red print bedspread, a dressing table and a small wardrobe, the window looked out on to walled gardens, and there were tall plane trees at the bottom of Miss Grady's, which stopped the Braemar being overlooked.

The shared bathroom and a separate lavatory were both at the front of the house, but Molly had a washbasin in her room, too.

Over a cup of tea and a slice of fruit cake, Molly chatted to Miss Grady, telling her about her job interview the next day. Miss Grady offered to make Molly something to eat but, as tempting as it was to avoid the need to go to a café, Molly refused, because she felt it was cheating. Besides, it was an adventure coming to London, and it would be a shame to stay in the room on a summer's evening.

It was just after ten when Molly got back to the guest house that evening. She had had egg and chips in a café, followed by apple pie and custard, and had then walked for what seemed miles, looking in shop windows. The café experience hadn't been frightening, though she had felt a little self-conscious eating alone. As for the fear of being robbed, that had vanished. She had kept a tight hold on her handbag, but she hadn't felt threatened in any way. As she climbed into bed, she felt very satisfied with herself at overcoming some of her fears.

The interview at Bourne & Hollingsworth was held in an oak-panelled room right at the top of the building. Molly had heard someone refer to it as the boardroom. In films, such rooms had a huge, oval, shiny table and men sat all around it, but the one at the London store had a very ordinary long table, behind which sat the three interviewers, and in front of it, one single chair for the interviewee.

'You do understand that being an assistant in a high-class fashion store is very different from slicing bacon and weighing up sugar and tea,' one of the interviewers, a hawk-faced woman, said.

She sat between two middle-aged men and was wearing a very smart black costume, her dark-brown hair in a bun. Her voice was what Molly's mother would call 'BBC'. Every word was pronounced with precision. All the questions she'd fired at Molly had been insulting to Molly's intelligence, but she had responded politely.

'Of course I know the difference between a fashion store and a grocer's,' Molly said, her patience beginning to run out. She was sure this hard-faced woman was appalled by the home-made navy-and-white dress and jacket and little white hat. She probably didn't like Molly's West Country burr either, so she might as well say her piece and be done with it. 'But even if the products sold are very different, customer care should be the same. I have been brought up to treat every customer as very important, to go that extra mile for them.'

To Molly's astonishment, the more portly of the two men gave a little hand clap, glancing round at Hawk Face to see her reaction. 'You are quite right, Miss Heywood. Customer care is the most important thing, but you do need to have a keen interest in fashion, too.'

'I always read fashion magazines,' Molly volunteered. 'I am keenly interested in it and hope that you'll give me the chance to prove my worth.'

'Will you wait outside, Miss Heywood? We'll call you in again later,' Hawk Face said.

Molly went back outside with a heavy heart and joined the five other girls waiting there. Despite all the patronizing questions from Hawk Face, she thought she'd given a good account of herself, and the men had seemed impressed with her

School Certificate results. But these other girls waiting all looked smarter, prettier and more confident than she was. She was just a country bumpkin in handmade clothes. It was tempting to leave now and avoid the humiliation of being turned down.

One by one, the girls went in, but they must have left the interview room another way, as they didn't come back out to where Molly was. Finally, when she was the only girl left sitting there, Hawk Face called her in.

'Well, Miss Heywood,' one of the men spoke up. 'We have decided to offer you a position here in Bourne & Hollingsworth, and would like you to begin in-store training with Miss Maloney, one of our fashion buyers, on Monday the seventeenth at 8.45.'

Molly's mouth dropped open in surprise, but she quickly pulled herself together. 'Thank you so much. I hope I can justify your faith in me,' she said, with as much dignity as she could muster.

Hawk Face half smiled. 'We hope for that, too, and that you will have the stamina to remain cheerful and attentive to our customers at the very busiest times. Your room in Warwickshire House, our hostel in Gower Street, will be available on Saturday the fifteenth. It's always better for our new girls to get settled in a day or so before beginning work, and it gives Miss Weatherby, our matron, a chance to tell you the rules over the weekend.'

Molly's mind was reeling when she finally left the London store and headed for the tube station. She was to get a starting salary of sixteen shillings per week, her board and lodging all found. She would share a room with another girl and be issued with a black dress as a uniform. Some of the other things she'd been told – days off, commission and laundry arrangements – had all gone straight out of her head.

As the nearest thing she had had to a wage back in Sawbridge was the odd half-crown from her father, she felt rich just thinking about earning sixteen shillings. On top of that, she would get staff discount off anything she bought in the shop.

But just being chosen was the real thrill. Those other girls were well turned out, they looked confident and poised, but the interview board had picked her.

Her new-found confidence swept her on to the tube without a false step. But when she came out of Whitechapel tube station she had to stand still for a moment to regain her equilibrium, because it was like landing in a stinking, overcrowded hellhole.

Nothing had prepared her for such squalid mayhem. It made her think of a huge anthill; there were people scurrying about and horse-drawn carts, cars, lorries and buses vying for routes between them.

Right opposite was a big, soot-blackened hospital and, even as she stood there, two ambulances tore into the forecourt, bells jangling. Adding to the tumult was a market which spread right along the street. She could hear the stall holders yelling out inducements to buy. But it was the smell which really turned her stomach and made her want to get right back on the under-

132

ground. A potent mix of horse droppings, sewage, human body odours, rotting rubbish and drains.

It was a warm, sunny day and there had been no rain for a while, so maybe that was why the smells were so bad, but everyone looked terribly shabby, too. Very old ladies and men bent almost double over their walking sticks were wearing little more than rags. Young mothers wheeling ramshackle prams didn't just have one baby in them but often a couple of toddlers and a big bag of washing, too. Everywhere Molly looked, the children were scrawny and pale.

She didn't like it one bit. She felt threatened by the sheer numbers of people, and it was all so dirty and squalid. She had to go and see Constance now, because she was expected, but as soon as that was over she'd rush away from this horrible place.

She asked a man selling newspapers outside the station for directions to Myrdle Street, which is where Constance lived.

'You sound like a farmer, ducks,' he said. 'You come up from Bristol?'

'Near there,' she said, surprised that he had any interest in her. 'Do you know it?'

'Never bin there,' he said. 'But I 'ad a mate in the army from there and 'e sounded just like you. Come up 'ere to work, 'ave you?'

After a brief exchange with him, Molly followed his directions to Myrdle Street, only to find that Whitechapel Road was a smart address in comparison to the side streets she was now walking along. There were so many houses missing in the long terraces, big timbers held up the remaining ones, and the weed-covered bomb sites in between were now impromptu playgrounds for huge packs of skinny, pale, sharp-featured children.

Molly looked up at the remaining houses and shuddered, because she could imagine how grim and comfortless they were inside. Old folk sat on the doorsteps of some of the houses, and the sight made her feel unbearably sad for some reason she didn't understand.

Myrdle Street was much the same as the others she'd passed through, but there was a gang of about twelve girls skipping over a long rope turned by two of the bigger ones. Molly paused to watch them for a moment, noting that they wore plimsolls on their feet, some with the toe cut out to give more room, they all had scabby knees, and every one of them wore a dress so faded and worn they looked like they'd fall apart in the wash. She was suddenly reminded that, however horrible her father could be, she'd always had enough to eat, good clothes and shoes. She hadn't realized until now what real poverty looked like.

The front door to 22 Myrdle Street was open. Molly tapped on it and, when there was no response, she went into the narrow hall a little way and called out to Constance.

'I'm back here!' a weak voice called back. 'Do come in.'

Molly nervously followed the voice to another open door at the end of the passage. It led to a rather dark room with a kitchen sink under the window. Constance was sitting in a wheelchair.

'I'm sorry, I can't get up very easily,' she said. 'You must be Miss Heywood?'

Constance was very small and thin. She wore a grey cotton dress and a grey cotton veil over her hair. Molly felt that she must belong to some religious order and that she was perhaps in her mid-sixties, maybe even older.

'Yes, I'm Miss Heywood, but please call me Molly. Thank you for agreeing to see me,' she said.

'It is my pleasure. Now, pull that chair up and sit down. Tell me, did you get the job?'

'Yes, I did,' Molly said, pulling the easy chair closer to Constance. 'I'm sorry that I addressed the letter just to "Constance", but I didn't know your other name.'

'I'm known round here to everyone as Sister Constance,' the old lady said. 'I'm a Church Army sister. We aren't like Roman Catholics: we don't live in nunneries but out in the parish we are sent to. This has been my parish for over twenty years now but, since I ended up in this wheelchair, my work is mostly of the listening kind.'

'I've always thought that good listeners are very valuable,' Molly said. 'Will you tell me how you got to know Cassie?'

'She came to live next door when Petal was just a few months old,' Constance said. 'I wasn't in the wheelchair then, and I walked down the street beside her one day. I asked her if she'd like to come to the young mothers' meeting at the church.'

'Did she go?' Molly remembered Cassie being very anti-Church.

Constance shook her head. 'No, she said she wasn't a "joiner", but we chatted as we walked, and I realized she was on her own without a husband and asked her if she got lonely.'

135

'I bet she said she didn't know the meaning of that word,' Molly said.

'No, what she said was that being alone can sometimes be far better for you than having others around you. I agreed with her, and I talked a little about how I pray when I'm alone, and how it clears my mind.'

'She didn't run a mile, then?' Molly said lightly.

'No! Despite her claims to be agnostic, she was a very spiritual girl. She understood about meditation, and had read widely on many religions. But let's leave that for a minute, Molly. Explain to me first about her death? I was so distressed to get your letter and, to be honest, it didn't make much sense to me. Why would anyone kill Cassie?'

'I thought the same myself,' Molly said, then explained everything, beginning from when she found her friend dead. 'The coroner said the bruising on her arms and neck was evidence of a struggle, then it seemed she either fell back on to the hearth or was pushed, and her head banged hard on it, breaking her skull.'

Molly paused. She could see that Constance felt as deeply about Cassie as she did, and that was all the justification she needed to continue to search for answers.

'What I don't understand, though,' she continued, 'is why the police have given up on looking for Petal. I kind of see why they've run out of steam in finding Cassie's killer, but they shouldn't have stopped searching for a six-year-old. They wouldn't be this way if she was the daughter of a doctor, or a teacher – someone that mattered. I hate it that they don't care about her because she's mixed race and her mother wasn't married.'

Constance reached out and patted Molly's knee. 'You mustn't hate. Pity people's ignorance and prejudice perhaps, and try to show them by example what is right, but hating just makes you feel bad inside and serves no useful purpose.'

Molly smiled weakly. She liked everything about this woman: her soft blue eyes that were full of understanding; her acceptance that she had to be in a wheelchair now after spending the best part of her life caring for the poor. 'I came to you because I'm hoping you can tell me stuff about Cassie which may make sense of everything. I want to be a detective and find Petal.'

'That sounds a good idea to me.' Constance smiled. 'Though I don't think I have any information that will help you. Cassie wasn't one for confiding things about herself.'

'But she must have told you where she came from, and something about Petal's father?'

'No, she didn't. Let me explain something, Molly. People who aren't born here in the East End come to live here for widely varying reasons,' Constance said earnestly. 'People like me, and nurses, doctors and social workers come here to serve the community. Some think it's sort of romantic or heroic to work with the poor, and they soon find out that's not the case and leave. Others, like me, come to love the people and stay. Other newcomers are immigrants, and they come because this is where friends and relatives have already settled and they want to join them. If you look around, you will see people from almost every corner of the globe: Jews, Arabs, Africans, Indians,

137

and many more.

'Other people end up here because they are too poor to go anywhere else. Finally, some are running away and see this as a good place to hide. But I doubt that any of these people, other than those who work here or were born here, actually want to live here. It is too tough and harsh.'

'Do you think Cassie was running away?'

'Yes, I believe so. But I don't think she was hiding from the police. She would chat happily to a constable on his beat. She certainly didn't slink away.'

'So that means she'd run away from Petal's father?'

Constance sighed. 'That does seem to be the obvious assumption, but I've found that women tend to admit such things once they feel safe with a new friend. She never spoke of Petal's father once, not even in a vague way. I came to the conclusion it was her parents she'd run away from.'

'I've thought of that myself,' Molly said. 'But her father died in the war, so maybe her mother?'

'Possibly. There were pointers to her having had a quite privileged childhood, though. She was well spoken, well educated, she had first-class manners. I would take a guess that she was brought up by a nanny or a housekeeper, though.'

'What makes you think that?'

'The lack of information about her mother, really. We all mention our mothers, even if only in passing. I asked Cassie once if she was orphaned, and she looked shocked. "I have a mother," she said. "She just doesn't figure in my life." I thought that was a very odd thing to say.'

138

'Yes, I agree.' Molly frowned. 'It sounds like she'd deliberately cut herself off.'

Constance nodded. 'Hmm. I thought maybe her mother was cruel to her when Petal was born – after all, an unmarried mother with a mixed race baby is often far too much for some people to deal with. Especially those higher up the social scale. But, if that was the case and Cassie had been thrown out because of it, you would expect her to be bitter. But she wasn't.'

'No, I never saw any bitterness in her either,' Molly agreed. 'Did she ever say where she grew up? What she'd done before she had Petal?'

Constance shook her head. 'She told me once she used to ride. The way she said that made me think she was brought up with horses, not just a ride now and then on a friend's or neighbour's horse. I don't think she ever worked for a living – another clue to a gentle, privileged upbringing. Those sort of girls don't work.'

'But while she was here, how did she live?'

'I think she must have had savings. Or she sold jewellery or other things to keep herself. She lived very frugally. She wasn't above collecting up fallen fruit or vegetables at the close of the market. But, speaking of food, let's have a cup of tea and some cake!'

Molly made the tea and, on Constance's instructions, got a fruit cake out of a tin and the best china from the sideboard.

She clearly lived very frugally, too. The one room was simply furnished: a bed covered in a dark-blue blanket, two easy chairs by the fire-place, a sideboard, a table and two chairs. There were lots of books on shelves and a couple of lovely watercolours of a picturesque village. There were also various religious pictures, but these weren't framed, just tacked to the wall. The room was clean and neat, although there were damp stains on the walls and a faint musty smell. Constance said she was fortunate enough to have two kind friends who came in and helped her wash and dress and kept the place clean. To Molly, it seemed a very sad and lonely life being in a wheelchair, and alone for much of the day. But Constance seemed happy with it.

'Do you get out?' Molly asked her as they waited for the kettle to boil. 'I mean, is there anyone who can take you out in your wheelchair?'

'Oh yes! Don't you get the idea I'm some sort of hermit. Most days someone will pop round and take me for a spin. Reverend Adams – he's the vicar at St Swithin's, takes me to church every Sunday, and I go home with him for lunch, too. People are very kind. That fruit cake, for instance, was a gift from a parishioner. I get people dropping in, too. It's a rare day when I don't see anyone.'

Constance kept asking Molly about her life and family, and it was all Molly could do to keep dragging the conversation back to Cassie. She found out that her friend had lived here for three years and only left then because she wanted Petal to go to a good school.

'The schools around here are overcrowded, and they don't attract good teachers,' Constance admitted. 'The government seems to have forgotten that we took the brunt of the Blitz here, and they are being very slow to clear the bomb sites and build new homes. Some families share one room with another family. There are children who don't even have a bed to sleep in, or share it with all their siblings. Most people don't have a bathroom in their home, babies get bitten by rats very often, and I'd say at least a quarter of the children are suffering from malnutrition. We keep hearing that England is almost bankrupt from the expense of the war, yet they found the money for a lavish Coronation. Don't get me wrong, I love and admire the royal family, but if I was in charge I'd put ordinary families first.'

'Well, we do have the National Health Service now,' Molly ventured, rather surprised that someone like Constance would criticize the Coronation.

'Yes, and it's a wonderful thing to have free medical care,' Constance said with a smile. 'But people's health would improve vastly with decent housing; too many small children are still dying of preventable diseases.'

This struck a chord with Molly. Cassie had often said similar things and, somehow, that confirmed how well she'd known Constance.

'When did you last hear from Cassie?' Molly asked.

Constance frowned, as if trying to picture it. 'I think it was late 1950. I've probably got her last letter here somewhere. She told me she didn't like living in Bristol, but she thought the countryside around it was lovely and she was going to look for somewhere to live there. I was a little hurt that she didn't write again. She had told me she wasn't good at keeping in touch, but I suppose I thought I was a special case.'

'From what you've told me, I think you were, and maybe the reason she didn't write to you was because she was afraid whoever she was running from might come to you. That would be a very good reason not to tell you where she was.'

Constance half smiled. 'You make it sound very cloak and dagger, Molly, but you might be right, because there was a man making enquiries about her around that time. He didn't come to me, but he questioned a few people in the road. They said they thought he was a private detective.'

'Really?' Molly exclaimed. 'What did people tell him?'

'They couldn't tell him anything, because they didn't know. I was the only person who knew she'd moved to Bristol, and I hadn't said a word to anyone. But people round here don't tell tales anyway, not if they like the person, and people did like Cassie. She slotted in here, Molly. Women liked her because she was straight-talking; she'd write letters for them if they couldn't do it. She helped children with their reading; she talked to them, too. She could make a fancy-dress outfit out of nothing and often helped people decorate their homes. A great many people missed her when she moved away, and those who I have told about her death are very sad.'

'It sounds as if people here are a lot broader minded than back home.' Molly sighed. 'She had few friends in our village. It's one of the reasons I want to move to London.'

'You may find the girls in Bourne & Hollingsworth are even smaller minded than your neighbours back home,' Constance said, arching one eyebrow. 'I've known a few girls who have worked in the big London stores and, for most, it's not as they imagined. But I'm sure you'll rise above it.'

'Don't say that!' Molly said in alarm. 'I thought it was going to be fun!'

'It might very well be,' Constance said soothingly. 'I've lived in the East End so long I can't imagine a life now where you can't speak your mind or be a bit different. All I can say is that if you don't like it, Molly, you come right back here. I'll help you find a job and somewhere to live.'

Molly didn't think it would come to that. But before she could make any comment a woman came in, greeting Constance as 'Sister'. Her name was Sheila. Molly thought she was in her late thirties, and she wore a flowery print pinafore and a headscarf over metal curlers.

'This is Molly, the friend of Cassie's I told you about,' Constance said. 'She wants to play detective and find Petal.'

Sheila looked hard at Molly. 'Terrible business,' she said. 'We was fond of Cassie and her little girl round 'ere. It were a nasty shock to 'ear she were dead. I reckon it all had to do with an inheritance. She were 'iding up when she were 'ere, but maybe she were too close to 'er 'ome and got spotted.'

'Where do you think she came from, then?' Cassie asked.

'I'd say down Sussex way. She mentioned riding her 'orse on the downs. And she talked about the sea. Didn't she mention Hastings and the marshes in that notebook she left 'ere, Sister?'

Molly sat up straight. 'Notebook?'

'Well, a journal I think you'd call it. Just scribblings of poetry, really, Molly,' Constance said. 'You can find it in the sideboard. I have no idea why she left it with me.'

'When you say she left it with you, would that be like leaving it here by accident, or wanting you to keep it safe?'

Constance frowned. 'I don't really know. She left it here one evening and when, a couple of days later, I mentioned I still had it, she just said, "Oh, you hang on to it for me." I gathered by that it wasn't important.'

'May I take it away with me to read?'

'Please do. Maybe as you are closer in age to her than me, you'll find something meaningful in it. I can't be doing with poetry that doesn't rhyme.'

Constance pointed to the sideboard and said Molly would find it at the back, under a biscuit tin.

The notebook had a brown leather cover and an elastic strap that held it closed. Molly opened it at the first page and read aloud:

'"Fletcher's box, where he keeps his socks, and the schemes and dreams that don't fit in his head.

'"His clothes, his tools and his mother's old jewels, he keeps in a suitcase under his bed."'

Sheila snorted with laughter. 'That's a bit peculiar. But it kind of rhymes.'

Molly laughed too. 'It *is* peculiar, but I like it just the same. It's very Cassie! But that's all there is to it, unfortunately.'

'Did she tell you she liked to write poetry?' Constance asked.

'She did mention it once. She had a diary – it

144

looked a bit like this notebook – she said she wrote her thoughts in it. It wasn't found in her home after she died.'

'Sounds like the geezer who killed 'er took it, then,' Sheila said. 'Tell us, Molly, were she 'appy down in Somerset?'

'Yes, I'd say so. People in the village were a bit mean to her, but she seemed to accept that was just the way it was. As long as they weren't nasty to Petal, she didn't seem troubled.'

'Were there a man in her life?'

Molly wasn't sure how to reply to that. She didn't want to tell the truth and shock Constance.

'I think she had a couple of admirers,' she replied hesitantly. 'But they were ruled out as her killer, and I never met them.'

'Sounds like she hadn't changed much,' Sheila said with a smile. 'She were always cagey about that stuff when she were 'ere. But I knowed there was a couple of blokes sniffin' around.'

'Oh, Sheila, you always like to add a bit of drama to everything!' Constance said with a little chuckle.

Molly talked to the two women for a little longer, but sensing that Sheila had come to see Constance for more than just a social call, she told them she had to go.

'Come back and see me again once you've moved to London,' Constance urged her. 'If I hear anything more about Cassie, I'll pass it on to you.'

'Don't let those snotty women at your new job grind you down,' Sheila added. 'Remember you've got chums 'ere.'

When Molly walked back down Myrdle Street

145

to Whitechapel Road, it didn't look as grim as it had earlier. If the two women she'd met today were representative of the neighbourhood, she was beginning to understand why Cassie had been happy here.

Chapter Seven

Molly had enjoyed her brief stay in London, seeing the big shops, Hyde Park and Piccadilly, but the time went too fast and, as soon as she got on the train at Paddington to go home, fear set in.

She knew her father was going to hit the roof because she had gone without his permission, and he'd be even angrier that she was going back to London to work, because that would mean he'd lose the person who did the lion's share of the work in the shop.

Molly tried to blot out what the homecoming would be like by reading Cassie's journal. But most of what she read was puzzling.

It was part diary, part a record of her state of mind, and part poems and prose, but there were no dates at all. One page she read at random said, 'Caught the bus, so many gloomy faces. Trapped by their family? Anxiety about money? Lack of love? I wonder how I look to others? Do my worries show in my face?'

It was a strange thing to record, yet it seemed appropriate, because when Molly looked around the railway carriage she saw lots of gloomy faces

146

and wondered if her own anxiety about the reception she would get at home showed in her face.

George had said that he wouldn't be able to pick her up on her return, so she caught the bus home and nodded off on it, only waking when she was approaching Sawbridge. It was nearly seven in the evening, so the shop was closed.

She approached the side door with trepidation, let herself in and, hearing the television on upstairs, hoped her father would be so engrossed in the programme he wouldn't want to miss it by having a row with her.

As she walked up the stairs she reminded herself that she wasn't going to be meek any more. She'd got to stick up for herself and show him she wasn't afraid of him.

But as she reached the landing he came out of the sitting room and glowered at her. He was wearing his usual grey flannels held up by braces, a white shirt and a cardigan. He wore a tie in the shop, but he'd taken it off now and, as always, he smelled of pipe tobacco.

'Well, where do you think you've been, young lady?' he growled.

'To London, for a job interview,' she said, trying hard not to shake with fear and to sound confident. 'I got the job. I start next Monday but go to the hostel on Saturday.'

'You'll do no such thing,' he said, his voice rasping with anger. 'This is where you live and work. I'm not having you gallivanting around London getting yourself into trouble.'

'Sorry, Dad, but it's all arranged,' she said,

more boldly than she felt. 'I want a decent career and a life of my own. I'm twenty-five, more than old enough to make my own decisions, but I hoped to get your blessing.'

'Blessing! I'll give you the back of my hand! You leave this house and you can never come back!' he roared out at Molly. She could see by his flushed face that he was likely to attack her but, although that scared her, her indignation at him using terror tactics to control her gave her the courage to oppose him.

'Why would I want to come back?' she retorted. 'All you've ever done is belittle me, use me and hit me. I don't ever want to see you again.'

She didn't move out of his reach fast enough and his fist hammered into her cheek, knocking her back against the kitchen door.

'Jack!' her mother yelled as she came rushing out of the sitting room. 'Have you learned nothing? Why can't you be a real man and admit you'll miss your daughter? You've already driven Emily away and now Molly will never come near us again.'

Molly stood up straight. Her cheek stung and she guessed she'd have a black eye by the following morning. Not the best way to celebrate getting a new job.

'You aren't going to get away with it this time,' she said, looking right at her father, daring him to hit her again. 'I'm going across to the police station now to report an assault. Let's see how you like being arrested!'

Jack made a move to grab her, but her mother caught his arm and held him back. 'No, Jack! Don't make it any worse. Or I'll be going over

148

there with her.'

He made a snarling sound and wheeled round, going into the sitting room and slamming the door behind him.

'Come with me, love,' Mary said, and drew her daughter into the kitchen. She soaked a cloth under the cold tap and, after wringing it out, held it to Molly's cheek. 'He doesn't really mean it,' she said weakly. 'He's upset that you're leaving.'

'When are you going to stop defending him?' Molly said, pushing the cloth away. 'He's an out-of-control brute, and I shudder to think what he'll do to you once I'm not here. I'm going over to the police now, if only so that they'll keep an eye on you while I'm away. But if you've got any sense, you'll leave him, Mum. If you don't, he might just kill you.'

'I made my marriage vows in church before God, and "For better or worse" was part of it,' Mary said quietly. 'It breaks my heart to know he's driven you and Emily away, but I have to stay. I'm his wife.'

Molly shook her head in despair. She'd already said everything there was to be said dozens of times, and she knew her mother would never be shaken from what she considered to be her duty. But before leaving for London she was going to have her father charged with assault. She had to make a stand.

'Then I'll take my case and go now. I'll ask George if I can stay at his house tonight, and I'll go back to the guest house in Paddington till Saturday,' Molly said. 'I'll give you my address and telephone number at the hostel. You know I'll

149

always help you, and meet you anywhere you like. But I won't come back to this house while he's still alive.'

Mary stepped forward and put her arms around her daughter, hugging her tightly and rocking her to and fro. Molly knew her mother was crying silently, and her whole being wanted to relent, to say she wouldn't take the job in London and she'd stay here. But as much as she loved her mother and feared for her, she couldn't back down to her father. To do so would mean a lifetime of kowtowing to him.

'I've got to go now, Mum,' she said, gently wriggling out of her mother's arms. 'If you need help any time, call George. It comes to something that I've got to start a new job with a black eye, but I'll keep that in mind if ever I start to weaken and think Dad wasn't all bad.'

Two days later, on Saturday, at six in the evening, Molly arrived at the hostel in Gower Street. She'd created a picture in her mind of an almost prison-like place, with bare wooden floors, garret-like rooms with no home comforts and a refectory-type dining room like you'd find in a Dickensian workhouse. But to her shock and surprise it was nothing like that; in fact, it could have been taken for a smart hotel, with its thick carpets, polished mahogany staircase and fancy lighting. She was greeted warmly by Miss Weatherby, the matron, a portly woman in her fifties who was wearing a light-grey dress with a white lace collar and cuffs.

'Oh, my goodness! What has happened to your face?' she asked solicitously.

'I tripped on the stairs the other day and banged into the newel post,' Molly lied. 'It looks worse than it is.'

Miss Weatherby touched it gently with her fingertips. 'I've got some arnica, which is good for bruising. I'll put a compress on it for you now, before showing you your room. You'll be sharing with Dilys Porter. She's the same age as you, but she's been here for over a year now and she'll show you the ropes. Dinner will be served very soon, so we won't waste any time. I'll see you again at ten tomorrow to explain all the rules and answer any questions you may have.'

Fifteen minutes later, holding a pad of cotton wool soaked in some kind of potion to her bruised cheek, Molly met Dilys in the room they were to share.

Dilys Porter was a small, blonde, blue-eyed girl from Cardiff, and she seemed very open and friendly. She, too, commiserated with Molly about her bruised cheek, and told Miss Weather-by she'd take good care of her new roommate.

The room was far nicer than Molly had expected: twin divan beds, a chest of drawers each, a shared wardrobe, a washbasin and a couple of easy chairs. The bathrooms were further down the hall. There was no view from the window, as it opened on to a well-like void at the centre of the building, but that didn't bother her at all.

'Unpack after dinner,' Dilys suggested. 'I'm not going out tonight, so we can get to know each other better, and I'll introduce you to some of the others.'

A further shock, but a good one, was the dining

151

room. It was vast, and all the tables were laid with silver and glasses, just like in a first-class restaurant. They even had waitress service. Molly could hardly believe it.

'It's good, isn't it?' Dilys giggled at her new friend's astounded expression. 'Hundreds of people work for the company, and it believes in treating and feeding its staff well. Lots of people say it's more like a hotel than a hostel. We have lots of laughs, too – us girls go out on the town quite a bit. I never expected it to be like this. I used to work in a chemist's in Cardiff, all old folk coughing and wheezing and complaining about everything, then home on the bus in the cold and wet. Then I get here and it's like paradise. In winter it's lovely and warm. I tell you, Molly, you won't catch me going back to work in Cardiff.'

Molly had reported her father to the police the night he hit her, and they had issued him with a formal warning that if he was to attack her again he would be arrested. She had stayed for two nights at George's house and, during the day, he had gone back to the house with her to collect the rest of her clothes. That morning, he had driven her to the station to see her off.

But Molly put home and her father out of her mind that evening as she tucked into a lovely dinner of steak-and-kidney pie, followed by rice pudding. She met some of the other girls on her landing and found out a little more about the job. From what she gathered, all the girls had to toe the line in the store, as the senior staff watched them like hawks and no one got away with anything. The girls complained that it was tough

152

being on their feet all day, being nice to customers who were often very rude, and it could also be boring when the shop wasn't busy.

'You always have to look busy,' Dilys said. 'Putting clothes back in size order on the rails, folding sweaters and blouses, polishing up glass surfaces. You daren't get chatting to another member of staff, not unless you want to be out on your ear.'

Molly thought she could cope with all that; after all, she'd had to do just about everything in her father's shop. But whatever the daytime hours were like, the evenings and days off sounded like fun. The girls went out dancing together. Once a week they could get a late pass till midnight, but on other nights they had to be in by ten thirty.

Because of her bruised cheek, Molly was put to work in the store room for her first three days. Staff rang down when they were running low on stock of something, and Molly and the other staff had to check to see if they had more there, and send it up to the appropriate department. Molly thought it was probably very useful to her, as she learned which departments upstairs were busiest, which managers were difficult and which were pleasant. Most of the store-room staff felt that they were looked down upon by the shop assistants, as did all the staff that worked in house-keeping or the kitchens. It seemed to be a triangular structure, with department managers at the top, then senior shop assistants, then the junior ones, right on down to the bottom, to the lowly porters who unloaded goods from the delivery lorries. There was a similar hierarchy with the office staff. They tended not to mix with

153

the sales-floor staff at all.

On her fourth working day, the bruise on her cheek now faded, Molly was sent to work in Haberdashery. Dilys commiserated, saying all the girls hated that department because it was all little sales of buttons, reels of cotton, zips and ribbons, and the customers expected the sales girls to be very attentive and knowledgeable, but Molly liked it. She had always made her own clothes, and she enjoyed being kept busy. When she wasn't serving anyone she opened up the drawers and cupboards to find out more about the stock.

Miss Bruce, the department manager, was something of a fusspot, and convinced that no one could ever know as much about haber-dashery as she did. But after working for a tyrant like her father, Molly found the woman easy enough to get along with.

Another advantage of working in Haberdashery was that the other girls didn't feel that she was a favoured one. Apparently, Miss Maloney, who was the Fashion manageress, did have favourites and gave them plum jobs. Those girls were viewed with suspicion by everyone else.

The part of the day Molly liked best was the evening, not necessarily going out with the other girls but sitting around the table having their evening meal, all chatting away about their day. Then they'd go back to their rooms, and quite often some of the girls would come in to Molly and Dilys for more chat, usually about make-up, clothes and boys. Molly had been a bit too young when Emily had left home to talk about such things, but she had loved having her older sister in

154

the bed next to her, the little chats in the dark, the cosiness of it. Sharing with Dilys brought that back.

On her second night in the hostel she and Dilys had got into their nightdresses and were having a cup of cocoa when Molly told her new friend about Cassie and Petal.

'Jeepers!' Dilys exclaimed, putting her hands over her face. 'Fancy finding someone who's been murdered! You think that only happens in films. Did you scream the place down?'

'I think I must have, but there wasn't much point, considering where the cottage was. No one would've heard me. But I was sick in the bushes!'

She went on to explain that Petal was still missing, and that she was on something of a mission to find her. Molly got out the only two photographs she had. One was of Cassie taken at the church fete last year, and the other was of Petal, a school photograph. Cassie had given it to Molly at Easter.

Dilys looked hard at the pictures. 'Petal is really sweet,' she said. 'I hope whoever's got her won't hurt her. Cassie was lovely – she reminds me of Ava Gardner.'

Molly smiled. 'She did look a bit like her, especially when she wore a tight sweater and a pencil skirt, but most of the time she was in a loose smock-type dress with wellingtons on her feet. She looks dark-haired there, but her hair was red. She used to dye it. I don't know what colour it was before. The truth is, I know next to nothing about her, really. Not where she came from or anything. But I've got a journal of hers and I hope to find some clues there.'

Dilys kept asking questions about Cassie and even when they'd eventually turned out the light her voice came through in the dark: 'Aren't you afraid that if you dig too deep the person who killed Cassie might kill you?'

Molly's first month passed so quickly she could hardly believe it. It was nice to be able to write home to her mother and tell her truthfully that she loved her job, had made lots of friends in the hostel and was happier than she'd ever been before. She wrote to George, too, telling him much the same, though she told him what she'd seen at the cinema rather than about the Saturday-night dancing at the Empire in Leicester Square.

The Empire was wonderful – the big band, the soft lights, the glittery balls turning on the ceiling, and very smartly turned-out young men to dance with, so different to the clodhopping boys back home. A few were a bit too fresh, thinking one dance and a drink meant they could take liberties, but all the girls from work looked out for one another and, unless one of them said she wanted to go outside or walk home alone with someone, they stuck together.

Molly had danced with a man called Harry on her first night. A week later she saw him there again and he asked her out for a drink. She'd met him at Oxford Circus tube station as arranged, on the following Monday, full of excitement and wearing a new pink dress that had been marked down in the sale. But, to her consternation, he was a little drunk even when they met, slurring his words and propping himself up by leaning on her

156

shoulder, and breathing beer fumes all over her. In the time she'd drunk one glass of Babycham he'd downed two pints of beer and a whisky chaser. Realizing that the evening could only get worse, when he left her to go to the men's room, she walked out of the bar and scuttled back to the hostel.

Dilys was sitting up in bed reading when she got in. 'Gosh! What went wrong? Didn't he turn up?' she asked.

When Molly told her what had happened, Dilys laughed.

'I went out with a man like that once. He was drunk, too, when we met, and got even drunker during the evening. As he was walking me home – or should I say "lurching me home"? – he threw up, and it splattered all over my coat.'

Molly grimaced. 'Yuk. I hope you pushed him into the gutter?'

'No, I was stupid enough to feel sorry for him,' Dilys admitted. 'But then he tried to kiss me, and that was so disgusting I came to my senses and ran off.'

Molly undressed and got into bed while Dilys told her about other disappointing dates she'd had. Molly loved listening to her; her sing-song Welsh accent was lovely. 'Another bloke didn't have a penny to his name, so we had to walk around in the rain. Another one turned up in his work overalls, and I was all done up to go dancing. I've had men asking me to lend them money for the evening; ones who didn't want to take me anywhere except a park to grope me. I tell you, it's enough to make you want to give up on

157

finding someone special.'

'I know this is a bit personal,' Molly said hesitantly, 'but have you ever gone the whole way?'

'Ooh, there's cheeky you are!' Dilys replied indignantly. 'I'll wait till I'm married, thank you very much. Me dad would go potty if I got up the spout before I was wed. How about you?'

'I haven't either,' Molly said. 'But then I haven't met that many men I feel that way about. There was a chap once, but he turned out to be a right sod. I met a writer called Simon, too, I thought he was perfect – handsome, from a good family – and I used to day-dream about him quite a bit. Turned out he was married, though, so just as well he didn't try it on with me.

'There is George, a nice policeman back home, though. I went to school with him. But now I'm here in London, everything and everyone from home seems to be fading away.'

Dilys nodded in agreement. It was the same for her. 'I was homesick at first, but not any more. I went back home for a week's holiday just after the Coronation, but after a couple of days I was dying to get back here. All my old friends seem so set in their ways, and Cardiff seemed very small.'

Long after Dilys had gone to sleep, Molly lay awake, thinking how odd it was that after only a month she couldn't imagine ever living anywhere but London. She loved the bustle and noise, the beautiful parks, lovely old buildings, even the element of danger in some of the backstreets of Soho. She had the feeling she could become anything she wanted to be here.

Back home in the shop, she'd only ever heard

158

about people's ailments, about their children and what they were cooking for dinner. Gossip was usually about such trivial things, like someone jumping the queue at the doctor's, a neighbour failing to give back something they'd borrowed, or the dog a few houses away that never stopped barking.

Customers in Bourne & Hollingsworth were often just as chatty, but they told her fun things, like they were meeting an old friend for lunch or they had come to London to buy something for a special occasion. Maybe they were just as dull as all her old neighbours when they were back home, but being in London was like living in a bubble that excluded dullness and mediocrity, and it made people dress up in their best clothes, smile because they were out to enjoy themselves and enjoy spending their money instead of begrudging it.

George had written to her every week so far. It was in his first letter that he told her that Simon had gone back to his wife and left the village. Molly felt that George had enjoyed telling her that – another reminder that people back in Somerset were small-minded.

But she had to concede that, small-minded or not, George was keeping a close eye on her mother. He reported back that Mrs Swainswick, the part-time help in the shop, had told him that Molly's father had been less grumpy since she had left, and her mother was less nervy.

'Perhaps,' George suggested, 'he's happier now he has your mum's entire attention.'

Molly didn't care what it was that had made

159

her father more amenable; it was a load off her mind to hear he wasn't being violent or abusive to her mother.

On her second day off Molly went back to White-chapel and spent the morning talking to Constance and finding out about the places Cassie used to go to: the library, Victoria Park in Bethnal Green, the market and the public baths. It was a bit of a shock to Molly to discover that people who didn't have bathrooms – and that was nearly everyone – had to go to the public baths. So, mainly out of curiosity, she made her way there first that afternoon.

There was a big woman with a large, shiny, red face behind the desk. Molly got out the photograph of Cassie and showed it to the woman. 'Have you seen this woman before?' she asked.

The older woman just glanced at the picture. 'Yep. Dozens of times. Why d'you wanna know?'

Molly explained what had happened to Cassie and Petal as briefly as she could. 'The police aren't doing much to find her killer or Petal, so I'm trying to discover more about her past which might help.'

The woman was horrified to hear that Cassie had been killed and immediately became much warmer. 'She were nice,' she said. 'And her little girl as cute as could be, and well behaved. But I don't know anything else about her, other than she lived in Myrdle Street. I'm so sorry she's been killed. Why would anyone kill a nice woman like her?'

It was disappointing that the bath attendant

knew nothing, but they chatted for a little while and Molly asked if she could see the baths, just so she'd understand how it worked.

'You pay your money, I gives you a towel and some soap, and I tell you which bath is free,' she said, leading Molly down a long corridor lined with small cubicles, a bath in each one. 'I turn the hot water on from outside. It's a set amount; you put the cold in yerself. I warn 'em not to drop their drawers on the floor or they'll 'ave to go 'ome with wet 'uns.'

Molly sniggered. It all looked so austere: white tiles, too-bright lights, bare concrete floor, a slatted wooden board to stand on when you got out of the bath. And just a couple of hooks to hang your towel and clothes on. But she supposed if you had no bathroom of your own it was all right.

'It ain't so bad,' the attendant said, clearly picking up on Molly's distaste. 'They can shout to their mates, 'ave a laugh with the other women. It's nice and warm in the winter, too. They can do their washing and ironing here if they want, through the doors at the end. You must be one of the bleedin' lucky ones that's got yer own bathroom and inside lav at 'ome?'

'Yes,' Molly admitted, feeling ashamed she'd been so transparent. 'Was Cassie all right about it? Or do you think she was like me, used to one at home?'

The attendant leaned back on a bathroom door and pulled some cigarettes out of her apron pocket. She took her time lighting one, looking at Molly all the while.

'I'd say she had no real idea how folk like us live

161

round here, 'cos the first time she come 'ere she looked scared to death,' she said eventually, puffing smoke into the air. 'She had Petal in a pushchair and I don't think she could work out whether it was best to bath her or herself first. She learned fast, though. By the time she'd been three or four times she was like everyone else, 'aving a laugh and a joke, making the best of it.'

'Did she ever tell you why she came to Whitechapel?' Molly asked.

'Why does anyone like her come 'ere?' She shrugged. ''Cos it's cheap. To disappear. You don't come 'ere 'cos you *like* to slum it.'

At the library they also remembered Cassie and, here, the head librarian had read in the paper about her being murdered. 'I couldn't believe it,' the woman said. 'She was such a clever, well-spoken young woman. But then I was surprised when I first met her that she had a mixed race baby – not what you'd expect from someone who likes to read Jane Austen. Obviously, she'd got in with bad people.'

Molly had a real desire to say she was surprised that a librarian could be such a bigoted snob, but that wasn't advisable if she was hoping to find out more about Cassie. Sadly, no one at the library knew anything more about her than that she took out at least four books a week and came in almost daily to read the papers.

Molly promised herself that she would go back to Whitechapel the following week and start asking about Cassie in shops and cafés, but when she mentioned to a couple of girls back at the hostel that she'd spent the day in the area, they both looked appalled. It seemed that everyone at Bourne & Hollingsworth thought of the East End as being dangerous and full of disease. It put Molly off a bit about going back, and it was another three weeks before she visited there again.

Yet Dilys thought Molly's quest to find Petal was a wonderful one, and often, when they'd got into bed, Molly would read bits of Cassie's journal to her, and they would discuss what she might have meant.

Molly had found references to Hastings and a place called Rye in some of Cassie's writing.

'Listen to this, Dilys,' she said one night. '"The wind whistles across the marsh, forcing the trees to bow down to it. The sheep huddle together for warmth, and the few flowers that grow there are tiny and stunted, as are many of the folk that live there. Only the prickly gorse defies the wind, its yellow, sweet-smelling splendour spreads in defiance."'

'What do you think of that?' she asked her friend.

'If I'd written like that at school I might not have got "Make more effort" written across my work.' Dilys giggled.

'Don't you think Cassie was using the bleakness of the marsh to convey the sadness of her own life? That the wind is like someone laying waste to all her dreams and aspirations, and she is the gorse defying them?'

'You sound like my English teacher, who used to tell me what Shakespeare meant. I never got it, and I don't get Cassie's stuff either.' Dilys giggled again. 'But I like you reading it and hearing your

163

ideas. Who do you think the "someone" is that's laying waste her dreams?'

'I don't know. Maybe her mother or some other relative?'

Molly wondered if Cassie's mother had been mad. She remembered once confiding in Cassie about her father, and seeing her friend wince as if she'd experienced the same kind of abuse. Of course, her father could've been the brute, before he went off to war. And if her mother hadn't defended her, then that could be why she didn't talk about either of them.

'It's a kind of mental illness,' Cassie had said, about violence. 'A rage inside your father that he can't put out, maybe because something bad happened to him years ago, and when it boils up and spills over, he attacks you.'

She told Cassie about how her father had been robbed of the week's takings from the furniture shop he'd worked at in Bristol and then blamed for the crime.

'My advice is, don't waste your sympathy on him,' Cassie had responded, shaking her head. 'Each one of us is given some sort of cross to bear; that is his, and he's allowed it to destroy his life. He was fortunate that it was later proved he was innocent and he got compensation. Not many people get that.

'I think he is the cross you have to bear, Molly. You can drag the misery he's created around with you or toss it aside and choose your own path to happiness. Your mother has chosen her path, what she believes is the right thing to do, and you must accept it and leave her to it.'

164

One of Cassie's poems was about crucifixion, and as Molly read it Cassie's remark about the crosses they had to bear came back sharply into focus. She thought it was about Cassie being forced to give up the comfortable life she'd had to keep Petal. But Petal was no crown of thorns; she was Cassie's delight, her reason for everything.

Molly was glad for Simon that he'd gone back to his wife, and hoped they'd find happiness again, yet she was disappointed he wasn't in Sawbridge any longer and she wouldn't be able to show him Cassie's journal. He was a literary man, and he might have seen meanings in it that eluded Molly.

But he was gone, just another closed door, and however kindly George was in inviting her to stay at his house so she could see her mum, if her father got to hear she was there, it might just inflame her father's temper.

George was another puzzle. He'd kissed her again before she left for London, and it had been a passionate kiss, not one from a mere friend. In the letters she'd had from him since, amongst the village news and amusing incidents concerning people she knew he had referred somewhat obliquely to not knowing how she felt about him. But he hadn't revealed what he felt for her, so how could she respond?

Molly had discussed this with Rose, a girl she'd got friendly with who worked in Hosiery. She had a similar situation with Robert, her young man back in Birmingham.

'I think we have to make up our minds what we want,' Rose said. 'Robert is a good man, all my family like him, and when I was living at home

165

and working at the Co-op, I thought he was the one. But now I'm here and have seen how some people live, I don't want to live in a couple of poky rooms with a bricklayer, however nice he is. I want style, nice clothes, to eat out in restaurants, and a house in a smart suburb.'

'If George had courted me when I was at home I might have been only too happy to marry him and live in a police house,' Molly said, squirming a bit, because she wasn't really comfortable with Rose thinking she was too good for Robert now. 'But he didn't, and even now he isn't saying he's always loved me, or anything positive.'

'Forget him. You don't want some dull policeman in an even duller place. We'll find ourselves a couple of dream boats at the Empire,' Rose said with a grin. 'We need to have a list prepared to tick off: good job, well educated, nice-looking, smart clothes, a car, parents with money.'

'If they've got all that, they probably only want a girl for one thing,' Molly said. 'We aren't that much of a catch, working at Bourne & Hollingsworth.'

'Speak for yourself.' Rose grinned. 'And I might be prepared to go the whole way if the man was worth it.'

Molly laughed, because she didn't believe Rose would ever go that far before marriage. Like most of the young staff here, she wanted fun, but of the innocent kind: going out to tea, the cinema or the theatre with a man, but nothing more. Molly had been told about a girl who'd been asked to leave back in the spring when it was discovered she was pregnant. The disdain and lack of sympathy for her expressed by many different girls was quite disturbing really, for surely some of them must have had moments with some boy, as she had with Andy, when she had almost succumbed.

In fact, Molly felt that if she ever felt that way again with a man who she knew loved her and who she could trust, she doubted she'd hold back. Besides, there were several girls back in Sawbridge who were pregnant on their wedding day, and their marriages were all happy ones.

Then, of course, there were Cassie's views on the subject. She made no secret of liking sex and, often, when Molly had been listening to her speaking about her relationships with men, she'd felt Cassie was the most honourable, truthful person she'd ever met.

In one of Cassie's poems she'd spoken of hypocrisy. 'I am shamed by those who speak out with others' voices, knowing that it is not their truth.'

She certainly didn't think Cassie would've approved of anyone searching out a man using a cold-hearted list of required assets. She would've said that kindness, passion, loyalty and honour were more important.

But maybe Rose and other girls that said similar things were just showing off, trying to make themselves sound more sophisticated.

Dilys was fascinated by Soho – the strip clubs, jazz dives, gambling places and the spivs and floozies who worked there. One evening about six weeks after Molly had started at Bourne & Hollingsworth, she persuaded Molly it was time they went to a jazz club.

'How can we not do it?' she said. 'Soho is right on our doorstep. Imagine how we'll feel when we are old if we hadn't dared to try it out?'

Molly liked the idea in theory, but there were always memos being posted up in the staff room about the dangers of Soho, advising staff to keep away.

'Okay, then,' Molly agreed, not wanting to seem dull and unadventurous. 'If we go on Saturday we can be out till twelve.'

Both girls wore new dresses for their adventure. Dilys was in turquoise shantung, a princess-style dress with a stand-up collar that framed her face, and a flared skirt which they thought looked very sophisticated. Molly wore a cream crêpe sheath dress with three-quarter-length sleeves and a sweetheart neckline, the most daring, slinky dress she'd ever worn. Even though it was a bit chilly they decided against wearing a coat or cardigan, as they wanted to show off their dresses.

They went to a pub first for a couple of Baby-chams to give them some courage, and at nine they sauntered off to find the Blue Moon Club just off Wardour Street.

It was a bit disappointing to find they were too early. The emptiness of the basement club made the grimy walls, sticky floor and the smell of stale drink and cigarettes more noticeable. It was also very dark, just a few dim lights here and there on the walls and candles on the tables. A jazz quartet was playing, and a waitress in a very short black satin dress like a skater's outfit plonked two glasses of red wine down in front of them and said, 'They're on the house,' in a very surly way.

The wine was horrible, but they sipped it anyway, and when Dilys looked around two men at the closest table to them grinned and raised their glasses in a toast.

'They're old enough to be our dads,' Molly said in horror.

Although both men were smartly dressed in dark suits, they had thinning hair and the slack jowls of men over fifty who drank too much.

'As long as they buy us a few drinks, does it matter how old they are?' Dilys said. 'We're here in a Soho night club at last! We don't have to marry them.'

Molly liked jazz – sometimes they had a jazz band playing at the Pied Horse – but the band here was much better, and when a girl singer came on after a couple of numbers to sing 'Frankie and Johnny' it got even better.

At the same time, the two men came over to the girls' table. 'That red wine they give girls in here is terrible. Let us get you a drink you like?'

'Well, thank you,' Dilys simpered. 'It is awful, and we'd love a Babycham.'

The taller of the two men introduced himself as Mike, waved his hand at the waitress and gave her the order, Babychams for the girls and whisky for them.

'This is my pal Ernie,' he said of his companion. 'We're down in the Smoke on a business trip and so I'm sure you won't mind if we keep you company.'

It wasn't a question, more an ultimatum, and both men sat down before either girl could respond. 'So,' Mike said, grinning at Molly. 'What are your names, and where do two such pretty girls come from?'

Close up, the two men looked even more worn and saggy; they had bad teeth, paunches and nicotine-stained fingers. From their accents, they sounded like they came from Birmingham, and Molly felt a little threatened.

'I'm Molly, from Somerset, and Dilys is from Cardiff,' she said. 'We are both nurses at the Middlesex Hospital. I'm a midwife and Dilys is a sister on the children's ward.'

Dilys bit her lip so as not to laugh. They had said on the way here they would make up a different job and place to live as they didn't want anyone tracking them down to Bourne & Hollingsworth.

'We like nurses,' Ernie said, and when he smiled his brown teeth were even worse than the girls had first thought. 'Do you live in a flat outside the hospital?'

'That would be telling,' Dilys said with a very naughty grin. 'Never tell a gentleman where you live, that's what my granny told me when I came to London.'

The drinks arrived just as the club started to get busier. The girls downed their Babychams quickly and, almost immediately, a second round arrived. The men had moved their chairs closer to the girls and Mike kept trying to take Molly's hand. All she wanted to do was listen to the great music and perhaps have a couple of dances, but it looked like they were stuck now with these two old men, and all the other tables had filled up, so even if they'd felt able to move there was nowhere to move to.

Molly drank the second glass of Babycham and

170

felt a little squiffy. The music was too loud to really make conversation, and she could see Dilys was uncomfortable with Ernie, too.

But the club was exciting, lots of very elegant women in beautiful evening dresses, their hair just perfect, and the men all looked so suave and sophisticated. But there was an undercurrent of something odd. She noticed that there were other girls who came in without male partners, but they weren't alone for very long; a man would always join them. Molly could tell just by watching that they didn't know the girls.

By her third Babycham, Molly knew she was drunk, and she could see that Dilys was, too. Mike and Ernie took them to the dance floor for a dance, and Molly didn't like the tight way Mike was holding her one bit.

'I need to go to the powder room,' she said to Dilys, giving her a surreptitious wink to make her realize she was to come, too.

'Get us another drink in, boys,' Dilys said, giving Ernie what passed for an affectionate tap on the cheek. 'Won't be long.'

'We've got to get out of here, they're horrible,' Molly said once they were in the Ladies. 'It's half past eleven anyway, so we've got to get back.'

'I'm too drunk to run,' Dilys said, slurring her words. 'I hope we don't get seen by Matron. She takes a dim view of girls drinking.'

'Come on, then,' Molly said, opening the door a crack to check the two men weren't watching. She could just see Mike's head. He appeared to be watching the girl singer. All they had to do was to skirt round the edge of the club, keeping

171

behind other people till they got to the door.

They bent over to walk to the door, but the ridiculousness of that made them giggle like schoolgirls. After a while, they reached the door that led to the stairs up to the street.

Just as they got to street level Mike shouted from the bottom of the stairs. 'Wait up, girls!' he yelled. 'We'll take you home in a taxi.'

'Run for it,' Molly ordered. She took Dilys's hand and they tottered along as fast as their high heels and drunkenness would allow.

It was only after they'd turned two corners and there was no sight of the men pursuing them that they slowed down.

'I've got a stitch,' Dilys said, bending over to get rid of it. 'My God, we can pick men, can't we? What a handsome pair they were!'

They laughed all the way back to the hostel. 'At least it was a cheap night,' Molly said, after they had got into their room, without being seen by Matron. 'Apart from the drinks in the pub, we didn't spend anything. But I think the girls on their own in that place are – you know.'

'What?' Dilys asked.

'Well, street girls,' Molly said, explaining that she'd seen girls come in alone and then a man would approach them.

'So maybe next time we try out some dive we need some nice male company,' Dilys giggled. 'I wonder how much Mike and Ernie would have been prepared to pay us?'

'They could offer me a thousand pounds and I'd turn it down,' Molly said. 'Did you see Mike's teeth?'

'I don't think he'd be using his teeth,' Dilys said. They were still giggling after they turned out the light.

That night in Soho and the awful Mike and Ernie was something the girls often reminded each other of and laughed about, but there were many more memorable evenings, dancing at the Empire, at safer jazz clubs and in pubs. They learned that the girls they saw that night were club hostesses who got a fee for keeping men company. Mike and Ernie must have thought that's what they were.

Dilys didn't quite fill the hole that Cassie had left in Molly's life, but in many ways she was an even more agreeable friend because they had no secrets from one another, they shared clothes, looked after one another and really liked being together.

Molly had been down to Whitechapel several more times, going to see Constance for tea and a chat, then asking questions around the neighbourhood, but although many people remembered Cassie and Petal, they couldn't throw any light on Cassie's past. It seemed almost unbelievable that anyone could become so embroiled in so many people's lives without giving anything of herself away.

Through reading the journal again and again Molly was certain Cassie had either come from, or had long holidays on, the coast in East Sussex. Her plan was to go there, but as the weeks passed and the store gradually grew busier, with people buying winter clothes and looking ahead to Christmas, she knew she wouldn't be able to do it till the new year.

It was frustrating and disappointing that she couldn't find out anything new about Cassie and so was no nearer in discovering what had happened to Petal, but at least everything was fine at home in Sawbridge.

Her mother wrote every week, and she said that Jack had become easier to live with since Molly had left. She said he was doing more in the shop; he'd even painted the walls and got smart new linoleum tiles laid. One time when Molly telephoned her she said she thought Jack had always been jealous of Molly and Emily because they took her attention away from him. That was why he was happier now.

George also wrote often, telling her not only the village gossip but echoing her mother's words in saying Jack was much less grumpy, sometimes even jovial. He also said her mother was looking more relaxed and was getting out some afternoons to go to Mothers' Union meetings and to visit her old friends. He always said he missed Molly and wished she'd come back for a weekend, and reminded her she could stay at his house.

Dilys said it was obvious he was in love with her, but Molly thought she was being silly, as surely a man told the woman if he loved her. But, sometimes, late at night when she couldn't sleep, Molly would think of George and his kisses, and wonder if she should say something in her letters back to encourage him.

But she didn't want him to think she was homesick and only latching on to him because of it. Besides, with her in London and him back in

Somerset, it was never going to work out anyway.

One night halfway through November, Dilys and Molly were just getting ready for bed, when Dilys suddenly blurted out that she had to warn Molly about someone.

Molly's three-month probationary period was up now, and she'd been moved from Haberdashery to Gloves a while ago. With autumn well under way, the department was a very busy one.

'Who?' Molly asked, and giggled. 'Is it Stan in the stores? He does keep leering at me.'

'No, he's harmless,' Dilys replied. 'It's Miss Stow. She can be a real vixen.'

Ruth Stow was the senior assistant in the Glove Department. She was a plain woman from Shropshire, in her mid-thirties. She'd worked at Bourne & Hollingsworth since she was seventeen, and she was always snooty towards the younger girls.

'Have I put a pair of gloves back in the wrong drawer?' Molly asked, grinning, because Miss Stow was always complaining about assistants who did this.

'No, that's your trouble: you don't. She thinks you're after her job.'

Molly pulled back the covers on her bed and climbed in. 'That's daft. All I want is to be moved to the fashion floor before long. What on earth gave her that idea?'

'You've had a lot of praise from customers, I think,' Dilys said. 'Miss Stow knows her stuff, but she's starchy. People like a bit of warmth and someone who takes a real interest in them.'

Molly frowned. She couldn't see what could have upset the older woman. She'd tried to be

175

friendly with her, not just behind the counter but talking to her here in the hostel. But her manner was always chilly and Molly had got the idea it was because she was the senior assistant and felt unable to mix with anyone more junior.

'It's not just in the shop,' Dilys said. 'You've become popular with most of the other staff, including some of those above us juniors.'

'Me, popular?' Molly asked.

Dilys laughed. 'Yes, very. Surely you've noticed that the girls always include you in anything going on and want to share a table with you at mealtimes. And I've heard some of the men are sweet on you, especially Tony in Menswear.'

Molly laughed. She was aware that Tony with the buck teeth was always gazing at her, but she hadn't considered that people asking to share her table was a sign of popularity; she thought it was just because there was nowhere else for them to sit. 'I have always attracted male lame dogs,' she said. 'Tony is good company, and he's sweet, but not my type. But, tell me, what should I do about Ruth? Should I try and talk to her about it?'

'I think that might just put her back up even more,' Dilys said. 'Just carry on normally and take no notice of her. Chances are she'll decide all on her own that you're no threat to her.'

'But who told you this?' Molly asked.

Dilys hesitated.

'Come on, tell me,' Molly urged her. 'I'm not going to confront whoever it was.'

'Well, it was Mr Hardcraft,' Dilys said reluctantly.

Molly had been merely amused until then but

176

now she realized that Dilys wasn't just repeating a bit of harmless gossip. Mr Hardcraft was the floor walker, and his job was to look out for any kind of trouble, be it theft or anything else likely to disrupt business.

'He wouldn't have told you that Miss Stow was gunning for me. My guess is he asked you questions about me. So tell me the whole truth now,' Molly insisted.

'Well, okay, but don't fly off the handle. He just asked me stuff like who your friends were and who you saw in the evenings.'

'What's that got to do with anything?' Molly was bewildered.

'I don't know. I told him when you go out in the evening you're always with one of us. He asked where you went on your day off, and I said you sometimes go to Whitechapel to see a friend there. Did I do wrong to say that?'

'No, of course not. You aren't the only one who knows I go to Whitechapel anyway, quite a few of the girls know, so it's a good job you said it in case he got it from someone else. Do you think Miss Stow's told him I'm keeping bad company?' Molly asked. She knew staff could get fired for that.

'Maybe, but if you're asked you've only got to say your friend is in the Church Army – that's not bad company. But forget about it, Molly. Everyone knows Miss Stow is nasty to anyone who shines too brightly.'

'I'll try to be especially nice to her in future.' Molly laughed. 'Maybe I'll keep going on about wanting to work in the Fashion Department so she feels less threatened.'

Chapter Eight

By the week before Christmas, Oxford Street and Regent Street were congested with shoppers from nine in the morning until closing time. Yet even after that, until ten or eleven at night, there were still people thronging the pavements to see the Christmas lights and gaze into the beautiful and brightly lit shop-window displays.

Molly was no stranger to being rushed off her feet at Christmas. Back in her father's shop at previous Christmases, sometimes it had seemed as if people were afraid they'd starve during the two days the shop would be closed.

Bourne & Hollingsworth, though, was much busier than she could ever have imagined, and she was astounded at how much money some people were spending. She and her sister had only ever had one present each from their parents, and a filled stocking from Santa Claus, the latter being mainly stuffed with cheap things like crayons, colouring books, a few nuts, sweets and a tangerine. But shoppers in London had long lists of things they were going to buy, and the cost seemed almost unimportant.

Every male customer wanted advice on which pair of gloves to buy his wife, mother or sister, yet few knew what size the recipients were. Women customers were more decisive and usually chose more utilitarian gloves, not the fancy red suede ones or those in white kidskin. Yet the Christmas spirit seemed to be in everyone, as they were mostly genial and patient, even when they had to wait a long time to be served.

Molly had been as excited as any six-year-old when the legendary lights in Oxford Street and Regent Street, which she'd always wanted to see, were switched on at the end of November. Coming from a small village where the only Christmas lights she'd ever seen were those on the tree in the village hall, to her, London's lights were like a glimpse of Fairyland.

Her delight grew as the display team at Bourne & Hollingsworth put lights and decorations up in the store, too. Each day, as Christmas inched closer and closer, there was a gradually increasing excitement in the air; people smiled and laughed more as they chose gifts or bought clothes to wear for Christmas parties. Molly got a warm feeling inside each time someone wished her a Merry Christmas, and when the Salvation Army band played carols right outside the store she got a lump in her throat.

Aided and abetted by Dilys, Molly had dared to buy the kind of dress for the staff party that, at home, would be unthinkable. It was red shantung with a low neck, a very full skirt and a wide, waist-clinching belt. Her father would have claimed she looked like a harlot, but after a few months in London she no longer cared about his opinion. The party was to be held on the evening of the twenty-third because many of the staff would be going home to their families after the shop closed on Christmas Eve.

As Christmas Eve fell on a Friday this year, most of the staff were taking advantage of the three-day holiday to do this. But both Molly and Dilys were staying on at the hostel. They told anyone that asked them why they weren't going home that a very long train journey after a full day at work was too much for them, but of course that wasn't the real reason they were staying in London.

In the past four months, the girls had become close enough for Molly to tell Dilys about her bullying father; Dilys had confided that hers was a drunkard and that her home in Cardiff was a slum. Admitting to each other that they hadn't come from a happy family when so many of the other girls boasted about how wonderful theirs were was liberating, and it bound them even more tightly together.

After telling each other about awful Christmases they'd had in the past, they resolved that this one would be wonderful. They hung paper chains up in their room, filled a stocking for each other with cheap little things, and they both had new dresses. There was also far more going on in London than there ever would be back home.

After the shop closed on Christmas Eve it was the tradition that everyone staying on at Warwickshire House would go down to Trafalgar Square for the carol service that was held around the huge Christmas tree. This was always followed by a pub crawl back, with a drink taken in every pub they passed.

Christmas dinner was cooked by the few kitchen staff staying on and, afterwards, everyone played party games. On Boxing Day, the Empire would

180

be open, and that promised to be a great evening as, a fortnight ago, the girls had met Frank and Robert, two men from Notting Hill who they really liked, and they'd arranged to meet them again on Boxing Day. Dilys had said gloomily that they'd probably forgotten her and Molly already, but Molly had sensed that both men were pretty taken with the girls and that they would be there.

Molly was just thinking about the staff party the next evening and how she'd look in her new dress when Dilys stopped at the glove counter on the way back from a late lunch break. 'Pst!' she hissed, to get Molly's attention, then pretended to be studying a display of gloves tumbling out of a small basket.

Molly sidled nearer, opening a drawer beneath the counter and pretending to look in it. 'What is it?' she asked, concerned that they would be told off if they were seen chatting.

'I just saw Miss Stow and Mr Hardcraft waiting for the lift together. I wouldn't have thought any-thing of it, but they were talking, heads close together, and looked back in your direction before getting in the lift.'

'So what?' Molly said. 'I expect they were just looking back to check there wasn't a queue of people waiting to be served.'

'Maybe, but I got a funny feeling about it – thought I'd warn you. Must go now.'

Molly smiled fondly as her friend scuttled off to the canteen. She thought that Dilys read too many thrillers and so saw intrigue everywhere. In fact, Miss Stow had been much less demanding recently. Molly thought it was because she'd finally

181

come to the conclusion that Molly could be trusted to put unsold gloves back in the right drawer, not be rude to customers and that she wasn't after her job.

It became even busier after four that afternoon. Schools had broken up for Christmas the day before, and so there were hundreds of mothers with children who had come up west to see the lights. It had started to rain heavily, so they were all taking shelter in the shops, and many of the children were badly behaved, touching everything and racing around.

'Where on earth is Miss Stow?' Julie Drysdale, the other assistant in the glove department, asked Molly. 'Look what those blessed kids have done to the counter!' She pointed to the sticky fingerprints all over the glass counter.

'They'd have done that even if she had been here,' Molly said as she went to serve a lady in a stylish, red, wide-brimmed hat. 'I love your hat, madam,' she said to the lady. 'We've got some gloves that would match it perfectly.'

'I'm sure you have, but I'm after some sensible, woolly gloves for my sister, who lives right up in the north of Scotland,' she replied, smiling at Molly.

Molly was just ringing up the sale when Mr Douglas, the security man, came along. Molly had never seen him on the shop floor before; he was always in his cubbyhole down by the staff entrance and exit. He was there to see that no one took anything out of the shop with them. Staff purchases went down to him, too; he had to make sure no one added anything to the bag after paying for their goods.

She finished serving the customer and wished her a Merry Christmas, then turned to Mr Douglas. 'A pair of gloves for your wife?' she asked with a wide smile. 'I hope you know her size.'

'No, Miss Heywood, I've come to fetch you,' he said. 'They want to talk to you upstairs.'

Molly looked at him. Staff were summoned upstairs to the personnel office for a variety of reasons, but the message usually came by telephone, or through the department manager. She'd never heard of anyone being escorted there by Mr Douglas.

'Now, please,' he said, more sharply.

Molly felt faintly sick as she went up in the lift, wondering what she could have done wrong. It was clear she'd done something but, apart from being five minutes late to the counter last Friday morning, she couldn't think of anything. But would she really be hauled out at such a busy time for something so trivial?

A voice from inside the personnel office responded to Mr Douglas's knock, telling him to come in. He didn't go in, though, just put his head round the door to say he had Miss Heywood with him.

'Go in.' He nodded at Molly, his face cold and blank.

Molly went in to find Hawk Face, the woman who had been on the interview panel, sitting behind the desk. She knew her now as Miss Jackson, one of the directors of the company, but aside from occasionally seeing her walk through the store, she'd had no reason to speak to her.

'Miss Heywood,' she began, not even asking Molly to sit down. 'It has been alleged that you have been putting extra goods which haven't been paid for into customers' bags. As I am quite sure you are in total command of your faculties, I have to assume the lucky recipients are friends or relatives of yours.'

'I'm sorry.' Molly frowned, not really understanding. 'There must be some mistake. I have never done such a thing.'

'But we have two independent witnesses who saw you do it.'

Molly felt her heart plummet. In a flash she guessed that the two so-called witnesses were Miss Stow and Mr Hardcraft, but why they should claim such a thing was a mystery to her.

'They're mistaken. I have never stolen anything in my life, and this is theft you're talking about, isn't it?'

'Of course it is. Any item taken from the store without payment or permission is considered stolen. A cunning way of stealing, too, as you personally would never have the stolen goods on you.'

'Then why didn't the witnesses call Security when they saw it happening?' Molly asked, but the shock of being accused of theft made her voice waver and her eyes prickle with tears.

'The first time, you were given the benefit of the doubt, but after that you were watched and, of course, you did it again, and again.'

'I did not,' Molly said with indignation. 'Whoever told you this is a liar and a troublemaker. Get them in here, and they can say it to my face. I don't have any friends or relatives in London to give anything to. The only people I know are members of staff.'

'That's not what I've heard,' Hawk Face said, her dark eyes flashing with steel. 'I've heard you have friends in Whitechapel.'

Molly was astounded. 'I know one person there, and she is a Sister in the Church Army,' she retorted angrily. 'And she's a frail old lady in a wheelchair. She can't even go out alone, much less come up to the West End so I can pass stolen gloves to her.'

'Come now! Do you really expect me to believe she is the only friend you have?'

'I have friends back home in Somerset.' Molly was aware that her voice was rising in her agitation, but she tried to control it. 'But the only friends I have in London are people who work here and live in Warwickshire House.'

'Don't you dare raise your voice to me, Miss Heywood. Or deny something which senior and trusted staff members have reported. I want you to go to Warwickshire House now, pack your suitcase and leave. You may count yourself very lucky we are not calling the police.'

'You aren't calling the police because you have no proof or evidence of theft,' Molly said, wanting to scream and stamp her feet at the injustice of it, but she wasn't the kind to do that. 'You only have the word of a spiteful spinster who doesn't like me because I'm popular with everyone else. And I expect she's influenced Mr Hardcraft into believing her story about me.'

Miss Jackson sat back in her chair, putting her two hands together to make a church spire, and

185

looked at Molly over them, a reflective expression on her face.

'Go quietly now, or I will call the police,' she said after a second or two. 'Aside from everyone seeing you taken away to the police station, you are likely to get a prison sentence and a police record. So just be grateful that I am being so lenient.'

She got to her feet, picked a brown envelope up from her desk and handed it to Molly. 'Your wages, made up till the end of the week. But I want you out of the store now.'

'I didn't do this,' Molly pleaded. She couldn't hold back her tears any longer. 'Please believe me, Miss Jackson. I promise on all that's holy that I have never given any goods to anyone, or taken them for myself. This is an act of spite by Miss Stow because she is jealous of me. I love working here. I wouldn't jeopardize my job by doing such a thing.'

'Go now,' the older woman said, and her voice was as cold as a January morning. 'Mr Douglas is waiting to escort you from the premises, both from here and from the staff hostel.'

Chapter Nine

Molly caught hold of Mr Douglas's sleeve as he ushered her out of the staff entrance and began walking her to the hostel.

'I didn't do this,' she pleaded with him. 'How can they throw me out of my job and home without any proof that I did anything wrong?'

He brushed her hand away from his jacket, his face cold and stern. 'If the floor walker and the head of department say you did it, then that's proof enough for me. I see thieves almost every day; they always deny their guilt. Now come along. It's my job to oversee you as you pack your belongings and to escort you from the hostel.'

'I haven't got anywhere to go,' Molly said, and the tears she'd tried to control spilled over and cascaded down her cheeks.

'No good blubbing,' he said brusquely. 'You've got your wages. Go home to your folks.'

Twenty minutes later Mr Douglas stood with his arms crossed, resolutely unmoved by her tears as she packed her clothes into her suitcase. She found his manner even more distressing because he'd always been so nice to her before; they'd often shared a little light-hearted banter at the staff door. She couldn't believe that he would turn against her like this.

What was she to do? She couldn't go home, not when she'd told her father she'd never come back while he was alive. She couldn't land herself on George and his family at Christmas either, not without being invited, and they weren't even on the telephone so she couldn't try sounding them out. And even if she had a fairy godmother living in the village, one who would welcome her with open arms and no strings attached, Molly would have to admit that she'd lost her job. The reason would soon come out and, before she could even say 'dismissed', it would be right round the village. No one would believe that she hadn't done something bad.

Once she'd got everything into her suitcase, she looked pleadingly at Mr Douglas. 'Please may I leave a note for Dilys?' she asked.

'Certainly not,' he said gruffly. 'The management doesn't hold with thieves fraternizing with employees. Pick up that case and get going.'

'Dilys will be upset if I'm gone without her knowing why,' she pleaded.

'She will know why. All the staff will be told. It encourages them to stay honest.'

Molly put her hands over her face in despair to imagine all the girls she'd come to know and like thinking she was a thief. How could this have happened? She had never done anything wrong.

Yet from deep inside her indignation rose up. 'What about innocent until proved guilty?' she snapped at the security man. 'If Miss Stow or Mr Hardcraft had really seen me slipping something to someone, as they claim they did, why didn't they stop that person?' Her voice rose in her anger and she moved closer to the man to drive her point home.

'I haven't even heard a description of this person! Not even whether it was a man or a woman. But then they couldn't describe them, or stop them, because they just don't exist. It's all fantasy, malicious at that. If they could do this to me, they're probably robbing the store blind between them. Have you thought of that?'

If her words meant anything to him, he didn't show it. His face was as cold and hard as granite. 'Come on, let's go,' he said and, putting his hand in the small of her back, he nudged her towards the door.

She took one last look at the room she'd been so happy in. Dilys's somewhat bedraggled poster of *Gone with the Wind,* and the photograph of Frank Sinatra she used to kiss goodnight. The paper chains they'd made together, looped right round the room, the two bulging felt stockings hanging from the knobs on the wardrobe.

So many stories from the past traded in this room; a few tears, but far more laughter. Now Dilys would be alone for Christmas, thinking her best friend was a thief.

Mr Douglas shut the front door of Warwickshire House the second she was over the threshold and, as the cold wind hit Molly's face, the enormity of her situation hit her, too. Tomorrow was Christmas Eve; she was jobless and homeless. What's more, it would be difficult to get another job after Christmas without a reference from Bourne & Hollingsworth.

Part of her wanted to hang around and see Dilys to tell her what had happened. But all the staff came back together in big groups, and if they'd already been told what she was supposed to have done, they would probably be as nasty as Mr Douglas had been. Dilys might even believe it was true. After all, she'd been the one warning her that something was afoot.

Molly made her way towards Euston, rather than going the other way, which might mean running into someone from the store. Her suitcase was much heavier than when she had first come to London, because she'd bought new clothes and shoes. The weight of it and the need to sit down and think about what she was going to do made her go into a café and order a cup of tea.

Once she had her tea and an iced bun, she counted her money, including the wages she'd been given today. They'd paid her for two weeks, as she'd worked a week in hand when she had first arrived in London, and along with what she already had in her purse, she had three pounds, four shillings and sixpence. But that was all: no savings, nothing more.

If Miss Grady at the Braemar would give her a room, she had enough money for roughly five nights. Maybe she could get a job in one of the restaurants around Paddington?

But what if she couldn't? Once her money ran out, she'd be destitute, like the men who slept on the park benches down on the Embankment.

A little later, she telephoned the Braemar from a telephone box, and Miss Grady answered.

'I'm very sorry, Miss Heywood,' she replied to Molly's request for a room, 'I'm full to bursting. So many people come to London at Christmas to see relatives, it's often my busiest time of the year. But aren't you going home?'

There was something guarded in Miss Grady's voice, as if she suspected Molly was in difficulties and didn't want to hear about it for fear of being expected to help. So Molly just said she'd left her job and was going on to a new one in the New Year. Even as she said it, she wondered how many more lies she was going to be forced to tell in the coming days.

Miss Grady didn't suggest another hotel, and Molly was so demoralized that she didn't ask.

The streets around Euston were becoming empty now that people had left their offices and all the shops had closed. She tried two guest houses close to the station, but they were full up, like the Braemar, but with even less friendly owners, who both said they couldn't recommend anywhere else.

She walked back down Tottenham Court Road, because it felt safer to be amongst people.

Since her first day of working in London she had completely lost her fear of the big city, but that fear came back now. Suddenly, everyone looked tight-lipped, cold-eyed, elbowing their way aggressively through the crowds. Her case was heavy, she was cold and hungry and she was fighting back tears.

As she reached the junction of Tottenham Court Road and Oxford Street, she looked right and saw that Oxford Street was still packed with people who had come into town to see the Christmas lights. They didn't have that mean and aggressive look she'd observed around Euston, but somehow their happiness and delight made her plight seem even more desperate.

Married couples arm in arm, a serenity in their expressions that said they expected this Christmas would be the best since before the war, because so many foodstuffs, including sweets, had come off ration. Sweethearts, hand in hand, looking at each other with tender smiles; old people huddled together for warmth, perhaps afraid this would be the last time they'd see the lights. And there were so many families, some of

191

their children sagging with weariness on their father's shoulders, others jumping up and down with the excitement of being out so late, but all gazing up at the lights with awe.

She remembered, when she and Emily were little, how excited they used to get as Christmas approached, making paper chains, sewing needle cases or making calendars for Christmas presents. If her parents had brought them to London to see the lights they would have been delirious with joy.

That same kind of joy was everywhere she looked, and it was unbearable when she didn't even have a bed to sleep in. Unable to stand another moment of it, she turned off Oxford Street towards Soho.

When she had first got here, people had delighted in telling her lurid tales about Soho. It was supposed to be a dangerous haunt of prostitutes and gangsters. But from what Molly had read in newspapers and travel guides, it also had the best night clubs and restaurants in London. She and Dilys had loved walking through it and, though they certainly sensed an element of menace in some parts, perhaps because of the neglected old buildings and unsavoury smells, their overall impression was that Soho was just a melting pot of people from all walks of life and of many different nationalities. They had observed elegant, aristocratic women in evening dress with their equally elegant male escorts sharing the grubby pavements with vagrants, snotty-nosed urchins and the kind of rough-looking women in aprons and scarves, fastened turban-style, that her mother had always called 'fishwives'. If there were prostitutes working here, then they weren't out on the streets wearing the kind of tight skirts and clingy sweaters Molly imagined such women wore. Dilys had always joked that maybe streetwalkers were like vampires, and they had to wait for the midnight hour to come out.

Molly was really hungry now; she hadn't eaten anything except a bun since noon. Her feet hurt, she thought a blister was coming up on her heel, her arms throbbed with carrying her case and she was icy cold. She could have stood it if she had been on the way to a warm place with a bed for the night but, knowing that the reality was a bench on the Embankment, she began to cry.

Wiping her eyes on her coat sleeve, she tried to sniff back the tears, but it was no good; she was too desolate to control her emotions, and she put her suitcase down, turned towards a shop window with a display of old books and let the tears fall.

'Is that bookshop so tragic it makes you cry?'

Molly's head jerked round on hearing the man's voice. Its owner was about thirty, stocky, with a round, very pink face, a receding hairline. He was wearing a camel coat with a velvet collar and looked concerned for her.

'What on earth could make you cry that hard?' he asked.

'I'm tired, hungry and cold,' she blurted out. 'And I've got nowhere to go.'

'Is that so?' he said, looking at her hard for a moment or two as if weighing up whether she was conning him. Then he smiled. 'Well, suppose we sort a couple of those things out by getting something to eat in a warm café, and then you can tell me why you've got nowhere to go.'

Her mother had told her a hundred times not to talk to strangers, but as she had found out today that people who know you well can be treacherous, too, her mother's advice seemed superfluous. 'That's very kind of you,' she said in a small voice, and dabbed at her eyes with an already damp hanky.

'I'm Seb,' he said. 'That's short for Sebastian, but no one but my granny calls me that. What's your name?'

'Molly,' she said, giving him a watery smile. 'Molly Heywood.'

'Well, Molly Heywood,' he said, bending to pick up her case, 'they do a good fish and chips just down here, and you can tell me your troubles while you eat.'

Five minutes later, sitting in a wooden booth at the back of a fish-and-chip shop, Molly felt more hopeful. It was very warm in the café, the fish and chips would be in front of her in just a few minutes and her cup of tea was just as she liked it: strong and very sweet. She liked Seb, too; he had a forthright manner, a lovely speaking voice and he was kind and a good listener. 'So why did they sack you?' he asked.

As Molly explained the reason and how humiliated she felt, she began to cry again. 'As God is my judge, I didn't let anyone have anything without paying. I don't know anyone in London aside from the other staff at Bourne & Hollingsworth, so who would I give stuff to?'

'That is really appalling,' he said, and took her

two hands in his and squeezed them. 'But I have a friend who works in Personnel. I could contact them for you tomorrow and find out the legal position. I'm sure you have to catch staff red-handed to be able to dismiss them. You might be entitled to compensation, or at least your job back.'

He sounded so confident and knowledgeable that Molly's spirits soared. The fish and chips were brought to them then, and she ate hungrily.

'Can you recommend a cheap guest house for a few nights?' she asked him, explaining how she'd called the Braemar already and it had been full.

'I can do better than that,' he said. 'I know some girls living in a flat just down the road from here. They're all around your age and they'll be happy to put you up for a while. They might be able to help you get a new job, too, if you can't go back to the shop.'

'Really! You'd do that for me?' she gasped.

He smiled and patted her hand. 'I never could resist a damsel in distress. And you've been treated very badly.'

As Molly polished off the last of her fish and chips she felt reassured that everything would work out fine. If she could get a job right after Christmas, and was able to pay rent, maybe these friends of Seb's would let her stay on with them permanently.

Although the street lighting in Greek Street was poor, Molly's first thought when Seb pointed out the flat, which was above a barber's shop, was that if the girls let her stay, her first job would be to clean the windows. Even in the dark she could see they were filthy.

A door beside the barber's was open, revealing a litter-strewn, bare wood staircase and peeling distemper on the walls.

'I know it looks a bit rough,' Seb said, 'but the landlord is too mean to get it smartened up. He claims the rent is too low to make it worth his while.'

'All of London is a bit rundown after the war,' she said. 'I'm quite used to it now.'

He led her up two flights of stairs, past three or four closed doors, and then knocked on one very battered one to the front of the building. It was opened by a dark-haired woman of perhaps forty. She was wearing a grubby pink dressing gown and had curlers in her hair.

'Hullo, Seb. What brings you round? If I'd known you were coming, I'd've baked a bleedin' cake,' she said. Her accent was pure cockney and her smile was bright.

'I found this young lady crying in the street; she's lost her job and has nowhere to go,' he said, half turning towards Molly. 'This is my friend Dora, and, knowing how kind she is, I was certain she'd give you a bed for a few nights.'

'Oh, you poor love!' Dora exclaimed, taking a couple of steps nearer to Molly, her dark eyes soft with concern. 'You come on in and we'll get you sorted. I got a spare bed up top as it happens, 'cos Jackie went home for Christmas.'

'I don't want to impose,' Molly said. She had a lump in her throat at this unexpected kindness. 'I could give you a bit of money.'

'I wouldn't hear of it,' Dora said. 'Now, come on in. The place is a mess, but it's warm and homely.'

Dora poured Molly a glass of sherry, saying it would warm her up and make her sleep well. Molly didn't really like sherry, but she was too polite to say so. As she sipped it, she surveyed the room.

Dora had been right in saying it was a mess. It was like Paddy's market, with clothes, make-up and unwashed dishes all over the place. The double bed wasn't even made but, clearly, Dora felt embarrassed by it and quickly pulled up the covers and smoothed out the pink satin bed-spread.

'Some days, you just can't seem to get into a routine,' she said with a chuckle. 'I bet you're a real tidy person, Molly?'

'Not at all,' Molly said diplomatically, though in fact she was. She'd had to be: clutter and sloven-liness were things her father had ranted about.

The warmth from the gas fire was making Molly feel sleepy. Dora and Seb were talking about noise from a club nearby; they said the music went on till four in the morning.

'You, my girl, are ready for bed,' Dora said, touching Molly's shoulder to rouse her. 'I'll show you up there now. Sleep's a great healer. Nothing will look so bad tomorrow.'

Chapter Ten

'She was so sleepy she didn't even take her clothes off, just lay down on the bed and zonked out,' Dora said when she returned from showing Molly the way upstairs.

'So the knock-out drops worked?' Seb grinned. 'I saw her grimace when you gave her the sherry. I didn't think she'd drink it.'

'Well-brought-up girls with nowhere to sleep will always down a drink, however nasty, out of sheer gratitude,' Dora sniggered. 'Thanks for bringing her my way, Seb. With her milkmaid complexion, good figure and lovely eyes, she's perfect for my more discerning customers. I don't have to ask if she's a virgin, it bloody well shines out of her; and I don't think she's got any fight in her either.'

'She told me she couldn't go home because of her father. My guess is he knocked her about.'

'Well, if she plays ball with me, she won't get no slaps from me or the johns,' Dora said. 'I'm going to phone Randall now to tell him I've got a Christmas present for him.'

'You're going to let him break her in tonight?' Seb was alarmed at this. He had procured many girls for Dora in the last couple of years, but they had all been hard little bitches. Molly was different.

He understood why Dora had a heart like stone. Her own mother had allowed a male friend to rape her when she was only seven. From that day till she finally ran away at the age of fourteen she'd been passed around from man to man like a toy. She had told Seb she'd decided then and there that, in future, she would make men pay dearly for what they wanted.

It was said she had a fine big house out Epping way, that it was beautifully decorated and furnished. But she was hardly ever in it; most of the time she slept here in Greek Street, in the same squalor as her 'tenants', as she liked to call them. She didn't turn tricks any longer – she didn't need to, as she took half of what each 'tenant' made, and none of them could cheat her because she knew every angle.

'That's why I gave her the drops.' Dora shrugged. 'If it ain't done tonight she'll realize what this place is tomorrow and she'll run. That'd be such a waste.'

'You're all heart, Dora,' Seb responded. Dora always gave him a good wedge for finding girls and, normally, he didn't have the slightest qualm about it. He took the line that, if he hadn't picked them up, someone else would. But, just this once, he felt bad.

'She'll hardly know what's happening with the dose I gave her. Get the first time out the way and she'll be fine.'

Seb wasn't so sure. In the short while he'd been with Molly she'd struck him as a bright girl with a great deal of natural dignity. He couldn't ever see her taking on some ten or so men a night, like the rest of Dora's girls did. But he'd brought her here for the money, and it was too late now to

199

back away. The best thing he could do was get home to his wife and sons.

'If I can have my cut now, I'll be off.' He got to his feet and buttoned up his overcoat. 'I told the missus I'd be home by ten tonight, and it's well past that now.'

Dora unlocked a small door in her sideboard and drew out a cashbox. She handed him twenty pounds. 'If she's got what it takes, I'll give you the same again in the New Year,' she said. 'And a merry Christmas to you, Seb.'

Molly woke with a start when the light was switched on. A man was standing in the doorway looking at her. He was perhaps fifty, a fat man with a high colour and thinning grey hair. He was wearing a navy overcoat, and the expression on his face made her feel alarmed.

'What do you want?' she asked.

'You, sweetheart,' he said, coming right into the room and closing the door behind him.

She was still half asleep, but in a flash of intuition she sensed what he was about, and also, to her horror, how the other girls in the house must make their living. She didn't know why it hadn't occurred to her when Seb had first brought her here.

'I'm not that kind of girl, so get out now!' she hissed at him. 'Or I'll scream and wake the whole place up.'

'I like it when girls fight me off,' he said, leering at her and reaching out to pull the blankets off her. 'Dora said you were likely to be a little hellcat.'

Molly was very woozy and her limbs felt like lead, but she knew she had to pull herself together and deal with this man. 'You lay one finger on me and you'll regret it,' she warned him.

'What are you going to do, sweetheart?' he said in a honeyed voice, one hand grabbing hold of her breast and the other pushing aside the blankets to get under her skirt. 'Screaming's not going to stop me – they're used to that in this place.'

It was something about the way he said 'screaming' that made her think of her father hitting her. He had never cared if she screamed either.

She'd learned to stand up to him, and she'd got away from him, and she wasn't about to allow some nasty stranger to do vile things to her without putting up the fight of her life.

She thrashed out at him and clawed his face, drawing blood. But he didn't even wince, just drew his arm back and slapped her hard, shoving her back down on to the mattress.

The slap stung, and she was really scared, but she didn't even put her hand to her cheek, much less cry out, as she didn't want him to see her weaken. She thought fast. She needed some kind of weapon, and she scanned the room looking for something she could use. There was nothing but a stout pole in the corner of the room, which she guessed was used to open the skylight. It was a bit unwieldy but, in the absence of anything better, it would have to do. She couldn't move, anyway, as he was holding her by the shoulders with both hands and pushing her down on the bed. She would have to wait for the right opportunity.

'My word, you are a nice little Christmas present,' he said, flopping himself down on her and trying to kiss her.

His breath stank, not just of drink and cigarettes but something like raw sewage, too. She turned her face, which was stinging from the slap, away from him, and forced herself not to struggle, as she felt she would have a far better chance of getting away if he thought he'd knocked the fight out of her.

'Don't hurt me,' she whimpered, realizing that he would have to let go of her shoulders to undo his trousers or to pull up her clothes.

'There's always a bit of pain the first time,' he said, and it sounded as if he enjoyed that thought. 'Just let me see that little virgin pussy.'

Molly almost retched at his breath and at the thought of him touching her. But to stand a chance of escape she had to play along with him.

'I'm really scared, but let me get my clothes off, or they'll be all creased up tomorrow,' she whispered.

'I'll undress you,' he said, and he moved off her, lying on his side, leaning up on his elbow to start undoing the buttons on her cardigan and blouse.

As he undid the last button he slid his hand into the top of her petticoat and tried to yank her breast out of her bra.

'Ouch!' she exclaimed. 'You're so rough.'

He withdrew his hand, as she hoped he would. 'Well, you take the rest of your stuff off, then.'

She sat up and made out she was going to take off her cardigan, and he seemed to relax a bit. She held out one side of her cardigan just long enough to stop him seeing her move her legs, which were still under the blankets, over the side of the bed. Then, in one swift movement, she flicked the blankets back and leapt to her feet.

She was on the side of the bed by the window. He looked at her in astonishment and laughed. 'You want to play games, then?' he said. 'I'll smack your bottom when I catch you, and that'll be easy, because you're trapped, silly girl.'

He got off the bed and began to sidle round the narrow space at the end of it to where she was.

Molly waited till he was almost close enough to grab her, then jumped up on the bed. He hastily moved back the way he had come, assuming she was making for the door. But as soon as he was there she jumped back to the floor where she'd been before and, once again, he moved back to try to catch her.

She repeated this twice more, as if it were a game. Each time, he was getting redder in the face and panting with the exertion.

'Can't catch me, Fat Man!' she taunted him, and bounced high on the bed, making the springs twang. He lunged forward across the bed to grab her, but this time she jumped off the bed on the side of the pole and snatched it up.

She'd worked out that she needed to disable him with just one blow or he would hurt her, so it had to be an extremely hard one. She knew she was strong: all that cycling and lifting heavy boxes back in Somerset had built up her muscles. Turning towards him and gripping the pole with both hands, she lifted it and brought it down on his head with all the force she could muster.

The sound as it hit his head was horrible, something like breaking china. He slumped forward on to the bed, his face into the blankets, and a thin red line of blood popped up on the back of his head and ran down to his neck.

She gasped, afraid she'd killed him, but although that was shocking, because she hadn't intended to go that far, she knew she couldn't wait to find out.

Quick as a flash, she moved round to where her shoes, coat, handbag and suitcase were still grouped together on the floor. She put her coat on, tucked her shoes under her arm and then, picking up her handbag and case, she made for the stairs.

She wanted to fly down them, to get out as fast as she could, but she controlled the urge and crept softly so no one would hear her and come to stop her.

There were sounds coming from behind most of the doors she passed – grunting, bedsprings creaking and the occasional yelp or moan, reminding her what had been in store for her, but when she got down to Dora's door there was silence.

Creeping, her heart hammering with terror, her legs like jelly and threatening to give way at any minute, she finally reached the last flight of stairs and got out on to the street.

It was only when the cold wind hit her that it dawned on her she'd been drugged. She had felt strange after drinking the sherry, and she remembered that Dora had supported her as she went up the stairs because she was wobbling as if she were drunk. But one small glass of sherry would never have had that effect on her.

What a naïve idiot she'd been to think that two complete strangers like Dora and Seb would help her just because they were kind people. Dora had clearly drugged her to make her compliant, and she was fairly sure the man she'd just hit over the head had paid Dora for her. That made her feel sick.

She had no idea what time it was – it had to be the early hours of the morning – but Greek Street was still busy with people, and she could hear music coming from several different places. All at once it was clear why people said Soho was dangerous, and passing through it in the middle of the night carrying a suitcase was virtually advertising that she was homeless. She was afraid that someone could be lurking in a doorway, ready to pounce on her.

Tears threatened, but she bit them back, remembering that Seb had spoken to her because he'd seen her crying. She picked up her suitcase and made herself walk purposefully down the street. She knew she had to get out of Soho and into a safer area.

Several men accosted her as she walked. One asked her how much; another asked if she wanted a bed for the night; and the others said things she didn't understand but knew by their tone of voice and their expression they were bad. She was growing more and more scared, so much so, she was struggling to breathe.

Finally, she came to a crossroads, and across the road she saw the blue light of a police station. She hurried towards it, hoping against hope there would be a policeman like George on duty who would be sympathetic to her plight.

Molly noted, once she was in the police station,

that it was Bow Street, and she recalled her teacher telling the class about the Bow Street Runners, the first policemen in London. A middle-aged police sergeant called Simmons with a saggy face like a bloodhound took her into a small interview room. He got her a cup of tea, commiserated with her about her swollen cheek, and seemed full of sympathy as she related what had happened to her.

But when she finished with how she'd run from the place in Greek Street, he looked at her very sternly. 'You hit this man over the head with a pole and left the house without checking he was still alive?'

Molly had thought the sergeant was totally in sympathy with her up to that point, but the way he spoke now suggested that he thought she was a potential murderess. She wanted to cry with frustration.

'Would you have expected me to stay till he came round?' she said with some indignation. 'He got what he deserved. Look! That woman Dora drugged me. Sebastian, the man who took me there, must have known what would happen to me. The only thing I did wrong was being stupid enough to think they were kind people putting me up for the night.'

'The address where it took place?' he asked curtly.

'Greek Street. I don't know the number, but there was a barber's shop beneath it. The woman was called Dora and the man who took me there was called Seb, short for Sebastian.'

'Dora, you say? Mid-forties, a buxom redhead?'

'Yes, that's her,' Molly said. 'Can't you go round there now and arrest her and the fat man?'

'Unless you killed the fat man, he'll be long gone now,' the sergeant said wearily. 'And it's just your word against Dora's that you were ever there. She'll deny it, of course.'

Molly couldn't hold back her tears any longer. She could hardly believe that, twice in one day, she wasn't being believed.

'Come now, don't cry,' the policeman said, his tone softer now. 'I can appreciate you've had a really bad scare and a hard time of it today. But it's not the end of the world.'

'A hard time?' she snapped back at him. 'I get accused of stealing at my job and get thrown out on my ear. I've got nowhere to go, and the one person who is understanding and kind turns out to want to force me into prostitution. If all that happened to you in one day, I think you'd cry, too.'

'Yes, I expect I would, Miss Heywood.' He sighed. 'But it's two in the morning now, and I don't really know what to do with you. All I can offer at this time of night is a bed in a cell. They aren't very nice, and there're a few drunks down there, too, but it's better than being out on the street in the cold.'

'Oh, thank you, but I'd happily sleep on the floor here,' she said gratefully.

'I couldn't let you do that. But I'll send some- one round to Greek Street, just to check you haven't left a man dying in that room. And we'll read Dora the riot act while we're at it. By the time it's daylight, you might be able to think of someone you can turn to for help.'

'There isn't anyone.' Molly dried her eyes and blew her nose.

'Well. I'll put my thinking cap on, too,' he said gently, and smiled at her. 'Maybe one of the churches round here has contacts with people who can help those in your position. Now come with me and we'll get some blankets and try to make you comfortable in a cell.'

An hour later, as Molly lay on the narrow bench in the cell covered by a blanket that smelled of feet and vomit, she wept again, this time in utter despair. She could hear a drunk shouting and singing further along the passageway, and every now and then another man would shout at him to shut up.

It seemed that she had no choice but to go home and throw herself on her father's mercy. Was his nastiness any worse than walking the streets with nowhere to go? Were his clouts as bad as attempted rape or being accused of theft? She didn't think he'd believe that she'd stolen any gloves; after all, she'd never stolen anything from him. But she would have to put up with an endless litany of 'I said you wouldn't be able to cope with London.' How he was going to enjoy that!

Molly woke with a start to find the sergeant shaking her shoulder. 'Come upstairs with me for a little chat,' he said. 'I've got to go off duty soon, and these cells are no place for a lady when the other occupants start to wake up.'

He led her back into the same small room where they'd been the night before. He told her to sit down while he got her a cup of tea.

'Have you had any more thoughts about some-one you could go to?' he asked when he got back, putting a mug of tea and a couple of ginger biscuits in front of her. 'Surely you know some-one in London?'

Molly was just about to tell him she'd decided she had no choice but to go home when she suddenly thought of Constance.

'Well, I do know a lady in the Church Army in Whitechapel,' she said cautiously. 'I don't know her terribly well, but she's kind and she might have some useful contacts.'

The sergeant nodded. 'Those Church Army ladies are good sorts,' he said. 'You know, Miss Heywood, I don't believe you stole anything, and I think your friend will believe you, too. You've had a nasty shock with Dora. I sent a couple of men to shake her up. As expected, the fat man had gone and Dora claimed no strangers had been in her house. But the men found the window pole still on the bed upstairs, and there was blood on it and on the blankets. Dora blustered that two of her girls had had a fight up there, but she knew as well as my men did that, without the fat man, we couldn't charge anyone with anything.'

'Isn't what she does against the law?' Molly asked.

'Soliciting on the street is.' He shrugged his shoulders. 'So is living off immoral earnings, which is what she's doing. But we can't prove that, or do anything about what goes on in private property.'

That seemed crazy to Molly, but then so did

209

giving someone the sack for stealing when there was no proof.

'Can I stay here till a more reasonable hour?' she asked. 'I can't go knocking on someone's door at seven or eight in the morning.'

'No, you can't,' he said. 'As I already told you, I'm off in a minute, but I'm going to take you upstairs now to our canteen and get them to give you some breakfast. Then I'm going to get one of my men to drive you to your Church Army lady. If she can't take you in, he'll take you on to someone else we fall back on at times like this. How would that be?'

Molly's heart swelled up with gratitude and her eyes prickled with tears. She hadn't expected such kindness. 'Thank you so much,' she managed to say, and had to cover her face to hide the tears.

A couple of hours later, after a breakfast of bacon, egg and sausage washed down by two large mugs of tea, PC Stanley delivered Molly to Constance's door in Myrdle Street. Stanley was a big, craggy-faced copper in his early fifties, and on the drive to Whitechapel he had tried to make her laugh with some awful jokes.

Molly's mother had always claimed that men telling jokes was a way of concealing that they couldn't hold a real conversation, and she was probably right in this instance, as Molly had learned nothing personal about PC Stanley.

When they stopped outside Constance's house PC Stanley said he would go and speak to her alone first. 'Sarge said I should, as it will sort of oil the wheels if I tell her you were in real danger last night and assure her we don't believe you

210

stole anything. If she really can't help you, it's easier for her to tell me that without you there.'

Molly watched PC Stanley disappear into the house and hoped he wouldn't try to tell Constance any terrible, unfunny jokes. She wasn't happy about putting the old lady in a position where she'd feel obliged to help her. It wasn't fair. Neither did she think she could bear to live in this terrible, grimy area for more than a couple of days.

PC Stanley came back to the doorway and beckoned for her to come in. Molly got out of the car with her suitcase and walked hesitantly towards the policeman.

'It's okay. She's happy to put you up,' he said. 'She said she likes you a lot and was shocked at what has happened to you. So go on in and I'll go back to the station.'

Molly thanked him and asked him to thank the sergeant, too, for his kindness. Then, as the policeman drove away, she made her way in to see Constance.

'You poor love,' the old lady said as soon as she saw Molly. 'Come and sit down by the fire and tell me all about it.'

Constance was sitting by the fire in her wheelchair. She didn't get out of it to hug her, she didn't even hold out a reassuring hand, yet just the way she spoke it felt to Molly as if someone had just wrapped a warm, soft blanket around her. All at once she didn't care how squalid Whitechapel was, or that she'd have to cope with no bathroom and an outside lavatory here. She felt safe and wanted.

All her other visits here had been on a different footing. She had been, to all intents and purposes,

211

like a distant relative doing her duty in coming to see an old lady, staying just long enough to be polite, then leaving. Yet by one o'clock on Christmas morning, after wheeling Constance home in her wheelchair from the midnight service, Molly felt that fate had smiled on her. It wasn't just a temporary place of refuge, somewhere she would want to leave as soon as she could. She felt that coming to the East End might actually be a really good thing for her.

All day, people had been dropping into Myrdle Street with food, offers of a shared Christmas dinner, to see if Constance needed any help, or just for a chat. These were nice people. They might be very poor, and often loud and coarse, but they had warm hearts.

Constance wasn't bound to the wheelchair; she could walk well enough with a stick to get to the lavatory, to stand up to wash and dress herself and make a cup of tea. But she was frail and her neighbours clearly wanted to show how much they loved her by doing as much as possible for her.

They didn't see Molly as some kind of interloper but as company for their friend, and when the story was told about her experiences the previous day, they were all in total sympathy with her. In fact, they were all impressed that she had got the better of the fat man in Greek Street.

Molly had spent the day not only meeting all the neighbours but decorating a small Christmas tree someone had brought round, helping wrap some toys for various small children Constance cared about, making up a narrow truckle bed for herself in the corner of the room and stowing her clothes away in a linen press.

Molly had always been involved with the church at home, not just going to services but singing in the choir and flower arranging, but she'd never been to a midnight service before. When Constance asked her to go with her, she agreed out of politeness, but she would rather have gone to bed. So it was a real surprise to find herself uplifted by the service. The carols, candles and flowers played a part, but it was more than that: she felt as if a burden had been taken from her shoulders and that whatever path she took after Christmas would be the right one.

She made some cocoa for her and Constance when they got in.

'It will work out for you,' Constance said as she got into her bed. 'You mustn't doubt that, dear. For now, you must just settle in here with me, rest and be comfortable. The New Year is the time for making plans.'

'I had such a cheek throwing myself on you,' Molly said, shame-faced. 'But there wasn't anyone else.'

'It wasn't chance,' Constance said. 'The whole thing – you finding my address in a book at Cassie's home, feeling you had to see me – it was all meant to be. The Almighty has a plan here; we just have to wait until He decides to let us know what to do next.'

If Molly had heard anyone else say such a thing, she would have scoffed. But Constance had a way of talking about God as if he was her best friend and she knew he could sort anything. Molly was beginning to believe that, too.

Chapter Eleven

By mid-January Molly's life had settled into a gentle routine. She couldn't claim it was a comfortable one, in a cold, draughty house with no bathroom and so much squalor and poverty all around her. But she was surprisingly happy.

Constance's belief that 'the Lord will provide' had rubbed off on her. Three days after Christmas she was walking by Pat's Café on Whitechapel Road and she noticed a card in the window saying 'PART-TIME HELP WANTED'. She went in immediately to enquire.

Pat Heady, who owned the café, was a woman in her early fifties, skinny, bedraggled and slovenly, and she was often very rude to her customers. The café was as grubby as its owner.

'What do you want to work here for?' Pat had asked Molly, looking at her with deep suspicion.

For two pins Molly would have turned and walked out. But she needed a job and, however grubby Pat and her café were, it was just a three-minute walk from home, and she needed to pay her way.

'Because I need a job,' Molly said, tempted to add that only a desperate person would want to work in Pat's.

'I only pay sixpence an hour, and it's hard work.'

'I'll take it.' Molly didn't think she had any choice.

'God love you!' Pat's eyebrows shot up in surprise. 'I thought a posh bint like you would sooner put a fork in her eyes than work here.'

'Desperate times call for desperate measures,' Molly said with a grin. She quite liked being called a posh bint; she thought she would tell George about it when she eventually got round to writing to him. 'When can I start and what are the hours?'

'Start tomorrow if you like. I want you ten till two, but if you're any good I might stretch that from nine to three,' Pat said. 'It's mostly cooking fry-ups.'

Molly could see that the frying pan on the stove was half full of lard and that there were four eggs floating around in it. She thought she could definitely improve the standard of the cooking by using less fat. But she kept that to herself. 'I'll be in at ten then. My name is Molly Heywood.'

She got home to find Constance beaming.

'The landlord has just been round. He said you could use the little box room on the next floor if you clean it out and give it a coat of paint,' she said gleefully. 'He doesn't even want any rent, because it's too small to let.'

'How wonderful!' Molly exclaimed. 'And I've just got a job, too. I'll pop up and see the room, because it'll be dark very soon, then I'll come back and make some tea and tell you about the job.'

The room was hardly bigger than a cupboard, with no gas light in it, but Molly thought once she'd scrubbed it out it would be fine.

Constance was delighted, too, that Molly had found a job. 'Pat could do with some lessons in hygiene,' she said. 'But the café is close to home

– a good thing in the winter months – and it's a chance to get back on your feet. Now let's think what we can put in your new room to make it homely.'

Pat required nothing more of Molly than the ability to cook things like bacon and eggs, sausage and chips, or cheese on toast, to wash up and ring up money in the till. It was as different from working at Bourne & Hollingsworth as it was possible to be. Almost all the clientele were male, either market traders or local workmen. They were rough, noisy, many with the table manners of pigs, but they appreciated Molly, the time flew by and she could walk home in five minutes.

She had to wait until Sunday to scrub her room out and give it a coat of whitewash. She slotted the truckle bed and a slender chest of drawers of Constance's in, and some hooks on the back of the door became her wardrobe. She bought a yard of cheap cotton in the market to make a curtain for the tiny window, and Constance dug out a bright-red blanket for her to cover the bed and create a cosier feel.

'It's an old ambulance blanket,' Constance explained. 'They used to have red ones to hide the blood. A rescue worker gave it to me during the war when I was bombed out, and I never thought to return it.'

The room was terribly cold, of course, and there was no way of heating it, but Molly put a couple of hot-water bottles in the bed at night, and she slept soundly. She was glad to be able to give her friend back her privacy, as both of them

216

sleeping and living in the same room had been far from ideal.

On her first night in the room, she thought about Cassie having lived next door; in fact, in the room on the other side of her wall. Molly couldn't help but feel it wasn't just chance that had brought her here but fate, and that she was right to keep on searching for the truth, because it would surface eventually. She hoped that if someone around here did know more about Cassie, or even the identity of the person who took Petal, they might make themselves known to her.

She kept the picture of Cassie and the one of Petal on the counter at Pat's Café, and every time a new face came in she'd ask them if they knew Cassie. Not many of them did, but there was a sprinkling of younger men who had known and liked her. Every one of them was shocked that she'd been murdered, and horrified that Petal hadn't been found.

That was one thing here in the East End that she really liked: people cared about children. Not just their own, but all children. In the main, they weren't concerned about colour or whether the mother was married either. But then, the East End had always been a melting pot of colour, culture and religion. Russians, Poles, Chinese, Jews, lascars, Africans and West Indians – many of them had arrived here as seamen and ended up staying. They had heard the evil racism that Oswald Mosley and his Blackshirts had tried to rouse the rabble with in the thirties, yet mostly they shut their ears. They had stuck together and helped one another through the Blitz, too. Molly was beginning to understand why Cassie had stayed here for so long, and also to realize how hurt she must have been by some of the narrow-minded people in Sawbridge.

One Sunday morning right at the end of January it had begun to snow while they were in church, and when they came out it was very thick on the ground and it was hard for Molly to push Constance's wheelchair. Ted Barlow, a neighbour from Myrdle Street, rushed over to help and, with a lot of laughter, as both Ted and Molly kept slipping, they got Constance and the chair home.

Molly had put a half-shoulder of lamb on a low gas to roast before they went out, and it smelled wonderful. The fire was banked up and, with a little poking, it was soon blazing.

'I think the snow is going to be around for a while,' Constance remarked as she looked out the window. 'It's a kind of blessing, isn't it? All the ugliness around us is hidden.'

'Not much of a blessing for those too poor to buy coal, though,' Molly said thoughtfully. Since living here, she'd become very aware of what poverty really meant. Back home in Somerset, it wasn't so clearly defined, as people grew their own vegetables and kept a few chickens. They might have little more than the clothes they stood up in, but they weren't hungry. She'd seen plenty of people round here who really were; they were gaunt with hollow eyes, stooped and slow with the desperate struggle to get through each day, with no hope things would improve. Hardly a day passed without her reading in the paper about an old person found dead in their home from malnutrition or cold. It preyed on her mind and she wished there was something she could do to help.

'You are right, my dear.' Constance sighed deeply. 'In the bitter winter of 1947 people were burning their furniture to keep warm. Bomb damage had left holes in roofs, and broken windows, and there was no one, or any materials, to fix things. I heard of families who got into one bed together as soon as they got home; it was too cold to do anything else. I was lucky the church provided me with coal. I used to ask people I knew were in a bad way round here for the evening.'

'I bet you were a tower of strength to people during the war,' Molly said. Constance always thought of others before herself. She would willingly give away her last crust of bread to someone in need. That was probably the reason people around here did so much for her, now that she needed help.

'Everyone did their bit during the war. I was nothing special.' Constance shrugged. 'But however grim you think it is, Molly, things *are* getting better. There is plenty of work now, the bomb sites are being cleared and new homes built. As for the new Health Service, that's miraculous. I often wondered how many died in the East End in the past because they didn't have a shilling for the doctor.'

'But that's awful!' Molly exclaimed.

Constance nodded in agreement. 'However, we should be looking to the future, not dwelling on the past. I think that, after we've had our dinner, we should sit by the fire and have a talk about what you want to do.'

It was nearly dark by the time they'd eaten their dinner. Molly got up from the table, lit the gas light and put another couple of lumps of coal on the fire.

When she looked round, Constance was scraping the last remnants of rice pudding from the dish. She laughed when she realized Molly had seen her.

'You're such a good cook it's hard not to eat every last scrap,' she said appreciatively. 'The lamb was so tasty, the roast potatoes perfect. My dear friends around here, although kindness itself, tend to be a bit limited in their culinary skills. Did your mother teach you to cook?'

'Yes – well, the basics,' Molly said. 'But we had a good domestic-science teacher at school who was always urging us to borrow cookery books from the library, and to experiment, too.'

'Working in Pat's Café doesn't give you much scope for creativity or experimentation.' Constance chuckled.

'I don't mind.' Molly smiled. 'I can improve things a bit by not giving people food swimming in grease. That's about the only improvement, though. I have suggested serving some home-made soup or stew. Pat said she'd think about it, but I doubt she'll agree.'

Constance laughed. She knew, as did everyone in the area, that Pat was lazy and against any kind of change. The only reason anyone ever ate in her café was because it was convenient and because, now and then, she employed someone like Molly, who could cook.

'Maybe it isn't worth the effort of trying to persuade her,' she said. 'After all, it's only a stopgap job. Have you given any thought to a new job, or a career?'

'I did think I might be suited to hotel work,' Molly said, with some hesitation. 'A small hotel, where I could do lots of different jobs – reception, cooking, running a bar and cleaning the rooms. By the sea somewhere in Kent or Sussex would be nice, especially if I could live in.'

'A great deal nicer than the East End,' Constance said with a smile. 'I'd miss you, of course, but I'd be happy to see you embark on something you really liked, and which has a future. I've been so pleased that you aren't talking about Cassandra and Petal so much lately. Something like that takes a great deal of getting over but, at your age, it isn't healthy to brood on it.'

Molly hesitated before replying. She might not have spoken to Constance about Cassie and Petal so much, but they'd been on her mind all the time.

'I don't talk about them because I've said everything I have to say,' she replied after a moment's thought. 'But I haven't forgotten them, or given up the idea of trying to find Petal. Every single day I show their pictures to people and ask them if they knew Cassie. In fact, that's exactly why I thought of a hotel in Kent or East Sussex. Many of Cassie's poems mention places there, so I think that's maybe where she came from. I've found out nothing here, but if I can discover where she used to live, I might be able to find some family members, too.'

Constance instantly looked worried, and Molly sensed she was going to say something she didn't want to hear.

'I think the idea of a hotel is a good one. But I'm not so sure about digging around for Cassie's relatives. We both sensed she had run away from something, or someone. Is it wise to go digging?'

'A child's life is at stake,' Molly said indignantly, surprised Constance didn't see it that way. 'For all we know, Cassie's relatives might not even know about her death, or that her daughter is missing, maybe murdered, or at least abducted. I suppose I just want to find someone who cares the way I do.'

'It's good that you care. I didn't mean that you shouldn't think about her and want to make it right,' Constance reproved her. 'But I have to say that when you first visited me here I felt you were making her the focus of your life because you had so little else in yours. That was perfectly under-standable, as you had no boyfriend, you had a difficult father – you even said your sister wasn't interested in you any longer. And Cassie had filled your life, just as she did mine when she lived here, so I know what a hole she left behind.'

Molly nodded. She didn't trust herself to speak in case she burst into tears.

'I had hoped that you'd find real happiness and good friends at Bourne & Hollingsworth,' Constance went on. 'I'm so sorry that went so badly wrong.' She paused, smiled and reached out to take Molly's hand.

'I know this place isn't what you're used to, and Heaven forbid that you get the idea that you've got to stay and take care of this old lady. But I will say that everyone who has met you here likes you. I think you have a tremendous amount to offer the world, because you are kind, thoughtful and very caring, along with being brave and intelligent, too. I don't believe you know what a good person you are – that's why I'm telling you this now. I think working in a hotel is a really good idea: you do have all the right credentials for it, and I think you'd be perfect for it. But I want you to choose a hotel that you like, in a place you'd like to live in. But not just so you can try and find Petal.'

Molly gulped back the lump in her throat. No one had ever said such nice things about her before, and she knew Constance meant it.

'Thank you,' she said. 'I'll take note of everything you said, but I have to try and find Cassie's family, if only so they can make the police open the case again and look for Petal. Something inside me tells me she'd want that.'

Constance sighed, then nodded. 'Yes, you're probably right, but just make it secondary to getting your own life settled. And, by the way, have you written to your mother or that policeman friend of yours back home? You should tell them where you are now, because if they write to you at the hostel, they'll probably get the letter returned to them marked "Gone away", and that is going to worry them.'

Molly blushed. She hadn't thought of mail being returned. 'I don't know what to say to them. I don't think they'll believe I stole anything, but all the same–' she broke off, not liking to admit her real fear was that they would all be horrified to think of her living in Whitechapel. George might even come up here to try to rescue her. That would make everything much worse.

Constance gave her a knowing look, making Molly blush again, because Molly was fairly certain the older woman understood her fears. 'You don't have to go into any detail. Just reassure them you're safe and happy. Your poor mother is probably frantic.'

A little later Constance glanced across the room to where Molly was sitting at the table, writing a letter to her mother. She could see by the way the girl's brow was furrowed that she was finding it difficult. Constance knew without a shadow of doubt that Molly hadn't stolen anything, and the injustice riled her. Her mother would surely know that, too, as anyone would who knew her well.

Although Constance had never had children, she understood that a child's hurt was felt just as keenly by the mother. Mrs Heywood must have spent her entire life in pain for the way her husband treated his daughters. Some would ask why she didn't leave him; that was easy to say but almost impossible for a woman with two children and no money of her own to do. Mrs Heywood probably thought, too, that it was better for her children to live with their father, and maybe she even believed he would change. How many thousands of women married to bullies believed that!

As for Molly's policeman friend, she sensed that Molly liked him a great deal, and he had to feel the same way, as he'd helped her get to London and wrote to her every week. Constance felt it was only a feeling of unworthiness on Molly's part that had prevented her from encouraging him. Constance smiled to herself.

Here she was, a frail old lady who had never married, sitting in a wheelchair, believing she had all the answers about courtship, love and marriage. But, in her defence, she had been privy to so many people's secrets over the last fifty years. She was a seasoned observer, and she liked to think she was also an excellent judge of character.

She had recently written to young Dilys at Bourne & Hollingsworth and told her she didn't believe for one moment that Molly had given goods to friends posing as customers. She said that one of the worst things for Molly was to be frogmarched from the building without even being able to leave a note of explanation for Dilys, who she had cared for a great deal. She asked that, if Dilys had felt the same about Molly, she should write to her or telephone. She ended her letter reminding her that true friends are rare and valuable and should be treasured.

If Dilys came back into Molly's life, it would help heal the wounds that the treacherous Miss Stow had inflicted on her, and maybe prove to Molly that she was worthy of love and affection. But there was something more Constance could do, and that was to use her contacts to help with Molly's future. Tomorrow, when Molly was at work, Constance intended to telephone someone she knew well and see if they had any vacancies.

February was even colder than January. Snow

turned to dirty slush and then froze again, leaving great piles of black ice at the sides of the roads. All the pavements were treacherous. Every day Molly heard horrible stories from people who lived in tenements about frozen lavatories and water pipes. She could tell by the smell of people who came into the café that washing wasn't a high priority any more. Even she, who had once been so fastidious, found it too cold to strip off in the scullery and wash all over every day. She went to the public baths with Constance every Thursday night, but even though it was lovely once she was in a nice, hot bath, it was so cold getting dressed and going home that sometimes she was tempted to skip it.

Constance often told her tales about how it was in the Blitz. She said that she didn't wash anything but her face and hands for over three weeks once, because she'd been bombed out and was sleeping in shelters.

'It was the same for lots of us.' She laughed. 'People came out of a night in the shelter to find their house had been flattened. They'd lost everything, but they'd still go off to work like nothing had happened. I saw women having a strip wash in the public toilets – they had nowhere else to do it.'

'In Bristol, people went out into the countryside at night because they were scared of the bombs,' Molly said.

'People left London, too,' Constance said. 'Not everyone was as brave as you are led to believe. I met women who were so terrified that they almost lost their reason. I would lead prayers in the shelters when the bombing was at its worst and, while most people found it comforting, there were some who tried to shout me down, saying there was no God.'

'Were you in the Church Army then?'

'Yes, but I can't remember if I also told you that I was a nurse back then. I was twenty-two in 1905 when my sweetheart, Ronald, died of pneumonia. We were planning to get married, but he died just a few weeks before the date we'd booked,' she said. 'That was my reason for turning to nursing. I thought that caring for the sick and injured would make me whole again, too. Perhaps it did, as nursing men with appalling injuries during the Great War brought me into the church to pray for them.'

'I think it would've stopped me believing in God,' Molly said.

Constance smiled, the kind of wry smile that said she'd had that response from many people. 'I can only speak for myself and, odd as it sounds, I felt something like a hand on my shoulder urging me to put my life in God's hands. I suppose, had I been a Roman Catholic, I might have entered a convent, but I was an Anglican, so it was the Church Army. They have always done evangelical work in places like slums, and I was sent here.'

'To try and make people turn to the Church?'

'To introduce them to God's love is how I see it. Some of the people I've met over the years have been right down in the gutter, as far down as it's possible to be. They might have a drink problem, be a criminal, have some terrible medical condition, or just be desperately poor, with absolutely no one to turn to. If I can make them see that God loves them, too, that their life is important to

227

him, often that raises them up and gives them the inner strength to improve their situation.'

'But you don't preach to people,' Molly said, puzzled how this evangelical thing worked. 'Well, at least not to any of the people I've met.'

'The simplest way to get the message across is by example.' Constance shrugged. 'They know I have as little as them, but they also see my contentment. Over the years I've been a friend to half the people in Whitechapel while they went through a tough period. For some, it was being bombed out in the war or having their husband brought home badly injured. Some have lost a child; others have a serious medical problem. Ordinary people encounter countless different hurdles but, mostly, they can cope if they have someone to talk to about it. I give them myself and God.'

Molly privately thought that Constance being willing to listen and sympathize was what worked, but if it was her faith that motivated her to do that, then just maybe God was there, too.

The morning after Constance had told Molly how she came to join the Church Army, she got a letter. She'd picked it up from the door mat with a couple of letters for Constance, and stood in the hall looking at the handwriting, which she didn't recognize for some time, before finally opening the envelope.

When she did, she gave a little shriek of joy and ran in to Constance. 'It's from Dilys, my friend at Bourne & Hollingsworth,' she said excitedly. 'How on earth did she get this address?'

'Go on and read it then,' Constance urged her, and wheeled her chair over to the stove, because the kettle was boiling for their tea.

Dear Molly [she read]. *I was so very relieved and happy to get a letter from your friend, because I just knew you hadn't stolen anything, I know that wicked Miss Stow made it up. But I didn't know how to find you, and I was really sad because I missed you so much and I was afraid you'd have to go home and face your dad.*

I spent the whole of Christmas Day crying. All those plans we had, the stockings and meeting those blokes at the Empire. It was just miserable. I never even wore my new dress.

None of the other girls believe you'd done anything either. All of them thought it was a terrible thing to do to you. I hope that makes you feel better.

I've got a new girl in with me now. Her name is Janice, and she's the most boring person I've ever met. She sits and knits, like that Madame Defarge in A Tale of Two Cities. *Even the jumper she's knitting is brown. Only really dull people wear that colour! I'm almost tempted to invite her out one night and then push her onto the tube line.*

I'll phone you on Thursday evening, and I hope we can arrange to meet up somewhere. I never wanted to lose touch with you. I thought we'd still be mates when we were old ladies. You thank Constance for me, tell her I said she is an angel for writing to me.

Your loving chum, Dilys

'Oh, Constance,' Molly sighed as she finished the letter. She wiped a stray tear from her eye. 'Thank you so much for writing to her. She doesn't believe I did it.'

'Would anyone believe that if they really knew you?' Constance smiled and poured tea into two cups. 'So, when are you going to see her?'

'She said she'll phone on Thursday,' Molly said, her eyes shining. 'I'm so excited.'

It was on Thursday that Charles Sanderson came into the café.

The man might have had a dirty face and been covered in brick dust, but he had the biggest, softest brown eyes Molly had ever seen and a smile that would light up the whole of Whitechapel.

'What's a pretty little doll like you doing in a Whitechapel caff?' he said, leaning on the counter and looking right into her eyes. Molly found herself opening and closing her mouth like a fish at the question.

'Did you say an egg-and-bacon sandwich?' she said, unable to think of any clever response.

'I certainly did, and is that a West Country accent I hear?'

She nodded, because he was looking at her so intently she couldn't speak.

'I went to the West Country once, but it was closed,' he said.

'We don't allow cocky cockneys in,' she retorted.

He laughed, and his lovely brown eyes crinkled up. 'So what made you come to the Big Smoke?' he asked, leaning even further over the counter, as if he might reach out and grab her.

'It's a long, dull story,' she said. 'Let's just say I didn't expect to end up making bacon-and-egg sandwiches.'

She turned away from him to the stove, put the bacon in the pan and began to butter the bread. 'A cup of tea?' she asked, turning back to him.

Two other men had come in behind him and he glanced round at them. 'Wish I could talk to you,' he said. 'When does it get quiet?'

'When I go home at three,' she said.

'Right, I'll meet you then.' He grinned.

He watched silently as Molly got his sandwich ready, served the two newcomers with sausages and chips, poured cups of tea for them all and rang up the money.

'You're very efficient,' he said as she handed him his sandwich. 'Along with being very pretty,' he added.

Molly couldn't help but laugh. He had such a cheeky grin, and his voice was deep and musical. 'You've got rather a lot to say for yourself, for a man covered in brick dust.'

All at once, eight or nine people came through the door and the man was forced to take his sandwich and cup of tea and go and sit down. Molly was too busy even to check what he was doing, and when she finally got a moment to go and clear the tables he had gone.

There was no sign of him when she left the café and, though she was a bit disappointed, she wasn't surprised. Men often said cheeky or flattering things to her; two or three had even asked her out. She thought it was merely showing off in front of their mates. In any case, she was expecting Dilys to phone tonight, and that would be more than enough excitement for one day.

She was just turning into Myrdle Street when

231

she heard the sound of someone running. She glanced around, and it was him. He'd washed his face and he was out of breath.

'I couldn't get away,' he gasped out. 'Glad I caught up with you.'

Molly's heart leapt. He wasn't matinee-idol kind of handsome, but he had such a nice face and she was flattered that he was interested enough in her to chase her down the road.

'Are you doing some building work nearby?' she asked.

'Yes, we've been clearing that bomb site just around the corner from the caff. We start digging the foundations for a block of flats next week.'

She couldn't help but be glad he was going to be around for a few more weeks. 'Do you live round here?' she asked.

'In Bethnal Green,' he said. 'But what made you come here? You're far too posh for Whitechapel.'

Molly giggled. 'I'm just the same as loads of other people who end up here. I just didn't have anywhere else to go.'

'Tell me about it,' he insisted, taking her hand and tucking it under his arm as they walked along the street.

'I'm nearly home now, and I can't ask you in, as I live with an elderly lady who is in the Church Army,' she said. 'Also, I don't even know your name!'

'It's Charley,' he said. 'Charles Sanderson of Bethnal Green, age twenty-seven, still got all me own teeth and, luckily, I was too young to join up in the war but did me National Service when it ended and got sent to Germany.'

'I like the potted history, but you still can't come in,' Molly said, grinning at him. 'I'm Molly Heywood, grocer's daughter from Somerset. I was working at Bourne & Hollingsworth but got the sack for something I didn't do. That's why I'm here.'

'They said you nicked something?'

Molly explained briefly. 'I really didn't do it, as God is my witness.'

'I believe you, but I'd like you just as much if you had done it,' he said. 'Those posh shops are right slave drivers, anyway. Treat their staff bad.'

'I really liked it there, and I loved living in their hostel. Constance was the only person I knew in London, so I kind of threw myself on her mercy. That was back on Christmas Eve, and now here we are at the end of February and I'm hoping to find a job in a hotel in Kent or Sussex.'

She stopped outside number ninety-two. 'This is me now,' she said.

'Come out to the flicks with me tonight?' he said. '*Genevieve* is on. Do you like John Gregson?'

'Yes, I do, and I'd like to see it, but I can't go tonight,' she said. Apart from Dilys phoning, she thought she should play hard to get, and she needed time to tell Constance about him.

'Tomorrow, then? If you're planning to run away from Whitechapel I've only got a short while to talk you out of it.' She looked into his soft, brown eyes and her stomach did a kind of somersault.

'You won't talk me out of it, but tomorrow is fine,' she said, wondering if her face showed what she'd just felt inside.

'We'll see about that,' he said with a wide grin. 'I'll pick you up at seven.'

Molly watched him as he walked away. He was tall, over six foot, with wide shoulders and slim hips. His brown hair needed a cut, the donkey jacket he was wearing looked worn out, yet still he had style and grace. She liked the way he walked: straight backed, head up, with a bounce in his step. He turned back to wave at her and she blushed, because he knew she'd been watching him. She waved back, anyway, and a bubble of excitement fizzed inside her.

'So, poor George back home will be cast aside?' Constance said, raising her eyebrows quizzically.

Molly had rushed in to tell her friend about Charley and, as always, Constance seemed to read her mind and see into the future.

'If George and I were meant for one another, surely it would have erupted years ago?'

'I suppose so,' Constance said. 'But you be careful with Charley. London boys are a lot pushier than country ones. Don't give him an inch. But if he does manage to persuade you to stay here, then he'll have my undying love.'

Dilys telephoned on the dot of half past seven. 'Oh, Molly, I've missed you!' she said, and the lovely Welsh lilt in her voice made Molly smile.

'I bet I missed you more,' Molly responded. 'I was quite resigned to never seeing you again. I didn't dare write to you in case they checked your post. Miss Jackson was probably in the Gestapo. Constance didn't tell me she'd written to you, and it was such a wonderful surprise.'

They chatted for some little time, Dilys telling her the gossip from the hostel and Molly telling her about her job in the café.

'Are you still looking for Petal?' Dilys asked.

'Yes, still asking around to see if I can get any leads on who might have taken her and why. Lots of people remember Cassie and her here, and really liked them, so they would tell me if they knew something, but they don't. But I think Cassie came from Kent or Sussex, by the sea. I'm going to try and get work down that way, then I can carry on searching and maybe find some family members.'

'You're certainly a loyal friend,' Dilys said. 'Most people would've given up by now.'

'I can't give up. I think of Petal's pretty little face, remember how much Cassie loved her, and I feel it's my duty to solve the mystery.'

'Will your sense of duty allow you to meet me on Saturday night?' Dilys asked. 'Dancing at the Empire? I could meet you outside at eight.'

Molly began to laugh.

'What's so funny?' Dilys asked.

'You, me, dancing at the Empire. Because I'm so happy you phoned. Is that enough reasons?'

Chapter Twelve

Two weeks after meeting Charley, Molly woke up to see her room bathed in a murky grey light. She groaned, as she knew that meant it had snowed again overnight.

She snuggled further under the covers, dreading the moment she'd have to get up.

It was March now, and she'd started to think that spring was just around the corner. But it seemed it intended to strike more blows before it slipped away. Molly was so tired of being cold, of the lack of sunshine, of hearing coughing and spluttering all around her and seeing small children with sore, red noses. It took away the joy she ought to be feeling.

She ought to be ecstatic that, just yesterday, Constance had said that friends of hers with a small hotel in Rye on the south coast would like to interview her for a job. If she got the job, she could live in warmth and comfort, and when spring eventually came she'd be in a beautiful part of England, having said goodbye to the slums of Whitechapel.

But she wasn't ecstatic. She was scared.

Not scared of the job – that sounded perfect. It was for an all-round assistant, barmaid, receptionist and chambermaid, which was ideal for gaining valuable experience. It would also be wonderful to get to know new people who weren't down-trodden, like they were around here.

There were two flies in the ointment. One was Charley. Molly didn't want to move away from him. The other was Dilys. Having only just got in touch with her friend again, she didn't want to lose her either. Both of them were very special to her. She knew Dilys would write and keep in touch, maybe even come down for a holiday, but Charley might lose interest if it was too hard to see her often.

She and Dilys had so much fun the night they went to the Empire in Leicester Square. Seeing one another again was like a magic potion that made them giggle like schoolgirls and talk as if they'd been in solitary confinement for a month. They danced with anyone who asked them but escaped to get back together again. There was so much to catch up on, and it felt as if there weren't enough time.

Dilys said when they parted at the end of the evening, 'You once said, "We'll still be chums when we're old ladies"; it was when we'd had too much to drink. But I believe it's true. Even if we find our Mr Rights, get married and have lots of kids, we'll still keep in touch. We'll look at each other when we're both sixty, and we'll think we haven't changed a bit, and I bet we'll still be giggling the way we have tonight.'

Molly felt the same: they might go their separate ways because of husbands or children, but there would always be that invisible chain which either of them could tug on to bring their friend right back.

It wasn't that way with men; for them, it had to

be all or nothing. Since her first date with Charley, when he took her to the pictures, she'd seen him almost every day. Mostly it was just drinks in a pub, or a cup of tea in the café when she'd finished work, but then, she would've stood on a street corner in a howling gale if it meant seeing him. He was bright, caring, funny, generous – everything she'd ever wanted in a boyfriend and he set her pulse racing, too.

The cold weather and having nowhere to go to be alone together was perhaps just as well, because one kiss was enough to set her on fire. She was pretty certain that if they had a warm, comfy place to be in, she'd be tempted to go all the way with him.

One of the very nicest things about Charley was that he behaved like a gentleman. His parents in Bethnal Green were, by his own admission, 'a bit rough'. He'd been evacuated at the start of the war to Sussex and the family he was billeted with were 'toffs', as he put it.

'I couldn't believe the house when I first saw it,' he said, his eyes shining as if he were recalling a very magical moment. 'A huge great pile – I could count twenty windows just on the front! They picked me because they wanted help in the garden and with their horses, and I was about the oldest, strongest boy amongst the evacuees.'

'Were they kind to you?' she asked.

'Fair more than kind. No demonstrative stuff, certainly no mollycoddling. But I think they liked me. I was fed far better than at home, I slept in a bed of my own – at home, I'd shared one with two of my brothers. But the best thing for me was learning about how people with money and position live and behave. I soaked it all up and promised myself that, one day, I'd live like that.'

'So what was it like when you went home?'

'Bloody awful.' He pulled a face. 'So many bomb sites. Whole rows of houses gone. Mum and Dad were virtual strangers, and they claimed I looked down on them and talked posh.'

'I expect they felt bad that someone else had been able to give you things they couldn't,' she said, in sympathy with them.

He gave a snort of disbelief. 'Not them – just put out 'cos I'd learned a thing or two while I'd been away, and one of them was that they both liked the booze more than they did any of us kids. They knew right away that when I got a job I wasn't going to meekly hand my wages over to them. Why would I, when it would only make them drink more?'

He paused to ruffle Molly's hair, and smiled at her. 'That makes me sound hard but, if you ever meet them, you'll understand. Anyway, I found some digs and got some demolition work while I waited to see if I'd be called up for National Service. I was well past the age then, but the family I was evacuated with didn't want to lose me, because I was so useful to them. They pulled some strings so I could stay with them, but once I left there and got back to London I knew I was likely to be summoned again. Sure enough, I was. But being called up was the second best thing to being evacuated. I learned to drive and maintain not just cars and trucks but cranes and other machines, too. When I got out I was taken

239

on straight away by Wates.'

Molly knew that Wates was one of the biggest building companies in London. They had contracts for clearing bomb sites all over the East End and then building flats and houses. One of Charley's workmates had told her that he'd worked his way up and been made foreman. She'd also observed from the attitude of all the men who worked under his supervision that they respected him and admired his desire to get on in life.

Part of Charley's long-term plan was to become a civil engineer and, to that end, he attended night school twice a week. His ambition and tenacity must have come from the influence of the people he was billeted with during the war; few other local men who worked as hard as he did by day would think of going back to school in the evenings when they could be in the pub with their mates.

To Molly, all this was very laudable, and she liked the fact that Charley seemed to be very serious about her, too. Yet men always expected their women to mould their lives around them, so he wasn't going to like it when she told him later today that, tomorrow, she was taking the day off to go down to Rye for a job interview.

She expected him to ask why she'd want to move away from Whitechapel and Constance when she already had a job she liked. As ambitious as he was himself, he wouldn't think any normal woman would want a career.

Molly had to go to the interview, or Constance would be offended after she'd gone to all that trouble to arrange it. And unless there was some serious drawback to the job, Molly had to take it. Not just to please Constance, but because she wanted far more out of life than cooking bacon and eggs in Pat's Café.

Yet how could she leave Charley when he made her legs turn to jelly and her heart almost burst when she saw him. And leaving him is what it would amount to, as she couldn't imagine him promising to come down once a week to see her.

Later that morning, as Molly made her way to the café, the misery of the icy wind and a few inches of snow was compounded by her falling over. She went down so heavily she thought she must have broken her leg and the pain made her cry. A man passing by helped her to her feet and offered some sympathy and, to her relief, her knee was just bloodied, and her stockings ripped.

Pat was less than sympathetic. She was a hard-faced woman in her sixties, with iron-grey hair always covered by a turban-style scarf. Several of her teeth were missing, those remaining were like dirty gravestones and she always had a cigarette dangling from her lips. On quite a few occasions Molly had seen her drop ash into a cooked breakfast.

''Ow many times 'ave I told you to put socks over your shoes when there's ice!' she snapped at Molly. 'It ain't no good crying to me now 'cos you've fallen over.'

Molly gritted her teeth, tempted to tell the woman she'd soon have to run the café herself if she got the job in Rye, but to do so would be a mistake, as Pat could be spiteful.

It seemed to Molly a very long day. Her knee throbbed, people complained about everything and the air in the café was thick with cigarette smoke. When it finally got to three o'clock, Pat told her she wasn't going to pay her for the next day.

Molly hadn't expected to be paid but, remembering all the times she'd stayed an extra hour when the café was busy without pay, she was hurt.

She bit back tears and hurried out, disappointed that Charley hadn't come in and concerned that he'd be worried if he didn't see her in the café tomorrow.

Making her way very cautiously down Myrdle Street, avoiding icy patches, she noticed an ambulance up ahead. Instinctively, she knew it was there for Constance.

Throwing caution to the winds, she ran the rest of the way, her sore knee and the ice forgotten. She reached the house just as the ambulance men carried Constance out on a stretcher.

'What's happened?' she asked frantically.

Iris from upstairs put her hand on Molly's shoulder. 'They think she's 'ad a stroke, ducks. I 'eard a thump and I went into 'er place and found 'er out cold on the floor.'

'Are you a relative?' one of the ambulance men asked.

'No, but I live with her,' Molly said. 'Can I come with her in the ambulance?'

''Course you can,' he said. 'Hop in alongside her.'

It made no difference that the ambulance man in the back with Molly said he thought it was only a

minor stroke, the kind from which people recovered completely. Constance was chalk white,
her mouth was twisted grotesquely and, although
she had regained consciousness, she didn't appear
to be aware of Molly or her surroundings.

The London Hospital was only minutes away,
in Whitechapel Road, but it seemed to take for
ever to get there. Molly held Constance's hand
between both of hers and talked to her, hoping
her voice would bring her friend back to normal.

But there was no response and, once the ambulance men had transferred Constance on to a
hospital trolley and wheeled her inside, nursing
staff took over and Molly was told to sit down
and wait until her friend had been examined.

They had arrived at the hospital around four in
the afternoon, but at eight thirty that evening
Molly was still waiting. Each time she'd asked
how Constance was she was merely told she was
'stable' and that she would be told when the
patient was fit to receive visitors.

Molly could see how busy the hospital was:
every few minutes either an ambulance arrived
with a new patient, or people staggered through
the doors with anything from a head wound to a
sick child in their arms. For much of the time it
was bedlam: people shouting for attention, children and babies screaming, and some of the adults
getting angry that they were being pushed aside
in favour of someone else.

Molly had lost count of how many times she'd
heard a nurse explain that they examined the
most urgent cases first, but that didn't satisfy

everyone. One man who appeared very drunk and who, judging by the blood pouring down his face, had been in a vicious fight, smashed a chair against the wall because he was left unseen too long. He was taken away by the police, and Molly wondered if there was a doctor at the police station who would patch him up.

She heard the young parents of a small boy rushed in by ambulance wailing; they clung to each other and her heart went out to them, but she couldn't manage even a few words of sympathy, because all she could think about was that Constance might die. Even if she did survive, she might be paralysed, or unable to speak, and that was just as bad in Molly's opinion. The prospect of death set her thinking once again about Cassie's death, and how she still hadn't done enough to try to find Petal.

It had just turned nine when, to her surprise, Charley turned up. He had a sprinkling of snow on his coat, and the frantic way he was looking around said it was her he was looking for. She rushed over to him, and he hugged her tightly. 'I only just found out about your friend,' he said. 'I didn't get to the café till five, and Pat said you hadn't been your usual cheery self. But I couldn't call round at Myrdle Street straight away, as I had to go to night school. So I popped round the moment I got out, and the woman upstairs told me what had happened. How is Constance?'

Molly explained that she was still waiting for news. 'I keep thinking that the longer I wait the better the news will be,' she said. 'But I'm not sure it works like that. Did Pat really say I wasn't my usual cheery self?'

'No, she actually said you were a bleedin' misery all day, but then she's not the kindest or most sympathetic of women. But you've been here for hours – have you had anything to eat?' he asked.

Molly shook her head glumly. 'I didn't like to leave her,' she said.

'There's a fish-and-chip shop just over the road. I'll tell one of the nurses we're popping out and that we'll be right back.'

Molly felt more optimistic when they came back to the hospital. She wasn't sure whether it was because Charley had listened to her fears about Constance, or just that she'd eaten and had a cup of tea. They sat down again to wait for news, and Molly blurted out about her interview the next day. 'I can't possibly go now, but Constance will be disappointed in me if she gets better and finds out I didn't.'

Charley didn't respond immediately. He looked like he was deep in thought.

'If you don't go tomorrow, they'll give the job to someone else,' he said. 'And you'll always think that you might have missed the best opportunity of your life.'

She hadn't expected him to say that, and she didn't know how to reply.

He took her hand in his, lifted it to his lips and gently kissed it. 'If I'm to be totally honest, I'd like you to stay right around the corner from me, where you are now. But you're worth far more than a job in Pat's Café, and you don't belong in

245

Whitechapel at all.'

She glowed at that, and was just about to ask when she'd see him if she went away when a young nurse came towards them. 'Sister asked me to come and get you,' she said.

'She's on the mend, then?' Molly asked.

The nurse acted like she hadn't heard. Molly looked at Charley questioningly. 'Is it okay for me to come, too?' he asked.

'Yes, of course,' the nurse replied, proving there was nothing wrong with her hearing. 'Sister wants a word with you before you go in, though.'

Alarm bells began to ring in Molly's head, and she hurried after the nurse, with Charley coming on behind.

The nurse led them to the ward sister's small office, which had a window looking on to the ward, but most of the cubicles' curtains were drawn, so they couldn't see Constance.

This was a different ward sister to the one who had been on duty when Molly first got to the hospital. Sister Jenner was older, perhaps mid-fifties, and stout, but with a round, soft face that seemed to radiate compassion.

'Sister Constance has rallied a little,' she said. 'We are cautiously hopeful, as she knows where she is now and she's managed to ask for you, Miss Heywood.'

Molly beamed at the sister. 'That's wonderful. I don't think she knew me when I came in with her.'

'It's progress, but you'll find her speech is badly affected by the stroke. Now, is this your young man?' she asked, looking at Charley.

Molly introduced Charley.

246

'Sister Constance is clearly very fond of Miss Heywood,' she said to him, 'so it will help to reassure her that her young friend is not entirely alone while she's in hospital, which I'm afraid might be for some time. Don't be shocked by her appearance, or too concerned if she suddenly falls asleep, and I would ask that you only stay for ten minutes at most, because she needs rest.'

She led them to the last cubicle in the ward. As she drew back the curtain Molly had to bite her lips not to cry out because Constance looked so dreadful. The pallor, she had expected, but not the way her face appeared to have caved in, leaving her jaw and cheekbones sticking out like a skeleton's.

'Molly,' Constance murmured. 'Come closer. Don't be afraid.'

'I couldn't be afraid of you,' Molly said, going right up to her and taking her hand. 'But you gave me quite a turn today. This is Charley, the man I told you about. He's come to see you, too.'

The ward sister's words had made Molly feel hopeful again. All the time she'd been waiting, she couldn't help but think how awful it would be to lose Constance. She was the one who'd helped her when she was at her most desperate; she'd shared her home, her food, become her friend, and made Molly feel loved.

She hoped she could soon find a way to express her gratitude.

Charley went to the other side of the bed and took Constance's other hand.

'I'd have liked to have met you for the first time under better circumstances,' he said. 'But I hope when you get home again I can call on you.

Molly speaks of you so highly.'

It looked as if Constance was trying to smile at Charley, but it was more like a grimace. 'It's good to put a face to the man Molly talks about,' she managed to get out, pausing after each word as if struggling to form each one. 'She tells me you are a gentleman, so I hope you'll look out for her for me?'

'You don't need to ask me, Sister Constance,' he said, bending to kiss her hand. 'I'll do that willingly. But you must tell her she has to go to the interview tomorrow and take the job if she likes it. You know Whitechapel isn't right for her, don't you?'

Constance's pale-blue eyes fixed on to his face. 'Yes, Charley, I do. But she's got a habit of thinking too much about what other people want. We have to set her free from that.'

'You hear that?' Charley looked across the bed at Molly. 'Sister Constance wants you to go.'

The old lady turned her head towards Molly. 'I do. I'm going to miss you, but I want you to have a good life.'

Her eyelids drooped down suddenly and Molly was so alarmed she rang the bell for the nurse. She came scurrying in but smiled when she saw Constance.

'She's only dropped off.' The nurse turned to Molly and Charley. 'Talking will tire her, but she'll remember that you visited. Her friend Reverend Adams is waiting to see her, so you should go home now and come again tomorrow.'

It was eleven o'clock when Charley got Molly

248

home to Myrdle Street.

'Will you come in?' she asked.

He put his arms around her and held her tight. 'That wouldn't be an appropriate thing to do tonight, as much as I'd like to. Besides, you've got to do what she said and go for that interview tomorrow.'

Molly smiled weakly. 'She's going to need a lot more help when she comes out of hospital. I'm going to feel really bad about leaving her.'

'She has dozens of friends in this area who will all come to help her, and the church will find a nursing home for her if she can't manage alone. Now, I'll be around tomorrow night about seven to see how you got on at the interview. Just take one day at a time, Molly. Things always work out when you don't over-think them,' he said, tilting her face up and bending to kiss her. 'Now go to bed and try to sleep. Good luck for tomorrow.'

Charley walked back up Myrdle Street to Whitechapel Road in deep thought. Would she go tomorrow? Or would a misplaced sense of duty make her stay?

He knew the East End had a habit of sucking people in and keeping them there. Sister Constance was a fine example. Molly could so easily go the same way, involving herself in saving people, be it drunks, tarts, criminals or the very poor. She had made a couple of pointed remarks about her father that had made him think the man was a bully, so it was possible he'd already trained his daughter for martyrdom. If so it would be second nature to her to feel obliged to take care of anyone who needed it.

She let Pat at the café treat her like a slave, and he had sensed that Molly had already half formed a plan in her head that she would take care of Constance when she was released from hospital. He couldn't let her do that; she was worth more than what she had now, and a job in a decent hotel could be the making of her. If she channelled all those special qualities she had into making guests feel they were the most important person in the world, she'd rise to the top in no time.

Chapter Thirteen

Molly felt a pang of trepidation as she looked up at the George Hotel.

It was a lovely old inn, probably dating back to the eighteenth century, its front covered in mathematical tiles. She wondered what they represented and thought she would ask. She imagined that the building must have an interesting history; it could even be haunted. But it wasn't that which scared her. She wasn't sure she was good enough to work in such a place.

Rye was a medieval walled town perched up on a hill and surrounded by windswept marshes. People in the West Country tended to think all the best towns and villages in England were there but, in Molly's opinion, Rye was the prettiest, quaintest town she'd ever seen and far exceeded anything the West Country had to offer. As she'd walked from the station up the narrow cobbled streets with their sweet little houses with bow windows and shiny brass on the front doors, she felt she had gone back a few centuries in time.

The sun had come out while she was on the train and, though it was still very cold and windy, the first thing she noticed as she stepped off the train was the fresh smell and the quiet. She'd got so used to London's soot-laden air, the noise of the traffic and the nasty smells that she'd virtually forgotten what fresh air or quiet was like. There was some traffic, of course, on the main road down by the station but, compared with White-chapel Road, it was like a country lane.

Already, without knowing anything about the job, she wanted to live here. She understood, too, why Cassie had mentioned this town so often in her journal.

Before going in the door to reception, Molly took a deep breath and braced herself. She hoped they didn't ask her to take off her royal-blue coat. She knew it looked chic with the matching beret and that it suited her, but the black sheath dress she was wearing underneath looked cheap. It had been cheap, she'd bought it from the market, but it hadn't created the sophisticated image she'd intended.

She walked up to the reception desk and said to a red-headed woman sitting behind it, 'I have an appointment with Mrs Bridgenorth. My name is Molly Heywood.'

As she had expected of such an old building, it smelled a little fusty, and the patterned carpet had seen better days, but the hotel had a good feeling

251

about it. It was almost like coming home. She nearly laughed at herself for thinking that, for she'd never ever felt there was anything special about going to her real home.

The receptionist spoke to someone on the phone then smiled at Molly. 'Mrs Bridgenorth has asked me to show you into the library and bring you some coffee. She'll be with you as soon as she can.'

The library was a small, book-lined room made cosy by a blazing fire. It wasn't large enough for anything more than a couch, two button-backed chairs and a couple of side tables. Everything, including the books, looked very old and shabby, but Molly thought that, on a cold day in winter, it would be the perfect retreat.

The receptionist came back with a tray, coffee in a pot, hot milk and a plate of ham sandwiches. 'Mrs Bridgenorth thought you might be hungry after leaving home early to catch the train,' she said. 'Tuck in. She won't be long.'

Such consideration for her well-being touched Molly; she was hungry and it was also lovely to be in such a warm room. Since moving to White-chapel, she couldn't remember ever being really warm.

Mrs Bridgenorth came in some ten minutes later. She was a statuesque woman in her forties with wavy fair hair and she was wearing a blue twinset, pearls and a tartan pleated skirt.

'Lovely to meet you, Molly,' she said, smiling and offering her hand. 'Sister Constance is obviously very fond of you – she couldn't speak of you highly enough. How is she coping with this bitter weather?'

Once they'd both sat down, Molly explained that Constance had had a stroke. 'She looked very poorly last night,' she said. 'I really didn't think I should come today, but she insisted.'

'Oh dear.' Mrs Bridgenorth looked utterly dismayed. 'I must try and get up to see her tomorrow, she's such a dear thing, and we've been friends since I was a little girl. I'm sure she told you, but she came to look after me one summer at the hotel my parents owned in Bournemouth. She was marvellous – kind, attentive and also great fun. My family never imagined she'd choose to spend her life in the Church Army. We thought she'd get married and have half a dozen children of her own.'

'It was such a shame her sweetheart died,' Molly said. 'She's devoted her whole life to other people since; she really is a saint. I'm awfully worried about how she'll cope after this stroke, but she's so well loved in Whitechapel I'm sure everyone will rally round.'

'Funnily enough, she was afraid you might fall into the same trap as she did,' the older woman said. 'She said, and I quote, "Evelyn, the girl is like a young twin of myself. If I don't give her a push into making a career for herself, I'm afraid she'll end up like me."'

Molly was a bit taken aback and it must have showed, as Mrs Bridgenorth laughed.

'That is exactly what she said, Molly. Maybe right now you feel that ending up like Constance would be no bad thing, but she was very aware that she had turned her back on a comfortable home, a husband and children, and she doesn't

253

want that for you.'

Mrs Bridgenorth moved on then to talk about the hotel and what duties Molly would have if she were to be offered and decided to take the job.

'My plan would be to give you experience of all aspects of the hotel at first, so that you totally understand how it works. So one week you'll be the waitress in the dining room at breakfast, followed by chambermaid duties for the rest of the morning. Then perhaps you'll serve behind the bar in the evening. Another week you'll be helping the chef in the kitchens with breakfast, lunch and dinner. Another week it will be reception work, learning to help organize wedding receptions and private parties. How does that sound to you? Constance did tell me you virtually ran your parents' grocery shop, so I have no fear that you wouldn't be able to cope here.'

'It sounds wonderful,' Molly said.

'We tend to be quiet in the winter, just a few commercial travellers staying, but then we perk up at Easter. After that, we're mostly fully booked right up to the end of September. But the restaurant is busy year round, especially at weekends, and we do have many wedding receptions here, too. I'll take you to see our Georgian ballroom in a minute; it really is a lovely room.'

A couple of hours later Molly was on the train back to Ashford, where she had to change for a train to London. She had been offered the job and was excited by it and the prospect of a new home, and had assured Mrs Bridgenorth that she did want to take it. She had agreed to arrive on Saturday, 27 March, in eight days' time, to start work on the following day.

She would be paid three pounds a week, all found, to start, which seemed amazingly generous to her. Furthermore, the bedroom she would have up on the attic floor was lovely. It was only small but had everything she needed, and the bed had felt very comfortable. As Mrs Bridgenorth had explained, her working hours would vary according to what jobs she was doing in a particular week. So, one week, she would have every afternoon off, plus a full day, to be arranged. The next she might work all day and have the evenings off. One Sunday in four she could have off, too.

Aside from John Masters, the chef, all the other staff were local and lived out. He had a couple of rooms down by the kitchen. The owners lived at the hotel, too. Mrs Bridgenorth had pointed to a door on the first floor and said it led to their apartment, but she hadn't taken Molly in there.

If it hadn't been for the question of when or if she'd see Charley once she'd moved, Molly would have been jumping up and down with glee. Did he care enough to travel a round trip of one hundred and fifty miles to see her when she had a Sunday off? If she had her day off during the week, would it be worth her taking the train to London to see him for just a couple of hours after he'd finished work? The trains from Ashford to Rye weren't very frequent and, if she missed the last connection, she'd have to stay on the station all night.

Molly went straight from Charing Cross to the London Hospital to see Constance and tell her

255

about her interview.

The night before, she'd been told that Constance would be taken up to a different ward, so she went straight to the inquiry desk. One of the two men there looked in a register, and then at Molly, with a slightly anxious expression, then said he needed to check with Sister.

When Sister Jenner came back with him Molly knew something bad had happened.

'Will you come with me, Miss Heywood?' she said, before Molly could even open her mouth to speak. She led Molly into a small cubicle and asked her to sit down.

'I'm very sorry, Miss Heywood,' she began, 'but Sister Constance died at ten o'clock this morning. I thought Reverend Adams would've contacted you.'

'I left home early this morning to catch a train and came straight here when I got back,' Molly said.

'Oh dear! You see, as Reverend Adams has a telephone, we were able to ring him this morning when we felt her condition was worsening. He came straight away, and was with her when she died.'

Molly couldn't speak for a moment; it was too much of a shock. 'B–b–but I thought she was getting better?'

'We thought that, too,' Sister Jenner said, reaching out to take Molly's hand and holding it comfortingly in both of hers. 'But we cannot always predict accurately what results a stroke can have, and she was already frail before it. Yet it appears that the cause of death was actually a heart attack.'

'I was at an interview for a job,' Molly bleated out, tears springing up in her eyes. 'She really wanted me to go. But I wish I hadn't now.'

'She would've been more upset to think you had missed it,' the sister said gently. 'She told me last night how fond she was of you, and that she thought your young man was a good one, too. You wouldn't want to see her living in pain, unable to communicate properly, would you? She will have no more suffering or indignity now. The reverend was holding her hand and praying for her when her moment came. Be glad that she went as she'd want to.'

Molly knew that what the sister said was right, but it didn't stop her feeling like she'd been kicked in the stomach.

Back home and sitting in Constance's room a little later, Molly felt her heart was breaking. It was such a spartan room, yet she'd never really thought that while Constance was there. She could see now, in the drab, comfortless room, that by giving her life to the Church her friend had turned her back on everything but the basic essentials of life.

Charley called round later and was horrified when she opened the door to him with red, swollen eyes.

'I'm so very sorry,' he said when she blurted out that Constance was dead. 'Such a shame you didn't get a chance to tell her about your interview. But please let me in and tell me about it.'

It didn't seem right to take him into Constance's room, but there was nowhere else, so Molly left

257

the door open, so none of the other tenants in the house would think she was taking liberties. She quickly told Charley all about the job, and how lovely Rye was, but she couldn't help but switch right back to talking about Constance.

'Look around this room,' she said, waving her arm. 'There's nothing of any value, not even a wireless. She would sit with her coat on rather than putting another shovelful of coal to the fire. Yet she'd use the coal if a visitor called, and give them the special biscuits or cakes that would have been given to her as a present. She lived her whole life for other people.'

Charley comforted her with a cuddle, and agreed that people as selfless as Constance were as rare as hen's teeth.

'And, on top of that, how will I be able to see you if I take this job?' she sobbed out.

'We'll have to do what people did during the war and write to each other,' he said. 'I can phone you at the hotel, too, I expect, and I'll buy a car and come down as often as I can. And later this year, when I've finished my night-school classes, I might be able to get work down that way with Wates. They've got projects coming up in both Hastings and Ashford.'

Molly brightened a bit at that. It meant that Charley was thinking long term about them. Yet, however much she wanted to be near him, she knew very well she couldn't bear to stay on in this cold, depressing house without Constance. As for working at Pat's, she couldn't wait to hand in her notice. So, unless she miraculously found another job here and somewhere better to live, she had no choice but to go.

'That would be something to look forward to,' she said, and, remembering the advice she'd read in magazines about men not liking to be pushed into corners, she realized she'd have to try to sound more positive. 'I'm sorry I've been such a drip, and a bit clingy, too. It's just the shock of losing Constance. I've got to look forward, not back.'

'So you'll be leaving next Saturday, then?' he asked, raising one eyebrow. 'If you like, I could borrow a motor and take you down there?'

'That would be wonderful!' she said, hoping she could hold her emotions in check when he left her there. 'I can't wait for you to see how pretty Rye is.'

Charley went home soon after. Molly went upstairs first, to speak to Iris, and then went off to bed. Her room felt even colder than it normally did, and she huddled under the covers and cried.

Iris had spoken to Reverend Adams, and it seemed the funeral would be the following Thursday and he had all the arrangements in hand. He was expecting over a hundred mourners, and he had asked the ladies from the church to lay on a tea afterwards in the parish hall. Iris was as grief-stricken as Molly, and with more reason, as they'd known each other for years. That was a reminder to Molly that she didn't have exclusive rights to Constance. Molly rang Mrs Bridgenorth to tell her, too. She was very upset, but she said she and her husband would come to the funeral, and she commiserated with Molly on what a shock it was, when they had thought Constance was going to recover.

In the days before the funeral Molly worked at Pat's and spent the evenings helping Iris sort out Constance's belongings. She had very little, and nothing of any value, but they put little ornaments, books and such like to one side to give as mementoes to people she was especially fond of.

Despite all the sadness at losing Constance, her funeral was uplifting, something Molly hadn't expected. The sun put in an appearance, and Molly thought half the population of Whitechapel must be there, crowding into the church, and everyone had something to say about how Constance had helped them in some way.

Reverend Adams spoke of her compassion, generosity and understanding of people. 'True understanding is a rare gift, to know why people behave in a certain way and yet not judge them for it. I believe it is a gift God only gives to very special people who he knows will use it well. And he couldn't have found a better person to give that gift to than Sister Constance.

'I know from brief conversations I've had with so many of you in the last few days that all of you have your own little story of what Sister Constance did for you but, as you remember it, and perhaps share it with others, please don't cry for her, because she wouldn't want that. Just be glad you knew her and take that special quality she had into your own life.'

Molly bowed her head during the prayers, but she wasn't praying, only thinking about what

Reverend Adams had said. Constance had welcomed her into her home and shared what little she had with someone who was to all intents and purposes a stranger. She vowed then that she would make her friend proud of her, because that was the best way to thank her for everything she'd done for her.

Reverend Adams spoke to Molly later at the tea in the parish hall. 'Many people here will miss you, Molly, when you move on to your new job. But you take all our good wishes for your future with you, and I know Sister Constance will be watching over you. Rye is a beautiful little town, and I feel sure you will be very happy there.'

A few days later, on Saturday afternoon, Charley bent to kiss Molly goodbye outside the George. 'Don't look so forlorn,' he said. 'You'll soon make new friends here and I expect, next time you come up to Whitechapel, you'll wonder how you could ever have borne to live there.'

He had borrowed a friend's car to drive her to Rye and, once he'd met Mr and Mrs Bridgenorth, he'd felt satisfied he was leaving his girl in good hands. They were nice people, the kind that understood that happy staff created a happy hotel which guests would come back to. They understood what a blow it was to Molly to lose Constance so suddenly, and he knew they'd be kind to her.

But they'd been nice to him, too, insisting on him and Molly having lunch with them. He'd half expected to be shown the door once he'd brought her suitcase in, but instead they welcomed him.

261

Earlier, he and Molly had walked around the old town and had tea in a shop, because of the bitter wind.

Charley knew that Constance's funeral had been very difficult for Molly. She had said that she felt she had no real position there; after all, she was the Johnny Come Lately, many of the dozens of mourners had known her friend forty years or more. She'd also had to witness her friend's rooms being emptied out, and all she had was that tiny, icy-cold room to retreat to.

Reverend Adams appeared to have been the only person who had an inkling of how Molly felt. He'd given her Constance's bible, which she'd been given as a prize at school. He told her that whenever she was feeling sad or lonely she was to open it at random and read a passage and there would be a message from Constance there.

Charley wasn't one for thinking about God and had never so much as opened a Bible since leaving school, but he sensed that the reverend had made Molly feel a little better.

But, now, he had to leave Molly to return to London, and he didn't like that she looked so terribly sad.

'I don't mean to look forlorn,' she said, trying to smile. 'I think I'm just worrying that I'll be useless and they'll give me the sack.'

'You know that isn't going to happen,' he said. 'Now, I'm sorry, but I've got to go. The lights on the car aren't very good, so I have to go fairly slowly across the marshes or I might end up in a ditch. The heater doesn't work either!'

Molly flung her arms around him and he

breathed in the sweet smell of her Blue Grass perfume. He wanted to tell her he loved her, but it was too soon for such statements.

'Write to me,' he said instead. 'And don't let the barman or the chef lead you astray.'

He jumped into the car then and coasted down the hill until the engine started, waving one hand to her.

When he glanced in the mirror just before turning the corner she was still standing outside the George and waving, despite the cold wind.

'I love you, Molly Heywood,' he said aloud. 'And, before long, I'm going to marry you and make sure you never look sad again.'

Chapter Fourteen

'You've finished the bedrooms?' Mrs Bridgenorth asked as Molly came down the stairs carrying the carpet sweeper and a basket of cleaning materials.

'Yes, all done,' Molly replied. 'Room six had spilt something sticky on the carpet, but I managed to get it off. Goodness knows what it was, but it smelled like cough mixture.'

'It never ceases to amaze me what people drop in their rooms, what they leave behind or try to steal,' said Mrs Bridgenorth with a little ripple of laughter. 'You're so quick, Molly. I thought at first you weren't doing the rooms properly, but I've made quite a few lightning checks and they are first class. Well done.'

Molly glowed. She was into her third week at the George now, and she loved it. She'd been given a pink-and-white striped uniform dress, an apron and a little matching stiffened hair band with a lace edge for her chambermaid duties, and she so enjoyed being dressed for the part. For bar work and reception duties, she had a black dress with a white lace collar and cuffs, and when she was waiting on tables she added a frilly white apron. Both dresses fitted perfectly and looked nice, especially the striped one.

Everything about the job was wonderful. The hotel was always warm, thanks to old Albert, who came in early in the mornings and cleared the grates, and lay and lit fires in all the main rooms. The guests' rooms had electric fires fitted into the fireplaces and there was even a small portable one in her room in the attic. The food was lovely, too, quite the best she'd ever eaten.

Her favourite job was waiting on people at breakfast as, often, they chatted and told her where they'd come from and what their plans for the day were. She liked serving lunch much less, as some of the people could be quite rude. Being a barmaid in the evening was good, although Ernest, the head barman, was a bit stuck-up. He'd told her five years ago he used to be the head cocktail waiter at the Savoy in London and only left because his then fiancée was a teacher in the junior school here in Rye and they wanted to get married.

Working on reception was interesting, as she got to greet the new guests and resolve any problems they might have. There was also quite a lot of work organizing wedding receptions and private parties, putting on special buffets or sit-down meals and dealing with the music and flower arrangements. She thought that, in time, this would become her favourite role, but there was so much to learn it would be a while before she was able to handle it all alone.

This coming Sunday, she had the day off and Charley was coming down to see her. Spring had finally arrived and, unless it decided to pour with rain, Molly thought she would pack a picnic for them and they could have it in Camber Castle.

Cassie had mentioned Camber Castle in her journal a few times. She'd jotted down that it was built by Henry VIII as a defence for one of his Cinque Ports, but also that people claimed Anne Boleyn had been locked up in it by the king when he grew tired of her. Mrs Bridgenorth said she doubted that was true, but people liked to make up interesting stories about places. It was just a ruin now; sheep sheltered from the sea wind inside its walls. Molly had walked out across the marsh to it the previous week on her day off. She'd eaten her sandwiches in the shelter of its walls, then climbed up on to what was left of the battlements to survey the countryside.

It had been a lovely spring day. Gorse had sprung into flower all over the marsh and the sweet perfume from its bright-yellow flowers hung in the still air. She loved the look of the black-faced sheep, apparently a much-prized breed known worldwide as Romney Marsh sheep, and lambing was in full swing. She saw twin lambs that

265

day which could only have been born minutes before her arrival, so little and wobbly and utterly adorable.

Perched up on the castle battlements, the sound of curlews and gulls filling the air, Molly had realized that she was truly happy, perhaps the happiest she'd ever been. She was coming to terms now with the death of Constance, and was even a little glad that any suffering her dear friend had gone through was over. She was no longer brooding on the unfairness of her dismissal from Bourne & Hollingsworth. Dilys was back in her life again – only yesterday she had had a letter from her – and she loved her new job and home. On top of that was Charley, who never failed to telephone at six on a Friday, as he'd promised, and so far she'd had three letters from him, too.

If it hadn't been for her sorrow about Cassie and thinking what more she could do about finding Petal, Molly's would be the perfect life. But even Mr and Mrs Bridgenorth seemed to understand how important these things were to her.

She had been intending to pick an appropriate moment to tell them what had happened, to see if she could enlist their help but, as it turned out, Mr Bridgenorth asked her some questions on her third day with them which led naturally into the subject.

Molly had been asked to take a tray of coffee and buttered toast up to the office for Mr Bridgenorth that morning, as he was working on the hotel's accounts.

'Hullo, Molly,' he said as she came in. 'How are you settling in?'

He was a tall, slender man with very bony features, not unattractive, but she'd been told he tended to be ill at ease with people, so she was quite surprised at his cheery interest in her.

Trudy, one of the cleaners, who had worked here for years, had told her the background of most of the staff at the hotel. She said that Mr Bridgenorth was an accountant and that, when he married Evelyn, who had been brought up in the hotel trade, he had agreed to handle the business side of the hotel, as long as she took care of the day-to-day running of it.

'I'm settling in very well, thank you, sir,' Molly had replied, putting the tray down on his desk. 'I'm finding it all so interesting, and it's super to be in such a warm, comfortable place.'

'I can imagine,' he said. 'My wife and I visited Constance a couple of times in Whitechapel, and we both felt chilled to the bone. How did you get to know her?'

'I found her address in a book after my friend Cassie was killed back in Somerset. I wrote to Constance, because it was clear they had been close friends,' she began.

'Oh my goodness!' Mr Bridgenorth had exclaimed, looking astounded. 'I had no idea your connection was so dramatic. Please, go on. Tell me the whole story.'

Molly gave him an abbreviated version of the story, knowing she ought to get back to work.

'And they still haven't found the murderer or the little girl?' he asked when she had finished.

'No, they haven't,' Molly said. 'Actually, I think Cassie came from round here. She kept a journal,

267

and in it she mentions Rye and the marshes quite a bit. I'm intending to ask about and show people her photograph in the hope that I might get a lead I can hand over to the police.'

'Gosh, that is interesting,' he said, then smiled. 'Well, in a gruesome sort of way. But you have photographs? Might I see them? You never know, she might be someone who worked here at some point.'

'I could go and get them now,' Molly volunteered.

She got the pictures from her room but, sadly, Mr Bridgenorth didn't recognize Cassie. However, he did applaud her persistence in trying to find Cassie's family and suggested places in town where someone might remember her.

It was his interest in both the case and her part in it that really warmed Molly to Mr Bridgenorth. She didn't understand why other staff said he was chilly or aloof.

Molly had telephoned her mother twice since she'd been at the George, each time in the evening, when she knew her father would be at the pub. She didn't talk for long, because long-distance calls were expensive and, anyway, her mother was useless at chatter: she dried up after a couple of minutes and Molly had to fire questions at her to keep the conversation going. Yet she did sense her mother's relief that Molly had left London for a nice part of the country and that she was happy in the hotel.

Cassie had often asked Molly why her sister, Emily, had left home and hadn't kept in touch.

Back then, Molly had never really admitted how very nasty her father could be, so she hadn't been able to explain adequately why Emily had cut herself off, or the rage she still felt against their mother.

Now Molly was beginning to understand and sympathize with her sister's feelings. She didn't feel angry at their mother, but she was finding talking to her on the telephone a bit of an ordeal, as it always brought on reminders of her father's cruelty and how her mother had just accepted it. And she was one for letting unspoken reproaches hang in the air, and there were long, awkward silences which Molly didn't know how to fill. Without going home and facing both of her parents, she couldn't ever hope for complete reconciliation, and no sensible person would go home if they knew their father was never going to meet them halfway.

When asked how the shop was doing, Mum merely said it was ticking over; she never spoke of new lines they were selling, or if anyone had failed to pay their monthly account, and Molly just had to hope her father wasn't alienating customers with his grumpiness, or hitting his wife.

The only thing her mother volunteered was to say how kind George was, always popping in when it was cold to see if he could carry coal upstairs for her and generally checking up on her. But even this sometimes seemed to be a reproach, as if her mother was hinting that Molly had let him slip through her fingers instead of encouraging his attentions.

Molly had told her mother a dozen or more

269

times that there was nothing but friendship between her and George. She did feel a little guilty that she'd never told him why she left Bourne & Hollingsworth; he must be as puzzled by it as her mother was. But then, she couldn't bring herself to tell either of them the truth, as it still shamed her to be labelled a thief. She couldn't ever say that she was coming home for a visit either, because it was too far to go and, anyway, she couldn't stay at home, and taking up George's offer to stay with his family wasn't really an option now that she'd met Charley.

That was another thing she ought to tell George about, but she didn't know how to go about it. If George saw himself only as her friend, there would be no problem, but she had a sneaky feeling he felt he was more than that, and she didn't want to hurt his feelings or make him jealous. Cassie would've roared with laughter about this. Molly could almost hear her friend berating her for being frightened of upsetting people. She would've pointed out that it made life unnecessarily complicated.

Reading through Cassie's journal again, Molly realized that her friend had spoken of Rye as a favourite place to visit, not as if she lived there. One entry said, 'Caught the early bus to Rye.' To Molly, this implied that Cassie had travelled from an isolated village with a limited bus service. She studied a bus timetable and a map of the area and found that buses going to and from Hastings were regular, as they were on the route to Tenterden. So, in all likelihood, Cassie came from somewhere on the marshes between Rye and Hythe. As she didn't mention the sea or beaches, Molly felt it must be inland, perhaps one of the tiny villages like Brookland, Old Romney or Ivychurch.

On her afternoons off Molly usually found somewhere new to ask about her friend and show the photographs. She'd already called at the library, and at the doctor's and dental surgeries in Rye, but she'd drawn a blank at all of them. No one recognized Cassie.

Now that spring had arrived, Molly was looking forward to exploring the surrounding countryside and villages on her afternoons off, and she thought the best way to do it was by bicycle, as the land was flat as far as the eye could see. Albert, the old man who lit the fires, had told her there were a couple of ladies' bicycles in the shed out in the backyard. Apparently, they were kept for the use of guests. All she had to do was check if it was all right for her to borrow one.

There was just one person who thought he might have seen Cassie before, and that was Ernest.

He'd squinted at the photograph for some time. 'Her face is familiar,' he said thoughtfully, 'but I've never met anyone called Cassandra, or Cassie. Maybe she was someone who came in a few times when I first got here five years ago. I don't think it could've been more recent.'

'She's dead now,' Molly told him, quickly telling him the story and that Petal was still missing. 'I want to try and find her family. If she did come from somewhere around here, surely someone would remember a black baby.'

Ernest agreed that they would and said he would ask his wife because, as a teacher, she had

271

contact with people from a huge radius around Rye. 'Usually, she doesn't forget anyone,' he said with a proud smile. 'We'll be out together, and someone she taught twenty years ago will come up to her. She always remembers them, not just their name but the things they were good at.'

'Then I hope she might help me with this,' Molly said. 'Local knowledge is invaluable.'

But, for now, seeing Charley was more important than questioning people about Cassie. She sensed from the tone of his letters that he was really serious about her, even if he hadn't actually said anything to confirm that. She was serious about him, too: he was the last thing she thought about before dropping off to sleep at night and her first thought in the morning. She wished there was another girl of her age working at the George, someone she could talk about such things to, but all the female staff were in their mid-thirties or older, all married women with kids, and, although they were warm and friendly, they were hardly the kind she could have a heart to heart with about falling in love.

In women's magazines and films love was always depicted as a kind of sickness, where the victim couldn't eat, sleep or function normally. Molly, however, was sleeping like a top, eating like a pig, because the food in the George was so good, and, if anything, she was functioning on a day-to-day basis more efficiently than she ever had. It was true that Charley was never far from her mind – her stomach did a little flip every time she thought about his kisses – and she really missed seeing him all the time, as she had in

Whitechapel. But was that love? Or just an infatuation that would fizzle out one day?

'You're looking very nice today, Molly,' Mr Bridgenorth said on Saturday morning. 'I take it your young man is coming to take you out?'

Molly had been leaving the staff room after eating breakfast when she ran into him in the corridor.

'Thank you, sir,' she said with a broad smile. She'd washed her hair the night before and slept with it plaited, so it was wavy, and she was wearing a new turquoise-and-white dress with a full skirt and three-quarter-length sleeves.

'Yes, Charley is coming to take me out,' Molly said. 'We're going for a picnic. It's such a lovely day we might even paddle in the sea. But can I do anything for you? Were you looking for something, or someone?'

'Yes, you, Molly. I wanted to tell you that, because Ernest thought your friend looked familiar, I looked through our records to see if a Cassandra March ever worked here. She didn't, I'm afraid. Well, not if that was her real name.

'But while she was on my mind I suddenly recalled hearing some gossip in the bar about a young unmarried woman out on the marsh having a mixed race baby. I think this was back in 1948, though I can't be certain. All I really remember is that it was something of a mystery because no one had seen the child except the housekeeper.'

'They must have had money, then, if there was a housekeeper!' Molly said.

'Some, I suppose,' Mr Bridgenorth replied.

'Probably a family with a sizable house and live-in help. The housekeeper might even have been a relative. As I recall, it was said there were mental problems in the family.'

'Cassie didn't have any mental problems,' Molly said with a touch of indignation. 'She was about the brightest person I ever met.'

'People tend to say that about almost anyone who lives out on the marshes. They say it's down to the wind.'

'How did anyone know the baby was black, or even if there really was a baby if they hadn't seen it?'

'I don't know.' Mr Bridgenorth shrugged. 'But my experience of gossip is that there's always some truth in it. Maybe the housekeeper talked. In any case, whether or not it's true, that girl's name definitely wasn't Cassandra, it was something ordinary – Carol, Susan, something like that – and the family name is Coleman.'

'Well, that's a good start,' Molly said, suddenly feeling hopeful now she had a name to go on.

'I'm not sure it is, Molly,' he said doubtfully. 'You see, I've talked this over with Ernest and, after some discussion with his wife, who, as you know, is a teacher, he came up with more detail about the family. The grandfather was a doctor, and his daughter married a man called Reginald Coleman. Rumour had it that the parents disapproved of him. Anyway, he enlisted in the war and never came back. Ernest says he was reported missing, presumed dead, but there were whispers that he had deserted because he had a woman in France.'

'Goodness me!' Molly gasped. 'So where is this house?'

'A couple of miles from Brookland, very isolated, not another house near it.'

'So why did no one around here respond when there were pictures of Petal and Cassie in the newspapers and they were asking for inform-ation?' Molly asked. 'Surely if Ernest thought she looked familiar, other people would recognize her, too?'

'Don't you think it's all to do with place?' he asked. 'If a body had turned up down the road here, everyone would be talking about who had gone missing, who it looked like. But a girl found dead some hundred and fifty miles away doesn't have the same impact. The newspaper gets wrapped round fish and chips and it's forgotten.'

'I suppose that's it.' Molly sighed. 'But thank you for all that information. I'll mull it over and decide what to do.'

Mr Bridgenorth smiled. 'Forget it for now and have a lovely time with your young man. I must get off and do some work now.'

An hour or so later, as Molly was packing a bag with the picnic she'd made, Trudy, one of the cleaners, called out to Molly, 'Your bloke's in reception. Lovely smile he's got!'

Molly's heart flipped with excitement and she hurried from the kitchen to meet him.

Trudy was right, Charley did have a lovely smile, and it seemed even wider and warmer than she remembered. 'You look gorgeous,' he said, and swept her into his arms.

275

'Not here,' she whispered, blushing furiously, as she knew Trudy and Anne, the receptionist, were peeping round the door to watch. 'I've made us a picnic!' She picked up the straw basket she'd dropped on the floor just before he hugged her.

'You look good enough to eat yourself,' he said and, taking the basket in one hand, and hers in the other, he led her outside.

'Sorry it's only a van.' He waved towards a small blue van with 'JACK SPOT GARAGE' stencilled on the side. 'I wanted to come in a Rolls Royce but, strangely enough, none of my pals have got one.'

Molly laughed. She wouldn't have minded if he'd turned up in a horse and cart.

She directed him away from the hotel, down the hill to the main road, and from there to Rye Harbour, on the way telling him the rumours Mr Bridgenorth had heard about a girl with a black baby.

Charley looked a bit apprehensive. 'I can't help thinking it would be better to leave well alone,' he said. 'The chances are it's not your friend's family and, if it was and Cassie left after some serious falling out, then you'll only be stirring up muddy water.'

'If it *is* her family, I just want to tell them about Petal and hope they'll push the police to do more.'

'Well, just be careful how you approach them, that's all I'm saying. If they didn't want to know the baby when she was born, they aren't likely to care that much about what happened to her. And some families don't like outsiders poking their nose in,' he said.

Molly was a bit hurt and surprised by his attitude. She'd expected him to be behind her one hundred per cent.

'We have to leave the van here and walk the rest of the way,' she said a little sharply as they drove into Rye Harbour. Charley glanced sideways at her, then pulled over on to a scrap of waste ground.

'I didn't mean to hurt your feelings,' he said. 'I suppose I'm afraid you'll get yourself into hot water. Just let me kiss you and make it up to you.'

Molly wasn't able to stay cross with him and allowed herself to be drawn into his arms.

The kiss was so sweet, and his tongue flickered into her mouth, making her heart beat faster and the outside world disappear.

'I won't be held responsible for what happens if we stay in this van,' he murmured some twenty minutes later as he rained kisses on her neck, 'so we'd better get out.'

It was just the best of days, warm and sunny with only the lightest breeze, and the way Charley was with her – the ready smile, the gentle caresses and his interest in her day-to-day working life – made her feel so very special. They ate their picnic on a grassy bank inside Camber Castle, laughing about everything and anything.

The kissing and cuddling was wonderful, too. Their bodies felt so close it was as if they were one person. 'I hate not seeing you every day,' Charley whispered. 'I've thought of nothing else this week but seeing you today.'

'I've been the same,' she told him. 'And now you're here I don't want to let you go.'

'It won't be for ever,' he said. 'I'm sure I can swing getting work in Ashford once I've passed my exam. I've been putting the word around that I want to move this way.'

'I still wouldn't be able to see you that much,' she reminded him. 'I have to work quite a lot of evenings and weekends.'

'Then we'd better get married,' he said.

Molly didn't know whether he was joking or serious, as he didn't laugh, and he didn't enlarge on it further. She didn't feel able to ask, though, in case he thought she'd taken him too seriously, so she changed the subject.

They walked on later to Winchelsea Beach and then on to Winchelsea, an ancient and pretty little town perched on a hill, as Rye was. They wandered around chatting and admiring all the old houses, then had tea and cake in a tea shop.

'There's so much space down here,' Charley said as they walked back along the road to Rye to pick up his van. 'In London you always feel someone is breathing down your neck. My idea of heaven would be a little cottage with no close neighbours. To have three or four children and bring them up knowing they were safe playing on the marsh or riding their bikes.'

'That sounds good to me too,' said Molly.

He turned to her, put one finger under her chin and tilted her face up. 'Then let's make it happen. Will you marry me, Molly?'

She was thrown. For some reason, in his idea of heaven, although she liked it, it seemed like the woman was almost an afterthought.

'Doesn't telling a girl you love her come before

a proposal?' she asked.

'That goes without saying,' he said, looking surprised.

'Well, it shouldn't. It's important.'

'Of course I love you. I think I fell for you the moment I clapped eyes on you in the café.'

She liked his words, but not the tone in which he said them. It sounded slightly insincere.

They hadn't said anything more about it, and when Charley said goodbye and drove off Molly was left feeling very confused. She had expected him to stay till at least ten, but he'd said he had to go at eight thirty, and she couldn't help but think he had something more exciting planned back in London than sitting in a pub with her on a Saturday night. Then there was that odd proposal.

It hadn't been mentioned again. They had kissed and cuddled in his van and things had got a bit heated. But he still didn't tell her he loved her, or ask if she loved him.

Why hadn't he?

Molly didn't have any first-hand experience, but in books and films men spoke from the heart when they said such things. It had sounded like an excuse when Charley said he had to leave because he had to be up early for work in the morning. But if it was true he'd been asked to work on a Sunday, why hadn't he mentioned it when he phoned on Friday evening?

She felt downcast. It had been a lovely day and he had seemed as happy to be with her as she was with him, until he'd said he had to go. But, now she came to think on it, he hadn't talked about

279

his own life at all, not today or ever, really. He spoke of the men he worked with, of jobs he'd had in the past, but he didn't volunteer personal information about his everyday life.

Molly went in through the hotel's back door, as there was less likelihood of her running into anyone and she couldn't trust herself not to cry if she was asked about her day. Fortunately, she was able to slink unnoticed up the back stairs to her room. Once inside, she fell on the bed and cried.

There was something not right about Charley, but she didn't know what. She knew he wasn't only after sex like most men: he could easily have lured her into it today, but he hadn't even tried.

Then there was the way he'd been about Cassie. On the face of it, he was just being protective, but she had a feeling that wasn't all of it. Did he have something to hide, and so not want her making a scene about anything in case it turned a spotlight on him?

He couldn't be married – no man would propose to another woman if he already had a wife. Or could he?

It seemed unlikely, but she couldn't think of any other reason that might explain things. Yet when she thought of his broad smile when he'd met her this morning and his tender goodbye kiss she felt ashamed that she was doubting him. Maybe she was the odd one?

Chapter Fifteen

A few days after her day with Charley, Molly borrowed one of the hotel bicycles and rode out towards Brookland. She had been on breakfast and chambermaid duties and, as it was a warm, sunny day and she didn't have to be back until seven to turn the beds down, she'd put on a blouse and some shorts and decided to explore.

The previous day she'd received a letter from Charley. He'd apologized for leaving so early and said the reason he hadn't told her earlier in the day was because he was afraid it would spoil things. He also apologized for proposing. He said it had just come out and, although he did want to marry her, it was all too soon, so would she please forgive him.

She didn't know what to make of that. She didn't like that he sounded so weak, but then she told herself that he was right, it was too soon to be talking of marriage and, today, she was trying to put it out of her head.

Being out in the fresh air, whizzing past orchards of apple and pear trees in full blossom, seeing lambs frolicking in the fields and feeling the sun warm on her face, arms and legs, she felt happy. Her mother had always said, 'What will be, will be.' And even though she'd found that little homily irritating in the past, today it seemed profound.

281

She stopped at the post office in Brookland to ask the way to the Colemans' house.

'You won't get no reply,' the postmistress said. 'She don't answer the door to no one.'

As the postmistress had a big, soft, motherly face, Molly didn't think she was being deliberately obstructive.

'Why's that?' she asked.

The postmistress put one finger to her forehead and made a screwing motion, the way people often did to imply someone was barmy. 'She's been that way for years now. I can't remember how long it is since she came into the village or passed the time of day with anyone.'

'Does she have a daughter?'

The postmistress looked surprised by the question. 'Yes, she do, but she went away years ago.'

Molly took the picture of Cassie out of her knapsack. 'Is this her?' she asked.

The older woman looked at it carefully for what seemed like minutes. 'I'm not sure,' she said eventually. 'She's got a bit of a look of Sylvia, but I couldn't say hand on heart that it's her.'

'Sylvia?' Molly repeated. 'Is that her daughter's name?'

'That's right.' The woman continued to look at the picture. 'It does put me in mind of her, but there's sommat wrong.'

'Is it the hair?' Molly asked. 'I know you can't see the real colour of this girl's hair. It looks so dark in a black-and-white picture, but she dyed it red, you see. What if it was much fairer?'

'Maybe that's it. Sylvia had lovely hair – the colour of butter, it were.'

Molly had no idea of the natural colour of Cassie's hair, but she felt she was getting somewhere. 'Can you tell me how long ago it was that Sylvia left here? You see, I'm trying to find the family of this girl in the picture and I don't want to be going to the wrong house.'

The woman sucked in her cheeks. 'Must be nigh on six years ago now, though no one is exactly sure, because of the way Miss Gribble was and still is.'

'Who's Miss Gribble?'

'The housekeeper. Local kids say she's a witch, and she's certainly disagreeable, tight-lipped as they come. Some folks round here think she's the reason Reg never come back after the war and why Christabel went crazy.'

Molly was getting excited. 'Look, the girl in the picture was my friend, and I knew her as Cassandra, Cassie for short. She was killed on Coronation Day and her little daughter went missing at the same time and has never been found. The police seem to have given up on the case, but I thought I'd try to find her family. Would you please tell me, did the girl you know as Sylvia have a black baby?'

The postmistress hesitated and her expression showed the conflict she was feeling. Molly guessed she had suddenly realized she'd already been indiscreet.

'It's okay, you can tell me,' Molly reassured her. 'I'm sure the family saw it as a disgrace and did their best to cover it up. But none of that matters now: a child is missing, maybe even dead. People must say what they know.'

'I really don't know anything.' The postmistress shrugged her shoulders. 'There was a story going around that Sylvia had a mixed race baby, but I always thought that was spite, because she were a bit wild and the family was so peculiar. I never really believed it. After all, where would Sylvia meet a black man around here? Besides, no one I know ever saw the baby, so there probably weren't one.'

'If Sylvia and Cassie were the same person, which I believe they were, then there really was a child, a little girl. Petal, she was called, and she was a lovely kid, bright as a button and a credit to her mother. Her grandmother may not have wanted her, she might send me away with a flea in my ear, but she ought to be told her daughter is dead and that her granddaughter is missing.'

'Fair enough. Put that way, I suppose she ought to know.' The postmistress looked rattled now. She was wringing her hands and bright red spots of colour had appeared on her cheeks. 'I'll give you the address, but it would be best if you wrote to Christabel Coleman rather than going there. She won't open the door to you.'

'Okay,' Molly said, though she had every intention of going straight there. 'I'm really grateful for your help, and I won't tell anyone the information came from you.'

She rode away slowly from the post office, the address of the Colemans' house in her pocket, mulling over what she'd been told. She wanted to believe she'd found out Cassie's real name, and her home and family, but she had no proof at all that Sylvia Coleman was Cassandra March. What she ought to do was go straight to the police and get them to find out for certain. She could almost hear George lecturing her, saying that this wasn't a job for amateurs.

But the police might take for ever to act, and Molly was desperate to know the truth. Besides, now, she wanted to see mad Christabel Coleman and the fearsome Miss Gribble.

It seemed that Cassie hadn't spoken about her family for good reason. Who would want to admit that their mother was barmy? But even if Cassie's mother was as mad as a hatter, she would never have expected her daughter to die young or her granddaughter to be taken away. So, however weird the family was, surely they'd want to help in finding the daughter's missing child?

Mulberry House was only about three miles from the post office, but it took Molly some time to find it, as the postmistress hadn't given her any directions. The entrance was down a small lane and a wall of thick, evergreen trees hid the house. It was only by pure chance that she noticed the faded sign by a large, rusting wrought-iron gate, and she got off her bike to peer through the rails.

The house was set back some hundred yards from the lane at the end of a drive that was over-grown with weeds and broken up in parts. The house was quite picturesque: mellow red brick, with fancy tall chimneys and lattice windows; Molly thought it must be over two hundred years old. Ivy covered most of it, including some of the windows, and, like the drive, it was neglected, with plants growing out of the gutters and roof.

It was obvious that neither house nor grounds had received any maintenance for years. What would have once been a lawn was now more like a field, with clumps of rough grass suffocating the daffodils, which must have been planted years ago and somehow managed to survive. Huge rhododendron bushes had spread and choked any other plants and bushes that may have once filled the borders. The rhododendrons were about to burst into flower, and Molly was reminded that Cassie had been thrilled when she found a couple growing in the woods behind Stone Cottage. Back then, Molly had thought her friend was just a bit of a botanist, but now it seemed clear that she'd been pleased to see them because they were a reminder of her childhood home.

Molly tried the gate and found it unlocked, but then she thought that perhaps shorts and a blouse were hardly suitable attire to give someone the news of their daughter's death and decided to come back the next day in a dress.

But she remained at the gate for a while, looking at the house and trying to imagine Cassie growing up there. It wasn't difficult: it was as extraordinary as Cassie, and her friend had always had an air about her, as if she'd known better things. She knew the names of plants and trees, could talk about composers, writers and artists in a way that ordinary people never did. She wished Cassie had told her about her father going missing in France. Had she heard the gossip that he had a woman over there? Did she hate the implication that he might have deserted?

Molly thought it looked a sad house. Maybe that

was just because of the neglect and the sketchy information she now had about the residents, but she couldn't possibly imagine any child ever playing noisy games in the garden or the house ringing with laughter.

It was going to be even sadder when she gave Mrs Coleman the news. She might have ordered her daughter to leave when she had an illegitimate child, but no mother, however hardhearted, could possibly be totally immune to grief.

Later that evening, after she'd turned the guests' beds down and helped out in the kitchen for a while, as the restaurant was busy, Molly wrote to Charley, telling him an edited version of the day's events. She didn't think he'd approve of her going back to the house to inform Mrs Coleman of her daughter's death, so she implied she was going to hand what she knew over to the police.

With police on her mind, she also wrote to George, because he'd known Cassie and had been as frustrated as she had when his senior officers had given up on finding Petal.

'I'm hoping that talking to her mother and this scary-sounding housekeeper will result in them demanding a better investigation into Petal's disappearance,' she wrote. 'If they don't seem to care, then I'll go straight to the police myself. I'll let you know what happens.'

She also penned a letter to Mrs Coleman, on headed paper from the George, in case she wouldn't answer the door and speak to her. In it, she told her about her friendship with Cassie, who she felt sure was Sylvia Coleman, her death on

287

Coronation Day and that Petal had disappeared.

She kept the letter short and to the point, asking Mrs Coleman only that, as Petal's grandmother, she should insist on further investigation by the police.

It was raining the next morning while Molly served breakfast, but one of the guests said they'd heard the forecast, which said that showers would be dying out by midday. By the time she'd finished the bedrooms she was delighted to see the rain had stopped, and she rushed off to change.

She selected a blue, checked, pleated skirt to wear as it was heavy enough not to blow up in the air and expose her stocking tops as she rode the bike, and with it a toning blue twinset. She tied her hair back with a matching blue ribbon. She looked at herself in the mirror for some time before leaving and, although she had butterflies in her stomach about what she had to do, she at least felt confident about how she looked. Her cheeks were pink again; they'd lost their colour in London, and her hair its shine. But it was shining now and the sun over the last few days had given her blonde streaks amongst the brown.

'It's going to be all right,' she said aloud. 'I doubt they'll be that weird. That's just stuff people love to say.'

When she arrived at Mulberry House she pushed the heavy iron gate open and wheeled her bike up the drive. She had a feeling she was being watched, but she couldn't see anyone looking out of the windows. She leaned her bike against a low stone wall which surrounded a weed-filled rose bed, then went over to the front door and pulled on the bell.

She heard it ring loudly enough to alert even someone hard of hearing, but no one came, so she rang it again, even harder. Again, no response. She rang it five times in all, and when there was still no response she walked round the side of the house to see if there was another entrance.

Catching a fleeting glimpse of a white-haired woman through a window, she rapped on the glass and called out. But the woman didn't respond so Molly continued round the house until she came to a kitchen door. It was propped open, and she rapped on it very loudly and called out.

Her early training never to step into anyone's house uninvited made it difficult for her to cross the threshold, so she stood there for a while calling out. Still, no one came.

Coming through the open door there was an unpleasant smell of fish. She could see a saucepan on the gas stove and guessed it was being cooked for a cat. She hoped so, as it smelled too disgusting to be for humans.

The kitchen was like so many she'd seen in country houses back home: a central table with a scrubbed top; painted cupboards and shelves lining the walls. Here, though, everything looked neglected, untidy and dirty and with peeling paint.

She spotted a brass handbell sitting on the sink. Maybe Miss Gribble and Mrs Coleman were deaf, but perhaps they would still be able to hear it.

Drawing on all her courage, Molly stepped inside, went over to the sink, picked up the bell and rang it loudly.

On the second ring – and it had been a very loud, long one – the white-haired woman she'd glimpsed through the window appeared.

'If the door bell isn't answered, it means we don't want visitors,' she barked at Molly.

Molly was scared but stood her ground. She was fairly certain that this was Miss Gribble, not Mrs Coleman. She was perhaps sixty, her face was deeply lined and weather-beaten, but she looked strong, with broad shoulders and thick, muscular forearms, revealed by a faded, short-sleeved blouse. She looked like a formidable woman, and the way she was glowering at Molly was frightening.

'I'm sorry to intrude, but I have something very important to ask Mrs Coleman,' she said, trying to keep her voice from shaking with fright. 'If it hadn't been so important I wouldn't have been impertinent enough to come in uninvited. So will you please fetch her and let me get this over and done with?'

'You can talk to me. Mrs Coleman isn't well,' she said.

'No. In a matter like this, it is important to speak to the right person,' Molly insisted. 'It's about her daughter.'

'We have nothing to do with her,' Miss Gribble snapped, drawing herself up very straight, as if doing her best to intimidate Molly.

'I know that, and the reasons for it are none of my business. But I am not leaving here until I've spoken face to face with Mrs Coleman.'

The door through to the house opened slowly,

and another woman came in. She was very dishevelled, with long hair the colour of dirty straw, and her shapeless maroon dress did her no favours, yet, even so, Molly could see Cassie's face in hers, and it shook her. The same speedwell-blue eyes, the pointed chin and an expression of disdain which she'd seen Cassie flash many a time at people when they were mean to her.

'What do you mean by coming here and demanding to speak to me?' she asked. 'Who are you, girl?'

The tone was so scathing, Molly suddenly felt almost happy to give her bad news. She pulled the photograph of Cassie out of her skirt pocket.

'My name is Molly Heywood, and I came to ask you to look at this picture and tell me if this is your daughter, Sylvia.'

She knew straight off that Sylvia and Cassie were one and the same person, just by the way the woman's expression changed as she glanced at the picture. Clear recognition, yet it was mixed with fear, perhaps foreboding, as if she were already anticipating tragedy.

'It is her, isn't it, Mrs Coleman?' she asked. 'I know her as Cassie. She was my best friend.'

The woman's expression changed to one of confusion, and she looked at the older woman as if seeking guidance.

'I'm very sorry to be the bearer of bad news,' Molly said, now wishing she were anywhere but here in this grubby kitchen with these two weird women. 'Sylvia was murdered last year, and her daughter, Petal – your granddaughter – was taken, presumably by the killer. I would've liked to sit

291

down with you and talk about this, but it seems that isn't going to happen. So I'd better go to the police and let them investigate.'

'Why go to the police?' Mrs Coleman asked. Now, her voice wasn't quite so harsh. In fact, Molly thought she sounded scared.

'Because this is a murder inquiry. The police have been looking for family members and now I've found you they need to talk to you.'

She saw alarm jump into those blue eyes that were so much like Cassie's and, just as she was about to ask a question, she felt a heavy blow to the back of her head. She reeled and saw both of the women in triplicate before everything went black.

Chapter Sixteen

Evelyn Bridgenorth popped her head around the door of the hotel bar. There were only about six or seven people there and Ernest was busying himself polishing glasses. As always, he looked very dapper in a dinner jacket and bow tie, his still-dark hair slicked back with Brylcreem. He'd been working at the George for fifteen years now, except for a gap of six years when he was called up. Evelyn often wondered how they'd manage if he retired or found another job, as he was a great barman and totally reliable.

'Ernest, have you seen Molly this evening?' she asked him.

He stopped polishing for a moment. 'No. Why? Is she missing?'

'Yes. It's odd, she's normally in the kitchen at this time of day, having a bite to eat before going up to turn the beds down.'

'Maybe she met a friend this afternoon and got chatting. She'll be back any minute – she's very conscientious,' he said.

'Yes, of course. And it doesn't matter if the beds aren't turned down right now. It was just that I wanted to talk to her about the Beauchamps' wedding next week, a few little wrinkles that need ironing out.'

'She went out on a bike, so she won't want to be riding it in the dark,' Ernest said. 'Of course, she could've got a puncture and had to walk back.'

'Oh, I do hope not.' Mrs Bridgenorth looked anxious. 'She's such a dear girl.'

By nine thirty, when Molly still hadn't returned although it had been dark for some time, Mrs Bridgenorth began to get really worried, and consulted her husband, who was doing some paperwork in his office up on the third floor. She explained that Molly hadn't returned for her evening shift. 'She isn't the kind to forget she had a job to do, Ted,' she said. 'If something unexpected had cropped up this afternoon, she would have found a phone box and telephoned us.'

Ted put down his pen and turned his chair round to give his wife his full attention. 'What about that boyfriend of hers?' he asked. 'Could he have turned up and whisked her off somewhere?'

'I doubt that very much, because she borrowed

293

a bicycle. And I saw her minutes before she left. She was plainly dressed in a skirt and twinset, didn't even have lipstick on, so she wasn't meeting anyone, and especially not him.'

'Didn't she tell you or someone else where she was going?'

'She said she was just going for a ride to explore. I did tell her the other day that it was a nice easy ride to Lydd, because it's all flat. But Lydd hasn't got much to keep you there for long.'

'There's the army camp,' Ted reminded her. 'Maybe a soldier picked her up.'

'Oh, Ted, she's not the kind of girl to allow herself to be picked up by a soldier, or any man, for that matter. She's too smitten with Charley.'

'Calm down, dear,' he said. 'It's not the first time we've had a girl go missing for the evening, is it?'

'No, of course not!' she snapped at him. 'But all those other girls had family close by; they swanned off because of some disagreement with someone. Molly hasn't got anyone near here. Neither has she fallen out with anyone. Now tell me, should I phone the police?'

Ted realized then his wife was very anxious about Molly and got up from his chair to give her a hug. 'And say what, Evelyn? She's twenty-six, not fifteen. They only consider someone a missing person when they've been gone for forty-eight hours or more. Let it go for now. I've got no doubt she'll come bursting in before long with some perfectly good reason for being late back. You'll see.'

Evelyn agreed to wait until the next day but, as

294

she passed the narrow staircase which led to the attic rooms, including Molly's, on an impulse she ran up the flight of stairs to see if there was anything in her room which might indicate where she was.

Molly kept her room very neat and tidy, but the little oak bureau which stood under the window had a writing pad, envelopes and a small diary left out on the drop-down flap, as if she'd been halfway through writing some letters.

Evelyn hesitated before opening it, as it seemed a terrible invasion of her privacy, but she didn't feel quite so guilty when she discovered Molly had only begun the diary since she had come to work at the George, and only used it to enter the duties she was doing each week and her day off. But, right at the back of the diary, Molly had written a few addresses.

Most of them were back in her home town in Somerset. The name George Walsh caught her eye, and she vaguely remembered overhearing Molly telling Trudy that she'd had a letter from George, an old schoolfriend who was now a policeman.

There were a few addresses in Whitechapel and Bethnal Green, Charley Sanderson's amongst them. If Molly had put a telephone number down for him, she'd have been tempted to ring him, but there was none. There was an address and a telephone number for Mr and Mrs Heywood but, as worried as she was, she knew she couldn't ring Molly's parents, not yet: it would only make them frantic.

Then she saw the name Dilys Porter and

remembered Molly asking how much it cost to stay a night in the hotel, as she'd like to invite her friend Dilys down. Evelyn had said if Dilys shared her room there would be no charge, and Molly had lit up like a Christmas tree.

Reluctantly, she put the diary back. Common sense told her she was over-reacting and that she should wait to see if Molly came back later that night before ringing anyone.

Molly wasn't going to be coming back that evening.

She found herself lying on a stone floor with a pain in the back of her head. She touched it gingerly, and felt a big lump, but she didn't know how she'd done it, or where she was.

She lay still for a little while, trying to remember, but the last thing she recalled was riding past orchards and seeing pink-and-white blossom. Had she had an accident on her bike? But if she had, where was she now? The room was quite dark, like a cellar, and it smelled musty. All she could see was a small window high up on the wall. If she'd come off the bike, surely she'd be either at the side of a road or in someone's house?

Trying to sit up, her hands touched her pleated skirt and that triggered a memory of standing in front of a mirror checking to see if she looked mature and sensible.

All at once it came back to her. She had come out to Mulberry House for the second time to see Cassie's mother. Miss Gribble had been fierce and defensive and Christabel Coleman hadn't wanted to talk to her.

She had a ghost of a memory of a blow to the back of her head and, presumably, she had been knocked out, as she had no memory of being moved from the kitchen to wherever she was now.

As the last thing she remembered was facing Mrs Coleman, it must have been Miss Gribble who hit her. But why?

It was like reading a book and suddenly finding that a couple of pages had been torn out. She could remember the two women, even what their kitchen looked like, but she couldn't quite put together what had led up to being hit.

Whether she could remember or not, though, the fact remained that she was in danger. No one knocked you out and put you in a cellar by mistake. Those two women were either stark staring mad or they wanted to shut her up. Or perhaps both.

She got to her feet and nearly keeled over with dizziness, probably a side effect of being hit. She stood still till it passed then made her way to the door. As she expected, it was locked, and she turned, leaned against it and surveyed her prison. How could she get out?

Some meagre daylight came in from a small, barred window high up on the wall, enough to see a collection of empty boxes for storing apples, some wooden crates piled up in the right-hand corner of the room and a workbench along the wall to her left. When the dizziness eased, Molly moved over to the bench, hoping to find a screwdriver or some other tool, but there was nothing, only thick dust, which showed this room was rarely used.

It was also cold and damp, but if the two women could dump someone in here with a head injury, they weren't going to be concerned about her comfort.

She could feel hysteria welling up inside her; the temptation to scream and bang on the door was almost overwhelming. But she tried to control herself and think things through. Why had the women attacked and imprisoned her?

It was possible they were so batty that they were prepared to do the same to anyone who had the cheek to enter their home uninvited, but she thought that was very unlikely. Shouting, threatening or brandishing a weapon was enough to eject an unwanted visitor. So it had to be to do with Sylvia, or Cassie. But why would Molly informing them she was dead provoke such a reaction?

Christabel obviously didn't have any normal maternal feelings, not if she felt her daughter had totally disgraced her by producing a mixed race, illegitimate baby and decided to throw her out. Yet although news of her daughter's death and the child's disappearance might make her feel guilty, remorseful or ashamed, surely it wouldn't make her aggressive towards the messenger?

Of course, it could have been a panic reaction on Miss Gribble's part. Perhaps she had lashed out involuntarily because she was afraid of scandal. The two women might have dragged her into the cellar while they considered what to do with her.

Molly decided she was going to believe that this was the case for the moment, and she turned to the door and started banging on it.

'Please let me out!' she shouted. 'I know you

didn't mean to hurt me, but I have to get back to my work, or they'll call the police. Just let me go and I'll forget this ever happened.'

She felt like screaming that the first thing she'd do when she got out would be to get a doctor to certify them and have them put into an asylum. But she knew that wouldn't help her cause.

There was no reply, and when she put her ear to the door Molly couldn't hear anything at all. It was possible, of course, that this cellar was just one of several underground rooms, and had such thick walls that sound from here couldn't penetrate up the stairs into the house.

She took off her shoe and began banging on the door as loudly as she was able. She did this for around five minutes, paused to shout out the same message as before, then returned to banging again.

After repeating this sequence around twenty times, her arm ached and her throat hurt; also, the foot without a shoe had become like a block of ice on the stone floor. She put the shoe back on and, picking up one of the wooden crates, used it to batter the door until it fell apart in her hands. Still no one came.

There were plenty more crates, but Molly's head hurt and she felt exhausted. She sank down on to the floor and sobbed.

She hadn't told anyone where she was going, so no one would know where to come looking for her. She'd told George in her letter that she had a lead on Cassie's mother, who lived in Brookland, and that she was going to see her, but that wouldn't alarm him, not unless he was told she hadn't come back. And who was going to tell him that?

Eventually, if she didn't turn up, Mrs Bridgenorth would alert the police. They would contact Charley, and when he told them she'd been determined to find Cassie's mother and thought she lived in a nearby village, the police might end up here.

But how long would that take? At the very least, it would be days. The thought of spending even one night in such a cold, damp place without food, water or a blanket was terrifying.

The cold floor was striking up through her skirt to her bottom now, and the light coming through the small window was fading. She had to make a plan for when total darkness fell.

Getting to her feet, she went over to the workbench. The top of it was wood – far warmer to sit or lie on than the floor. She pushed the apple boxes to one side and found a piece of rag. She wiped the dust off the bench, then pushed all the crates away, hoping to find anything – rags or sacks – to keep her a bit warmer, or a tool to pick at the door lock. But there was nothing.

She prowled round the cellar then, looking for anything useful, but there was nothing other than cobwebs.

She picked up a crate, intending to start banging on the door again, and something dropped to the floor with a slight tinkle. She couldn't see what it was, as the light was so bad, but she groped around with her hand and eventually found it.

It was a hair slide – just a little red circle like a Polo mint, with a metal clasp across the back. It looked familiar, but maybe that was just because she had worn such hair slides when she was little.

Grabbing a box, she began to bang and shout again. It made her feel warmer, even if it did no good. She thought she would do it in the middle of the night, too; with luck, it might annoy them so much they would come down.

Once complete darkness fell, Molly was unable to maintain her calm. She wanted to relieve herself; she was cold, hungry and thirsty, and very frightened. It seemed to her as she lay hunched up on the workbench that if a person could knock you out and drag you to a cellar, they were capable of leaving you there for ever. Compared with that, her fear of spiders seemed silly, but still she kept imagining them creeping towards her in the dark.

She couldn't see her wristwatch now, but it couldn't be more than nine at night, as it hadn't been dark for that long. She wished she could fall asleep, but it was too cold for that.

She thought of Constance and how much she'd believed in the power of prayer.

'Not a sparrow can fall from its nest without Him knowing,' she'd said, on many an occasion.

'If you know about the sparrows, what about me?' Molly asked God. 'I haven't done anything bad, I was trying to put things right, so please help me. Make someone work out where I am.'

All at once, almost as if God had heard her prayer, she remembered why the red hair slide looked familiar. Petal had always worn two of them in her hair, one on either side.

It could, of course, be pure coincidence that a

hair slide like Petal's had been dropped here. But she didn't believe it was. She just knew Petal had been here.

At four o'clock in the morning, while Molly was shivering uncontrollably and thinking she just might die of it, Evelyn Bridgenorth was lying awake, worrying. She had stayed up till after twelve in the hope that Molly would turn up or telephone, then, as all the guests were now in bed, she finally locked the hotel door and went up herself.

Ted was already asleep, and she didn't want to disturb him by putting the light on and reading. So she just lay there, waiting for sleep to overtake her, but it didn't; her mind was racing too fast.

She heard the church clock strike four and wondered how she was going to run the hotel when she'd had no sleep. If Molly did come breezing in the next morning, she'd get a real tongue-lashing for putting her through this.

At ten o'clock Evelyn Bridgenorth rang the police station to report Molly missing.

'It's not unusual for young women to just take off,' the sergeant said, clearly not having taken on board what she'd just said about Molly being a reliable and conscientious girl. 'It'll be a man, I expect. He'll have sweet-talked her into dropping everything and, when she comes back, she'll tell you a cock-and-bull story that she was on an errand of mercy.'

'Miss Heywood left on a bicycle. She took no clothes or overnight things. She didn't even have a coat with her,' Evelyn said crisply.

302

'Oh, we've had plenty of women go missing when they said they were just out to buy a pint of milk and still wearing their pinny. No accounting for what goes on in women's minds.'

Evelyn was tempted to tell him that she was imagining going down to the police station and throwing the contents of a chip pan over him. 'I want you to look into it,' she said through gritted teeth.

'Tell you what, Mrs Bridgenorth, as it's you, if she isn't back in two days, I'll see what I can do.'

'You don't suppose Molly's disappearance has got anything to do with her looking for her friend's family?' Ernest asked Mrs Bridgenorth that evening when he opened the bar. 'She hadn't given up on finding them. I've heard she's been asking around the town about the family quite recently.'

'Yes, I know about that. Ted told me. But I can't see that there'd be any connection between that and her disappearance. I mean, her friend was killed back in Somerset.'

'Maybe so, but if the dead girl's family live around here, Molly may have stumbled into something they want kept hidden,' he said. 'What are you going to do?'

'I'm going to call the police.'

'But I thought they wouldn't do anything.'

'Not the Rye police – they're a bunch of disbelieving idiots. If she isn't back tonight, I'm going to call Molly's policeman friend in Somerset and hear what he has to say. I'm also going to ring her friend Dilys and see if she knows anything.'

Molly was beyond crying now that darkness had fallen for a second night. The previous night had been long and tortuous, and the daylight hours that followed it almost as bad. Every now and then she had banged on the door and screamed, but it was no use. Now she was so hungry and thirsty she could think of little else but food and drink, and the cold made it impossible to fall asleep and forget about it for a few hours.

She now knew without a doubt that she'd been left here to die. Maybe when the two women had dragged her here unconscious, they thought she was already dead. In any case, the fact they hadn't been back to check on her proved that was what they wanted.

Yet, however utterly miserable she felt, Molly's mind was still active, and it seemed to her that no one would react quite as aggressively as those two women had unless they had something very serious to hide. She felt certain now it was they who had attacked Cassie, and taken Petal.

When she'd walked around the back of Mulberry House Molly hadn't really noticed much beyond the garden being overgrown. Yet out of the corner of her eye she was sure she had seen a black car, an old Austin or something similar. The two women could have found out where Cassie was living and driven to Somerset.

She asked herself what would have made them attack Cassie. Surely a mother would only drive all that way out of love, wanting to be reunited with her daughter? Maybe Cassie hadn't been able to forgive her for turning her back on her when Petal was born, and had told them to leave.

Perhaps a fight had broken out because Cassie had told some home truths, and one of the women had hit her so hard that she had fallen on the hearth. Then, perhaps, realizing Cassie was dead, they had taken Petal with them so she couldn't tell anyone what had happened.

What had they done with the child? That was the most important question now.

Having seen how they lived, and how irrational and volatile they were, they could well have killed her. With miles and miles of marshland within a stone's throw of the house, they could have buried her little body anywhere and no one would ever find it. That would explain their panic when she'd arrived.

But there was also a small chance she could be here in this house, locked up just as she was.

That image was almost worse than her being dead. She had been taken over ten months ago, and the thought of Petal being terrified and locked up for all that time was terrible. It would surely be better if she had been killed right away. Yet the thought persisted that she was alive, and very close by.

One night when she had been working behind the bar at the George, an elderly gentleman with a very upper-crust accent had started chatting to her. He was a retired lawyer who had been born in Rye, a former captain in the First World War who, when invalided out, went to university and studied law, later returning to his home town to set up his own practice. He was an interesting man, clearly very intelligent and astute about people. Amongst other things he spoke about that night was the high proportion of mentally unstable people living on the marshes with whom he had had contact through the courts.

'When I was a boy, people talked about "the Marsh Folk", usually with words like "barmy", "touched" or "queer",' he had said. 'There were peculiar old women we believed were witches, men who talked to themselves, odd folk who came into town on market day and seemed to be in a world of their own. It was said to be the constant wind on the marshes affecting the inner ear that made them that way. Nothing much has changed since then. There are still some very strange people living in remote places on the marshes, whole families of them. They're not necessarily bad people, but they're certainly weird and out of step with the modern world.'

Molly had been amused by this, and she had seen a few people in town on market day that seemed to fit his description. So maybe Christabel Coleman's strange, reclusive nature was caused by this, too, at least in part. Perhaps Cassie would've gone the same way if she hadn't moved away.

As soon as the first rays of morning light came through the small window Molly dragged herself off the workbench. She felt terrible: cold, stiff and aching all over. She had fallen asleep inter-mittently during the night, only to wake suddenly and feel even colder than before.

Holding on to the workbench, she tried some ballet exercises to loosen up her stiff limbs. She sensed that hunger and thirst had put her into starvation mode to reserve what little was left in her and that this was why she felt so weak. But she was aware that she had to make more effort to escape, or she would die here.

First she attempted to drag the workbench so that it was under the small window. Although she knew she wouldn't be able to get through the bars, if she broke the glass, someone might hear her shouting.

The workbench weighed a ton but, inch by inch, she managed to pull it nearer to the window. Finally, it was close enough and she climbed on to it to break the glass. The window was still right above her head so she couldn't see out but, using her shoe, she thumped the glass as hard as she could until it gave way and shattered. She pushed the remaining shards of glass out, then tried to rattle the bars, hoping against hope they were weak. Sadly, they were rock hard, fixed right into the stone window surround, not just into the wooden window frame. It occurred to her that, with no glass in the window, it would be even colder now, and rain would come in. But slim hope was better than no hope at all, and without the glass she might be able to hear the postman or milkman and raise a hullabaloo.

Next, she got down to examine the wooden crates and apple storage boxes, hoping she might find a long nail to try and unpick the door lock. But she was overcome with exhaustion, the cellar began to swirl and she was forced to lie down again and rest.

As she lay there it flittered across her mind that when people said they were hungry they really didn't know the meaning of the word. Real hunger was like something gnawing at your insides; it stopped you thinking of anything else. She supposed, as it grew worse, you would eventually hope for death.

Chapter Seventeen

George Walsh put down the phone after speaking to Mrs Bridgenorth and stood for a moment considering what to do.

When he had got Molly's letter the previous day the only emotion the contents had stirred was amusement. He felt that she'd swallowed a far-fetched yarn, a myth like the one spread around in this village about Enoch Flowers. It was said that his sweetheart had fallen into a threshing machine and he'd picked up her two severed legs and carried them and her down the high street.

It wasn't true; his sweetheart had died of Spanish 'flu in 1920 but, somehow, this grisly story still circulated. There were even some who claimed that he had let Cassie have Stone Cottage because she looked like his sweetheart.

George knew that Molly was obsessed with Cassie's death and Petal's disappearance, so it was hardly surprising that she was willing to believe a story about a nutty widow and her formidable housekeeper who lived in a remote house on the marsh.

Now he knew she was missing, though, he wasn't quite so ready to scoff at what she'd written to him. Mrs Bridgenorth had spent her whole life in hotels, so she wouldn't scare easily, yet he had heard real fear in her voice. She had said that Molly was always so conscientious, that she wouldn't have just gone off to see a friend without telling anyone. And none of her friends lived only a bike ride away.

George knew the correct thing to do was to go into the police station and tell Sarge all he knew, and that Molly had now been missing for nearly forty-eight hours.

He knew that Sergeant Bailey agreed with him that the investigation into Petal's disappearance had ended far too quickly and hadn't been very thorough. But he wasn't going to like it that Molly hadn't shared any further information about Cassie with the police.

Even if Sergeant Bailey went straight to someone senior to demand that they organize a search for Molly in Brookland, by the time the ball had been passed to the police in Rye, another twenty-four hours would have passed, maybe more.

Mrs Bridgenorth had already contacted all the hospitals in the area to check that Molly hadn't been knocked off her bike and taken in for treatment. She'd also telephoned Molly's friend Dilys, who worked at Bourne & Hollingsworth, and left a message for her, just in case Molly had gone to her. But George knew, as did Mrs Bridgenorth, that if by some chance Molly had felt compelled to go off somewhere, she would have telephoned the hotel. So it stood to reason she was in difficulties. And if the local gossip about Christabel Coleman and her housekeeper was true, it was even possible that they had been the ones who killed Cassie and took Petal away.

However, Sergeant Bailey and the rest of the local force weren't necessarily going to believe any of this. They were likely to delay doing anything while they discussed it with the Rye police. Molly might be dead by the time they made a move, so George felt there was only one solution, and that was that he go down to Rye immediately to find her.

He was on three days' leave, and he'd planned to spend it refelting the shed roof. But the roof could wait, and he'd write what he knew in a letter to Sergeant Bailey and get his mother to take it in to the police station. By the time Sarge read it, George would be almost in Rye.

Hastily, he grabbed a writing pad and wrote down as much as he knew, and his fears that the two women might have imprisoned Molly because they were afraid she might bring the police in to investigate them. Then he apologized for rushing off down there but pointed out that Molly was one of his oldest friends and that he was on leave.

His mother was very concerned when he gave her the letter and told her the gist of what was in it.

Janet Walsh was a typical countrywoman: plain, strong, hardworking and no-nonsense. She had always liked Molly Heywood; indeed, she had once or twice admitted that she'd always hoped that one day George would marry her. But she was very aware that, because George was a mere constable, his superiors would take a dim view of him riding off to rescue a girl he went to school with, just because he thought she was in trouble. That is, of course, if she was in trouble. For all Janet knew, and George, too, for that matter, she might have run off with some sweet-talking man.

'Now, son, this is madness,' she said, shaking her head. 'Why can't you let the police down there investigate it?'

'Because I could sense that something bad had happened to her the moment her boss told me she was missing. I've got three days' leave, Mum, and how I spend it is my business. I couldn't live with myself if Molly was killed while I sat on my hands, along with the local police force.'

'Why should she have been killed, George? Aren't you being a bit melodramatic?'

'Cassie was killed, remember,' he replied. 'And Petal was taken away, Heaven knows where. If these two women were responsible for that, they wouldn't have liked Molly turning up, would they?'

'No, I suppose not.' Mrs Walsh sighed. 'But now you've given me something more to worry about.'

'If you give that note to Sergeant Bailey a couple of hours after I've left, he'll make sure there's back-up down there. Now, please would you make me a couple of sandwiches and a flask of tea to take with me. It's a long ride.'

'You aren't thinking of going all that way on your motorbike, are you?' His mother's voice rose in horror. 'I thought you'd be going on the train.'

'The bike is much quicker,' he said. 'There's no direct train to Rye.'

He got together a few bits and pieces he thought he might need, including a map, a toothbrush and a change of clothing, a jemmy, a screwdriver and a bolt cutter, and put them into the pannier on his motorbike, then went in to put on his leathers.

When he came back downstairs his mother met him in the hall and handed him a sandwich box and his flask.

'Drive carefully, son,' she warned him. 'Ring us when you get a chance. I'll be praying you find Molly unharmed.'

'You'd better tell her mum about this,' George said reluctantly, as he put on his helmet. 'She needs to be prepared, just in case.'

'The poor woman.' Mrs Walsh sighed. 'Her husband's such a miserable devil, and now both her girls gone and unlikely ever to return. And now this. It's enough to crack her.'

'I know you'll do a good, diplomatic job,' George said. He could see by the way his mother was biting her lower lip that she wasn't far off tears. 'Now, don't go worrying about me. I'm a grown man.'

She shook her head and half smiled. 'Not to me you aren't,' she said, then, taking a step closer to him, she patted his cheek. 'But you are a brave, gallant one, and that makes me proud.'

It was around eleven thirty when George rode out of Sawbridge, and within the hour he was riding over Salisbury Plain, towards the south coast. It was no hardship to him to go such a long way on his bike. Under happier circumstances, he'd have loved it, as he rarely got to ride long distances. Thankfully, the splattering of rain that had been falling when he set out stopped soon after he

312

bypassed Bath, and now the sun had come out.

'I'm on my way, Molly,' he murmured to himself. 'Just hang on, and don't do anything reckless.'

Molly had been busying herself from first light trying to find a long nail in one of the boxes. In over three hours she had only managed to gouge out three nails, and they were all short ones. But then she spotted one with a far larger head, which suggested it would be longer, and she worked and worked on it with the aid of one of the others.

It had rained quite hard in the night, and she'd stretched up and held out her shoe to try and collect some rainwater in it. She got about half a cupful, and nothing had ever tasted better, even if it was tainted with the smell of leather. Then the rain eased off to just drizzle and she couldn't hold her arm out long enough to collect more than a few drops.

But it was something: just that small amount of water had made her feel a bit better and, without it, she doubted she'd have been able to stick at trying to get the nails out.

Her fingers were sore now, and she had several splinters, but when she finally drew out the nail and found it was one and a half inches long, and thick, she felt triumphant.

Picking locks always looked simple in films, but it didn't turn out to be. She pushed the nail this way and that, but the mechanism didn't move. After an hour working at it she'd had enough; she was dizzy and she had cramps in her stomach. In a moment of frustration she shoved a thin,

313

wedged-shaped piece of wood from one of the boxes into the keyhole and banged it in with her shoe. To her surprise, she heard a dull click.

She couldn't really believe she'd somehow managed to unlock the door, and when she tried to turn the knob she fully expected it would stay put. But, to her delight, it turned. She'd got the door open!

Her instinct was to just rush out, but she forced herself to take some deep breaths, to put her shoe back on, despite it being wet, and to gather her thoughts.

It must be around midday. The two women were bound to be in the house and she had no idea of its layout, not even whether the front door would be on her right or her left. She knew that, in most houses, the cellar was reached via a door in the hall or the kitchen, and that that door was likely to be locked, too.

Peeping through the open door, she found that there was some light in the cellar corridor because the other three rooms down there all had their doors open. The one opposite had a small, barred window like the one in the room she was being held in. When she crept out, she saw that the remaining two rooms were much the same, one a small store room for preserves. It was very tempting to grab a jar of plums or gooseberries to eat, but getting out was her priority.

The other two rooms held nothing but a few sticks of old furniture, and she passed on quickly to the stone staircase at the end of the corridor. She crept up it and paused to listen before trying the door.

To her right there was the sound of running water and a clattering of dishes, so she guessed that it had to be the kitchen and that someone, or perhaps both women, was in there.

That meant the front door would be to her left. But, as country people rarely used their front door and normally locked and bolted it, she didn't think she should rely on that door. Even supposing the keys had been left in it, it might be swollen through lack of use and she could waste valuable time trying to get it open.

She continued to listen carefully and, just as she was almost giving up on hearing anyone speak, Miss Gribble did. She said something about needing to use up the stew.

Christabel responded, 'She won't eat that.'

'If she doesn't, she can go hungry,' Miss Gribble said sharply.

Molly was crouching down on the stairs, her ear to the keyhole. She was so hungry she felt she would eat a boiled cat if it were offered to her, but the conversation she'd just over-heard made her forget her hunger: it was evidence to her that Petal was not just alive but in this house.

She forced herself to stay still and think about it. They might not be talking about Petal, of course; the person who wouldn't eat the stew could be a friend or a relative. She mustn't go charging about half cocked. She needed a plan.

Yet the thought that little Petal could be alive and in this very house made her pulse race.

If she could get through this door, there was a strong possibility she could get clear away, as she could probably run a lot faster than the two older women. At least, she could have done before she had been starved for a couple of days.

But it wouldn't be easy to escape with Petal, if she was there. First she had to find her and then, somehow, they'd have to get out without being spotted. The two women weren't going to give up without a desperate fight: they must know that there would be a long prison sentence for them if Molly managed to get out and fetch the police. She'd already been on the receiving end of one blow to the head, so she could testify to Miss Gribble's strength.

So the choice was either to flee on her own and get help or to find Petal and, with her, take a chance on outrunning and outwitting the two women.

The first seemed the more practical option, but if the women found out she'd gone they might take Petal and flee. They knew the marshes well and could probably remain hidden for a long time, but what would happen to Petal in that time?

Cassie's heart told her that she had to find Petal and leave with her. If she was in this house, she'd been through enough. She deserved to be rescued by someone who loved her.

Gingerly, Molly turned the door knob, not for one moment thinking it would just open. But, to her shock, it did. Presumably, the two women had forgotten to lock it, or maybe they'd thought that, if she wasn't already dead, she had no chance of getting out of the cellar room.

'Well, I've got news for you two,' she murmured to herself, opening the door just a crack. She could see she was in the hall: it had gloomy, dark, varnished wainscoting with dark-green wallpaper above it. Opposite the cellar door was a mahogany demilune table with a huge, hideous brass eagle perched on a fake log.

She could only see the kitchen doorway and about a foot into the room, but she could hear both women. It sounded as if one of them was chopping something on the table and the other was walking about. Molly opened the door a bit wider, and now she could see it was Miss Gribble chopping vegetables at the table and Christabel pacing around.

Then she had to pull the door almost shut, because if either of them looked her way they would see it was open.

'Oh Christabel, do stop stalking around like that!' Miss Gribble snapped. 'I don't know what's got into you today.'

'She won't talk to me. She cowers away from me,' Christabel burst out.

'I told you right at the start that a child of that age remembers too much about her mother,' Miss Gribble said impatiently. 'Anyway, I think she's half-witted.'

Molly seethed at that insult. It was all she could do not to charge into the kitchen and lay into both women.

'Come into the garden with me. It's lovely out there today, and I'll push you on the swing. That always calms you down,' Miss Gribble said.

At that, Molly's eyes widened in shock. They had stolen a child and one was suggesting she pushed the other on a swing to calm her down! Were they both completely mad?

317

But, mad or not, it was the opportunity Molly had been waiting for. She listened to the women's footsteps receding and opened the cellar door far enough to see the women go out the back door and into the garden.

She came out into the hall, shut the cellar door behind her and turned right towards the front of the house and the staircase, which she expected to be facing the front door. It was, in a central position, with a further two closed doors to the right and left of it across the hall. The staircase was polished dark oak, large and imposing, with a narrow, almost threadbare carpet runner on the treads fixed in place by brass stair rods.

Molly went up the stairs like the wind, not stopping at the bedrooms on the first floor, because she guessed they'd put Petal in an attic room.

The narrow staircase leading to the attic was bare wood, and food and drink had been slopped on it. A glance out of a back window revealed Christabel sitting on a swing hung on a big oak tree, and Miss Gribble pushing her.

As fast as she could, Molly ran up the last few stairs. 'Petal!' she called.

There were four doors up here, but she expected Petal would be in one of the two back rooms. She heard a scuffle, little more noise than a mouse would make, from the second of those rooms. The door was locked and there was no key.

'Petal,' she whispered at the door. 'It's Auntie Molly come to get you. This door is locked and I need to break it down. Stand away from it.'

The only reply was a little whimper.

Molly didn't even stop to think of what injury

318

she might do to herself but took a few steps back and then charged into the top door panel with her shoulder. It cracked, and so she did it again. This time it caved right in, and there was little Petal standing there, eyes swollen with crying, thin and very dirty, in a smocked dress which was several sizes too big for her and almost reached the floor.

She looked dazed and unbelievingly at Molly.

'You'll have to jump up and wriggle through this hole,' Molly told her. 'Come on, be quick! They're out in the garden, but they might have heard me break the door.'

Petal came through the hole as quickly and smoothly as a cat and threw herself into Molly's arms, her arms tightly around her rescuer's neck.

'We'll talk later,' Molly whispered, kissing the child's head and trying not to cry with joy at finding her alive. 'For now we've got to be fast and silent. Can you do that?'

Petal nodded, perhaps too overcome by shock to speak.

Molly picked Petal up to hold her on her hip and crept down the staircase. She could see the front door was, as she had expected, locked and bolted. The chances were she'd be struggling with it for too long and they'd be caught.

When she'd glanced out at the garden, she'd seen that the swing was about twenty-five yards from the kitchen door and, if she remembered rightly, there were bushes between them which would shield her and Petal from view. She hoped they'd have enough time to run round the house, down the drive and away.

They had just reached the hall when, to her horror, Miss Gribble appeared. Molly's blood ran cold, because she had a long poker in her hands and, judging by the ferocious look on her face, she'd heard the door being broken and had every intention of using her weapon.

Molly shook with fear. There was no doubt in her mind that this woman would think nothing of killing both her and Petal. She jabbed out with the poker at Molly, and Petal squealed and clung more tightly to her.

'I should have dealt with you when you first got here, but I will now, and that brat!' the woman snarled at her. She had big, yellow teeth like a savage animal.

'Please let us go,' Molly said. She knew that nothing she said would make any difference, but she hoped the woman would think she was docile and stupid enough to allow her to prod them down the hall and back towards the cellar.

The big brass eagle would make a good weapon if Molly could reach it and, even if Christabel appeared, Molly had the idea she was a bit thick, so Petal could probably run past her. 'I told loads of people I was coming here, so the police will be here before long,' she said, playing for time. 'But if you let us go now, I'll tell everyone I found Petal out on the road.'

'Save your breath. You won't have it for long!' the woman roared at her. It was as if she was possessed: her eyes were rolling and she had spittle coming out of her mouth. She was lifting the poker up above her head ready to whack Molly with it.

Molly put her lips close to Petal's ear. 'Run when I put you down. Get help,' she whispered.

Petal made a little grunt, which appeared to indicate that she'd understood, and as Molly jumped to one side as the poker came down to hit her, she let Petal drop to the floor.

The poker whistled past Molly's shoulder by a whisker, but Miss Gribble was undeterred and lifted it again, at the same time pulling open the cellar door with her other hand.

'Get in there!' the madwoman shrieked, prodding out with the poker.

'Please, please, not in there again!' Molly screamed out. 'It's dark, there's spiders and rats.'

Petal was clinging to her side, and Molly couldn't tell her to go without revealing her hysteria to be an act. 'Please, please, I can't bear it!' she yelled, and she grabbed hold of the demilune table as if to prevent herself being hauled back into the cellar.

Petal suddenly took off like a jack rabbit, through the kitchen and out the back door. Miss Gribble lifted the poker, but hesitated, as if unsure whether to catch the child or deal with Molly. In that instant Molly picked up the brass eagle, which weighed a ton, and flung it at the woman's face.

It had the most dramatic effect. There was a crack, Miss Gribble's nose splattered like a squashed tomato and she slid down the wall behind her like a drunk on a Saturday night.

Molly gave her only the briefest glance then ran for the back door. But, as she stepped over the threshold, she saw Christabel standing there, and in her hands was an axe.

Chapter Eighteen

George reached Hastings just on four. He was stiff from the long ride and it seemed hours since he had drunk the last of the tea in his flask. He stopped on the seafront to look at his map, and was pleased to see that Brookland was only about another half an hour away.

His mind had been on Molly constantly the whole ride. He kept on remembering little incidents, like when they were about six and he fell over and cut his knee badly while they were out playing. She had washed the cut in a stream and tied the belt of her dress round it like a bandage. Always the nurse and the comforter.

She had often tried to get him to play Mummies and Daddies, too, and he remembered how she'd told him off for not coming in and asking, 'Why isn't my dinner on the table?' Of course he hadn't realized then that her father was so difficult and demanding, not like his own, an easy-going, kind-hearted man who always had time for his kids.

Later, when he did know what a tyrant Mr Heywood was, he asked his mother if Molly could come and live with them.

'I'd have her like a shot. She's a lovely girl,' his mother had replied. 'But you can't take children away from their parents just because they are grumpy and sour. I only hope that, when you have children of your own, you'll be like your father with them, and not like that pig.'

His mother said she had gone out of her way to befriend Mary Heywood when she and her family had first arrived in the village. She said that Mary had been a sweet, kind woman, but even then she had become like a little mouse when Jack was around. Yet Mary had made good friends in Sawbridge: they watched over her and popped round to see her when they knew Jack wouldn't be there. Everyone said what a kind heart she had; she'd slipped many a customer a few extra slices of bacon or a few ounces of cheese when she knew they were having a hard time. She passed on the girls' clothes when they outgrew them to those who were struggling, and there was hardly a new mother in the village that hadn't had a lovely hand-knitted pram set from her.

Since Molly had gone off to London, some people had told George that Mary seemed distant and withdrawn, but he hadn't found this himself, and he'd gone in to see her often to check. He felt that she was happier now than she'd been for a long time, going off to Mothers' Union meetings or popping in to see friends.

She had told him herself that she didn't want Molly to come home. 'She needs to make her own way in life and not worry about me,' she said. 'Besides, Jack is a bit better since she's been gone. So you can stop checking up on me!'

He hadn't stopped, of course; he just made out he was coming to the shop to buy something.

Brookland was easy enough to find, as the marsh was as flat as a pancake and the old church, with

its strange, wooden three-part tower, which reminded him of a child's stacking toy, stood out like
a beacon. He asked a man out walking his dog if
he knew where Mrs Coleman and her housekeeper lived.

'They won't open the door to you,' the man
said. 'Completely cuckoo, both of them.'

'Are they now?' George said. 'Well, I'm with
the police, so they'll have to open up for me.'

The dog walker shrugged and gave him directions to Mulberry House. It turned out George
had already driven past the house, so he turned
his bike round and set back off. He hadn't gone
far when a little girl darted out of a side lane and
ran towards him, waving her arms.

He slowed right down, as it was quite clear she
was in great distress, and as he got closer, to his
shock, he realized it was Petal.

He pulled up and jumped off his bike.

'Petal, sweetheart,' he said. 'I'm George, the
policeman from back home in Sawbridge. I came
to find you and Molly.'

'She's in there!' The child waved her hand towards the high stone wall beside the road. 'She
came and got me, she told me to run for help, but
the nasty lady has got her now.'

George took in the neglected dirty state of the
girl, the long, far too large dress, and no shoes.
However much he wanted to go straight to Molly's
aid, he couldn't leave the child here unprotected.

'Jump on behind me and hold on tight,' he said,
getting back on his bike. 'There's a shop along
here. I'll take you there and get them to phone
for more police. Can you be a brave girl for a

little bit longer?'

She nodded and climbed silently up behind him. He looked down at her thin, brown arms clasped around his waist and felt a lump rising in his throat.

It took only a couple of minutes for him to flash his warrant card at the stunned shopkeeper and to ask him to phone 999 and explain that PC George Walsh had left a missing child called Petal with him while he returned to Mulberry House. He told the shopkeeper to tell them he was assisting Molly Heywood, who was being held captive there. An ambulance might be needed, too.

George roared back to the house, left his motorbike by the gate and ran around to the back door.

There, on a paved area by the back door, he found Molly lying in a pool of blood and a wailing woman crouched a little way off with her head on her knees and an axe lying beside her.

Kneeling beside Molly, he found that she had a pulse but it was very faint. The blood was coming from a wound on the top of her head. He couldn't tell how deep it was because of her hair.

'You're safe now, Molly,' he said to her, even though she was unconscious. 'It's George, and I've got Petal safe and sound, too, and I'll have you in hospital in no time.'

As he waited for assistance, he heard a sound from inside the house. He went in to see what it was and found another woman slumped on the floor. She was older than the first one, and her face was a bloody mess where she'd been hit. She was conscious, but appeared to have taken leave of her senses. She was just making a keening sound and didn't respond when he asked her name.

The woman outside didn't appear to have any injuries, but she was still just crouching there, rocking herself to and fro. He removed the axe, just in case she thought of using it again. He guessed that Molly had thrown the big eagle thing he'd seen on the floor in the hall at the other, older woman to escape, and that this younger one had hit her as she came through the kitchen door.

It seemed to take for ever for the emergency services to arrive, and he sat at Molly's side, urging her to hold on until help came. Looking at what he could see of the house and thinking of the unbalanced state of the two women who lived here, he felt sick to think that Petal had been kept here for months, and he was astounded that no one had reported seeing her.

But, above everything else, above even his anxiety for Molly and Petal and the need to get the two older women into custody, he felt so proud of Molly. She had said she was going to find Petal, and she had. She'd stuck at it like a dog with a bone, even coming to work down here because she had what he thought was a crazy idea that Cassie had lived here. How wrong was he? It was Molly who should become a detective.

Then, all at once, he heard the clanging of an ambulance bell and a police siren.

'That's it now, Molly,' he said to her. 'You'll be in hospital in no time and I'm not leaving you.'

George sensed the detective inspector's hostility even before he opened his mouth to speak. He was middle-aged with a military-style moustache and had introduced himself as DI Pople.

'We got the message about this from Somerset. So why did you feel it was necessary to come?'

George gritted his teeth at the man's arrogance and stupidity.

The ambulance men were getting Molly into the ambulance now and George was ready to follow it on his motorbike. He'd already asked them to pick up Petal as they went past the shop.

'It was as well I did, or she might have been dead before you got here. But you must excuse me, I'm going with her and Petal.'

'You are not. You will come back with me to fill me in on the background,' DI Pople said briskly. Two other police cars had arrived. The younger woman had been handcuffed and led to one of them, and two policemen were trying to get some sense out of the older, injured woman while waiting for a second ambulance to arrive.

'Sorry, sir, but my duty is to my friend, who is badly hurt, and to the little girl she risked her life to save from these two madwomen,' George said. 'I'll contact you as soon as I know Molly is going to make it.'

It was midnight before George was finally assured that Molly was out of the woods.

The doctor at Hastings Hospital who came to tell him was elderly but had bright-blue eyes and a warm smile. 'She'll be having a few headaches for a while and she's not going to be amused by how much hair we had to cut away to stitch her scalp, but she'll be fine after a nice long sleep.

She became unconscious not just because of the head wound but through severe dehydration and lack of food. The poor girl must have been through a terrible ordeal.'

'And Petal?'

'She isn't speaking at all, but that isn't unusual for a child after a long and frightening experience, but apparently she wolfed down scrambled eggs and three glasses of milk after she'd had a bath and then threw a tantrum until we let her go in with Miss Heywood.'

'You've let her stay with Molly?' George asked.

'Of course. After what she's been through, the best place for her is close to someone she trusts. As I understand it, she owes her life to Miss Heywood, so we've put a little bed in her room for Petal.'

'But how is she physically?' George asked.

The doctor frowned. 'She's severely undernourished – her weight's more appropriate for a four-year-old – she has a rash, possibly an allergy to something she was given in that house, and bruises, which suggest rough handling. But I'm confident that with more food, a good night's sleep and some loving care, by tomorrow, when she wakes up beside Miss Heywood, she'll start to open up. Now, where are you staying, young man? I believe you rode up from Somerset on a motorbike?'

'That's right, sir,' George said. 'I've been offered a bed for the night at the hotel where Molly works in Rye. Mr and Mrs Bridgenorth are frantic about her, so I'd better get off there now and give them the good news. But I'll be back tomorrow. When are visiting hours?'

'For you, anytime. She's in a private room, of course. That makes it easier for Petal to be in there, too.'

'I suppose Petal will have to go into care?' George asked, his eyes prickled at the memory of those little arms around him earlier in the day. 'She calls Molly "Auntie" but she isn't a real aunt unfortunately, just her mother's closest friend.'

'Let's not worry about anything just now. First, both of them need to get over their ordeal. You've been something of a hero today, too, and I'm sure you are exhausted. I'll see you tomorrow.'

George spent the night in Molly's bed at the hotel.

He was exhausted, but he forced himself to stay awake long enough to savour the smell of her on the sheets, to note the tidiness and the feminine touches that were so much part of what he loved about her.

Before he came to bed he had told Mr and Mrs Bridgenorth all he knew, and Mr Bridgenorth had told him that he was going to drive up to find Charley the next morning, as he needed to be told what had happened.

It was a real blow to hear that Molly had a boyfriend and that she hadn't told him. But, to save face, he pretended he had known and nodded as Mr Bridgenorth spoke of him.

'We kept hoping he'd ring,' Mrs Bridgenorth said. 'We did send him a telegram. Clearly, he isn't at his home or he would have responded.'

George went straight to Rye police station as soon as he'd eaten his breakfast. DI Pople hadn't come in yet, but Sergeant Wayfield, a tall, thin man with a face like a bloodhound, was there to take his statement.

'There isn't much to it, really,' said George to the sergeant. 'I was on my way to Mulberry House when Petal ran out of the lane in distress.' He went on to explain the rest, ending up with him following Molly's ambulance to Hastings Hospital.

'So how did Miss Heywood discover the child was being held at Mulberry House? And why didn't she speak to us before she went off there?'

George went further back in the story to when Molly had found Petal's mother dead and the child missing last June. 'She felt the police didn't do enough,' he explained. 'And I have to agree it looked that way. Anyway, Molly got it into her head that she was going to find Petal, and she didn't divulge the small pieces of evidence she found to anyone, not even me. As far as I know, a Church Army lady who Molly had stayed with in London helped her get the job at the George, but it looks to me as if Molly must have already discovered that Cassie came from somewhere round here.

'Anyway, a couple of days before Molly disappeared she wrote to me. She said she thought she'd tracked down Cassie's mother, someone called Christabel Coleman, who had a daughter called Sylvia, who was the same age as Cassie, and it was rumoured she'd had a black baby. She said she was going there in the morning to see her.'

'And how did you discover that Miss Heywood

had gone missing?'

'Mrs Bridgenorth phoned me; she found my number in Molly's address book. She said that no one here at the nick had taken her seriously when she reported that Miss Heywood hadn't come home, so I think she rang me in desperation. As I was on leave I came straight away, asking my mother to inform you.'

'I sense an implication that you didn't trust us to act immediately?'

George looked the sergeant in the eye. 'Wouldn't you have done the same if you were in my shoes?'

The sergeant scratched his head, but didn't answer the question. 'Well, it was very high-handed of you. You might have made the situation very much worse, or put yourself in danger. Thankfully, Miss Heywood was very resourceful. We found the cellar room she was kept in, and the child had been imprisoned in an attic room.'

'All the time?' George asked, horrified at the thought.

'We can't be sure one way or the other until she's ready to talk, or one of the women does. There's an old doctor's surgery in the house, full of drugs and medicines, so it's possible they gave the child something to keep her quiet. We found a pair of baby reins in the room, too, so we think they used them to walk her around the garden sometimes. She was fed sporadically but, judging by her weight, not nearly enough. As for bathing her or washing her hair, that appears not to have been done for some weeks.'

'But that woman is her grandmother!' George said angrily. 'How could she treat a child that

331

way? And just how long was she intending to keep her like that?'

The sergeant shook his head. 'Mrs Coleman was taken straight to an asylum. She'll be seen by a psychiatrist and, in due course, we might have a better idea of what her intentions were. Miss Gribble may give us some answers; she is, by all accounts, devoted to Mrs Coleman. She's something of a dragon but, it appears, not insane. Her injuries are superficial and later today she'll be taken to Holloway Prison, where she'll be held on remand while we ascertain the full extent of her crimes.'

'Then, if I may, I'll be off to see Molly and Petal. I'll be staying another night in Rye. I'll be at the George if you need me.'

'Before you go, do you have an address for the Church Army lady? We might need to contact her as a character witness.'

'She died back in winter,' George said. 'Just as Molly got the job here. If you need a character witness there are dozens of people back in Sawbridge who'd be happy to tell you what a good, honest person Molly is.'

'Well, thanks for the statement,' said Sergeant Wayfield. 'Please pass on to Miss Heywood that we're all hoping she'll get well soon.'

'I'll thank her for doing your job for her, too, shall I?' George asked, unable to resist making a jibe.

Wayfield looked him up and down, his mouth bent into a sneer. 'If she'd come in here with that photo and explained to us that she felt the girl's mother lived near here, we would have checked it out. As it happens, we've already found the child's birth registration, and her name wasn't Petal March but Pamela Coleman. It was a home birth and the father's name is marked as unknown, as the mother wasn't married.'

George decided to quit while he was ahead, and said goodbye. The police here seemed to be annoyed with him for muscling in on their territory. It didn't seem to have occurred to them that, if he hadn't acted as he did, Molly and Petal might be dead now.

Chapter Nineteen

Ted Bridgenorth arrived at Charley Sanderson's address in Bethnal Green and winced when he saw how squalid it was. It was a shabby, three-storey terraced house in a row of eight equally run-down ones. The other side of the street had fared even worse for, though the bomb sites between some of the houses had been cleared of rubble, weeds had taken over, and only partially covered the piles of dumped rubbish.

As it was a pleasant day a great many people were sitting out by their front doors on boxes or chairs, and dozens of children were playing in the street. A gang of children had surrounded the car as he drove into the street and, though they appeared to be admiring it, Ted wished he'd come on a school day instead of a Saturday, as they might just let his tyres down while he was talking to Charley.

He rapped on the door of number twelve.

'There's no one in. Who you after?' a strident female voice called out from the street.

'Charley Sanderson,' he called back. 'Do you know him?'

'Well, I do 'is washing, so I 'ope I do.' A woman with red hair broke away from a group of other women and came towards him. She was in her twenties, an attractive, shapely woman with a look of Rita Hayworth.

'Are you his girlfriend?' Ted asked. He really hoped Charley hadn't been playing fast and loose with other women, but he wasn't the kind to tell tales or to cause trouble for another man.

'No fear,' she laughed.

'Well, that's good, as I came to tell him that Molly's in hospital. I sent him a telegram, but I think he must've been away as he didn't get back to me. Do you know how I can get hold of him?'

She moved in much closer to him. 'Is it an emergency?' she whispered.

'Well, yes, something really nasty has happened to Molly, and she needs him.' Ted thought the woman was being a bit odd, but then he wasn't used to London girls of her class.

'Then you'd better go round and knock him up at Balaclava Street,' she said. ''E'll be at number five, it's only a couple of streets away. 'E'll be with 'is mate Alan.'

She gave him directions and, as he was getting back in the car, she leaned forward to speak to him through the window. 'Is Molly 'is sister?'

'No, his girlfriend,' Ted replied.

To his surprise, the woman spluttered with laughter.

Ted drove off, a little puzzled by the woman's attitude, but found Balaclava Street easily. It was almost identical to the first street he'd been to, and equally squalid, except that the houses here were only two storeys.

He rapped at the door of number five and was just about to rap again when the door was opened by a very attractive young blond man wearing a pair of trousers but with his chest and feet bare.

'What can I do for you?' the young man said.

Ted was taken aback by his effeminate manner, and the way he spoke. If this was Alan, he understood why the red-haired woman had laughed. 'Are you Alan?' he asked.

'Yes, who wants to know?'

'I was told that Charley Sanderson is your friend. Is he here?' Ted asked. 'I have a message for him.'

'Charley!' Alan yelled, still looking at Ted. 'Someone to see you.'

Ted heard someone's feet coming down the stairs. When the man got to the hall he was buttoning up his shirt. His feet were bare, too.

'I sent you a telegram,' Ted said hesitantly, so shocked he wanted to drive off in his car. 'You didn't reply.'

Charley looked puzzled for a moment, and then suddenly apprehensive. 'Oh, couldn't place you for a moment,' he said, then flashed that wide smile of his. 'It's Mr Bridgenorth, from the George in Rye. I haven't been home, so I haven't seen a telegram. Don't tell me something has happened to Molly?'

'It has, I'm afraid.' Ted hastily told him the bare bones of it. 'We heard this morning she was going to be all right, but I'm sure she'd appreciate a letter, a phone call or visit from you.'

Charley's eyes were wide with shock. 'Of course! I'm just sorry I didn't get the telegram. I would've come straight away. What a terrible business!'

The young, blond man was standing just back from Charley, his anxiety showing clearly in his face. Ted had met other homosexuals since he'd been in the hotel trade and didn't have a particularly strong view on homosexuality. His attitude was, each to his own, as long as no one wanted to try anything on with him.

But this was totally different. Both he and his wife had got the distinct impression that Molly and Charley loved each other. Molly would be destroyed if she knew he preferred men to women.

'I must go now,' Ted said, unable to get away fast enough. 'It's busy at the hotel, and my wife and I had planned to visit Molly this afternoon.'

He saw Charley glance over at Alan. He couldn't have looked guiltier if he'd been caught in the act.

As Ted got into his car Charley shot over to him and leaned in at the window, just as the red-headed woman had.

'I know what you are thinking, but it's not like that,' he said.

'Oh, really?' Ted raised a questioning eyebrow. 'Do you think I was born yesterday?'

Charley turned scarlet. 'Alan and I are just

336

friends, nothing more,' he insisted in a shrill voice. 'I love Molly and want to marry her.'

'I don't doubt you care for her, as my wife and I do, too,' Ted said. 'But I saw for myself how it was between you and Alan, and marrying a woman you have no physical desire for is doomed from the start.'

'You don't know how it is with Molly and me,' Charley said belligerently. 'I ought to knock your block off for suggesting I'm homosexual.'

'Charley, stop right there,' Ted said firmly. 'I know, and you know, so there's no point denying anything. I don't give a damn about your preferences, but I do care about Molly. So you've got to be fair to her and let her down gently.'

He didn't stop for a reply but drove away quickly, feeling faintly sick. It wasn't about Charley's persuasion – the man couldn't help that – but only that he was trying to cover his tracks and avoid the risk of being prosecuted by being seen to be a happily married man. Such a marriage would be a disaster, especially for someone like Molly.

The question was, what should he do about it? Tell her, or keep quiet and hope Charley was man enough to do the right thing?

Evelyn was probably naïve enough to imagine that a good marriage would 'cure' Charley, but Ted knew that couldn't happen. In the days when he was an accountant he'd had two clients who had married, perhaps even fooling themselves they'd be cured. But neither of them was: one was caught by the police and went to prison; the other committed suicide in the end because he was so unhappy. He guessed that their two wives

337

had been through hell.

Any intelligent, humane person could see that the law against homosexuality ought to be abolished. But while it was still in place Ted felt that he must protect his employee. She was worth far more than a cowardly man who wanted to hide his dark secret behind a flimsy veil of marriage.

The irony of it was that Molly already had a man who loved her truly, someone she'd grown up with and knew all about and was ideal for her. Ted felt sure she could love him, too, if he would just make his feelings known.

'Over to you, George,' he said aloud. 'Over to you.'

On Sunday afternoon Molly remarked to the nurse that she was feeling almost like her old self again. Food, drink and lots of sleep had restored her spirits and, even though her head hurt where she'd been hit and probably would for some time, even after the stitches came out, it wasn't too dreadful. 'I could almost convince myself I imagined the whole thing. Well, that is, until I look in a mirror and see my bald patch.'

The nurse laughed. 'And there's this little one to remind you,' she said, nodding towards Petal, who was snuggled up on a small bed beside her.

Molly smiled. Petal looked so adorable in a pair of red pyjamas someone had donated, and clutching a teddy bear Evelyn and Ted had bought her.

'It's a funny thing,' Molly said. 'Once you aren't really hungry any more, you can't quite remember what it was like.'

'I believe childbirth is much the same,' the

338

nurse joked. 'I'd avoid that one if I were you. It might make you remember being hungry, too.'

Molly laughed. She felt she had a dozen reasons to be joyful. She'd finally found Petal, she had Charley, and a job she loved with people who clearly cared about her. Mrs Bridgenorth had left a message at Warwickshire House for Dilys to contact her, and her friend had rung last night just before the Bridgenorths came to visit her. Dilys had sent her love and said she would come down to Rye on Wednesday, her day off. Molly had also had a telegram from her parents, and she was inclined to believe her father was as worried about her as her mother was.

Petal wasn't right, of course. What child could be after such a terrible, long ordeal? She didn't sleep calmly, she woke frequently with bad dreams and was fearful when anyone new came into the room. Sometimes she sat staring into space, and who knew where her mind was going to.

But she was talking to Molly, even if she wasn't to anybody else, and she'd told her about the car ride from Sawbridge to Brookland. She said Christabel kept talking about someone called Sylvia who was going to come and join them very soon, and that they were all going to the house she'd lived in when she was a little girl.

'But she told me lies,' Petal said indignantly. 'Sylvia was what she called my mummy, and she said Sylvia was going to join us. Miss Gribble told me the truth in the end, she said Mummy was dead because she'd got a bang on the head. She said if I didn't do what she told me, she'd kill me, too. They gave me horrible food, and when I couldn't eat it Miss Gribble brought it back the next day when it was cold and made me eat it or have it again the next day when it had gone off. She said I was a spoiled brat and she was going to teach me how nice girls behaved, and if I didn't learn she would beat me.'

Molly felt sick to think that Petal's hideous ordeal hadn't been just for a few days but for months. She could imagine, too, the struggles Petal had had with that fearsome woman. She must have felt totally abandoned, locked up in that attic room, scared out of her wits whenever she heard a footstep on the stairs.

Luckily, she hadn't seen what had happened in Stone Cottage, as she'd been out in the car. But Petal cried when she told Molly about how the two women had tricked her into thinking they were taking her to the Coronation party but just kept on driving.

'She slapped me really hard, too,' Petal sobbed out. 'Just for saying I wanted Mummy. I didn't know why she was being so mean to me, or where they were taking me. It was so scary.'

Petal didn't know how they'd found her and her mother, or why they'd taken her away with them. She said that Christabel and her were out in the car while Miss Gribble was talking to Cassie, and they stayed there until Miss Gribble came out and then drove away. It was a blessing she hadn't seen her mother lying there by the hearth with her head caved in. That was something even an adult would struggle to get over.

An examination of Petal when she was admitted to the hospital showed numerous bruises on her small body, proof of many cruel attacks on her since the women had got her into Mulberry House. She said Miss Gribble took her out into the garden most days, but always on a pair of baby walking reins or, latterly, with a rope around her waist so she couldn't make a bolt for freedom. She said that the first couple of times she had screamed really loudly, trying to attract a passerby, but the beating she got for it put her off trying again.

The strangest thing was that Petal had seen very little of Christabel, in fact so little that Petal had the idea that 'the younger lady', as she called her, was locked up like her, and felt sympathy for her. It was quite clear that, although Christabel had gone along with keeping Petal at Mulberry House, she hadn't had a hand in any of the cruelty.

Molly wasn't sure that any child, however strong and determined, could go through all that and remain normal. But, for now, Petal derived comfort from getting into bed with her and listening to stories.

What would happen next was anyone's guess. Molly had already been told in no uncertain manner by a social worker from the Children's Department that they would make the decisions on her future. Molly didn't think they were going to think it important that Petal stayed in close contact with her mother's friend. She wondered, too, if anyone would care enough to try to rebuild Petal into the happy, well-adjusted child she'd been before all this? Just thinking about that made her so sad.

Molly was lying back against the pillow day-dreaming that she and Charley would be allowed to adopt Petal once they were married when the ward door suddenly opened, and there he was. He looked very smart in a dark-grey suit and striped tie.

Molly was unable to hold back her tears.

'I'm sorry,' she said, wiping her eyes. 'It's just that it was only thinking about you that kept me going while they had me locked up. And I was afraid I'd never see you again.'

She expected him to embrace her, to tell her that no one was ever going to frighten her like that again, but he didn't, he just stood at the side of the bed with his arms against his sides looking awkward, distant and embarrassed.

'You didn't think there was something funny about George coming to rescue me, did you?' she asked, thinking that might be why he was being so chilly. 'I've known him since I was five, and I only wrote to him about getting a lead on Cassie's family because he worked on the case when she was killed and Petal disappeared.'

'Why would I think there was something funny about you keeping in touch with him?' he asked, but his eyes seemed cold and he didn't flash that brilliant smile of his.

'Well, you don't seem your usual self,' she said. 'But then, I'm not exactly my old self either, what with the bald patch and Petal being tucked in here with me. Say hullo to Uncle Charley,' she said to the child, who was sitting on the end of her bed doing some colouring.

'I'm not her uncle,' he said.

342

'Well, I'm not her aunt either, really, but I hope she'll always think of us that way and come to stay with us when we get married.'

Charley didn't respond, and the brooding silence was as startling as a cold shower.

Molly couldn't think of any reason why he should be like this and she was cut to the quick.

'Why don't you go out the door, turn round and come in again as the Charley I know,' she said, hoping that would break the ice.

'I don't think I can do that now,' he said.

'What, go out and come in again?'

'No, I mean, get married,' he said. 'I said it without thinking it through. It was a bad idea. I have to work away too much to settle down.'

'But you said you were going to get work in Ashford or Hastings,' Molly said in puzzlement.

'Yes, I know. I didn't think that through either. It wouldn't work.'

She looked hard at him. It crossed her mind that he couldn't be the kind, lovable Charley she knew but an imposter who looked like him. Her Charley would've swept her into his arms, wanted to know every last detail about what she'd been through. He certainly wouldn't be telling her he'd had second thoughts about their future.

'Are you trying to tell me it's over?' she asked, though she didn't believe he could be.

His eyes wouldn't meet hers, his mouth was set in a straight line and, all at once, she realized that was exactly what he'd been trying to say.

'Yes, I guess so,' he muttered, hanging his head. 'It's just too hard with you being down here and me in London.'

She wanted to cry, to tell him she loved him and he was making a big mistake. But she wasn't going to allow herself to do that. Firstly, it would upset Petal; she might even think it was her fault. Secondly, she had too much pride to beg.

'Just go now, Charley,' she said firmly. 'I thought we had something special. It seems I was wrong. Silly of me.'

'I'm sorry, Molly,' he said, and it came out like a whimper. 'I was never the man you thought I was. It's better this way.'

He left quickly then, and Molly lay back on the pillows and tried to smile at Petal. 'Men, eh!' she said. 'Looks like I had a lucky escape from that one.'

Petal moved up the bed and lay down beside Molly. 'You've still got Uncle George, and he's much nicer than that man.'

George came in later to say goodbye, as he was driving home in the morning.

'You've been crying!' he exclaimed, noting her puffy eyes. 'Is your head hurting?'

She *had* been crying. Petal had gone with a nurse to help with the tea trolley and, as soon as she had, Molly found she couldn't hold back her hurt and disappointment about Charley, and she cried buckets. 'No, my head is okay – sore, but not too bad. It's just Petal. I can't bear to think of her being put in a children's home.'

'Nor me,' he agreed. 'It's not right after what she's been through. Nice foster parents would be all right, though. I wondered if I could put out some feelers in Sawbridge when I get back. It will be in the papers tomorrow that she's been found, and people in the village will be very happy about that.'

Molly smiled weakly at him. He meant what he said. He always did. And he was right: foster parents in Sawbridge would be ideal. Petal would see her old friends and teachers again, and be accepted, too, which might not happen as readily elsewhere.

'I'll suggest it to the social worker,' she said. 'And pass on your telephone number to her.'

'Is that all that's upsetting you?' asked George then, picking up her hand and playing with her fingers. 'Did Charley come to visit?'

'I should have mentioned him in my letters,' she said, realizing that Ted and Evelyn Bridgenorth must have told him she had a boyfriend. She hoped they hadn't said it was a serious romance. 'I didn't say anything because I suspected it wouldn't last, and I was right. He just told me he made a mistake thinking we had a future together, he works away too much. Or maybe he just didn't like my bald patch. Anyway, it's over.'

He looked at her in puzzlement for a moment or two.

'I'm so sorry, Molly,' he said. 'You might not have said anything to me, but I got the idea from the Bridgenorths he was important to you. All I can say is that he's an idiot and doesn't know a real gem when he finds one.'

'I think I saw something in him that wasn't really there,' she said glumly. 'His timing is terrible, though. You'd think he'd have waited till I was out of hospital. He didn't even ask me anything about what happened at Mulberry House.'

George sat on the bed and scooped her into his arms, rocking her gently for a few moments. He smelled really lovely, of fresh air and some kind of perfumed soap. She didn't want the hug to end, even if it was making her feel weepy again.

'Come home for a few days and rest?' he suggested after a few minutes. 'My mum's offered to put you up, and you could see your mum, too. I rang her this morning to give her a progress report. She sent her love and said how much she wanted to see you.'

'That sounds lovely, but I'll have to talk to the Bridgenorths. It's coming up for their busy time.'

'I think you'll find they'll insist you have a break,' he said. 'They are very fond of you, Molly. They told me last night that you are the perfect employee – adaptable, good-natured, intuitive and totally reliable. They believe you could manage a hotel yourself with just a little more experience. Does that cheer you up?'

'You cheer me up, George,' she said, and kissed his cheek. 'You've been the best of friends.'

George turned to her, intending to kiss her on the lips, but Petal came running in just then and hurled herself at him, forcing him to turn away from Molly and pick the child up.

'I was telling the nurse I had a ride on your motorbike,' Petal said excitedly. 'Can I have another ride soon?'

Molly smiled. Petal appeared almost back to normal today, but of course her happy mood might end as suddenly as it had come. But it was good to see her trusting enough to perch on

George's lap. He had a way with children. In fact, now she thought about it, he had a way with everyone.

'I can't make any promises, because I've got to go home tomorrow and be a policeman again,' he said, stroking Petal's hair tenderly in a way that made Molly want to cry again. 'But I'm hoping I can take you for a ride very soon.'

When George left a little later, he bent over to kiss Molly on the lips, lingering just long enough for Molly to feel a little flutter inside her.

'Look after yourself and, if you want to come home for a holiday, just ring.'

'I never said how marvellous it was that you rode all that way to rescue me,' she said. 'Thank you so much.'

'You did very well just on your own.' He smiled. 'Picking locks, walloping Miss Gribble and getting Petal away from there. Just wait till I get back and tell the lads at the station.'

'I wish–' she broke off, afraid to say what had popped into her head.

'You wish what?' he asked.

'Wishes don't come true if you tell them. And you'd better get going before the nurse chases you out. Visiting time is over.'

He had only been gone ten minutes when a nurse came in and told her there was a telephone call for her in sister's office.

Molly hurried there, wondering if it would be her mother, but it was Evelyn Bridgenorth. 'I just wanted to tell you I've asked the Children's Department if Petal can stay with us until they find the right permanent home for her,' she said.

347

'And they agreed?' Molly asked, amazed her employer would be so kind.

'Well, they haven't actually signed on the dotted line, or whatever it is they do, but they've agreed in principle. They do realize she's likely to have a serious setback if she goes to a stranger, and although they pointed out that licensed premises are not the ideal choice of home, they feel the bond you have with her more than makes up for that.'

'That's the best news ever,' Molly gasped. 'But are you sure about this? It's a big commitment.'

'We were rather selfishly thinking you'd do most of the taking care of her,' Evelyn said, with laughter in her voice. 'Once the doctors feel she's fit enough, she'll go to the primary school, anyway. But it's mealtimes, after school and weekends that she'll need you. Obviously, we'll adjust your hotel duties to fit in. How does that sound?'

'Marvellous,' Molly said, suddenly feeling like whooping with joy. 'I was worried sick about where they would send her. She's going to be so happy. And so am I.'

'And she deserves to be. Of course, it won't be permanent, only till they feel she's stable and they've got the right foster parents for her.'

'Sister said earlier that there's a possibility they might discharge us both tomorrow. Will we know then for sure?'

'Yes, don't worry. Just ring the hotel if they say you can come home, and Ted will come and get you. You and I will need to pick out some clothes and toys for Petal. I'm looking forward to that.'

'I'm looking forward to being back at the George,' Molly said.

'Not half as much as we're looking forward to you coming back,' Evelyn said. 'All the staff and customers have been pestering us for news. You've become quite a celebrity.'

Chapter Twenty

'Miss Gribble!' DI Pople snapped at the woman on the other side of the desk. She had closed her eyes, as if to shut him out. 'You don't seem to appreciate how much trouble you are in. Murder, abduction, imprisoning and ill-treating a young child and assault and imprisoning an adult. You could hang for this. But, whatever you've done, I want to know the reasons for it. It's only by co-operating with me fully that there is any possibility that you will find some sympathy with a jury when this comes to trial.'

Her eyes opened. 'I never meant to kill anyone,' she said woodenly. 'I was trying to put things right.'

'I fail to see how any of your actions could be seen as an attempt to put things right,' DI Pople said. 'But maybe if you went back to the beginning, from the time of Petal's birth, and explained how things were then, when, presumably, your mistress, Mrs Coleman, was in full command of her senses, I could understand.'

Miss Gribble had been kept in hospital in a private room for a week after the police had arrested her at Mulberry House. Her facial injuries were not serious but she had lost consciousness and, as she suffered from angina, the doctors felt she should stay under observation, though with a police guard outside the room.

She had refused to say anything while in the hospital: no explanation, no denial, nothing. She wouldn't even speak to the nurses. On her discharge she was taken back to the police station and a solicitor was called for her, but she still refused to talk. Finally, she was charged with murder and abduction and taken to court, where she was remanded in custody.

Owing to the seriousness of her alleged crimes, she was being held in London's Holloway Prison, and this was DI Pople's third visit there to try to get her to talk. But today she seemed to be weakening just a little, enough to make him hopeful.

'As I understand it, you have been housekeeper, companion and friend to Christabel Coleman for over forty years,' DI Pople said, trying a different tack. 'I can understand that you formed a strong bond during that time. You were there when her father was killed in the Great War, you helped Christabel through her mother's death, the birth of Sylvia and, a few years later, when Mr Coleman, Christabel's husband, was reported missing, presumed killed in action in the last war, you remained at Mulberry House, still caring for her and protecting her. I would say that you were mother, father, sister and friend to Christabel. Am I right?'

'Yes. She means everything to me,' Miss Gribble replied, but she looked at the floor as if she wasn't in the habit of admitting such a thing.

'And you'd do anything for her?'

She nodded.

'You won't be able to help her at all if they hang you,' he said. 'She'll have to stay in the asylum, and no one will visit her. There'll be no one to care if they neglect, starve or hurt her.'

Miss Gribble's head shot up and, suddenly, there was fire in her eyes.

'She shouldn't be in there, she did nothing wrong. She won't last more than a few weeks without my care and attention.'

'Are you saying you acted alone in tracking down Sylvia? And in killing her and taking Petal? Are you trying to tell me that Christabel didn't know you were holding her granddaughter in an attic and being cruel to her? Is that what you're saying?'

The older woman clammed up. She was clearly bright enough to realize that, by insisting Christabel knew nothing of any of it, she would be admitting to having done it all herself.

'If the psychiatrist at the asylum finds Christabel fit to stand trial, she will be charged jointly with you for these crimes and, although you may escape the noose, you'll both spend the rest of your days in this prison. You'll be separated, too. You won't be able to protect or care for her here.'

Miss Gribble hugged her arms around her and rocked on the chair. She was a very plain, big-boned woman, and her white hair, scragged back in a bunch at the nape of her neck, only served to draw attention to her grey-tinged complexion. DI Pople had seen on her medical record that she was sixty-seven, but she looked strong and her arms were very muscular.

'What am I to do?' she bleated out, all her former belligerence gone. 'Christabel is innocent of any crime, she's just like a child. She trusted me to do whatever needed doing. Whatever you do to me, she will suffer more.'

'Tell me the truth about everything and then I can make sure she gets the help she needs,' DI Pople wheedled. 'Now tell me why Sylvia ran away with her baby, and how you managed to find her. It must have been hard, as she'd changed her name.'

'She left because I tried to curb her wildness.'

'Okay,' DI Pople said. He guessed this woman had put Sylvia through hell because she'd had an illegitimate mixed race baby. 'So what made you want to track her down again? Surely the problems you'd had with her when Petal was born would still be the same?'

'Christabel wanted to see her. I tried to make her see it wasn't a good idea, but she kept on and on, so in the end I agreed. I got a private detective to find her.'

'Did it take him long?'

Miss Gribble pulled a face. 'Yes, the man spun it out in order to take Christabel's money. His name is Frank Wilson; he was a retired policeman living in Ashford. He died just after he gave me his report. That was back in April 1953, so I expected Sylvia might have moved on from the address he'd given us. But we thought we'd go and see, anyway.'

'Did you drive?'

'Yes. Christabel can't. I learned after her husband went missing.'

'Any reason you chose Coronation Day?'

'Yes, I knew the roads would be quiet. But it was much further than I expected.'

'And the plan was? Just to see Sylvia and Petal, or to bring them back to Mulberry House with you?'

'To see them, maybe have a little holiday down that way. I didn't expect Sylvia to come back, she was always strong willed, even as a little girl. But Christabel was sure she would. All the way there she kept talking about redecorating Sylvia's room, and where the child would go to school. I kept warning her Sylvia wouldn't come, but she took no notice of me.'

'What time did you get to Sylvia's house?'

'Just on noon. We'd left at first light, because we were afraid we wouldn't find it. Mr Wilson had given us a map of where the cottage was. Good job he did; it wasn't easy to find.'

'So this man Wilson had been there himself?'

'He didn't say, but he must have done, as the map was hand drawn.'

'Okay, so you arrived at Stone Cottage. Now tell me exactly what you saw, and how Sylvia reacted to seeing you and Christabel. And then what happened.'

The woman just sat there, her eyes almost closed, and DI Pople thought she wasn't going to say anything further. He waited, trying hard not to snap at her again and remind her that he didn't have all day.

'It was pouring with rain,' she suddenly blurted out, her eyes still half closed, as if she'd gone back to that day and was about to relive it.

353

She and Christabel had been at the beginning of a steep, muddy track which ran down under overhanging bushes, giving it an almost tunnel effect. She was hesitating to drive down because of the mud.

'Can we be sure this is the right track, Gribby?' Christabel had asked. She had invented the affectionate nickname 'Gribby', when she was a child. Since she had grown up, in company she used 'Miss Gribble', or 'Maud', but when it was just the two of them it was always Gribby.

'Wilson said there was a milestone on the hill just by the track, and we saw that,' Gribby said.

'But what if we get stuck in the mud?'

Despite hesitating because of the mud, Miss Gribble was irritated by Christabel's question and began to drive down. 'We won't. Stop worrying,' she replied.

Christabel worried about everything. Whether she'd be too hot or too cold, if she should wear blue or green, that the car wouldn't start, that they'd get a puncture. She was incapable of doing anything, or going anywhere, without constant reassurance that everything would be fine.

Gribby had assured her early this morning that her blue print dress and toning cardigan would be perfect whether it was hot or cold, that she looked lovely in it, that the car would start and that, if they did get a puncture, Gribby would know what to do. She hadn't anticipated so much rain and mud, but she wasn't going to admit that.

'What a funny little place,' Christabel said as they came out of the overhanging bushes into a clearing and saw Stone Cottage nestling into the woods and the little garden, pretty with flowers. 'Rather picturesque, though. Fancy Sylvia planting flowers! She never used to be interested in the garden.'

Gribby turned the car around, leaving it in a stony area so they wouldn't get stuck. She wanted to get this visit over and done with as quickly as possible, to let Christabel see that Sylvia was coping with the child, that she was happy living here, and then they could go.

As they got out of the car, both putting up umbrellas, the side door on the cottage opened and Sylvia stood there in the doorway.

She looked startlingly different. Her blonde hair was dyed red, and they'd interrupted her styling it, as one side of her face was framed with curls, the other side still a mass of silver curlers. She was wearing a simple floral dress and her feet were bare. Six years had added maturity to her face, a confidence that was apparent even before she spoke.

'What brings you here?' she called out. 'If it's trouble, then get back in the car and go.'

'Oh, Sylvia, don't be so hostile!' Christabel called back. 'I've missed you so much, and I just wanted to see Pamela.'

'Her name is Petal now – as I'm sure you are aware, if you tracked me down here. Come in out of the rain but, I warn you, I wasn't expecting visitors and we're going to a Coronation party in the village this afternoon.'

Christabel tried to embrace Sylvia as they went into the house, but she backed away.

'I can't be doing with all that false stuff,' Sylvia

355

said, her eyes flashing. 'You, Gribble, were vile to me and cruel to Petal, and you, mother dear, were an apology for a woman, let alone a mother. So say your piece and then go. I want nothing to do with you, and nothing from you.'

Christabel let out a sound, part sob, part expression of shock. 'I want to see Pamela!'

'There's no child here called Pamela,' Sylvia hissed at her. 'And I'm not Sylvia any longer, but Cassandra.'

'May I see Petal, then?' Christabel asked.

'Just for a few minutes, and if you frighten her I'll throw you out,' Sylvia warned. 'Petal, sweetheart!' she called out at the bottom of the stairs. 'There's some people who want to meet you.'

Miss Gribble felt nothing but resentment when the child came down the stairs. The little girl was all smiles, her tight curly hair fixed up in a sort of top knot with a red ribbon. She wore red shorts and a red-and-white striped blouse.

But what really upset her was the way Christabel reacted.

'Oh, isn't she beautiful!' she gushed. 'Come here, you darling girl.'

'I'm going to be Britannia in the fancy dress this afternoon,' the child announced. 'Mummy made my costume. Would you like to see me in it?'

'I would indeed,' Christabel said eagerly. 'You know, I've wanted to see you for such a long time.'

'Enough of that,' Sylvia said with a note of warning in her voice, and moved between the child and Christabel. 'You relinquished all rights six years ago.'

'I need to talk to you in private,' Miss Gribble

said to Sylvia in a low voice. She felt she had to let the girl know she wanted nothing more than to let Christabel see her and the child and then they would go. But she couldn't say that in front of Christabel. 'Where can we go?'

'Nowhere in this cottage – it's too small,' Sylvia replied.

'Could Christabel and Petal go and sit in the car, then?' she asked. 'I've got things I must tell you, and I can't with Petal listening. Please? Just for a few moments.'

Sylvia looked a little apprehensive but nodded her agreement. 'Okay. Petal adores cars, and it can't do any harm as long as she sticks to asking about school and stuff.'

She went over to Petal and stroked her face. 'Look, sweetie. Would you just go and sit in the car with this lady for a few minutes so I can talk to her friend?'

Petal nodded and readily took Christabel's hand. She was giggling as Christabel held the umbrella over them both to run to the car.

Sylvia turned to Miss Gribble the moment they'd gone. 'Now what do you want?' she asked. 'If you think I'm coming back, you'd better think again. I wouldn't cross that threshold if my life depended on it.'

Miss Gribble's hackles rose immediately, just as they always had when Sylvia showed a lack of respect for either her or her mother. She'd been a wilful child who had always gone against any form of authority. As she got older, she'd become scornful because her mother was weak, and she'd done her best to drive a wedge between herself

357

and Christabel. Miss Gribble tried to control her rising anger, because she knew Sylvia would never agree to her terms if she thought she was being put under pressure.

'It's your mother's nerves,' she said. 'You and the child are all she thinks about – she's always asking about her, crying for hours sometimes. I'm afraid she might have a complete breakdown unless you allow her some contact with you both. I'm not saying you have to come to the house. You could stay nearby, and she could come to you.'

'Even if I had the money to go all that way, why would I even consider seeing a woman who allowed you to mistreat and manipulate me?' Sylvia snarled. 'I don't care if she has a break-down, a mother's job is to protect her child, and she didn't, because she preferred to go along with what you, a bloody monster, told her to do. You were inhuman, and you are never going to inflict the kind of things you did on me on Petal. I hated you my whole childhood, and now I'm old enough to rationalize it all I hate you even more.'

Lashing out was what Maud Gribble always did when anyone upset her. This was why she kept her distance from people. Mostly, the lashing out was just shouting abuse or throwing something. Any form of physical violence she generally managed to control. But Sylvia's words cut right into her, and she couldn't hold back.

She sprang at Sylvia, catching hold of her two upper arms and shaking her like a rag doll. She must have done that hundreds of times while Sylvia was growing up. But, this time, she couldn't stop.

Sylvia's head began lolling to one side, and Miss Gribble let go of her arms, took her head in her two hands and slammed it backwards.

It was the horrible crunching sound that alerted her to the fact that she'd banged Sylvia against the edge of the stone mantelpiece and not the wall. She let go of the girl and she dropped to the hearth like a sack of potatoes, leaving a trail of blood across the fireplace.

Panic took over. She glanced out and saw Christabel and Petal happily chatting in the back of the car. They hadn't come to try and take Petal away, but she knew it would make Christabel very happy if they could drive away with the child.

'So that's what I did!' Miss Gribble said, finishing up her story. 'I collected up a few bits of Petal's from upstairs and picked up a diary of Sylvia's, because I thought it might have some information about her in it. Then I went to the car. I said I was driving Petal down to the village party and that her mum would follow on when she'd done her hair.'

DI Pople was astounded at the way Miss Gribble had graphically described the scene, both seeing and then killing Sylvia. It was almost like hearing a play on the wireless. There was no doubt that what she said was the absolute truth. He thought she was utterly mad, in as much as she had no real conception of the evil of what she'd done.

He was so astounded he felt faint.

'Tell me, then,' he said, pulling himself together so as to continue. 'Did Christabel have any idea of what you'd done?'

'None. She did ask why she couldn't say good-

359

bye to Sylvia, but that was all. Petal got a bit anxious when I didn't stop at the village hall, but I said it was too early for the party and we'd have a little ride in the car. Later I told her that her mother was following us down to our place the next day on the train.'

DI Pople gulped. 'And what did she say to that?'

'She starting crying and making a fuss because she hadn't got her fancy-dress costume and she was missing the party. I had to smack her.'

'You casually killed the mother and took the child away?' DI Pople was incredulous.

'I didn't mean to kill Sylvia, and I certainly didn't want to take the child. But I had to, didn't I? I couldn't leave her there.'

'So when did you tell Christabel that you'd killed her daughter?'

'I didn't. I told her that Sylvia had admitted she was struggling to keep body and soul together and couldn't get a decent job because of Petal. I said I'd suggested we took Petal home with us, then, once she'd found a good job, Sylvia could come down to see us.'

DI Pople shook his head, amazed that Christabel would believe this. But, clearly, she'd been conditioned since she was a small child into doing whatever Miss Gribble said.

'And, once you got home, how did you explain away the need to keep Petal hidden from view?'

Miss Gribble gave him a pitying look. 'Because of her colour, of course.'

'How long did you think you could keep her hidden? What about school? If she became ill? Surely Christabel isn't so crazy she wouldn't consider these things?'

'I told you, she's always relied on me to make decisions.'

'And what decisions had you made about the child's future?'

'I'd already realized I would have to kill her.'

Chapter Twenty-one

'I hate September,' Molly sighed as she looked out the ballroom window at the rain lashing down in the street. 'It's a sort of preview to all the grim stuff winter's got in store for us.'

Evelyn, who was sitting at one of the tables behind Molly planning the seating arrangements for a wedding party at the weekend, laughed.

'Oh, you doomy thing!' she said. 'We often get lovely weather right through October. You're only feeling that way because the weather has been so good and, now Petal is back at school, you feel a bit lost.'

Molly looked round at her employer. 'Maybe. I do feel a bit lost without her, but the way I feel isn't to do with Petal.'

Caring for Petal had been the best thing that had ever happened to Molly. From the moment she got her up in the mornings right through till she kissed her goodnight and tucked her in, she felt happy. She couldn't really put a finger on what it was that made her feel this way. Perhaps it was just a need in her to care for someone, or a substitute for a family of her own. But she loved taking Petal to the beach, reading to her, playing dolls with her, everything about being with her. 'Don't get me wrong. I'm thrilled, of course, that she's settled down so well and the nightmares have stopped, but–' she stopped suddenly, too embarrassed to go on.

'But what?' Evelyn asked.

Molly shifted her weight from one foot to the other and wrung her hands.

'Come on, tell me,' Evelyn insisted. 'After the stuff you've been through I can't believe you can't tell me the reason you're feeling down in the dumps.'

'It's just stuff that I can't get out of my head, and it's driving me mad. Like, why did Charley pack me in? Was it something I did or said? One moment he was talking about marriage and then crash, bang, wallop he's changed his mind. It doesn't make any sense.

'Then there's George. When he was here, I got the feeling he wanted to take things further, but in his letters since there's nothing, not a hint he might want me to be his girl. And my parents seemed to care when I was in hospital, but that seems to have faded since.

'And, to cap it all, there's the trial for Miss Gribble and Mrs Coleman. When's that going to happen? And what sort of things am I going to be asked?'

'Sounds like you feel you're shut in a waiting room and there's nobody to tell you how long you've got to wait,' Evelyn suggested.

'Sort of.'

Evelyn thought for a moment. 'As far as George goes, maybe he thinks you're still smitten with Charley and haven't ever thought about him in that way. My suggestion is that you go home, perhaps stay with George, and make it very clear to him that you're interested. While you're there, you could try and make the peace with your father, show both him and your mum you're prepared to meet them halfway. As for the trial, that isn't something you should concern yourself with. It will only take place once the police have gathered all the evidence.'

'You don't have any idea why Charley packed me in, then?'

'Why do you need to know why? It won't help you.'

'It might stop me making the same mistake with another man.'

Evelyn frowned. 'It wasn't a mistake on your part. The fault lay with him.'

Molly looked at her employer hard. They had become much closer since Petal had come to live at the George, and she now had a keen intuition when Evelyn was hiding something. She had it now: Evelyn was avoiding eye contact.

'You've said that before, and Mr Bridgenorth has, too,' Molly said sharply. 'If you know something, you should tell me.'

Evelyn laughed, a light little trill that might mean she felt she'd been caught out. 'Oh, Molly. You didn't use to say boo to a goose, and now you've found confidence enough to pick me up on things I say. I'm glad of that – you were once far too meek and mild. I like this new assertive person.'

Molly had no intention of backing off just because of a bit of flattery. 'Then tell me what fault lay in Charley?'

Evelyn hesitated, biting her lip.

'Go on, spit it out,' Molly insisted.

'He was homosexual,' Evelyn blurted out. 'We didn't want to tell you, but it isn't right that you keep blaming yourself.'

Molly's eyes almost popped out of her head. She was utterly astounded. 'Surely not! I can't believe it. What makes you say such a thing?'

Evelyn explained what had happened the day that Ted had gone over to Whitechapel to tell Charley that Molly was in hospital. She recounted it carefully, making sure Molly fully understood that there had been no mistake. 'There was no doubt about it,' she ended up. 'I'm terribly sorry, Molly. It isn't an easy thing to tell anyone, especially someone you care about.'

Molly had turned pale. Her eyes were wide and glassy, and she ran her fingers through her hair distractedly, as if trying to think up a reason why it couldn't be so.

Evelyn waited. She wanted to embrace the girl and take away her hurt, but that would be like trying to put a plaster on a broken leg.

'I can't believe it! Surely you're wrong!' Molly exclaimed, and tears came into her eyes. 'But I know you and Ted wouldn't tell me this unless you were absolutely sure.'

She paused, taking deep breaths as if trying to calm herself. 'Poor Charley!' she finally burst out. 'What a terrible thing for him! He can't help how he was born, can he? And I'm sure he didn't know what to do, or who to turn to.'

Evelyn was moved by Molly's ability to feel sympathy for Charley even when she was so hurt. 'That's very understanding of you,' she said. 'I think I'd be tempted to stamp my feet and ask why he'd led me up the garden path and talked about marriage. But you must always remember he did the right thing by you in the end, and that was because he was genuinely fond of you. Both Ted and I have met quite a few men in the hotel trade that are that way. They have to hide it, of course, but they're usually true gentlemen.'

Molly began to fold some napkins. She looked very pensive for some time. Evelyn got on with the seating plan, but she kept glancing over at Molly, afraid she might break down when the reality of it hit her.

But, to her surprise, Molly suddenly looked up, bright eyed again, as if she'd given herself a mental shake.

'Then it was for the best,' she said. 'Imagine how awful it would've been if we had got married and it was all a sham? It doesn't bear thinking about.'

'No, it doesn't, and I'm sure Charley is feeling as bad as you are about it,' Evelyn assured her.

'I don't feel bad exactly, just rather foolish,' Molly said. 'I don't seem to be any good at working men out. Am I going to make a prize fool of myself with George, too?'

Evelyn smirked. 'Hardly – the man is nuts about you.'

'But the distance between us?' Molly said.

'You're putting the cart before the horse.' Evelyn laughed. 'Go home for a weekend, see how it goes, and if it's meant to be the pair of you will come up with solutions to the problems.'

Molly frowned, deep in thought. 'Of course, we'll both be witnesses at Miss Gribble's trial. Maybe I could wait and see how it goes with him there, up in London, where no one is watching. It would be easier than back home in Sawbridge.'

'A brilliant plan,' Evelyn said, delighted that Molly was finally being positive about the situation with George. 'London can be very romantic, especially at night. Walks along the Thames Embankment, an intimate Italian restaurant, or St James's Park in the moonlight. Ted and I had some lovely times there.'

Molly smiled. 'I'm not sure the Old Bailey could be thought of as romantic, especially as we'll both be put through our paces by the barristers.'

'Yes, but think of the relief when it's all over.' Evelyn sighed. 'That'll be the night for romance and looking to the future. I know I'm sick of people talking about the case in the bar, asking me questions, giving their point of view, which is mostly inaccurate. And it must be a hundred times worse for you, Molly.'

'It is tiresome when people stop me in the street or outside the school gates – they do it even when Petal's with me,' Molly said indignantly. 'I really hate that they haven't the sense to realize she shouldn't be hearing this stuff. I suppose they'll forget about it as soon as the trial is over, though.'

'I believe the only thing holding it up is that the police are still waiting to get a statement from Christabel Coleman. One of the local bobbies told me she became hysterical when she was told Miss

Gribble killed her daughter. She hasn't been fit for questioning since, and they've got a lot of loose ends to tie up that only she can help with.'

'How could she have not known? Or that Miss Gribble was ill-treating Petal? They were all in the same house, for goodness' sake! The woman is a total loony!'

'Perhaps, or maybe it's just years and years of being conditioned into accepting her house-keeper's views and behaviour.'

'Do you think the she-devil will hang?'

Evelyn shrugged. 'She should – she's an evil woman and no mistake – but so many people are against hanging now, she might just get life.'

'I wonder what will happen to Christabel. I do wish she'd find her voice and tell us all her side of the story. I'm quite sure that Cassie would never have wanted her mother to end her days in an asylum.'

At the time Molly and Evelyn were discussing Christabel Coleman, DI Pople and his sergeant, Brian Wayfield, were waiting in a small room at Hellingly Hospital near Hailsham in East Sussex to see her.

Christabel's ward sister had reported that her patient had become much calmer and had been talking about Miss Gribble, and this was passed on to the police.

Both policemen had visited other mental insti-tutions, most of which were very grim, but Hellingly had been built as recently as 1906 and was not only in a rather splendid building which had its own railway, hairdresser's and beautiful

367

grounds, but it also had a reputation for taking good care of its patients.

The room they were in was on the ground floor and had a big window looking out on to the grounds. It was decorated in an attractive pale blue with a darker blue chintz-covered sofa and armchairs. If they hadn't observed a few patients shuffling about, talking to themselves, the two policemen could almost have imagined it was a private hospital.

Christabel was brought in by a plump, middle-aged nurse. 'I'll be outside if you need me,' she said to the patient. 'But you're well today, aren't you, Mrs Coleman?'

Christabel nodded. She looked quite attractive. Her fair hair shone and curled around her face, she was wearing a little lipstick and a pale-grey pleated skirt and baby-pink jumper. She certainly didn't look insane, only nervous, as she sat down in one of the armchairs and folded her hands in her lap.

'I understand that I must talk now about what happened when we took Petal away,' she said, her blue eyes fixed on DI Pople. 'But I hope you believe that I really didn't know Gribby, I mean Maud – sorry, Miss Gribble – had killed Sylvia.'

DI Pople was surprised to find her so articulate. From everything he'd been told, he had expected her to be simple and for this to be why Miss Gribble had been able to manipulate her.

'You can call Miss Gribble whatever you feel most comfortable with. And yes, we do believe that you didn't know she killed Sylvia,' he said. 'But weren't you suspicious when you got back to

Mulberry House and Miss Gribble imprisoned Petal in an attic room?'

'She said it was because people would talk if they saw a black child and, when I kept going up to see Petal, to read to her and play with her, Gribby got cross with me.'

'But surely you could have insisted that Petal was brought downstairs and treated properly? Also why weren't you concerned that Sylvia hadn't turned up to get Petal?'

'Well, that's the strange part. You see, I started to feel peculiar about that time. Sort of woozy and strange. Gribby said I was ill and that I must go to bed to recover. I had to, because I couldn't stand up sometimes, and everything seemed so muddled and cloudy. But since I've been here in the hospital I've gradually stopped feeling like that, so I think she must have been drugging me.'

DI Pople had been told by the doctor that tests on Christabel Coleman's arrival had revealed narcotics in her bloodstream. The doctor thought it was withdrawal symptoms that gave the impression she was insane, because she'd been given this drug for a considerable time. DI Pople had himself been into Christabel's father's surgery in the house. It was very old-fashioned, a time-warp room from Victorian times, with a big mahogany desk and shelves from floor to ceiling filled with medical books and rows of medicines. In the drawers and cupboards they'd found countless bottles of pills and, presumably, Miss Gribble, when a much younger woman, had managed to discover what a great many of them were for.

DI Pople studied Christabel now. She must

have been very attractive as a young woman. How sad it was that her life had been blighted because of an inability to stand up for herself.

'It seems to me, Mrs Coleman,' he said carefully, 'that you've allowed Miss Gribble to take over your whole life. Tell me, when your husband was alive, what did he have to say about her?'

'He didn't like her at all,' Christabel admitted. 'He called her the Black Widow. In fact, she tried to stop me marrying him by hinting he had other women. I expect you know my father was a doctor? Well, he and Mother liked and trusted Reg, though Gribby would say the exact opposite, so I took no notice of what she said and we got married. A year later, in 1926, Sylvia was born and we were terribly happy. Reg was always firm with Gribby then, expecting her to know her place as housekeeper. She did help me with Sylvia sometimes, but not much. Then Father died and, soon after, Mother too, and I suppose I leaned on Gribby more than I should've done. Then, when the war started and Reg was called up, she just sort of took over. She ate with Sylvia and I, she came in the drawing room with us, she became like a mother.'

'You must have been very upset when your husband was reported missing. You leaned on Miss Gribble still more then?'

'Well, yes,' she said with a shrug. 'I was terribly upset. I kept crying, I felt so terribly alone. But Gribby took care of me and, looking back, I think she might have been giving me some sort of drug then, too, because I became very, very muddled. One night, I was sure Reg came back. It was so clear to me – he came into my bedroom and kissed and hugged me. He said that he'd got separated from the rest of his unit at Dunkirk. I can remember him saying he was going downstairs to find something to eat. The next thing I knew it was morning and he wasn't there. Gribby said I'd dreamt it.'

DI Pople looked pointedly at Sergeant Wayfield. The two men excused themselves and went outside the room to confer. 'Could Reg Coleman have returned and Miss Gribble killed him?' he asked.

'Well, they said he was missing, presumed dead, but if he did get separated from his unit he could have made it back home.'

'In the Great War it was common enough for men to go missing and never be found, dead or alive, but it was fairly rare in the last one. There was one report on file that he was seen in Folkestone some time after the rest of his unit got back. But it was thought to be false information when he didn't surface again.'

'Why would Gribble kill him?'

'To have Christabel to herself? Because she was afraid Reg would kick her out? We've already established that the woman is capable of such a thing.'

'But we can't take the word of a woman who's a bit cracked for it.'

'She isn't cracked at all. Though, considering that Gribble was lacing her food with some kind of drug, it's surprising she isn't. We ought to have thought of that when we found so much medicine left in the doctor's old surgery. A sly woman like

Gribble would delight in finding out the side effects of various drugs and experimenting with them. But there's nothing to stop us digging around in the garden of Mulberry House. We'll go back in to Christabel now, but start the ball rolling afterwards.'

'Is everything all right?' Christabel asked sweetly when they came back in. 'I bet you think I've gone right off my rocker, imagining Reg came home.'

'Not at all. But can we move on a bit, to the point when Petal was born. It must have been an awful shock to have an illegitimate child in the family?'

She nodded and hung her head.

'Do you know who the child's father was?'

'I can't talk about that. It's too painful,' she said, her voice rising in agitation.

'The shame? People talking?' DI Pople said. 'I can imagine. So when Sylvia took off with her baby, it must have been a relief for you and Miss Gribble?'

She nodded again, mutely.

'So why, if you were glad, did you decide to look for her six years later?'

'I wasn't glad she left, I was terribly sad, and it just got worse and worse. Gribby kept telling me to snap out of it, but I couldn't. I was afraid I was heading towards the asylum, and that only seeing Sylvia and the baby and knowing they were all right would save me.'

DI Pople then questioned Mrs Coleman about the trip to Somerset. Her account of finding Stone Cottage, seeing Sylvia and Petal and then going out to sit in the car was virtually identical to what Miss Gribble had said.

'But didn't you find it odd that Sylvia didn't come out to say goodbye to Petal and you?'

'It was raining so hard, Gribby said she'd told her to stay indoors. She said we were taking Petal to the Coronation party and would come back for Sylvia later in the afternoon.'

'But weren't you horrified when Miss Gribble drove on out of the village?'

'Absolutely. Petal screamed blue murder about going to the party and wanting her mother. Gribby stopped the car and smacked her. She whispered to me so Petal couldn't hear that Stone Cottage wasn't fit to keep pigs in and Sylvia couldn't make ends meet so she'd suggested we took Petal and then Sylvia could go to London and get a job and come home at weekends. She said Sylvia was relieved because her life there was such a struggle. She didn't even have electricity, or a bathroom!'

'So you were glad?'

'Well, yes. I'd seen how ramshackle Stone Cottage was. Then Petal snuggled up to me in the back of the car, and it all felt so good and right.'

'When did you find out that Sylvia was dead?'

'I didn't. Later, when Petal was asleep, Gribby said that Sylvia was selling herself to make a living, and she'd become nasty and hard-faced. She also claimed that Sylvia had asked for fifty pounds for Petal, and she had given it to her.'

'And you believed your daughter was capable of that?'

Christabel shrugged and made a gesture with

373

her hands. 'It had been six years since I'd seen her, and she hadn't written once. She was living in a tumbledown shack, and I believed that Gribby was telling the truth about how she was living. I thought Sylvia had acted in Petal's best interests.'

'So when did you begin to doubt that?'

Christabel wrung her hands and looked frightened. 'A few days after we got home, really. When Gribby was so stern and wouldn't let Petal come down with us I remembered how things had been between her and Sylvia. I started to wonder why Sylvia would risk Petal being treated as she now was. I did have a big argument with Gribby about it, I said if Petal was going to live here she should be downstairs and going to school. It was after that I started to feel poorly, and I suppose I wasn't capable of taking in what was going on, because I don't really remember anything much from that time.'

'Were you aware that Molly Heywood had come to the house and Miss Gribble had imprisoned her?'

'No, I knew nothing of that. When I first got here I had a vague, dream-like picture of picking up an axe and a girl lying on the ground in the garden, but it was like that picture of Reg coming back – it didn't seem real. Even now I know I did hit her with the axe, and she got Petal out of the house, it still seems like a story about someone else.'

DI Pople nodded. He felt that Christabel Coleman was an honest woman. Gullible, too trusting and weak, but as much a victim as Petal and Molly.

'Miss Gribble did kill Sylvia. She admitted she

saw red at something Sylvia had said. She described how she shook her, holding her by the arms, then banged her head back against the fireplace. We are fairly certain that she intended to kill Molly Heywood, too, and she even admitted that Petal would have to go also. In view of this, we think she could also have killed your husband when he came home from France. Because of this, we would like to ask your permission to dig up your garden.'

DI Pople watched Mrs Coleman's face carefully and saw, in turn, horror, disbelief and then anger flood it.

She closed her eyes for a moment, took a deep breath and then exhaled slowly. 'Do it. And if you find my Reg there, then I shall wish I had taken that axe to her.'

Chapter Twenty-two

'It so wonderful to see you, Molly,' Dilys said breathlessly, throwing her arms around her friend on the platform of Rye Station. 'I'm dying to know what the police are doing about those two madwomen, and whether Charley has realized that you are the best thing that ever happened to him and returned to the fold.'

Dilys had come down to see Molly just after she got out of hospital. Molly had been smarting from Charley's rejection, anxious about Petal and still feeling poorly, so, as lovely as it was to see

Dilys, the visit hadn't been all they'd both hoped for.

'I'm so glad you came again,' Molly said, picking up her friend's overnight bag with one hand and tucking the other through her friend's arm. 'There's so much to catch up on, and I wasn't really myself last time.'

'Gosh, Rye is pretty!' Dilys said as they crossed the road into one of the many cobbled streets lined with tiny, ancient cottages leading up to the church. 'No one ever told me there were nice places outside of Wales. I'll have to spread the word.'

Molly giggled. She knew it was a joke, but then, people back home in Sawbridge seemed to believe there was nowhere else in England as lovely as the West Country.

'I've got the rest of today off,' she told her friend. 'So what would you like to do? Mooch around town? Ride a bike down to Camber Sands? Catch the bus into Hastings? I haven't even got to pick Petal up from school – Mrs Bridgenorth said she'd do it.'

'Surely she's old enough to come home on her own?' Dilys asked.

'Yes, she's old enough, she's recently had her seventh birthday, but after all she went through we don't want some mean kid saying something nasty to her and setting her right back. Every now and then she still gets a bit sad and scared, so we have to keep an eye on her.'

'Poor kid. I think it's amazing she's come out of it so well. But speaking of coming out of things well, I've got a surprise for you.'

'You're coming down here to work?'

Dilys laughed. 'No, nothing to do with me. It's good news for you. Miss Stow has been caught handing goods over to a friend.'

Molly stopped short in shock. 'Really? She blamed me and she was doing it herself?'

'That's right! She got transferred to Handbags just recently. There was a bit of a stink when they did a stock check on Gloves, but it was assumed by everyone they'd been stolen by customers – after all, they're quite small and easy to hide. But then Mr Hardcraft caught her and her friend red-handed. Miss Stow had rung up a cheap plastic handbag but she'd put a really dear leather one in with it. It turned out she'd been doing it for some time.'

'That bitch blamed me!' Molly exclaimed, her cheeks turning red with anger. 'They threw me out the night before Christmas Eve. I went through hell.'

'I know. Everyone's talking about it at Bourne & Hollingsworth. Nobody ever believed you'd done it, anyway, except of course Mr Hardcraft and Miss Jackson. But wait, it gets better, they checked her room and they found all sorts of stuff she'd nicked. She'd been putting it down her girdle to get past security.'

'I bet they don't even bother to apologize to me,' Molly said with some bitterness. She had never been able to forget the shame and humiliation of being made to leave the company.

'I think you're wrong there,' Dilys grinned. 'You see, a lot of people saw the story in the newspaper about you rescuing Petal, so when this thing about

Miss Stow broke two days ago everyone was up in arms on your behalf. They're going to have to do something for you. After all, you could go to the newspapers.'

'I wouldn't do that. It was bad enough being accused in the first place, and I certainly don't want the world and his wife to learn about it now.'

'I so much wanted to phone you and tell you.' Dilys's eyes were sparkling with the news. 'But I wanted to see your face when I told you, so I waited.'

'So what does my face say?'

'It did say you'd like to kill Miss Stow, but that's gone now, you just look kind of weird.'

'Something like this happened to my dad,' Molly admitted. 'He was accused of stealing the takings from the shop he worked at. He and Mum had a terrible time of it. He never got over it. I think it's what made him such a nasty, sour apology for a man.'

'Whatever Miss Stow put on to you, it hasn't made you like that,' Dilys insisted. 'In fact, if it weren't for that crabby cow, you'd still be at Bourne & Hollingsworth. You wouldn't have met Charley, come to work here or found Petal.'

'Remind me to send her a bouquet,' Molly said sarcastically. 'That is, instead of cheering as they cart her off to Holloway Prison.'

Dilys laughed. 'Let's forget about that and go to Camber Sands on bikes. I've got a new swimming cossie, and I look like a beauty queen in it. I think it's warm enough to prance about with next to nothing on and get chatted up by a couple of lads.'

'Good thinking,' Molly said, suddenly aware

that what her friend had suggested sounded like a lot of fun. She hadn't had any of that for quite some time. 'And tonight we'll hit the hot spots of Rye and get silly drunk.'

On the day that Dilys had arrived to visit Molly, unbeknown to them, digging work had started at Mulberry House.

Two days later, when DI Pople drove into the grounds there, his heart sank. It was pouring with rain for the second day running and the garden was a complete quagmire. It looked as if a family of giant moles had been digging, throwing up small mountains of soil, and in between were huge puddles. His men had tried to fill in each hole they'd dug with the soil from the next one, but it hadn't really worked. All the trees and shrubs that had been planted pre-war hadn't been disturbed, but it was still a vast site, and there was still a great deal more ground to cover.

DI Pople got out of his car and, standing on the gravel drive, put his wellington boots on. He had been expecting complaints about the futility of the search and, before he'd even crammed a sou'-wester on his head and buttoned up his raincoat, the first came.

'No one has dug down more than a foot here for donkey's years,' the first remark came, from a burly constable called in from Hastings.

'Keep at it!' Pople yelled back, and surveyed the scene, hoping for inspiration.

His men had done a thorough job so far, under terrible conditions, and there would be hell to pay about the cost of the search if nothing was discovered. So he looked as he walked, trying to imagine himself having a dead body to dispose of. It would be very heavy for a woman to drag, and she'd need to get it hidden quickly without being seen. She would also need to bury it somewhere where it wouldn't be dug up accidentally at a later date.

Putting the body in an outhouse or shed while she dug a grave seemed a likely scenario. Dunkirk, where Reg Coleman was last seen, had been in June, and a body left lying around at that time of year would soon start to smell.

He walked around the house and noticed that a laundry room complete with an old wood-fired boiler was attached to it. He'd noticed a more up-to-date gas boiler in the kitchen but, although the outhouse was now obsolete, it had probably been in use during the war years.

There was an old greenhouse, a potting shed and an old chicken house in the back garden, too. At the right-hand side of the house was the garage and not very far from it, with its back to the garden wall, was a summer house.

He looked from one to the other. The greenhouse he rejected, as anything inside could be seen through the glass. The potting shed was less than five feet long, too short for a grown man to lie on the floor. During the war, people had relied heavily on their chickens, so Miss Gribble was unlikely to have disturbed them by shoving a body in there.

He went over to the summer house to examine it carefully. The felt on the roof was in good condition and the walls had been repainted pale blue in the last three or four years. The cane furniture inside was probably pre-war, but the cushions were clean and looked newer. There were books on a shelf, a couple of jigsaw puzzles on a table, all signs it had once been a loved place, but, judging by the amount of cobwebs, it hadn't been used for a few years.

It seemed a likely spot to put a body: not far to drag it from the house, and not visible from it either, as there was a big oak tree at the side of the house blocking the view from the windows. He noted, too, that there were a few feet of crazy paving in front of the door. No concrete, just stones laid on the grass, and trodden in well over the years. He could understand someone putting down stepping stones, but it was odd to make a rectangle with them.

'Over here!' he yelled to two of his men. 'I've got a strong hunch we might find something under these stones.'

They put up a tarpaulin to work under and, from the first spade of soil after the paving was removed, the men remarked how much easier it was to dig here than elsewhere in the garden. DI Pople could feel their growing excitement as keenly as his own.

'I reckon she were a professional gravedigger,' one of the men joked as they went down and down.

It was just a few minutes after his jovial remark that his spade hit something. 'Looks like a blanket wrapped round something,' he shouted from the now four-foot-deep hole. 'Best pass me down a trowel to scrape away the soil.'

An hour and a half later, a skeleton was fully exposed and awaiting the pathologist. There were still bits of khaki uniform attached to it which hadn't rotted away, and brass buttons, belt webbing and a pair of boots.

'No doubt that it's Reg Coleman,' DI Pople said as he sheltered under the tarpaulin and gazed down at the skeleton. 'It will be interesting to discover how she killed him. Anyone want to place a bet on it? Stabbing, shooting or poison?'

There was a round of speculation on the subject.

'Bet he was over the moon to get back from Dunkirk in one piece.' The voice of one of the constables rose above the rest. 'Poor geezer, happy as Larry, thinking only of getting his leg over, and the bloody housekeeper does for him. That's what you call tragic irony.'

'Makes you wonder who else is buried out here,' someone else chipped in.

'It does indeed,' DI Pople murmured to himself. 'It does indeed.'

Three days later, armed with the police pathologist's report, which confirmed that the body in the garden was indeed that of Reginald Coleman, DI Pople went back to Hellingly Hospital to see his widow. He had Sergeant Wayfield with him as a witness because he hoped that, by presenting the poor woman with evidence of just how evil her beloved Miss Gribble was, she might feel able to disclose other things which maybe, out of misplaced loyalty, she had kept to herself.

Christabel looked even calmer than she had on

the previous visit. Her eyes were bright, her smile was warm and there was a glow about her.

'I've been feeling very much better,' she said. 'I think this is due to finally being able to face up to the folly of allowing Miss Gribble to run my life.'

DI Pople thought that she might not feel quite so well balanced when he told her about the latest development but, however much sympathy he had for her, he had to press on.

'I am very sorry to tell you but we have found your husband's body in the garden of Mulberry House,' he said. He wanted to tell her as gently as possible but whichever way he put it she was going to be distressed. 'He was stabbed in the chest, and we have no doubt that this was done by Miss Gribble.'

Christabel's glow vanished like the sun going behind a cloud. She clamped her hands over her mouth and her eyes filled with tears. 'She killed my Reg?'

'I'm afraid so,' said DI Pople. 'She buried him in front of the summer house.'

Christabel cried then, a low, keening sound that somehow illustrated how badly she had been betrayed by the woman who professed to love her. DI Pople stood up and put his hand on her shoulder in an effort to comfort her, and the sergeant asked the nurse waiting outside to bring some tea.

'I never had any suspicions about her,' Christabel said, wiping her eyes. 'And the awful thing is that I chose to believe the rumour flying around the village that he had bunked off from the army to be with a woman in France. Isn't it terrible that

I believed that of him instead of grieving?'

'If it were me, I would wonder who started that rumour,' DI Pople said.

Christabel looked at him in horror. 'You think it was her?'

DI Pople shrugged. 'I think it's very likely. It would stop you from trying to find out more about his disappearance.'

'Oh God, I've been such a fool,' said Christabel Coleman, holding her head between her hands. 'I let her guide me because I trusted her implicitly. Why couldn't I see what she was doing? She even turned Sylvia against me.'

'I don't think you should blame yourself for that,' he said, afraid he'd pushed her close to the edge again with his revelations. 'Most mothers would be upset if their unmarried daughter got herself pregnant.'

She looked at him with an expression of utter exasperation. 'For a policeman, you aren't that quick,' she said. 'Sylvia didn't get pregnant. I did. Petal is my child.'

For all his years of experience of witnesses telling him the most unexpected and often outrageous things, DI Pople had never expected to be shocked like this, and by this gentle woman.

'She's your child?' he said stupidly. 'But how? I mean, who–' He broke off, unable to find appropriate words to ask how she could have even met a black man.

'My goodness, you're shocked,' she said, and gave a humourless laugh. 'The lady from the big house having an affair with a black man! Well, I did, and, for your information, he was a good man.

384

I met him towards the end of the war in Ashford. He was an American airman, handsome, charming and fun. I hadn't had any fun at all since Reg disappeared. I was in no man's land, neither a confirmed widow nor an abandoned wife. A friend in Ashford talked me into going to a dance with her, and that's where I met him.'

'What was his name?' DI Pople asked, trying to overcome his shock and to pull himself back into the role of interrogator.

'Benjamin Hargreaves,' she said, without any hesitation. 'Once a fortnight I would meet him in Ashford, just to talk. We didn't become lovers until just before he had to go home, in 1946. I cared for him a great deal, but we were both very aware of the prejudice there was against black people mixing with white. He came from the South, near Atlanta, and he said if he were to try and take me home with him I'd have a miserable life. Of course, I had Sylvia to think of, too, she was just twenty then, and there was Gribby, who I felt I owed so much to, and I couldn't tell her.'

'So she didn't know?'

'No, she didn't find out until long after Benjamin had gone home, when I was six months pregnant and it began to show. Even then I didn't tell her who the father was, or that he was black. She went mad as it was. If I hadn't been so far gone I think she would have forced me to have an abortion. Poor Sylvia was caught up in the middle of it. She listened to Gribby going on about how people would talk about me, and Sylvia argued that it didn't matter and we could bring the baby up together.'

'She sounds a good, kind girl,' DI Pople said.

'She was. I even confided in her that the baby would be black, to prepare her. That was when she suggested we could tell people it was her baby. She said she didn't care what people thought. She was always like that – she didn't give a damn about what she called small-mindedness. She even suggested that we got rid of Gribby, sold the house and moved to London. I was tempted, I can tell you. But I couldn't sell the house, because Reg was missing, and it would have taken a bomb to get rid of Gribby.'

'So you agreed that Sylvia would say the baby was hers?'

'Yes, somewhat reluctantly, but once Gribby knew about it, she ganged up with Sylvia. It was probably the first time they were ever in agreement about anything. I wanted a quiet life, and I thought everything would come right once the baby was born. So I stayed in so no one saw me, and waited for the baby.'

'Are you telling me you had Petal at home, with no midwife or nurse?'

'Yes. Well, it wasn't my first baby. I knew the ropes, and so did Gribby. It was an easy, quick birth, and she was a beautiful baby.'

'And how did Miss Gribble take it?'

Christabel's eyes filled with tears again. 'She went mad because the baby was black. She called me terrible names, she ranted and raved. It was awful, and now I know what she's capable of, I think she might have killed the baby but for Sylvia. She stood up for me. Young as she was, she was as fierce as a tiger, and she never gave Gribby a chance to be alone with Petal. That was why Sylvia ran away with her in the end. She couldn't stand the strain, and she said to me that Petal deserved a better life than having someone constantly disapproving of her. She said I was pathetic for allowing Gribby to rule me and that no one would ever tell her what to say or do.'

'Did you register Petal's birth?' DI Pople asked. He was beginning to have such admiration for Sylvia, and a great deal of sympathy for Christabel, too.

'Sylvia did, as her mother. She slipped out and went on the bus to do it before Gribby could stop her. We had been calling her Squirrel as a pet name, but Sylvia registered her as Pamela Coleman, and of course they put "father unknown" on the birth certificate. I assume Sylvia began calling her Petal March when she ran away with her and, at the same time, she changed her own name to Cassandra March.'

DI Pople felt that he had everything he needed from Christabel now. A statement would be drawn up and signed by her and, in the meantime, he would try and get a confession from Miss Gribble that she'd murdered Reg Coleman. He hadn't told Christabel that she had stabbed him repeatedly, as if in a frenzy. Some things were kinder not to mention.

However, one thing he felt he should do was to encourage young Molly Heywood to go and see Christabel. She needed to know about her dead friend's mother, and Christabel could do with knowing more about both her daughters.

As for himself, he felt drained. In his entire

career he had only been involved in five murders before this, and all of them had been fairly straightforward cases. This one had been hell, not because it was difficult but because one psychopathic woman had manipulated and destroyed an entire family.

If Gribble hadn't killed Reg, he might very well have pushed her out, and he, Christabel and Sylvia could have had a happy life together. Instead, Christabel became a virtual prisoner and Sylvia was forced to take responsibility for her half-sister and hide away, hoping they'd never be found. Her life, too, had been blighted, and then wiped out.

As for poor Petal, no court was ever going to give her back to her natural mother, but what would they decide her fate was to be? She was happy now with Molly Heywood and the Bridgenorths, but that was a temporary arrangement. Was she going to spend the rest of her childhood being moved around, haunted by the memory of the cruel woman who snatched her away and locked her up and never fully understanding why the woman she called her mother had died?

Molly was surprised when DI Pople called on her at the George. On the local news the previous evening it had been reported that the body of a man believed to be Private Reginald Coleman had been found in the garden of Mulberry House. She had been shocked to the core and wondered how someone as wicked as Miss Gribble had managed to get away with her crimes.

When she took Petal to school she was aware of people looking at her and that groups of women had their heads together talking but would break off as she came near. No one dared to ask her any questions, which was just as well, because she knew no more than they did. But it was an uncomfortable experience, and she fervently hoped no one would try to talk to Petal about it.

Because this latest development had nothing to do with her, she hadn't expected a visit from the police and had continued her chambermaid duties as usual. Then she had been called down to see DI Pople.

They sat in the small office behind reception and he told her about Reg Coleman's body being found and how he'd gone to see Christabel to break the news to her.

'It was then that she told me that Petal is her daughter, not Sylvia's,' he said. And, seeing Molly's complete shock, he added, 'And your face reflects how I responded to the news.'

'Good God!' Molly exclaimed. 'That is the absolute last thing I expected to hear.'

He filled her in with a little more detail and then asked if she would consider going to see Christabel at Hellingly. 'You don't have to, but I think it will be beneficial to both of you. She really needs to know about both Sylvia and Petal. You might say she doesn't deserve to, and I wouldn't blame you after she walloped you with that axe. But I've noticed that you're a compassionate person, and I think talking to her will help you understand how all this came about. In my opinion, she's been as much a victim of Miss Gribble as Reg Coleman, Sylvia, Petal and you were. She isn't barmy, she's been fed drugs which kept her partially sedated, and now she's free of them she's articulate, sensible and horrified at her part in all this.'

Molly considered this for a moment or two. 'I hope she doesn't think that by getting me on side she can have Petal back?'

'She doesn't even know I'm asking you to see her and, besides, no judge on earth would allow Petal to go back to her, even if she'd become a saint. She's just a woman who has been badly used, and I know you will understand how that can happen.'

It crossed Molly's mind that George might have told DI Pople a bit about her home life.

'Okay, I'll go on my next day off. It can't hurt me, can it? At least I can make her see what a good mum Cassie was to Petal and, now I know her background, I think Cassie is the one who should be sainted!' She laughed then, and told DI Pople how much Cassie would've hated anyone saying such a thing.

'When are you seeing George again?' DI Pople asked. 'I liked him, he's got real guts.'

Molly shrugged. 'He's not my boyfriend. We're just friends from school.'

DI Pople raised an eyebrow. 'I believe he thinks of you as more than that. I'd happily have him in my team down here if he wanted a transfer.'

Molly could only smile. She wished just one of these people who thought her and George were meant for each other would give him a nudge.

Chapter Twenty-three

'They tell me it was you I hit with an axe,' Christabel said when Molly was shown into a small room at Hellingly to meet her.

Molly agreed that it was, thinking that this was the strangest introduction to anybody she'd ever had.

'I'm so very sorry,' Christabel added after a moment or two, as if it had taken that long for her to realize that an apology was necessary. 'I can't offer any real excuse other than I wasn't myself.'

'That will do,' Molly said, and held out her hand to the older woman. 'I was very fond of Cassie – your Sylvia – and Petal, too. My name is Molly Heywood.'

Molly had only had the briefest glimpse of Christabel the day she arrived at Mulberry House, and then again when she escaped from the cellar there. She had formed the idea from the first meeting that she looked similar to Cassie, but she hadn't had enough time to study Christabel. She had time now, and she was glad of it.

Christabel Coleman and Cassie were about the same height and size, five foot five and of slim build. But Cassie had strength in her face, where in Christabel's there was weakness. Cassie had a habit of sticking out her chin as if to show the world what she was made of, and she had a voluptuous, almost pin-up girl, appearance. Yet, looking at her mother now, Molly saw that Cassie had inherited her delicate bone structure, baby-blue eyes and wide mouth. Cassie had made herself more noticeable with her dyed hair, and with her unusual dress sense. Christabel had her mousy hair pulled back from her pale face in a single bunch, which did her no favours.

Molly had been told that this woman was forty-six, but she looked older, because she had deep wrinkles around her eyes and her mouth. The beige shirtwaister dress she was wearing aged her even more, but then Molly was fairly certain it wasn't her own, just something she'd been lent by the hospital.

'DI Pople thought it would be good for us to have a talk,' Molly said. 'And I think he's right. Cassie never talked about you, and I assumed that was because you'd fallen out when Petal was born. Instead she talked about books, poetry, art, music and mystical things. Was she always like that?'

Christabel half smiled. 'Yes, she was. She read anything and everything, going off to the library in Rye as soon as she was old enough to catch the bus alone. I think growing up on the marsh makes for artistic leanings. It's the wildness of the terrain and the weather. I used to walk for miles as a girl and write poetry about what I saw, just as she did.'

'She was very much a loner, but I always felt it wasn't really from choice, but necessity. Would you agree with that?'

'I think so. You see, she was just thirteen when war broke out and, if it hadn't been for that, she could've made it to university. She might have been a teacher; she used to say that's what she wanted.'

'She did a good job teaching Petal,' Molly said. 'She could read fluently before she started school, and she loves history, too. Her teacher at the school in Rye tells me she's very clever and eager to learn.'

'She's with you, staying at the George, isn't she? How is she? After everything she's been through, and so much of it my fault, I don't feel I've even got the right to ask.'

Molly found herself warming to this woman she had thought she would hate and despise. She seemed a very honest woman, as Cassie had been. She might be a weak person who had allowed herself to be manipulated and controlled, but there was goodness at her core.

'She's quieter than she used to be. She watches people, as if she's making sure about them, before speaking. She still has the occasional bad dream, and now and then she has tantrums that we have no real explanation for. I think it's pent-up anger and frustration because she doesn't understand what it was all about. Sadly, neither I nor anyone else can fully explain it to her, she's too young to grasp it all.'

Christabel's eyes welled up with tears, but she brushed them away as if she'd decided she had no right to cry about a child who was suffering because of her.

'Will you tell me about her and Sylvia, or Cassie, as you know her? I mean, how their life was before Miss Gribble and I turned up.'

The raw longing and eagerness in her face

393

touched Molly. 'I will if you promise to tell me about Cassie before she ran away with Petal. How she reacted when you told her you were having a baby, how you both talked about it and how she came to run away. You see, you may be Petal's real mother, but I'm the only link with the life Petal remembers with Cassie. If you tell me how it was, one day I can sit Petal down and explain the whole thing in a way she can understand.'

Christabel nodded. 'You are a remarkable young woman,' she said eventually. 'I can see why my daughter chose you as a friend. If the dead are able to look down and watch us, I think she would be very proud to have known you, and so grateful that Petal is in your care.'

Molly blushed at the compliment. She'd thought she would be irritated by this woman's weakness, but she wasn't anything like the drippy, mad person she'd expected.

'Okay, so where do I start? Cassie did rather take the village by storm. She not only wore tight sweaters and skirts and made no apologies for being a lone mother, but she had a "Don't get on my wrong side" attitude. Yet she got round a local farmer who no one else has ever managed to charm, and he let her rent Stone Cottage.'

'Were people nasty because Petal was mixed race?'

'I can't lie to you: they said horrid things behind Cassie's back. My father, who is the village grocer, was just about the nastiest. But most people were nice to Petal. Of course, she is a little charmer, so bright and sunny natured. And she was a novelty, remember! Some of the villagers had never seen a black person before, and those who did only had memories of GIs stationed in Somerset for the last couple of years of the war and, as you'll remember, they didn't get very good press. But, as I said, Petal's a little charmer, so you can rest assured she didn't suffer any real prejudice. Her teacher liked her and the other children played with her. I don't think they even noticed her skin was a different colour to theirs.'

'Well, that's a relief.' Christabel sighed. 'Benjamin – that was her father – used to tell me hurtful things that had been said to him, and of course, back in America where he came from, white people's attitudes to Negros were appalling.'

'Cassie put her head up and sailed through everything, and if she'd lived she would've made Petal do the same. I really admired her for that, and for her intelligence. I loved being with her, she knew so much. She was living in the East End of London before I met her; after her death, I stayed with a lovely old lady who had befriended her while she was there, and everyone who knew her only had good things to say about her.'

Christabel smiled to hear that. 'How did she live, though? I mean, where did she get money? Did she have a job?'

'Where she got her money was a bit of a mystery to me,' Molly admitted. 'She was very frugal. In Somerset she grew vegetables, made new clothes out of old ones, and she used to go into Bristol once a week on the bus, so she may have had a cleaning job there, or a man friend. But she never said.'

'Did she talk about men friends?'

'Yes, but I never met any of them. She liked men; she preferred their company to women's, in general. She was very ahead of her time in that way.'

'You mean she slept with them?'

Molly blushed.

'You can say it. I was a fallen woman myself,' Christabel said with a light laugh. 'I worshipped Reg, and we were "carrying on", as my mother used to call it, well before we got married. I was pregnant on our wedding day, and barely eighteen. I took it very hard when Reg went off to war. We'd been everything to each other – best friends and lovers – and I missed that.' She paused, as if remembering.

'We never intended to spend our entire married life in Mulberry House with my parents,' she went on after a moment or two. 'But Sylvia came, then the bad times in the thirties. Reg was a carpenter, and we couldn't have survived on our own.'

'Your father was a doctor?'

'Yes, he was, and my grandfather before that. The practice had always been at Mulberry House. Back when I was a little girl, father went out on his rounds in a pony and trap. They had me quite late in life and, being the only child, I sort of felt obliged to stay with them. And, of course, they loved Sylvia. Then they died, a year apart, in 1935 and '36, and the house became mine. It was our intention to fill it with children and live happily ever after.'

'But you had Miss Gribble, the Wicked Witch, in the house with you...'

Christabel held her head in her hands as if the thought of everything that woman had done was too much to bear.

'Reg was always saying I should make her go,' she said after a few moments. 'He said she gave him the creeps because she watched every move we made. He was right, of course, but she'd been there my whole life, and even before that with my parents. Where would she go? At her age, she wouldn't find another job.

'Then war broke out and Reg joined up and went off to France, so I was glad of her being there. It was a big house to be alone in with a child. But I'm wandering off a bit. You want to know about Sylvia.'

'It's all interesting,' Molly said. 'Some other time I'd love to hear how it was for you during the war but, for now, tell me about how Sylvia reacted when you got pregnant.'

'I told her before I told Gribby and swore her to secrecy. Sylvia was always very mature for her age, and I didn't have to point things out, she just got it. She was excited about having a baby brother or sister, but scared, too.'

'What of?'

Christabel shrugged. 'Mostly of what people would say. And of Gribby too – we both knew she wasn't going to be a bit pleased I'd been with a man. Since Reg had gone missing, she'd become more and more forceful, taking over everything, as if it was her house. I should have put a stop to it, but I was grieving for Reg and it was easier than confrontation. Then, one day, when I was at least six months gone, she noticed.'

Molly observed that Christabel had leaned back in her chair, closed her eyes and had begun speaking as if she were reliving that day.

'We were doing the washing. Gribby was hooking the clothes out of the boiler with the boiler stick into the sink, and I was rinsing them. Sylvia was standing by at the mangle, ready to turn the handle when I fed the rinsed clothes into it.

'It was early January and a wild, windy day, and when I accidentally sloshed water on to my clothes, I yelled because it was icy cold. Gribby turned to me and, where my wet overall had stuck to me, she saw my tummy sticking out.

'"You little whore!" she said and leapt forward and slapped my face really hard.

'"Do that again and I'll hit you!" Sylvia screamed out. When I glanced at my daughter, she had the copper stick in her hands and was holding it, ready to strike Gribby. I remember, she was wearing a flowery red crossover overall over a dark-green jumper, her face was flushed from the steam in the kitchen and her hair had gone into tight curls.

'"You'll never lay a hand on my mother again or you'll be out on your ear so fast you won't know what's hit you," she snarled.

'My face was stinging. I was icy cold from my wet clothes, but I was so proud of my daughter being so bold and brave in standing up for me.

'"Yes, she's having a baby," Sylvia carried on, jabbing the copper stick at Gribby. "And we're going to look after him or her between us. If you don't like the idea of that, there's the door," and she pointed the stick at the back door. "Go and get yourself another job and another home, but just remember no other family will tolerate your interference or your bullying."

'"How can you speak to me like that when I've given my whole life to you and your family?" Gribby whined. "I'm only worried that everyone in the village will be talking about your mother. She won't be able to bear that. And I don't interfere or bully either of you. I don't know how you can say that."

'"You don't know any other way!" Sylvia shouted. "You bullied Granny and Grandpa, then Mum. But you won't do it to me. I won't stand for it."

'She didn't stand for it either.' Christabel opened her eyes again, seemingly unaware she'd been going back in time and reliving the scene. 'When my baby was born and Gribby saw how dark-skinned she was, she looked at me with utter disgust. But I'd confided in Sylvia some time before, and she picked the baby up to cuddle her and gave Gribby a look that would turn anyone else to stone.

'Gribby went mad, saying terrible things I can't repeat. But Sylvia ordered her out of the room, and took charge. I didn't think of it at the time, but I came to realize later that she never, ever left Gribby alone with the baby.'

'You think she was afraid Gribby would smother her or something?'

'Yes, I think so. I wasn't doing well with feeding her, and I remember Sylvia told me she thought it was best I put her on a bottle and then she could do the night feeds so I could get strong again.'

'Was that in preparation for Sylvia taking her away with her?'

'No, I don't think so, not then, only so she could take the baby into her room at night. I think she thought Gribby might come into my room and do something while I was asleep. Sylvia locked her door. I know, because I tried to go in there one night.'

'So Sylvia was looking after Petal right from the start?'

'Oh yes, she said even before Pamela was born that she'd say the baby was hers so people wouldn't talk about me. Sylvia never did anything in half measures, so I think she believed if she was going to tell people it was her baby then she must act like its mother.'

'DI Pople said that she registered Pamela's birth. Did she tell you she was going to?'

'Oh yes. She made me promise I would keep a constant eye on the baby that day because she couldn't take her with her. She also told me I wasn't to tell Gribby where she'd gone. I'm not sure why that was.'

'Maybe she was already planning to run off and didn't want Gribby taking the birth certificate from her?'

'Perhaps.' Christabel shrugged. 'But you must understand that, back then, I didn't believe Gribby could hurt anyone – well, no more than a slap, like she gave me. But Sylvia did. A couple of days before she left she said, "It's not safe for Pamela here, I've seen the look on Gribby's face, and she hates her." I told her she was over-reacting but she just shook her head and said, "You've

400

always been blind to her faults."'

'But did she tell you she was going to take Petal and run away?'

'Yes, the day before. Gribby was out doing something to the car. Sylvia was washing some baby clothes in the sink. "I'm leaving with Petal tomorrow," she said. "Don't try and stop me, Mother, I know it's for the best. She's registered as my baby now, so you can't do anything. If you gave Gribby her marching orders, I'd stay, but I know you can't do that, she's got too strong a hold on you."'

'Where was she planning to go? Did she have any money?'

'She wouldn't say where she was going, but she had money in a post office account from when her grandparents died. She said she'd contact me as soon as she was settled, and that if I made Gribby go she'd come back.'

'Did she contact you?'

'Yes, she called from a phone box. If Gribby answered she always put the phone down. She would tell me that Petal had got a tooth, or was eating solids, things like that, but never about where she was. Always the same question: had I made Gribby go? Of course, I hadn't. I couldn't, she was too strong for me to deal with.'

'Constance, the Church Army sister who befriended her in Whitechapel, said she thought Cassie was waiting for something. Was that for you to get rid of Gribby?'

'I would imagine so. I got lower and lower during that time. Guilt, sorrow and fear are a potent mix and I now suspect that Gribby was feeding me something to keep me calm and under control, as everything seemed very cloudy and disjointed. About the time Petal would have turned three Gribby talked about getting a private detective to find her. She kept saying she was sorry she'd been nasty about the baby, that it was just the shock and she wanted to make amends. She even talked about doing up a bedroom for Petal, and how wonderful it would be to have a small child in the house again.'

'Did the detective find her?'

'Not that one. We hired several, and they all drew a blank. They weren't that good, I suppose, just took my money and sat on their backsides. I had my last phone call from Sylvia on Petal's fourth birthday. She said there was no point in her ringing me any more because nothing was going to change. She had to think of Petal's future, school and such like. She was tired of sitting on a platform for a train that would never come.'

Molly could almost hear Cassie making that last remark. 'That must have been just before she came to Somerset.'

Christabel began to cry then, tears streaming down her cheeks. 'If only I'd been braver,' she whimpered. 'We could have had a good life together. We didn't have to stay out on the marsh. We could have sold the house and moved anywhere we fancied. Now I've lost both my daughters and I'm going to prison. All because I was gutless.'

Molly's heart swelled with sympathy for this broken woman. She couldn't think of anything to say that would change Christabel's life, but she got up and went to her and took her in her arms.

'I get angry with my mother, too, because she

402

stays with my father, who's a terrible bully,' she said softly. 'I suggested we got a flat together in Bristol, but she won't leave him, so I know how Cassie must have felt. I've been weak, too, working for Dad without a proper wage, letting him control my life. If it hadn't been for Cassie's death I'd still be the same, so I understand how it was for you.'

'You are such a kind girl,' Christabel said into Molly's chest. 'I hope that, whatever they decide about Petal's future, she'll be allowed to keep in touch with you.'

'If I'm asked my opinion about you at the trial, I'll say what Cassie would've said, that you were weak, but that that isn't a crime or a sin. And if I can play any role in Petal's life, and I do so hope I can, I'll find a way that you can share in it, too.'

Chapter Twenty-four

The train to London was crammed with people going Christmas shopping. Molly had brought a book for the journey, but she couldn't concentrate because of the butterflies in her stomach, so she stared mindlessly out of the window.

Miss Gribble's murder trial was to start at the Old Bailey tomorrow, Tuesday, 6 December, and George would be meeting her at Charing Cross Station today to take her to the hotel he'd found for them both to stay in until the trial was over.

She didn't know if it was the trial or meeting

George that was causing the butterflies. Both were scary, but in different ways. At the trial, she just had to answer questions truthfully but in front of a great many people. With George, there would be no one observing or commenting, but ever since the day he had rescued her from Mulberry House he had rarely been out of her mind, and she felt it might be love. He hadn't made his feelings clear to her, though, and now they would be alone together every evening for the duration of the trial she felt it was time to push things forward. However, if she made a move on him and he didn't respond, she was going to be so embarrassed.

She felt they were meant for each other, and George had said something similar in his last phone call to her about today's arrangements. 'It was always you and me,' he'd said. 'We held hands when we went into school the first day. We always told each other our problems. You were my partner in ballroom-dancing lessons.'

She'd joked that they could hardly base their future on such flimsy connections. But, after she'd put the phone down, she was sorry she hadn't just agreed with him.

It was very cold. Under her new red houndstooth-checked coat she wore a twinset and a straight wool skirt with a petticoat beneath that. Recently, since it had turned cold, she had taken to wearing slacks when she went out of the hotel, but Mrs Bridgenorth had said they weren't smart enough for London, so she just had to put up with an icy bottom and legs. At least her feet were toasty, in fur-lined boots.

Looking out the window and seeing sheep huddling together for warmth in the muddy fields, she smiled, remembering the song 'Gilly Gilly Ossenfeffer Katzenellen Bogen by the Sea', which Petal had woken her with this morning.

It was such a silly song, by Max Bygraves, but Petal loved it. She was a good singer, so much so she was singing the first verse of 'In the Bleak Midwinter' solo at the carol service in St Mary the Virgin on the Sunday afternoon before Christmas.

Molly was sure she'd be crying with pride when she heard her.

The question of what was going to happen to this child was another huge worry. It made the questions of whether George cared for her, and whether she would be struck dumb when she was asked questions at the trial pale into insignificance. Mr and Mrs Bridgenorth loved Petal, but they still saw her stay with them as a temporary arrangement, until something more suitable turned up. So far, nothing had, but Molly almost had heart palpitations whenever the children's officer visited, afraid she'd come to take her away.

Christabel was to be a witness in Miss Gribble's trial, but the solicitor for the prosecution had told Molly that she wasn't going to be charged with any crime. It was quite clear to everyone who had questioned her that she'd had no knowledge of her husband's murder, and that the later crimes of abducting Petal and imprisoning Molly had been done without her knowledge or help.

'She's been punished terribly for her weakness already,' the solicitor had said sympathetically. 'Her husband and older daughter murdered, the younger one taken from her. She'll have a sad and lonely life in her house on the marsh. Even if she sells it and moves away, the sadness will go with her.'

Molly totally agreed with him, and it made her sad, too. Not for the first time, she wondered what Cassie would've made of it all. Molly suspected she would be angry that, after all she'd gone through to keep Petal safe, her little sister's future still hung in the balance.

When Molly stepped off the train at Charing Cross, George came haring through the crowd and enveloped her in a bear hug. 'I thought today would never come,' he said. 'Sarge asked why I was so excited about a trial – after all, I've been to dozens of them. He must have forgotten I've always had a thing about you!'

Molly glowed. 'Well, I've had a thing about you, too,' she responded. 'No wonder Londoners think Somerset folk are very slow!'

He carried her case and shepherded her down into the underground to make their way to the hotel, which he said was in Russell Square. 'Sarge told me about it. He stayed there a couple of times while he was at trials in London. I was surprised at how nice it was. Your room is right next to mine, and there's a bathroom just opposite.'

Molly wondered if the closeness of their rooms would mean he'd be trying to get into hers. But she decided she wouldn't mind if he did.

The hotel was nice; nothing lavish, but the reception, with its highly polished floor and desk and shiny brass fittings gave a very good impression. It was lovely and warm, too, and Molly's bedroom was clean and cosy, with a thick red eiderdown on the bed and tapestry curtains.

She and George went out in the evening to get something to eat, but it was so cold they went into the first place they found, a small café with a very limited menu.

'Sausage and chips, egg and chips, fish and chips, ham and chips,' George read out. 'It wouldn't do to hate chips in here, would it?'

'Good job I love chips, then,' Molly said. 'My dad never allowed us to have them, he said they were a wasteful way of cooking potatoes. I could never see that, unless of course you count eating more than you would with plain boiled ones because they taste better.'

'He's a very opinionated man,' George said thoughtfully. 'I went into the shop yesterday before I left and, just to be polite, I told him I was coming up to London for the trial. It's been the talk of the village, of course, because the local papers rehashed all the stuff about Cassie's death and Petal disappearing the minute they found Reg Coleman's body. They portrayed you as a heroine for rescuing Petal from Miss Gribble.'

The waitress came over to them at that point and they gave their order for sausages and chips and a pot of tea.

'So what did he say?' Molly asked once the waitress had gone.

'"Waste of taxpayers' money giving the woman a trial," and he said it in that snooty way he has. "They should take her out and hang her. Can't think what they need you there for either. You should be down here investigating who has been stealing my coal."'

Molly laughed because George had sounded exactly like her father. 'So who has been stealing his coal?'

'No one. Your mum has just been putting more on the fire because it's cold. She told me so herself. When he goes out to the pub she goes down and fills up the coal scuttle.'

'She shouldn't have to be carrying coal scuttles up the stairs at her age!' Molly exclaimed. 'He said four years ago he was going to get a gas fire put in. Do you know what stopped him?'

'The cost of the fire?'

'No, because some women were talking in the shop about how much less work there is without a coal fire. Hardly any dusting, and no clearing out ashes or laying the fire. He went right off the idea then, afraid Mum might spend part of her day sitting down reading a book.'

'Surely not!'

'I promise you. He made out that a gas fire costs more than a coal fire to run, but that just isn't true. But I'm going off the subject ... did he ask about me?'

'No, but I asked if he had a message for you, and he said, "Why would I send a message?" I pointed out that being a witness is a horrible ordeal for most people. Guess what he said?'

'That I shouldn't have stuck my nose in other people's affairs?'

George grimaced. 'You know him so well. I don't know how you stood him all those years. He's utterly joyless.'

'I thought about leaving so many times, but

Mum was always the problem. I thought he'd be nasty to her. Is she all right, George?'

George leaned across the table, put one finger under her chin and tilted her face up. 'She's fine. For some peculiar reason, he's been nicer to her, or at least so she tells me. She reckons he was always jealous of you girls, wanted her all to himself.'

'That's obscene.' Molly laughed.

'Since I've been in the police force, I've come across lots of men like your dad.' George smiled. 'They lash out because they feel inadequate. They say nasty things because they think it makes them sound like big men. Deep down, they're insecure little twerps, but the saddest thing of all is that they don't see what they've got. Like your dad: he's got a lovely wife, two daughters to be very proud of – especially you – and a good business. Though it's a wonder he's got any customers, he's so rude or offhand to most of them.'

'I wish I could go home to check on Mum, but it's difficult. She'd be upset if I didn't make the peace with him and stay there, but I know I couldn't do that.'

'You could always stay with my folks and get a job locally. That would satisfy your mum.'

The waitress chose that moment to come with their meal, giving Molly time to think about how she could hint to George that she wanted more from him than just friendship.

'Would it satisfy you? I mean, me being in the spare room?'

Molly was aware that the question hadn't come out in the seductive way she'd intended but,

409

considering the length of time they'd known one another, she would've expected him to at least laugh. Instead, he blushed furiously and looked very uncomfortable.

She was mortified, yet at the same time she felt indignant that he couldn't rise to the occasion with a joke, some banter, anything that would stop her feeling like a first-class idiot.

It had spoiled the evening. George changed the subject to ask how Petal was, and Molly did her best to sound animated and happy when, inside, she felt hollow. George went on to tell her about two farmers in a neighbouring village who were caught up in a bitter feud. It had started when one of the farmers found his prize-winning sheepdog dead, apparently poisoned, and he was so convinced the other man had done it out of jealousy he retaliated by setting fire to his hay barn.

Normally, Molly would've been all too eager to hear the full story, but she wanted George to be the way he had been at the station, when he'd hugged her, to see that light in his eyes that said he thought the world of her and was excited to be alone with her in London for a few days. So she didn't show any enthusiasm for his story. In fact, she yawned and looked pointedly at her watch.

They barely spoke on their way back to the hotel and, although George hesitated outside her door, shuffling his feet and looking sheepish, he didn't say anything more than goodnight and that she shouldn't get too worked up about being cross-examined in court the next day, as she probably wouldn't be called for a day or two.

Molly slept soundly despite everything, and woke refreshed. After a very big cooked breakfast she and George decided to walk to the Old Bailey, as it wasn't very far and they would be sitting down waiting for most of the day. Molly wasn't one to keep up bad feeling with anyone, so she chatted normally, as if the night before had been a pleasant one.

George was in his uniform, as he was officially on duty as a witness, and he looked very smart. 'Once witnesses have given their evidence they can watch the rest of the trial,' he explained as they walked along. 'It's quite interesting watching and listening to the two opposing barristers. Sometimes, they're just like actors, only playing to the jury instead of an audience. But I doubt I'll be here to hear the closing speeches and the verdict. I expect I'll be summoned back home.'

'Oh, that's a shame,' Molly said. 'I thought we had a week or so up here.'

She purposely didn't say 'together', in case that was too familiar.

'Unfortunately, police witnesses are usually called right at the start. This case is a bit more complicated than most, as Miss Gribble has pleaded not guilty to abduction, claiming that Christabel had the right as Petal's mother to go and get her from Cassie. She claims, too, that she never touched Cassie; she just tripped over and fell. She's also pleading not guilty to murdering Reg Coleman, though how she can maintain that story I don't know, not when his body was found in the garden.'

'I suppose she could claim that someone else

killed him and put him in the ground. How are they going to prove it was her after all these years?'

'I think the forensic team have got something up their sleeve and, besides, when the jury hear she locked Petal upstairs for months and was going to leave you to die of starvation I can't see them finding her not guilty of stabbing and burying Reg when she alone had the motive and opportunity to do it.'

'Whatever happens, it's going to be tough for Christabel today,' Molly said. 'I'd hate to be in a position like hers. Miss Gribble is almost like a mother or big sister to her, and she must have loved her.'

'I'm hoping that now she realizes just how badly she's been betrayed, and that Miss Gribble stole her whole life it will make her speak out when she is called to give evidence.'

'It's funny to think such a weak woman could produce a daughter like Cassie,' Molly said. 'She used to tell me to stand up for myself and demand my rights. I used to think I was weak, just like my mum.'

'You are like your mum in that you care about other people,' George said, taking her arm as they crossed a busy road. 'That isn't weak. And you've got to remember that women of your mum's age were told from birth that being a good wife meant never criticizing or opposing their husband.'

'I suppose that's okay if you've got a reasonable husband like your dad.'

'Don't ever tell my dad that! Mum is the boss in our house. She's just good at making him think he is. She was even the one who proposed!'

Molly giggled. 'Really?'

'Yes, really. Apparently, he'd been hinting at it for months, but never came right out with it. He hadn't even dared to say he loved her. So she got cross with him, and just said she was tired of it all, she loved him and wanted to get married, but if he didn't feel the same he was to admit it and then clear off.'

'That was brave of her! Most women would feel a man was just stringing her along if he didn't speak about his feelings, or that he was rather pathetic.'

George's head whipped round to look at her. Molly felt herself blushing and she hoped that, by just looking ahead, she would appear nonchalant.

Neither of them was called on the first day of the trial; they just had to sit and wait. At first Molly enjoyed watching people coming in, wondering who they were and what crime they were involved in, but that soon wore off and she began to feel cold and bored. The time passed very slowly, even with George to chat with.

Her mind wandered and she began to think how far she'd come since that first time in London for her interview at Bourne & Hollingsworth. She'd been scared to eat in a café, terrified she'd get lost on the underground and convinced she stood out as a naïve country girl. What a lot she'd seen and done since then! She'd been sacked from her job, almost raped by the man in Soho, gone to live in the East End and then got the job at the George. And she'd done what she

413

set out to do: to find Petal and see Cassie's killer brought to justice.

There had been some terrible times but some very good ones, too. She'd made a friend for life in Dilys, and Ted and Evelyn had become almost family. She could thank Cassie and Constance for expanding her mind and making her realize that she wasn't weak. London had played its part in rounding her out but, although it would always be an exciting place to visit, she was very glad she didn't have to live or work here any more.

She could imagine Cassie smiling down at her. She felt her friend would think she'd turned up trumps. Not just for saving Petal, but for saving herself from becoming a cowed little mouse like her mother.

That evening she and George went to the pictures. He wanted to see *On the Waterfront,* starring Marion Brando, but Molly insisted she had to see *Carmen Jones,* with Dorothy Dandridge, and somewhat reluctantly George agreed.

She loved it, as she knew she would, because the music was so moving, and she cried several times. George admitted as they came out that he had been close to tears, too, and that he had loved the film, but said he was going to drag her to see *On the Waterfront* the following night.

He hadn't held her hand or even put his arm around her in the cinema but, when they got back to the hotel, he kissed her goodnight outside her room.

It was a delicious kiss, slow, sensual and toe curling, but George pulled away from her and smiled

414

down at her. 'Bed for you. I wish I could come in and share it, but I promised your mum I wouldn't take advantage just because we were in a hotel together.'

'I think I'm old enough to decide for myself whether I would welcome a man in my room,' she said jokingly.

'I agree, but a promise is a promise and, anyway, we may need to have our wits about us tomorrow,' he said. 'But can I just add that there would be nothing I'd like better than to spend the night with you.'

Molly closed the bedroom door behind her and stood leaning against it for a moment in a daze. He'd finally admitted he wanted her. Was that because she'd put him under pressure by talking about weak men? Or because he really meant it?

They had barely got to the Old Bailey the next morning when the prosecuting barrister, Mr Barrington-Sloane, came to tell Molly she was to be called first.

'I want the jury to see straight away that there is no doubt Miss Gribble is a ruthless and cunning murderess who had total control of Christabel Coleman. So I will first ask you to tell the jury about Sylvia Coleman and Pamela, then lead on to you finding Sylvia Coleman dead in Stone Cottage. I aim to go on from there to how you came to be imprisoned by Miss Gribble, but there is a possibility the judge will not allow that evidence today. We'll see how it goes.'

Molly's stomach began to churn with fright. Yesterday, as she and George were waiting, he had told her tales about defence lawyers throwing doubt on things witnesses had said. He'd assured her that she'd be all right as she was simply reporting what she'd seen at Stone Cottage and no one could twist it, as it was fact.

'Don't look so scared,' Barrington-Sloane said. He was scary, too, tall and very thin with a nose like a beak. With his robe, wig, and half-moon spectacles perched precariously on the end of his nose, he reminded her of a crow. 'You'll be fine,' he went on. 'Just look at the judge and speak up.'

Molly didn't think she'd be able to speak up, or to call Cassie and Petal by their real names. She couldn't even think of them as Sylvia and Pamela, let alone remember to use those names.

It began very well. Barrington-Sloane encouraged her to set the scene by explaining how Sylvia and Pamela hadn't turned up for the Coronation Day party, and how Molly had gone up to Stone Cottage on her bicycle to find them and found Sylvia dead on the floor and Pamela missing.

The defence lawyer, a short, stubby man, said he had no questions, so Barrington-Sloane moved straight on to getting Molly to relate what happened when she went to Mulberry House with the intention of meeting Christabel Coleman. Molly went on to say how she was attacked by Miss Gribble and knocked unconscious, only to come to later to find herself locked in a room in the cellar.

'Will you tell the court what it was like in that cellar?' Barrington-Sloane asked her.

'It was very cold,' she said. 'The only thing to sit or lie on was a wooden bench. I couldn't sleep because of the cold, and I was hungry and thirsty.'

'You were in there for two days,' Barrington-Sloane said. 'Were you confident you'd be either let out by Miss Gribble or rescued by someone else?'

'No I wasn't confident about being rescued,' Molly said. 'I thought I would die in there, as no one knew where I was.'

'But after your second night in there you did manage to pick the lock and escape,' Barrington-Sloane said. 'Did you run out of the house to get help for the child you believed to be held there?'

'No, I stayed in the house and went to find her,' Molly said. 'I guessed they must be holding her in one of the rooms upstairs, and I went to look for her.'

'And when you found her locked in, you broke down the door to set her free, isn't that so?'

'Yes, sir.'

'But your troubles weren't over just yet: you had to get out of that house, with the child. She was undernourished, neglected and frightened, but you carried her downstairs. And what then?'

'Miss Gribble was there, a poker in her hand,' Molly said. 'I whispered to Petal that she was to run when I put her down. Luckily, that was enough of a distraction for Miss Gribble, and I managed to grab a heavy ornament and throw it at her. It stopped her in her tracks.'

Barrington-Sloane told the remainder of the story, asking Molly to confirm that Christabel Coleman had knocked her unconscious with an axe. Later, she and the child had been taken to

417

Hastings Hospital by ambulance. The defence lawyer, Mr Myers, began his turn by spending a few moments strutting around the court, his hands behind his back, before starting his cross-examination. Molly quaked, fearing he was going to bring up her having got the sack from Bourne & Hollingsworth, or some other incident from the past which would suggest that her word couldn't be trusted.

'Miss Heywood,' he said, with the kind of sneer smile that confirmed her worst fears about what he intended to bring up, 'we have heard that you diligently took part in the search for Pamela after her abduction, but I would like to know why you weren't so diligent when you found a letter in Stone Cottage that was a link to Sylvia Coleman's past. Why didn't you take this letter to the police?'

'Because I knew they wouldn't follow it up,' she replied. 'They'd already lost interest in the case by then.'

'I'm sorry. I hadn't been informed that you were an expert on police procedure,' he said sarcastically. 'So, instead of informing those who have access to a huge network to track people down, and the benefit of forensic science to assist them, you chose to play detective?'

'I suppose so. I thought Sister Constance, the lady the letter came from, would be more likely to open up to me.'

'Can you tell me the date on which you found the letter?'

'No, sir, but it must have been July or so.'

'July or so. In 1953?'

418

'Yes, sir,' she responded, her heart sinking even further.

'Didn't it occur to you that by withholding this piece of evidence you might be responsible for prolonging the length of time that vulnerable little girl was held captive? Or, even worse that during that time she might have died?'

'Sister Constance didn't know anything,' Molly retorted. 'Even if I had given the letter to the police they wouldn't have found Pamela through Sister Constance.'

'Is that so?' Mr Myers asked, fixing her with dead, shark-like eyes. 'Isn't it true you were given a notebook belonging to Miss Coleman?'

Molly felt nauseous now. 'Well, yes, but it didn't have addresses or anything, just odd references to things she did, places she'd been to. It was very hard to understand.'

'And you didn't believe that an experienced detective would have been able to decipher a young woman's jottings faster than you?'

'Like I said, the way the police had left the case led me to think they would just ignore me.'

'Yet you went to school with Constable George Walsh, who was involved in the investigation. You were such close friends that he rode his motorbike to Rye from Somerset when he suspected you were in trouble. Are you telling me he wouldn't have taken your concerns seriously?'

Molly squirmed. She couldn't even be indignant at the barrister's questions, because he was right. She should have given that letter to the police and she should have at least informed George what she was up to.

'With hindsight, I should have shared all information I received or had worked out for myself with the police,' she admitted. 'But I didn't imagine I was going to find Petal – or Pamela, to give her her correct name – in a village out on the Kentish marshes. I was just trying to find my friend's relatives.'

The defence lawyer said he had no further questions, and Molly was able to leave the witness stand.

At four o'clock the judge adjourned for the day. George had given his evidence that afternoon, and tomorrow morning both sides would make their closing speeches. Molly had hardy said a word since giving her evidence that morning and, although George hadn't been in court to hear what the defence lawyer had asked her, he'd been at enough trials to guess why she was so withdrawn.

It was dark when they came out of the Old Bailey, and very cold. George led her across the road to a café nearby for a cup of tea.

'You mustn't take it personally,' he said once they'd sat down, taking her hand across the table and squeezing it. He had wanted to cuddle her as soon as they got out of the court, but he couldn't, not while he was in uniform. 'Lawyers are like that with everyone. They have to pick at things witnesses have said and done, it's the only way to draw out the full picture so the jury can make a fair assessment of the guilt or innocence of the person in the dock.'

Molly gave a weak smile, but he could see she

felt humiliated. 'Want to tell me?' he asked. 'Or would you rather forget?'

She told him the gist of it and admitted the lawyer had been right: she should have taken the letter from Constance to the police.

Well, it is a shame you didn't give it to me,' he said. 'I would've pushed for the London mob to go and talk to her. But I can see why you didn't – it was hardly a thorough investigation. I've seen the police put more effort into a burglary or a road accident.'

'He said Petal might have been found much earlier but for me withholding that letter. It makes me feel terrible to think I prolonged her suffering.'

George reached out and wiped a tear away from her cheek with his thumb. 'If you hadn't acted, she might never have been found,' he said. 'So stop blaming yourself and let's go back to the hotel so I can change and you can put on something warmer, then we'll go up to the West End, see the Christmas lights and have a swanky meal somewhere.'

'I thought you wanted to see *On the Waterfront?*' she asked.

'Not as much as I'd like to see you smile again,' he replied.

Chapter Twenty-five

Molly woke to hear banging on a door close to her room.

'Mr Walsh!' a woman called out.

She pricked up her ears at George's name.

'There's an urgent telephone call for you,' the woman continued.

Molly turned on the bedside light to look at her watch. It was six in the morning.

While they had been having dinner the previous night in an Italian restaurant just off Oxford Street, George had said he thought he would be called back to Sawbridge in the morning. 'I wish they'd let me stay to hear the verdict, but it's as if the DI wants you to have all the worry about being a witness but not the pleasure of the result.'

But if this was George's DI calling him, Molly thought it was a bit extreme to ring so early. He could have left it till after breakfast.

She heard George come out of his room and go down the stairs, she turned the light off and snuggled down again.

The next thing she knew George was tapping on her door. 'Open up, Molly,' he whispered. 'I have to talk to you.'

Assuming he wanted to say goodbye, she got out of bed, pulling the eiderdown around her, as it was freezing cold. She wondered if she was brave enough to go back to the Old Bailey on her own to hear the closing speeches and the verdict.

She unlocked the door and George came in. He had a jacket on over his blue-and-white striped pyjamas, his hair was sticking up and his face was very pale.

'What on earth's wrong?' she asked. 'Why did they phone you so early? Is it an emergency?'

He didn't answer for a minute, just looked at her as if unable to speak.

'George, you're frightening me. What is it?'

He ran his fingers through his hair distractedly. 'I've got to tell you, but I don't know how to,' he said.

'Tell me what? Is it Petal?' she asked in alarm, clutching the eiderdown around her even more tightly. 'Has something happened to her?'

He came closer, and his face was contorted with anguish. 'No, it's not about Petal, it's your parents.' He paused, putting his hands up on his head as if trying to force himself to get the words out. 'I'm so sorry, Molly. There's no easy way to say this. The shop caught fire last night and they both died.'

For a few moments Molly thought she was dreaming. Yet George had pulled her to him tightly as he spoke and his tweed jacket felt real enough against her cheek, and she could hear him breathing hard as he leaned his face against her head.

'A fire?' she exclaimed. 'How could that happen?'

'It started in the store room at the back of the shop. The firemen think your dad must have left the electric fire on in there and it was too close to a cardboard box or something. Once it got going, it found plenty to burn, and the staircase up to the flat is right over the store room.'

'You mean they were trapped upstairs and were burned alive?' Molly moved back from him and looked at him in horror.

'I think they were overcome by the fumes long before the flames reached them,' George assured her. 'They probably didn't even wake up.'

Molly went over to the window and pulled the curtain back. She thought she ought to cry, but she felt curiously numb, as if she'd been told about a couple of strangers. It was still dark outside; all she could see of Russell Square was a golden circle of light beneath the lamp post outside the hotel. But she could hear the rumble and clinking sound of the milkman's float on its round.

'Molly! Speak to me!' George said.

'What is there to say?' she asked, turning towards him. 'It's one of those times when there are no words. Mostly, I hate Dad, but I wouldn't want anyone, not even my worst enemy, to die like that. And Mum! What did she ever do to deserve such a death?'

'I know. It's so cruel,' he agreed. 'Oh, Molly, she certainly didn't deserve such a death. She should have grown old surrounded by grandchildren who loved her. She should have been around to see you and Emily make the peace with your father, and for him to change his ways. But we'd better get dressed and get a train back there. I'll go down and get a tray of tea first.'

When he had left the room Molly tossed the eiderdown on to the bed and began pulling on

424

some clothes. She got as far as putting on some slacks and a jumper when, suddenly, the enormity of what had happened hit her like a tidal wave, and the tears came.

It was over fifteen months since she had left Sawbridge, and she hadn't seen her parents in that time. She'd spoken to her mother on the phone, written dozens of letters, but that wasn't the same as seeing her, putting her arms around her and kissing those soft cheeks. She could offer perfectly good reasons why she hadn't been home – lack of opportunity and money and, of course, the bad feelings about her father – but now they all looked like petty excuses.

George came back into the room carrying a tea tray. Seeing her tears, he put it down and took her in his arms, rocking her silently.

'This is so awful,' he said. 'I can't imagine anything worse, and I can't think of anything to say which would make it better. But let's have some tea. I'll find out what time the trains are, and ring the Bridgenorths for you.'

'I always thought when I went home again it would be in triumph because I'd got a good job and a future,' Molly said brokenly. 'I wanted to rub my dad's nose in it.'

'You have got a good job and a future,' he said. 'And don't make the mistake of blaming yourself. No one could've been a better daughter than you were. Your dad really was a nasty piece of work – his death doesn't change that. But of course you're going to grieve, for what is past and for what could've been. Your mum was a lovely lady; she'll be missed by so many people. I know you

425

must feel you've got no one now but remember you've still got me.'

Molly clung to him, soothed a little by his calm manner and his kindness.

'Cup of tea now,' he said, edging her back so she could sit on the bed. 'I'll pack your stuff for you.'

It was late afternoon, dark and very cold when they arrived back in Sawbridge. There were Christmas lights up in the high street, and most of the shops had cheerful Christmas window displays. But Heywoods, which had always been the most prominent shop in the street, was in darkness. There was just enough light from the street lamps to see that all the windows were broken, the frames burnt, and there were marks where the flames had licked right up to the first floor.

'It looks much worse at the back,' Jack Ollerenshaw volunteered. He was a friend of George and had come to pick them up from the station. 'But you don't want to even think about that now, Molly.'

Mrs Walsh hugged Molly wordlessly for several minutes before drawing her into the living room, taking her coat and making her sit down.

The room was very neat and tidy, and a delicious smell of roasting meat was coming from the kitchen. 'You must think of this as your home, my love,' Mrs Walsh said. 'My hubby and I feel deeply for you, and if we can do anything to make you feel just a bit better, you just shout.'

'Thank you, Mrs Walsh, I really appreciate your kindness. I'm very glad I had George to travel home with. It would've been awful on my own.'

'You are to have George's bed, and he'll go in with our Harry,' she said. 'I don't know what the procedure is in cases like this one. You weren't here, so there would be no point in the police asking you questions, though I expect you'll have to contact the insurance company. Will there be a post mortem, George?'

'I imagine so,' he said, frowning at his mother, as if to warn her to keep off such subjects. 'I'm just going to nip along to the police station to let them know we're here. Will you be all right, Molly?'

Four days later Molly wanted to scream each time someone asked her if she was 'all right'. Of course she wasn't. How could anyone be all right when their parents had just died in a fire?

She wasn't just angry at people who asked such a senseless question, but with her father. A fire investigator had found a whisky bottle in the store room. It had broken in the heat of the flames, but there was evidence that the bottle and a glass had been on the desk and the pathologist had found that her father had been drinking heavily.

Even if Molly had been away for a long time, she could imagine the scene as clearly as if she'd been in that store room. He would've been skulking there with the one-bar electric fire keeping him warm while he drank his whisky. He had always made out he did paperwork on his nights in there, but Molly knew he just sat and got drunk. Upstairs, her mother had to go to bed to keep warm when the coal ran out because he was so miserly with it.

The investigator's report said they believed that Mr Heywood had forgotten to turn the fire off when he went upstairs. He may have accidentally kicked it too close to one of the many cardboard boxes in the store room. It would have taken as much as an hour for the first box to go from singeing to bursting into flames but, from that point on, there would have been no stopping it, because the room was full of flammable goods, including a tank of paraffin.

It was some small comfort that her parents hadn't been burned. They had died of smoke inhalation in their sleep, and the closed bedroom door had kept the flames at bay.

The shop, staircase, kitchen and sitting room were all gutted – only her parents' room and Molly's were intact because the doors had been closed, although they were badly smoke damaged. The whole building was unsafe and would have to be demolished.

George managed to find out where Molly's sister, Emily, was living – Molly had no address or telephone number for her – and sent a telegram asking her to ring. Emily telephoned the Walshes' house when she received it but, although she was as shocked and horrified as Molly, and concerned about her sister, she refused point blank to come back, even for the funeral.

'What point would there be?' she said in a cold voice. 'I hated Dad. Have you forgotten that he threw me out just for seeing Tim? He put me through hell my whole childhood, and he stopped Mum and you contacting me once I'd gone.'

'I know, but come back for Mum and me now,'

Molly pleaded.

'No, I won't. Mum should've stuck up for me. She didn't even write to me more than once a year. I wrote and asked her to the wedding, said she could come with you. She never even replied.'

'You married Tim?' Molly was shocked to hear that. 'I didn't know. She told me you hadn't written. You can bet your boots Dad took the letters! Oh God, Emily, if I'd've known I would have come to you, but I thought you didn't want me or Mum in your life.'

'I'm sure Dad did take the letters, but that doesn't excuse Mum. What sort of a mother abandons one of her children?'

Molly was too upset to continue. George took the view that she couldn't make Emily come to the funeral, and maybe it would be for the best if her sister stayed away if she was so bitter.

'Write to her once it's all over,' he suggested. 'Maybe you can salvage something then.'

Molly didn't know what she would have done without George. He was everything she needed – adviser, confidant, brother, friend and sweetheart all rolled into one. He cuddled her when she cried, listened when she wanted to talk, took her for brisk walks when he felt that fresh air and exercise would help, and often made her laugh when she least expected it.

His parents and brother, Harry, were all kind, too, attentive but not intrusive, caring but not to the point of suffocation. They fended off nosy neighbours and gossip-mongers, too, because, as if the fire wasn't enough for people, there was the trial, too, which the newspapers went to town reporting.

Miss Maud Gribble was found guilty of the murder of Reg Coleman and the manslaughter of Sylvia Coleman and sentenced to be hanged. But, for the locals, the real shock was that Petal had been Cassie's sister, not her daughter, and she'd been trying to keep the child safe.

Suddenly, even those who had said the nastiest things about Cassie were admiring her courage and kindness. Mrs Walsh got quite angry that they couldn't have been more tolerant and caring while she was alive.

'I hate this about people,' she ranted. 'They can make a person desperately unhappy because of some blind prejudice and then, when something happens to change that opinion, they never admit they were wrong, or apologize. It makes me see red!'

Evelyn Bridgenorth had rung twice to offer her condolences, to keep Molly abreast of how Petal was, and to remind her she had a job and a home to come back to. 'It's crazy here at the moment, everyone talking about Miss Gribble and Christabel. If they don't know anything, they make it up. I'm hoping that, after the hanging, it will all die down. It's not good for Petal.'

Molly's parents' funeral took place on 18 December. It was raining heavily and very cold. The church was packed, giving Molly some comfort that, even if people had disliked her father, they chose to put that aside for her mother's sake.

George held her hand firmly and, even if she

had doubted his feelings for her before, she could now see his love for her in his face. She had chosen the hymn 'Love Divine, All Loves Excelling', because she knew her parents had chosen it for their wedding. She would never learn now what had turned her father into such a hard, cruel man but, for today, she tried not to think of him that way but to remember that her mother had loved him.

As for her mother, Molly could remember only good things. Being handed a buttered scone still hot from the oven and a cup of tea when she came home from school on a cold day. Picnics in the woods, going to Weston-super-Mare on the bus in the summer holidays, picking strawberries at a nearby farm and her mother teaching her to ride a bicycle.

She may have been weak, but she was so loving, and when Molly glanced around the church she saw many of her mother's friends crying.

Some of them had laid on food and drink in the village hall after the interment. The cakes and tarts were all home-made, the tablecloths hand embroidered, brought out to honour Mary Heywood. Even the china was Sunday best. Molly noted it all, and knew her mother would have been very touched.

One by one, people came up to her and offered a hug or a loving little anecdote about her mother. Every one of them said how proud Mary had been of Molly. They also said how much they admired her for rescuing Petal.

No one asked why Emily wasn't there, and they didn't comment on her father either. Maybe they would discuss them when they got home, or in the pub over the next few days, but Molly didn't care about that. She'd laid her parents to rest, and her mother, at least, had gone with everyone remembering her for her kindness and warmth.

Enoch Flowers even made her laugh. He'd put on a suit, which obviously passed in his eyes for 'best', but it was shiny with age, had mildew marks on the jacket and stank of it, too. He approached Molly to compliment her on getting justice for Cassie and rescuing Petal. He said Cassie would rest easy knowing she had such a good friend.

'Yer ma was a kind soul, too,' he said. 'Many's the time she slipped me a few rashers of bacon or a lump of cheese when the old man weren't looking. She seemed to always know when I was skint. Now yer dad was a miserable bastard and no mistake. I can't bring meself to lie about him just to cheer you. Wouldn't be right, but you just make sure when you get the insurance money that you go over to his grave and pour a drop of whisky on it to thank him for sparing you the need to care for him when he was an old codger like me.'

A little black humour was just the lift she needed, and she planted a thank-you kiss on his heavily lined cheek. 'I like it when people say what they really mean,' she told him. 'That would've made Cassie laugh, too.'

'You and young Walsh oughtter get married,' he said, wagging a very grubby finger at her. 'Plain as the nose on me face you was meant for each other. And why don't you adopt little Petal and give her a good home? You'll have some brass coming from the insurance and, besides, I know you've always had a soft spot for her.'

George was just walking towards them, and he smiled because he'd heard what Enoch had said. As the old man moved away, George took her hand.

'Sometimes old folk see things clearer than us,' he said, still smiling. 'And I know the only thing I want for Christmas is you.'

Chapter Twenty-six

May 1955

'Ready?' Ted Bridgenorth asked as he opened the door of the limousine and reached in to take the wedding bouquet of pale-pink roses from Molly.

'Willing, and able, too,' she laughed, lowering her feet to the ground, then, scooping up the skirt and train of her dress, she stood up.

It was a beautiful day, not a cloud in the sky. St Barnaby's in Sawbridge was a pretty eleventh-century church, but it looked even prettier than usual as, today, the churchyard cherry trees were a mass of pink blossom. On either side of the path to the lychgate stately white tulips pushed through a mass of dark-blue forget-me-nots.

Petal was waiting at the lychgate with Evelyn Bridgenorth and Dilys, hopping from one foot to the other in excitement at being Molly's smaller bridesmaid. She looked a picture in a duck-egg-blue satin dress and with a garland of white

433

rosebuds in her curly, dark hair. Dilys's dress was the same colour and style, except it had a scoop neck rather than the high one Petal's had.

'I'll lift your train until we get to the church porch,' Ted said, bending to gather it up. 'We don't want it sweeping the path and taking leaves and God knows what into the church.'

'I hope George hasn't changed his mind and fled,' Molly said with a wide smile, knowing that would be impossible.

Ted laughed. 'I think there would be a posse at the gate ready to turn us away if that were the case.'

'There's still time to change your mind and let me marry George,' Dilys joked.

'I believe in sharing with friends,' said Molly, 'but I wouldn't go that far, not even for you. But his brother, Harry, is available still!'

Evelyn arranged Molly's train at the church porch and put the end of it in Petal's hands.

'Now, don't forget you put it down when Molly reaches the altar, where George will be waiting. Uncle Ted will take his place alongside Harry, the best man, ready to give Molly away. You take her flowers and take a couple of steps back to stand in the aisle, alongside Dilys, like the very important person you are!'

When Molly heard the church organ begin to play the Wedding March she turned her head and blew a kiss to Petal, who had a smile almost as wide as the River Avon. Evelyn nipped past her and into the church, and Ted crooked his arm and smiled. 'Shall we go, Miss Heywood? Your last few steps with that name.'

Nothing had ever felt so right. To be in the church which had been such a major part of her childhood with George, the boy who had held her hand on her first day at school, waiting for her at the altar rail.

He had proposed to her on Christmas Eve, and he'd done it properly and reverently, getting down on one knee outside the church, just as they were going in to the midnight service. He had even bought a ring, a small sapphire surrounded by tiny diamonds and, amazingly, it fitted perfectly.

All through the service he had kept reaching for her hand and smiling. It wasn't possible to erase the sadness of her parents' deaths entirely, but it went an awfully long way towards it.

It was a lovely Christmas, the best she'd ever known. The Walshes were a lively, warm family, and they were anxious to draw her in with them and keep her for ever. After so many dreary Christmas days with her own parents, her father carping about everything and her mother afraid to laugh or agree with anything Molly said, it was like soothing ointment on a wound.

Now, finally, they were to be married.

When the vicar asked the groom to lift Molly's veil, George felt his heart swelling up and becoming tight in his chest because Molly looked so lovely. He had always thought of her as the prettiest girl in Sawbridge but, in her ivory satin dress, she looked simply beautiful. Her skin was radiant, her hair fixed up in some kind of topknot with her veil but with little curls escaping onto her pink cheeks. And those beautiful blue eyes were fixed on him as if he were a god.

The church was packed. It was, after all, the wedding that even the most cynical people in the village had wanted to take place.

Earlier today, George's father had given his opinion about the impending marriage. 'Son, if I'd been asked to pick the right girl for you, Molly would have been my first and only choice. She's got a mind, a caring heart, a ton of patience and a pretty face. You belong together.'

George might have always believed she was the girl for him, but it had been a long road and, even after the engagement, there had still been hurdles in the way.

Miss Gribble was hanged on 2 January. The newspapers had a field day with it, rehashing every last bit of information about her, Christabel, Sylvia and Molly, and plenty of newer, juicy stuff that had surfaced during the trial.

Molly was struggling enough with all the dreadful memories it brought back, and she wasn't prepared for all the extra gossip and speculation in the village. It got to the point where she couldn't leave the house without someone accosting her. And these people often grew indignant and quite nasty when she said she had nothing to say about it.

Things got so bad she opted to go back to work in Rye. She used the excuse that she needed to work, but George knew it was more because she was afraid Petal might be having the same difficulties.

He understood. It was quite feasible that Petal might get to hear things that would upset her, and Molly could explain things in a way a little girl

436

would understand. Another reason to leave Sawbridge was the burnt-out shop; each time Molly passed, it was an unwanted memory of how her parents had died.

George had swallowed his disappointment, agreed she should go and put in for his sergeant's exam, which he'd been talking about taking for over a year. Without Molly in the house he had no distractions from studying for the exam, and one weekend in four he drove his motorbike down to see her.

One loose end about Cassie was finally stitched up during that time – the question of why she had gone to Bristol every Thursday and where she had got her money from. An elderly gentleman called Thomas Woods had rung the Sawbridge police station just after Miss Gribble was sentenced.

'I should've come forward before,' he said to the desk sergeant. 'I didn't because I thought my friendship with Cassandra would be misinterpreted. I am almost completely blind, and she came to read to me, through a librarian in Bristol library. She was a real treasure. She not only read to me but wrote letters for me, did a bit of cleaning and became a dear friend, because she loved books as much as I do. I paid her well because I valued her.

'A friend who had watched Miss Gribble's trial closely told me that the defence barrister had implied that Cassandra's income had come from immoral earnings. It was then that I felt I had to put the record straight. No woman should be wrongly accused of such a thing, especially when that woman was as kind and intelligent as Cassandra was.'

That last piece of the jigsaw meant a great deal to Molly. It rounded everything off; all her questions had been answered. It was another good thing she could tell Petal about, and perhaps they could even go to see Mr Woods one day.

That last mystery about Cassie might have been cleared up, but George found himself thinking that the situation he and Molly were in, being so far apart, would never change. He had begun to think that the journey would seem to grow longer each time and leaving her ever more painful. Yet it did change. He passed his sergeant's exam and shortly afterwards was offered a posting in Hastings, just a bus ride from Rye.

Both he and Molly saw the new posting as heaven sent, and decided to marry as soon as possible. The insurance money from the shop had come through, and Molly's share, after sending half to Emily, was enough to put a deposit down on a house. George had enough savings to buy furniture and pay for the wedding. They booked a honeymoon in Hastings so they could look for a house while they were there.

Everything was arranged in the three weeks it took to have the banns read at church. Molly got both her dress and Petal's made in Rye, and Janice, George's mother, took on the arrangements for the flowers and wedding cake. It seemed to George that Molly was on the phone to Janice about all this more often than she was to him.

His parents were a bit sad that the couple would be setting up home a long way from Somerset, but they'd always known that George couldn't possibly stay in such a quiet backwater if he wanted to advance his career. George guessed that they also thought he and Molly needed to move to a town where they weren't known, to build a new life and make new friends. It was close enough to Rye that Molly and Petal could visit Ted and Evelyn, but at the same time they wouldn't feel they had their every move watched.

Now, finally, they were here in the church, which was packed with friends and relatives. Sunshine was streaming through the stained-glass windows, making pools of vivid colours on the old stone floor and the air was heavy with the scent of the flowers.

Their vows made, George put the ring on Molly's finger, and he felt so happy when the vicar said that they were now man and wife he felt like cheering. He couldn't stop smiling as he walked with his new wife to the vestry to sign the register. Harry and Dilys were their witnesses, but Ted and Evelyn took Petal's hands and followed on, leaving Mr and Mrs Walsh taking up the rear.

Petal had behaved impeccably throughout the service, but the second the vicar had shaken hands with everyone before they left the vestry she took up a position in front of the group, wearing a somewhat belligerent expression on her face.

'So now George is Molly's husband, how long will it be before I go to live with them and call them Mummy and Daddy?' she asked.

A kind of communal giggle went round the vestry. Evelyn put her hand over her mouth to suppress it, but everyone else just grinned and looked at Petal.

'I thought I told you we had to wait until later?' Evelyn said.

Molly looked from Petal to George, frowning with puzzlement.

'We've got permission from the Children's Department,' George admitted. 'Ted, Evelyn and I were going to break the wonderful news at the reception, but it seems Petal couldn't wait any longer.'

'You mean, she'll be our little girl?' Molly's voice rose almost to a shriek in her joy. 'And live with us in Hastings?'

George swept Petal up with one arm and put the other around Molly. 'Yes, she's going to be our little girl and, we hope, a big sister to any babies that come along later.'

'So that's why none of you seemed concerned when I kept talking about how long it would take me to get to Rye from Hastings in the morning?' Molly said with mock-indignation. 'You all knew I wouldn't be going because I'll have better things to do than go to work!'

'We weren't ruling out the idea of you coming in for the odd day and in the school holidays, to keep your hand in,' Ted said, grinning broadly. 'But, with a new home to organize and Petal to care for, I don't think you'll be wanting to do chambermaid duties any more.'

Molly noticed that Mrs Walsh was laughing. 'You knew about this, too?' she asked.

'Yes, George told us a week ago, and we're thrilled. He's been badgering the Children's Department ever since you got engaged. But we'd better get out of this vestry and let the confetti

440

throwing commence, before all the guests come charging in here.'

Molly kissed George. 'I love you, Mr Walsh. I loved you before, but I love you even more now. Petal is the best wedding present ever.'

George opened the door, and the organ player, who had been playing quietly all the time they'd been in the vestry, upped the volume to alert everyone that they were coming out.

Petal gathered up the train of Molly's dress and walked proudly behind the newly married couple.

As Molly and George walked slowly down the aisle, everyone got to their feet to look and smile at them. Everyone was there: friends from school, others they had made since, George's fellow policemen pals, customers from the shop, neighbours and fellow shopkeepers.

'It'll be sad to leave them all behind,' Molly whispered to George.

'Not that sad,' he whispered back. 'It will be good to start again with a clean sheet.'

The publishers hope that this book has given you enjoyable reading. Large Print Books are especially designed to be as easy to see and hold as possible. If you wish a complete list of our books please ask at your local library or write directly to:

Magna Large Print Books
Magna House, Long Preston,
Skipton, North Yorkshire.
BD23 4ND

This Large Print Book for the partially sighted, who cannot read normal print, is published under the auspices of

THE ULVERSCROFT FOUNDATION

THE ULVERSCROFT FOUNDATION

... we hope that you have enjoyed this Large Print Book. Please think for a moment about those people who have worse eyesight problems than you ... and are unable to even read or enjoy Large Print, without great difficulty.

You can help them by sending a donation, large or small to:

**The Ulverscroft Foundation,
1, The Green, Bradgate Road,
Anstey, Leicestershire, LE7 7FU,
England.**
or request a copy of our brochure for more details.

The Foundation will use all your help to assist those people who are handicapped by various sight problems and need special attention.

Thank you very much for your help.